AFTER THE WEDDING

COURTNEY MILAN

For Anita Hill,
who should never have had to stand alone.

For Emily Murphy, Dahlia Lithwick, Nancy Rapoport, Leah Litman, Christine Miller, Kathryn Ore, Kathy Ku, and everyone who spoke anonymously—thank you.

For Matt Zapatosky,
for emailing me out of the blue.

And for me, for answering.

CHAPTER ONE

Surrey County, England, 1867

Lady Camilla Worth had dreamed of marriage ever since she was twelve years of age and had been shunted off to the first family who reluctantly took her in.

Marriage? She had quickly learned not to be persnickety in her choice of fantasies. It didn't *have* to be marriage.

When she was younger, she had used to imagine that one of the girls whose acquaintance she made—however briefly —would become her devoted friend, and they would swear a lifelong loyalty to one another. When she lived in Gloucester, she daydreamed about becoming a companion—no, an almost-granddaughter—to an elderly woman who lived three houses down.

"What would I ever do without you, Camilla?" old Mrs. Marsdell would say after Camilla learned to crochet properly and thereby wormed her way into her heart.

But old Mrs. Marsdell had never stopped frowning at Camilla suspiciously, no matter how well she crocheted, and

Camilla had been packed up and sent off to another family before she had a chance to charm anyone.

One person was all she had ever wanted. One person, just one, who promised not to leave her. She didn't need love. She didn't need wealth. After packing her bags nine times and boarding trains, braving swaying carts—or even once, walking seven miles with her aging valise in tow—after nine separate residences, she would have settled for tolerance and a promise that she would at least have a place to stay.

Of course she also hoped for marriage as she grew older. Hope had always whispered sweet and promising words to her, and she always gave in.

She stopped think of marriage the way children did, dreaming of white knights and declarations of undying adoration and houses to look over and china and linen to purchase. She hoped for it in the most basic possible terms.

She wanted someone to choose her. She wanted not to be sent away again. Her husband didn't need to love her; he just needed to say, "We should stay together for the rest of our lives."

Hope was forever beckoning, and having allowed herself to hope for so little, she had believed that surely she could not be disappointed.

It just went to show: Fate had a sense of humor, and she was a capricious bitch.

For here Camilla stood on her wedding day—wedding night, really. Her gown was not white, as Victoria's had been, and really shouldn't be called a gown, as tiny down feathers still clung to it from when she'd aired the bedding. Her hands were so dry they caught on the rough fabric of her apron; her throat was parched. She had no trousseau packed in trunks, no idea what sort of home—if any—awaited her.

She was getting married and still her dream eluded her.

Her groom's face was hidden in the shadows.

Late as this wedding was on this particular night, a few candles lit in the nave did more to cast shadows than shed illumination. He adjusted his cuffs. The linen fabric gleamed white against the brown of his skin, and seemed whiter still when he folded his arms in disapproval. She couldn't see his full expression in the darkness, but his eyebrows made grim slashes of unhappy resignation.

It might have been romantic—for versions of *romantic* that conflated *foolhardy* with *fun*—to marry a man she had known for scarcely three days.

What Camilla knew of her groom was not terrible. He'd been kind to her. He had made her laugh. He had even—once—touched her arm and made her heart flutter.

It might have been romantic, but for one not-so-little thing.

"Adrian Hunter," Bishop Lassiter was saying. "Do you take Camilla Winters to be your wife? Will you love her, comfort her, honor and protect her, and forsaking all others, be faithful to her as long as you both shall live?"

She would have overlooked the lack of a gown, a trousseau, almost anything. God knew she had given up hope of such luxury. She would have forgiven anything except...

"No," said her groom.

Anything except this: Just like everyone else in the world, her intended didn't want her.

The moment felt like a distant dream. It was happening to someone else, someone very, very far away, someone standing in Camilla's body and feeling Camilla's feelings.

Behind Mr. Hunter, Rector Miles lifted the pistol. He didn't quite aim it at her reluctant groom; he held it askew, angled in the vague direction of the man in a way that managed to be a threat without quite amounting to a promise. His hands gleamed white on the barrel; the flickering light made his fingers look like maggots writhing on the tarnished steel.

"That's not the way this is done," the rector said calmly. "You will agree and you will sign the book, damn your eyes."

"I do this under duress." His words sounded clipped and harsh. "I do not consent."

Camilla couldn't even call him her intended. Intent on both their parts was woefully lacking.

"I'm sorry," Camilla whispered.

He didn't hear her. Or maybe he heard and didn't care to respond.

She wouldn't have minded so much if he didn't love her. She didn't want white lace and wedding cake. But this wasn't marriage, not really. She'd stayed with her uncle, then his cousins, then...well, she could recite the chain of people who had not wanted her around until her eyes stung and their faces blurred together.

She'd been with Rector Miles longer than almost anyone, and she'd tried her hardest. She honestly had. This time, she had thought. This time, she'd stay for certain.

Instead, she was being wrapped up like an unwanted package again and sent on to the next soul.

After being passed on—and on—and on—and on—for all these years, she should have outgrown all illusions about the outcome in this case.

The candlelight made Mr. Hunter's features seem even darker than they had appeared in the sun. In the sun, after all, he'd smiled at her.

He didn't smile now.

Camilla was finally getting married, and of course her husband didn't want her.

Her lungs felt too small. Her hands were shaking. Her corset wasn't laced tightly, but still she couldn't seem to breathe. Little green spots appeared before her eyes, dancing, whirling.

Don't faint, Camilla, she admonished herself. *Don't faint. If you faint, he might leave you behind, and then you'll truly have nowhere to go.*

She didn't faint. She managed to breathe—in and out, in and out. She said *yes* when it was her turn to do so, and the pistol never jerked in her direction. Eventually, the dizzying spots went away. She managed not to swoon on her way to sign the register. She did everything except look at the unwilling groom whose life had so forcibly been tied to her own. That was it; she was married.

There were no congratulations. There was no wedding dinner. There was just that look in Rector Miles's eyes—the one that said Camilla deserved no better. She'd heard him say it often enough; she'd never let herself believe it. She took a deep breath and looked upward. She'd avoided thinking the worst of herself all this time. No point starting now.

"Camilla." Kitty, the other maid in the household, had been present to serve as a second witness. She reached for Camilla's hand as they passed. "I'm so, so—"

But Rector Miles just glared at the woman. "Kitty was going to say that she packed your things. Your valise is outside."

She followed him out into the night. It was late summer, but it had been unseasonably cold and rainy and the wind still raged. The rectory was in the middle of wide, rolling pastureland south of Surrey. A small collection of houses surrounded them, but it was five miles to the nearest town of any real size. An icy breeze whistled coldly down Camilla's neck, and she shivered.

"There's an inn three miles away," Bishop Lassiter said. "They might allow you to take rooms for the night."

Mr. Hunter made no response.

The rector who had given her a home for the last year and a half did not even look at Camilla. He had told her earlier how disappointed he was in her behavior. And there was no chance for Camilla to speak with him now, because her new husband, without saying a word, shouldered his own bag and started walking down the road without her.

That was how Camilla left the tenth household that had taken her in: on foot, at nine at night, with a chill in the air and the moon high overhead. She picked up her valise, gritted her teeth, and did what she did best: she hoped. So. She had a new…husband? Should she call him a husband? Maybe this would all work out. Just because it had never worked out yet didn't mean—

She shook her head, coming to her senses. Daydreaming, at a time like this? Mr. Hunter had started walking without so much as a glance at her, and he was now ten yards distant.

She was being left behind. Never mind what they could someday be to each other. Would he talk to her tonight? Would he want to consummate the marriage without even looking at her? Bile rose in her throat at the possibility.

His long legs ate away at the ground. She scrambled to catch up. The handle of her valise began to burn a line in the palm of her hand. Switching shoulders, then trying to rest the weight against her hip, didn't help.

She didn't dare complain. She didn't want to be left behind, not so soon. If she was abandoned again, in less than an hour…

She had almost no money.

She had no idea what she would do.

Halfway to the inn, he stopped. At first, she thought he might finally address her. Instead, he let his own satchel fall to the ground. He looked up at the moon.

His hands made fists at his side. "Fuck." He spoke softly enough that she likely wasn't supposed to hear that epithet.

"Mr. Hunter?"

Finally, he turned to her. She still couldn't make out the expression in his eyes, but she could feel his gaze on her. He'd lost his position and gained a wife, all in the space of a few hours. She didn't imagine that he was *happy* with her existence, but acknowledging it was a start.

He exhaled. "I suppose this...is what it is. We'll have to figure this mess out."

That was what she was: not a wife, not a companion. She was a mess. She inhaled once more, and tried, desperately, to reach for the thing that had sustained her for years: hope. She had never given up; she had never stopped trying.

Her fingers tightened on her valise.

She would make this work. She'd made everything work thus far, hadn't she? She'd just keep trying—harder this time—and...

Camilla exhaled into the cold of the night.

Hope felt very far away. How on earth had her life come to this?

Ah, yes. It had started three days ago, when Bishop Lassiter had arrived on her doorstep with Mr. Hunter in tow...

CHAPTER TWO

I t had started seven days ago, when Adrian Hunter received a telegram from his uncle.

The runner arrived just as Adrian sat down to breakfast with his brother. Adrian read the telegram once over coffee. He had a number of more pressing concerns—eight of them, to be precise. He had just approved the advertisement that announced that the world-famous Harvil Industries would have a booth at the autumn exhibition to reveal their newest line of fine china. They would have new vases, new bowls, new everything. The pride and centerpiece of the collection, the advertisement boasted, would be a set of eight enameled plates in gold leaf.

This would have been exciting, except Harvil did not yet have a design for eight plates. It did not have a design for *one*. Adrian and his team had not yet agreed upon on an artistic course. In point of fact, the Harvil artists had managed to accomplish precisely one thing with regards to those plates: Argue.

He didn't have time for his uncle's problem. But uncles

were family, even if the uncle in question had yet to publicly acknowledge Adrian's existence.

Adrian set the telegram to the side of his plate. *This* plate was one of the misadventures from a prior season—a review piece produced on too little sleep and too much artistic license. It featured a peacock with two heads and no tail.

Adrian spread butter on his toast, and considered. He read the words again as he ate a poached egg, sunlight spilling on the mahogany table. He read it a third time as he sifted through the remainder of his correspondence.

Mr. Alabi wanted him back in Harvil. Mr. Singh had finished the roof repairs there. He set aside a letter about sourcing copper carbonate, and looked up.

His older brother was watching him with an impatience that he didn't bother to conceal.

Grayson broke the fourth time Adrian picked up the telegram. "For God's sake. What precisely does uncle dearest want now?"

"He requests my presence, as soon as I can be spared."

Grayson's nose twitched.

Adrian could remember what Grayson had been like before they'd been separated by bloodshed and the many leagues of the Atlantic Ocean. Grayson was eight years his elder, but people had used to remark upon how similarly they looked—same broad nose, same sparkling brown eyes alight with curiosity, same lips, same rich brown skin.

Then war had come. Adrian's older brothers—Henry, Noah, Grayson, and John—had left to fight in a cause they all believed in.

Grayson had been the only one to return. The change in him was nothing Adrian could easily put his finger on. His features were all still the same; it was just the way he used them that had changed for good.

Right now, his elder brother scowled at him. "Did uncle *dearest* use the word 'please,' by any chance?"

Adrian fought the urge to inspect the paper once again. Alas. He didn't need to. "It's a telegram, Grayson. Every word is an expense, and frugality is a virtue."

"Ah. I had not heard of our uncle's horrible reversal of fortune. It must be significant, that he can no longer afford a half pence for manners."

Adrian took another bite of his egg in lieu of answering.

Grayson sighed. "You're going, then? You know Denmore only wants something from you."

His brother wasn't *wrong*. Adrian wasn't an idiot, and he knew their uncle better than Grayson.

Their mother's brother was the Bishop of Gainshire. He was busy to a fault, dedicated to his work. Yes, he *did* use people—and yes, he *had* used Adrian in the past—but he used himself hardest, working long hours.

It stung a little, the memory of the last time Denmore had seen Adrian. But it only stung a little, and Denmore was family.

"I visited him regularly for five years," Adrian said mildly. "I *do* know him. Better than you do."

Grayson snorted. "That's your gentle artist's soul speaking, there. You're too trusting."

"*You're* too suspicious." Adrian smiled. "And I'm not an artist. Have you seen my attempts at sketching?"

Grayson was not to be diverted. "He'll string you along with vague promises, and you'll *let him do it*, because he's—" Grayson caught himself on these words and looked away, his hand curling into a fist.

Grayson had never provided details of what had happened during the Great Rebellion back in the United States. Adrian had scoured the newspapers and the occasional letter avidly for news, but he only knew what anyone who hadn't participated knew—that after the Southern states seceded, brother had fought brother, that blood had flowed and bodies had piled up. He knew from letters that his brothers had sent that even among Northerners who didn't condone slavery, the black soldiers who joined their ranks had been ill-treated.

Three of his brothers had perished. Grayson had left looking like Adrian, and he'd come back like this—hard and untrusting, with a haunted look in his eye when he thought Adrian wasn't looking.

Now Grayson reached across the table and took hold of the telegram without asking. He read it with a curl in his lip before tossing it aside. "Denmore would ask you for your heart without paying a half-penny to say please. Whatever it is he wants of you? You don't need to give it."

"I'm a grown man. I don't *need* to do anything."

Grayson looked into Adrian's eyes across the table. There it was—that *look,* that sense Adrian had harbored for years that his brother had lost himself, and still needed to be found.

After a moment, his brother sighed. "You're going anyway. I don't want you to be hurt." Grayson looked away. "I just want to…"

Protect you, he didn't say, but Adrian could fill in the end of the sentence. Grayson had always looked out for him.

If it had just been himself remaining of his family, maybe Adrian wouldn't have gone. He knew, after all, what his uncle was. Hell, he had spent most of his years in England. He *wasn't* a gentle artist's soul, no matter what Grayson thought. It could be a hard, ugly world, especially for black men.

Adrian had been spared the worst of it; he knew that. That made him feel more of an obligation, not less.

"You don't need to look out for me," Adrian said mildly.

Grayson shook his head, smiling. "Shut up, sprout. That's my job. Don't you have work, in any event?"

Adrian had too much to do. He'd already put off his return too long; after Grayson left England this time, Adrian wouldn't see him for years to come.

Every worker at Harvil Industries depended on their continuing success. If they hadn't started producing plates in a month...

"Say no," Grayson said. "You don't have time. God knows you've frittered enough of it away, staying with me while I oversee the cable-laying contracts. You *know* Denmore."

Adrian did.

His uncle was flawed and self-centered, occasionally...but *good* still. Human, in other words.

And Adrian knew Grayson—knew the scars he bore on his soul, the ones he refused to talk about.

"Don't worry," Adrian said, with a half-smile. "I can take care of myself."

Protecting an older brother was dangerous work. Grayson would never allow it, if he knew Adrian was attempting it. That just meant he needed to be all the more diligent about it.

Adrian had been lucky—so lucky. He had *lived.* He'd been deemed too young to go to war. He'd had every advantage. Every time he thought *maybe I shouldn't,* or *maybe I don't have the time,* he reminded himself how much he had. He always asked himself if maybe, he could take on a little more.

He always came to the same conclusion—yes, he could manage more.

Adrian could trust a little, could show his brother that he could loosen his hold on that hard knot of his suspicions. Their uncle was human, but he was a good man at heart. And maybe, if Adrian kept trusting...maybe one day he'd see Grayson smile the way he had used to.

Grayson just sighed. "Well. When he pretends he doesn't know you a *second* time, you'll undoubtedly be too upset for me to chastise properly. So I'll say now what I won't say then: He's already shown his true colors. What he did was unforgivable, and I can't believe you're giving him a —what is it now?—a fourth chance. I told you so. You should have listened."

"Mmm." Adrian nodded. "I'll save my speech for when we know the outcome."

Grayson just shook his head. "Take care of yourself, little brother. I love you."

"I love you, too." Adrian stood. He reached out and set his hand on his brother's shoulder. A little more, he thought. He couldn't protect Grayson outright, but he'd trust where his brother couldn't. He'd trust a little more, and hopefully that would help.

∽

"Mr. Adrian Hunter to see you, my lord."

All the reassuring words Adrian had spoken to his brother earlier that day were not enough to suppress his sense of disquiet at that introduction. The footman who conducted Adrian to the many-windowed room on the third floor overlooking his uncle's grounds no doubt thought nothing wrong with what he'd said; it was, after all, the truth.

Just not all of it.

Adrian had visited his uncle for months at a time, starting when he was fifteen. It had not been a planned sojourn; war had broken out back in America, and his entire family had been determined to help. Adrian had been deemed too young to fight. His father had told him that *his* part in the war effort would be to keep the portions of the family business that were in England running smoothly.

His mother had given him another task. "Your charge is just as important," she had told him before she had boarded the ship. "Your uncle is a respected man; if you can change his mind, it will make a difference."

It had *not* been just as important, he had later realized; his parents had wanted to make sure that at least one of their sons survived the conflict. Boys his age and younger had fought. It had all been a lie to keep him from doing anything stupid, like trying to join his brothers as they blockaded Confederate forces.

During those years in England, Adrian had visited his uncle. Denmore, the Bishop of Gainshire, had been unerringly kind in private. In private, he'd talked lovingly of Adrian's mother—his favorite sister, the sister whose loss he still mourned. In private, Adrian had asked why Denmore thought he had lost his sister when she was still *alive* and *willing to speak to him,* and had listened to the frank response.

His uncle had provided Adrian with some incredibly valuable lessons in how English society functioned.

One of those lessons was that being married to the wrong person was worse than being dead. Adrian hated it, but society wasn't kind, and his uncle hadn't tried to soften the blow. He'd taught Adrian to argue, to *think,* and to understand how the English thought in turn.

He'd cried and hugged Adrian when Adrian, impatient and determined, had left his uncle's estate in order to take over his father's bewildering responsibilities at Harvil; he'd embraced him every time he returned.

All that loving affection had happened in private.

In public, Adrian had been presented to all and sundry as first his uncle's sometime page, then his part-time amanuensis.

In the seven years since Adrian had first visited his uncle, Denmore had never so much as mentioned their familial relationship in public. He had not let his own servants know the truth—not by so much as a flicker of a smile in their presence.

It had been thirteen months since they had last seen each other, and still his uncle let no spark of joy light his expression at the sight of his nephew. He did not rise from his desk; that would break his public façade.

Bishop Denmore would not show such affection for a man who had been a mere page.

Instead, he inclined his head. "Mr. Hunter," he said calmly. "Do come in. It's very good to see you. I'll be with you in a moment."

The footman was still present; Adrian stood stiffly beside the door. He could hear Grayson's admonition in his head.

He's going to hurt you.

Of course he was. Denmore annoyed Adrian every time they met by pretending they were not uncle and nephew. But Adrian could handle a little hurt if it eventually led to progress.

For now, he inclined his head.

"Bishop," he said instead.

"Come, Mr. Hunter." His uncle raised an eyebrow. "After our long acquaintance, we need not stand on such ceremony. Call me Denmore and be done with it."

Beside Adrian, the footman shifted uncomfortably.

The request was a mark of familiarity. It would seem a kindness, an extraordinary condescension from a man of such exalted rank to a mere servant. The footman—his name was Walter Evans—believed Adrian didn't deserve such respect.

Adrian knew this because he'd said so, repeatedly.

Know your place, Adrian had been admonished when he was younger. *Don't take advantage of the charity of a good man.*

"As you say, Bishop," Adrian said.

Denmore sighed. "Well, Evans. Close the door behind you. We've business to discuss."

Adrian and the bishop remained in place, a stiff, awkward ten feet distant. They waited until the door closed behind Evans, until they heard the servant's footsteps receding in the distance.

Then, and only then did the bishop stand. He crossed the room and pulled Adrian into an embrace. "Adrian," he said. "It's been too long."

It had been more than a year, and it had been a long year.

Bishop Denmore was almost a head shorter than Adrian; his wispy hair was white and textureless. His skin was paper-pale and creased with age, and he moved gingerly, evidence of his gout.

It was hard to believe they were related.

The bishop released him to an arm's length. "You're looking well, my boy."

Adrian felt the corner of his mouth twitch. "I'm twenty-two. I'm hardly a boy."

"No." Denmore let go of his shoulders and gave him another appraising look. "No, you are not. You've grown to be so much more."

Knowing they were uncle and nephew, not employer and employed, had left a mark. Denmore had pretended not to know Adrian when they met by chance at an exhibition a year ago. He had, in fact made an elaborate inquiry as to how a man like him had come to run a china-works near Bristol, so that the friend who accompanied him would not guess at their relationship.

The next time Adrian visited, he had given his uncle an ultimatum.

"Someday," his uncle had said sadly. "I will. I promise."

Someday had not yet arrived.

The bishop turned away. "You've arrived not a moment too soon. You always seem to know precisely when I need you."

"That would be because you asked me to come."

Over the last year, Adrian had had ample time to consider his situation in life. He knew how lucky he was. His family had money from their various business endeavors. His mother had inherited property, which had been added to his great-great-uncles' holdings.

Adrian had a loving, overbearing brother and a massive extended family.

He didn't *need* Denmore, not for anything.

Still, he had asked Denmore for that one thing, and he'd asked for it repeatedly. He'd asked when he was fifteen, and when he was sixteen, and again and again for years and years. His uncle had never said *no;* he had always said *later.* Not now.

Not now, not with the war in America still raging. Not now; Denmore needed time to bring his older brother, the duke, into the scheme. Not now; Denmore was being considered for elevation to bishop, and he could do so much more once he was appointed.

Not now; he was too new in his position; he did not dare make waves.

Not now, not now. But…someday. Someday, he had promised. Of course the time would come *someday.*

"So," Adrian said, eyeing his uncle. "Last time we talked, I asked you to acknowledge my family. My mother, me, my brother. Is it time yet?"

His uncle smiled slowly. "It's time."

Oh, thank God. Adrian could just imagine the look on Grayson's face when he brought *this* news back. He could not hold back his delighted smile; he felt as if his whole face would crack with joy. He hadn't precisely been estranged from his uncle this last year over this very issue, but he'd pulled back. He hadn't visited. His letters had been a little cold. He *hated* being cold.

"I always said the time would come," his uncle said, patting Adrian's hand. "I always said I would acknowledge you one day, and never mind the consequences. You know I love you, do you not?"

Adrian's nose twitched on that word: *consequences*. They hadn't *really* argued about consequences last time.

When he'd been his uncle's amanuensis-slash-nephew-in–hiding, he had needed to construct arguments in letters on his uncle's behalf. Denmore had taught him to hide his passion behind rational argument. Adrian always tried to meet people on the ground they knew best. Last time Adrian had met his uncle, they had debated the matter as if it were a question set before Parliament and they were indifferent observers hashing out the benefits and detriments.

"So." Adrian folded his arms. He imagined the rationality his uncle preferred settling over his shoulders like a cloak, hiding the furious joy that threatened to break through his calm. "How have you planned the announcement? Have you consulted with your brother the duke yet?"

"Ah…" Denmore blinked.

"Will you tell them that your sister did not perish, as your father claimed so many years ago?" Adrian had thought about this for so long; he had so many ideas as to how to proceed. "Or would you rather start by introducing my father and brother? I know you worry about the connection with trade, but the trade my family engages in is of a particularly honorable sort. My father is a respectable gentleman who has devoted his life to a just cause—"

"Adrian."

Ah. He hadn't sufficiently hidden his enthusiasm. Adrian bit back his excitement.

"There is no way to soften the blow our family's reputation will suffer when the news is out," his uncle said. "A duke's daughter ran off with a black abolitionist thirty-five years ago. My father told everyone she was dead rather than admit the truth. It will be a scandal no matter how it's announced."

Adrian took a deep breath. No point getting angry at the truth, even if his own uncle was the one saying it in that way. Except…it was not entirely the truth.

"My mother did not run off," Adrian said mildly. "My mother was a widow. It took my parents three years working together on the matter of abolition before they decided to marry, which they did—legally, properly." Rational; that was the way to convince his uncle. "You of all people know it matters how an issue is presented. My mother married a man who cared about a cause. How does that pose a problem?"

"It won't matter that they were married."

"As for my father, he—"

"Nor that your father was a man of property."

"That's not the point." Adrian lived in his own skin, damn it. His father could have been supreme emperor of the entire world for all that British society cared. The fact that his father was black would be a scandal, no matter how it was laid out. He *knew* that, but still—"I know it *won't* matter to some people, but it *should,* and if we are to have any chance of changing the way things are, we must talk of my parents as people first."

His uncle just looked at him briefly, then turned away.

From his uncle's point of view, this must seem a frightening step. It hurt a little, that this man who had been so kind still saw Adrian as an object of fear and not just a nephew—but Adrian had been lucky in his life. He could handle a little more personal hurt, if it led to the right result. His uncle had agreed to acknowledge him, and that was a good step forward. Adrian could acknowledge the hurt once the joy had come.

"Very well, then. If you've decided to do it, then it's a matter of accepting the consequences as inevitable. I suppose Lassiter is no longer a problem?"

Bishop Lassiter was his uncle's rival in the church. He had been Denmore's excuse for the last two years. There was no rivalry so bitter as one between two men equal in rank and seniority, who opposed each other on every principle.

Adrian's uncle brightened. "I'm so glad you mentioned him. That's the very thing I need to discuss with you. He won't be a problem...soon."

Adrian looked over. There was a light in his uncle's eyes.

His uncle leaned in excitedly. "Do you by any chance recall that favor you did for me on accident several years ago?"

"No," Adrian said swiftly. *No, he wouldn't do it*, he meant, but his uncle took it as simple denial.

"When those men took you for a servant and divulged those very embarrassing details in your presence. Well." His uncle slipped a piece of paper across the table with a self-satisfied smile. "Here," he said. "Lassiter is advertising for a valet."

It took Adrian a moment to process those words. To understand what his uncle was asking him to do.

He shook his head. "Impossible."

"I've taken the liberty of obtaining references on your behalf," the man said, as if Adrian had spoken of a practical impossibility instead of the fact that his soul rebelled against the thought of entering service to spy on another man. "Lassiter won't connect the letters to me at all. And there's a fashion for black servants in London at the moment. Lassiter is vain enough to indulge."

Adrian turned his head away as much as he could without being rude. "I could not possibly pose as a valet."

"My Henry will give you tips," his uncle said. "And you won't need to fool Lassiter for long. You're so bright—you'll pick up anything you need to know in no time at all."

"No. Absolutely not."

"You don't have faith in your own intelligence?"

"It's not that. It's this: I'm not a servant. And I *really* don't like lying."

"Of *course* you aren't. I'm not asking you to *be* one. I'm just asking you to *pose* as one. Be rational about this, Adrian."

Rational. It was always rationality with Denmore, and the word was only brought out when his uncle proposed something that left a bad taste in Adrian's mouth.

"I have business that requires my attention," Adrian said. It was not a lie. He had four weeks until production had to start on his series of plates, and there were still no designs.

"Isn't Grayson around now? He can handle it."

"Yes, but—" *But Grayson has no artistic sense*, Adrian didn't say, because it was one thing to make fun of your brother to his face, and another entirely to do it to someone outside the immediate family. "But Grayson is only in England because he's overseeing the final production of the cable-laying ship and securing the contracts for the business to proceed. He hasn't time to handle what is going on at Harvil, too."

"Is your business worth more than knowing that the Church of England is led by men of good character? I know Lassiter's doing *something*. I even have some idea as to what it is—he has a little too much money, and he has explained it by claiming excessively lucky investments for too long."

Adrian shook his head.

Denmore nodded, as if he heard everything Adrian wasn't saying.

"I know it's a great deal to ask of you. I know how lowering it must feel for you. But it's no more than you ask of me. If I could diminish Lassiter's influence, I could choose to lower myself and accept you."

Accepting me is not lowering. Adrian took another deep breath. He loved his uncle. He loved his uncle. Still, sometimes he didn't like him much. For a moment, his emotions rose in his throat.

Years ago, his mother had charged him with changing his uncle's mind. To bringing him around to the cause. *He has influence in the Church,* she said, *and think what it would mean if he used it properly.*

Grayson openly scoffed at his uncle's claims that *someday* he would acknowledge their branch of the family—Grayson, who had no trust any longer.

Adrian had always wanted to believe that his uncle—the uncle who had been so kind in private—could become the sort of man who would be kind in public, too. *I told you so,* he could hear Grayson saying, when he returned with this tale.

"I should hope," his uncle said, "that you would love me as much as I have loved you."

"I do," Adrian said, annoyed, "but—"

But he didn't have a good argument. Not the kind Denmore could listen to, at any rate. His love felt like a chain wrapped round his neck, yanking him in line.

"If you love me," his uncle wheedled, "do this one thing for me. Not even for me. Do it for *yourself.* Do this one thing, and I'll acknowledge you. I promise."

"That's—you should..." But Adrian knew there was no use arguing. There had never been any point in arguing.

Don't tie these things together, Adrian wanted to say. *It makes me feel sick.*

But feeling sick was an emotion, not an argument. His uncle wouldn't listen.

Don't ask this of me. You've hurt me enough. Emotion, not argument.

Don't use me this way. Don't use me at all. He had no arguments, only emotions.

Adrian knew his uncle. If he said no now, his uncle would take it as proof that he had never wanted acknowledgement, not really. Adrian could remember lying in bed at the age of fifteen and dreaming that his uncle would take Evans aside and just *tell* him. *Don't treat him like that. He's my nephew, not my charity case.*

It *hurt*, what his uncle was asking of him. But Adrian had been hurt so little, and others had been hurt so much. If he could make a difference...

He wanted Grayson to know that people could change, that a little trust would not go amiss. Here was his chance to have that.

He would do anything for his brother. Even this.

"If I do this, you must promise not to back away. Not this time."

"Of course not." The bishop looked utterly shocked. "I would *never*. It will be over before you know it, and we'll greet the world with joy together."

"Right." The word tasted sour on Adrian's tongue, but this was what he'd wanted. Recognition. Grayson. The part that hurt would be over soon enough, and once it was past, Adrian wouldn't need to think of it again.

"Joy," he said carefully. "I look forward to that."

～

A drian had to tell Grayson something, he thought. Something...short.

Eventually he settled on sending him a letter, one with no return address.

I will be a while, he wrote. *A week, possibly more. Will return to Harvil after to finish the designs. I'll explain when it's all finished.*

He did not know how to end his missive; anything he could add sounded foolish.

Don't tell me so yet, he finally wrote. *Not until all is said and done. It will all turn out beautifully, I'm sure.*

He wished he felt as sure as he pretended. He provided no return direction. He didn't want Grayson to know what he was doing, after all.

To Mr. Alabi at Harvil Industries, he sent another letter: *Another business matter has arisen. You all have never needed me anyway. We'll finalize designs when I arrive in two weeks. There won't be a moment to spare. Thanks for your understanding.*

And that was how it started for Adrian, the week before the wedding—with a mistake and a promise.

CHAPTER THREE

For Camilla, it started three days before the wedding —on a Monday, with another mistake.

It was already half-two, and it would have been *nice* if someone had told the household staff that guests would be arriving that day. Warning given a week ago would have been preferable; even notice provided yesterday would have been acceptable. For God's sake, a hint this morning at breakfast would have been better than what had *actually* happened, which was that the carriage pulled up outside just as Camilla was serving pudding at lunch.

Rector Miles had jumped up from the table. "Right!" He'd smiled broadly. "Bishop Lassiter is here now. Is everything in readiness?"

Nothing had been in readiness.

The sheets in the spare room had not been aired; no particular plans had been laid for supper except a course of roast chicken and rolls. The household had erupted into chaos, and Camilla had not had a moment to think in the time that followed.

"Camilla," Kitty was saying as Camilla dashed up the

stairs, staggering under her load of linen. "Camilla, why are the extra servants' beds not made up yet? I asked you *three hours* ago."

Kitty was not the housekeeper. She was just another maid-of-all-work like Camilla. But she had been around longer than Camilla, and so took it upon herself to order Camilla about when she had the chance.

"Because they're not," Camilla answered shortly. "But they *will* be."

"See that they are. Then come help me polish the silver. It'll be needed for tonight. Think how it will reflect on us if so much as a single fork has spots."

"It won't."

"Pardon?"

"It won't." Camilla popped the door to the male servants' room open with her hip. "It won't reflect. If there's spots? There will be no reflection?"

No response. Thank God Kitty had not heard that dubious attempt at humor.

Camilla shook out a sheet and wrangled it into place with a practiced air. When she'd been young and in an entirely different situation, she'd dreamed of marrying well and running a household far larger than this one. That had obviously not happened, and there was no point looking back to bemoan could-have-beens. But she could put on a square sheet, tight and perfect, in forty seconds flat. It wasn't much to be proud of, but then, Camilla found her pride where she could. It was nice to be good at *something*.

She reached for the second sheet.

"Camilla!" Cook's call drifted up the servants' stairs. "Camilla, you're needed *now*. Someone must bring the tea in for the bishop, and you're the only one with the manners for it."

"One minute!" She shook out her sheet.

"No minutes! Now!"

Sheets. Silver. Serving. All of which had to be done *now*, because the rector hadn't had the decency to inform his staff of an impending visit.

Camilla slammed the sheets down and growled. "I don't have *time* for this shite."

"Who does?"

It was an amused voice behind her, an unfamiliar voice. A man's voice—and since this was the male servants' room, perhaps she should not have been so surprised. Still, she jumped, startled.

The man who stood in the doorway was utterly striking. He was tall and dressed in dark blue with contrasting crisp white linen. He was African—or, no, probably not that, Camilla amended, thinking of his voice.

He'd sounded very British. Just two words, and she could hear a hint of West Country in his accent. Those vowels reminded her of the years she'd spent in Bath when she was fifteen. The other girls had laughed at her then, saying Camilla was putting on airs with her language. She had tried to sound like them. When Camilla had been dragged to the other side of the country after that, her new compatriots had laughed at her and told her she sounded like a country bumpkin.

This man just sounded friendly. He was watching her with a smile.

Funny, how much more striking that contrast of crisp linen was with his brown skin than it would have been for a white man. He made everyone else seem utterly pallid by comparison.

She'd seen black people before—servants and sailors and speakers. She'd never cursed in front of one until now. Camilla had always blushed easily; she felt her cheeks flame. How utterly uncouth he must think her.

"I—" She swallowed. "Just now, you may have heard, ah—"

He looked visibly amused. "I'm absolutely positive that I heard you say, 'I don't have time for this trite...'" He trailed off, gesturing.

She couldn't help herself. It was just a little kindness, to pretend he hadn't heard her, but little kindnesses were still kindness. She couldn't help herself; she smiled. "Oh, is *that* what I said? Of course. I don't have time for this trite... But now I'm confused. That's not a complete sentence. This trite *what?*"

"You didn't say." Maybe it was because his eyes sparkled. Maybe it was because Camilla had always bloomed under any sort of attention. Maybe it was because she'd been working furiously without so much as a half-second to breathe for the last hour. But she found herself blushing. Again.

"That doesn't sound much like me." She met his eyes, aware that speaking like this was a bit too forward. She was too tired to care. "I'll have you know that I usually end my sentences with nouns when it's called for. You must think me entirely ungrammatical. We can't have that."

"Ah." He shrugged. "I assume you would have finished what you were saying had I not interrupted you. The fault is all mine."

"If you had not interrupted me," Camilla continued, "you would have heard me say, 'I don't have time for this trite bullshit.'"

Uncouth, forward, impatient—everyone always counseled Camilla to hide what she was. She'd never been able to do it properly. If this man hated her, best he discover it quickly—before her imagination caught fire and she let herself get hurt with her own expectations.

But instead of backing away, he actually laughed at this,

his eyes crinkling up in a way that made her smile back at him.

"If you haven't guessed from Cook's shouting," she said, "I'm Camilla. That's Miss..." *Worth*, she did not say. It had been more than a year since she introduced herself by her real name. She couldn't be Camilla Worth anymore; Camilla Worth would be an embarrassment to her family. "... Winters," she finished. "Miss Winters to you."

"Mister..." He paused, imitating the way Camilla had drawn out her fake name. "Hunter, His Grace's valet."

A valet. To a bishop. *Well* above her current station, she reminded herself, and she had best remember not to be foolish. She really needed to get away before Mr. Hunter made her smile again.

But—"I look forward to speaking with you," he said, and he sounded as if he meant it.

Camilla always got carried away with herself. It was her worst flaw in what was undoubtedly an unending sea of unmendable flaws. She wanted so badly to be *wanted*. She'd been told again and again to stop, to have some decorum, and she rarely managed it. Likely she never would.

There was nothing particularly appreciative about the glances Mr. Hunter gave her; she should not allow herself to imagine that his gaze actually lingered on her. For heaven's sake, she was the only thing in the room. What else was he to look at?

Still, he smiled at her one last time, and she couldn't help but smile back. He was a valet to a bishop. That put him far above her station, and he was too handsome for her anyway. Besides, how long would he stay? Days, at best.

It was foolish to imagine that a little conversation was akin to flirtation. But Camilla had been foolish before.

Her glance, she knew, was possibly a little too familiar.

"Unlikely. We'll never speak again. I will perish from over-work before we have a chance to exchange another word."

There it was again. She was flirting.

"I'll be back to finish the sheets," she said, because talking of beds would *definitely* make the situation better. "When I die, make sure that Kitty gets my wire brooch. She's admired it so."

"I'll make up the beds."

"You're too kind. I'll—"

"No," he said with a twinkle in his eye, "you don't under-stand. If you perish, I'll have to get the bishop's formal blacks ready for the funeral. It's far less work to just finish the sheets."

He wasn't flirting, she reminded herself firmly. That sparkle in his eyes didn't mean anything.

"In that case," she said, "I'll leave you to it, and maybe we can have that word later."

He smiled. "Maybe we can."

God, Camilla was an idiot.

She had a moment to look up, dazedly, into his eyes. They were brown, flecked with gold, and when he smiled, it felt as if the whole world was smiling with him. Idiocy.

It took a particular sort of perverse obstinacy to fall in love at first sight. It took absolute pig-headedness to do it again and again and again. To imagine affection from nothing and then hope for it repeatedly.

It was, in short, Camilla's usual rebelliousness—to believe, after all this time, that someone would like her. It wasn't the first time she'd been taken with someone simply because he was kind and handsome and a stranger.

None of the people familiar with her liked her at all. It would *have* to be a stranger who decided she was worth something, if it were ever to happen. And it had been so long, her chance *had* to come up—

"Camilla! Tea! *Now!*"

The shriek up the stairs jolted her out of her state of daydreaming. Camilla jumped and ducked her head. "I'm —that is—"

"Goodbye, Miss…Winters," he said softly.

She shouldn't. She really should not. "Au revoir, Mr… Hunter." She could not help her hopeful smile, the lift in her heart. She could not help grinning as she ran down the stairs.

He was only going to be here for a short time. Then he'd leave. Besides, if he was employed by a bishop, he *had* to have an impeccable character.

She was flighty, flirty, and terribly good at fooling herself. Camilla *knew* this about herself. She'd learned it all too well. But a few hours, maybe a few days.

How could it hurt her to be happy for a few days?

～

Five minutes later, Camilla ducked into the rector's office, where the two men were ensconced deep in conversation.

Summer sun was shining through the window, laying a cross-hatched pattern on the surface of Rector Miles's desk. She set the large tray there, then gathered up the teapot.

"As far as charity works for the parish," Rector Miles was saying, "I honestly cannot imagine doing more than we are doing at the moment."

Camilla did not think much of the rector's plans for charity. It was flaw number forty-nine in her, she supposed—a tendency to judge others when she had more than her own share of defects to correct. She *tried* not to judge—a little bit —but alas.

That would no doubt be engraved on her tombstone: *Camilla tried to be good, but not for very long.*

It was particularly hard for Camilla not to judge Rector Miles on the matter of charity, though. She and Kitty were both his charity projects, and while she did see some charity in his actions, she was *still* essentially an underpaid servant. She knew she should to be grateful to him, but...

"No," the bishop replied. "I've seen what you do, and there is no benefit in devoting any more funds to the matter."

Camilla was grateful to Rector Miles. She *was*. She *had* been in trouble when he rescued her. He'd made her see all the possible consequences of her behavior. He'd taken her in, and he patiently spent time thinking of her.

No point returning to what she *had* been. She'd made a mistake—several mistakes—but she was trying to do better. She'd focus on that.

"Then we are agreed." The two men nodded at each other.

Camilla set spoons and saucers down, aligning them precisely, then arranged the little ceramic dishes of milk and sugar between them.

It had not been *trouble* trouble that the rector had saved her from. At least, it had not been immediate danger. Just the kind that put her immortal soul in peril, even if it had made her mortal being temporarily happy.

"I've been thinking of the best way to handle the situation," Rector Miles was saying. "It could potentially become a larger issue."

Mr. Hunter had seemed kind. Just thinking of a man's shoulders could not endanger her mortal soul, could it? They were just shoulders. Shoulders were above the waistline. *Far* above the waistline. Surely it would be entirely innocent to think of them. Would it not? Camilla fetched the sugar biscuits and set them above the tea things.

"And here I thought the matter was already decided," the bishop said.

The tea-tray had been laden with treats today, but who

had put it together, Camilla didn't know. One didn't serve sandwiches tossed higgledy-piggledy on a plate to a bishop. She shook her head and arranged them into a spiraling star.

The bishop was right, even if he hadn't been addressing Camilla. She'd already made her decision. She was *trying* to be good. She didn't *want* to have to think of her mistakes, and that meant no flirtations. No shoulders. No nothing.

Down that path lay danger to her immortal soul. If she were a better person, she'd accept what she ought to be with a glad heart. But there were times Camilla quite resented her immortal soul.

Sometimes, Rector Miles spoke of the conflict between good and evil as if an angel and a devil stood, one on each shoulder, whispering suggestions. For whatever reason, Camilla had been assigned an entire regiment of devils. And her angel was—at best—defective. Still, it tried its best.

"There will always be people who donate to the church," Bishop Lassiter was saying. "They'll do so loudly, to appear virtuous to those around them. Mrs. Martin is no different. Trouble is always possible, but we should handle her as we have all the others."

It was sobering. Camilla had to find her virtue elsewhere —in overheard conversations, perhaps. Camilla laid the scones in a straight line and made sure the jam and clotted cream had not spilled from their containers.

Trouble was *always* possible, and here she was, trying to justify her choices once again.

"But," Rector Miles said, "she's demanding—"

"Don't give in."

That was what Camilla had to remember. Her first impulse was wicked; her second no better. She usually didn't start questioning if she was on the right path until ten minutes later, when she'd already made a fool of herself. At least now she was questioning what she was doing, even if it took her some time. That was improvement, was it not? She had just met Mr. Hunter. She had no business flirting with him.

One last check of the little cakes, and she nodded.

"We have official policy in place precisely for times such as these," Bishop Lassiter said. "We cannot disclose the information she requests for reasons of parishioner privacy. It's that simple."

Camilla set the tray of sandwiches in front of the men with a flourish.

Bishop Lassiter stared at the silver tray, at the attractive display of sandwiches, then raised his head to contemplate her. He blinked and frowned, as if seeing her for the first time. "Girl. What are you *doing* here?"

"Me?" Camilla had thought that putting out tea things was self-explanatory. "Sandwiches, Your Grace?"

"She's just laying out the tea, Lassiter," Rector Miles said.

The bishop glared at Camilla as if she'd done something terribly wrong. As if he could intuit the legion of demons on her shoulder, urging her on to sin.

Oh look, whispered one of those demons. *Here's a man you have no inclination to flirt with. How bad can you be?*

Horrible. She was absolutely horrible. Camilla ducked her head to hide her wicked smile. "My apologies."

"Camilla," Rector Miles said, a little harshly. "I think you have enough to do without dawdling over the scones. Get on with you."

"Yes. Of course." She curtsied again, then darted away. Stupid devils. She was going to be good, so good.

All she had to do was *not* flirt for the next few days. How hard could that be?

~

The servants' table at dinner was a crowded affair. It did not bring back Adrian's happiest memories to be seated at benches belowstairs, the air smelling of onions and yeast, packed thigh-to-thigh with the other servants.

The looks the other servants gave him were all too familiar—uncertain at best, suspicious at worst. The questions were no better—*where are you from?*

The footman who asked was unwilling to accept Bristol as the answer, even though it was the truth.

The fact that Adrian was, essentially, lying about his family made the endeavor even more fraught. He had never been particularly good at lying. The faster Adrian figured out what Lassiter was about, the sooner he could drop this stupid disguise and get back to his life.

It was, as his uncle had said, something to do with money. He was sure of it now. It was always something to do with money. Money made idiots of men.

The money didn't make sense in Rector Miles's household, either, and that always set off little alarms ringing in his head. Two maids, a housekeeper, a cook, two footmen—that was an utterly massive staff for a single widowed rector. Then there was the china upstairs, the sheets—brand new everywhere, turned just once even for the servants, the *food*—

"My apologies," the cook was saying, "it's nothing but potatoes and cheese. We'd no notice of visitors, and this was the best I could manage."

Who apologized for potatoes and cheese?

"I've had far worse," Adrian said, "at far superior households." True.

"Well," muttered one of the rector's servants, "*that's* no surprise, as—"

The woman he'd met earlier—Miss Winters—thumped

the man on the arm with a metal spoon. "Don't be an ass, Salton."

The cook gave Miss Winters a slightly less casual tap with her spoon. "Don't use language like that, Camilla. Not around guests. Whatever will the bishop's men think of us?"

Adrian had made it a point to settle on the bench just opposite the delightful Miss Winters. She was pretty—dark hair that he suspected would fall in waves if she ever let it down from that white cap, and eyes that twinkled even though she was trying to look demure. She even had a little color to her skin, as if she weren't afraid of sun.

He would have sat near her even if he wasn't searching for information. As it was, she'd proven talkative earlier, and gossip was the best place to start.

"I mean it," Adrian said, shifting in place. "I've visited deans who set a worse table, and who had not so fine a staff. You must all be very proud."

Gossip was a delicate business, and Adrian didn't usually indulge. Still, even the most loyal, closed-mouthed servants, the ones who would never speak an ill word, would not hesitate to boast of their employer out of pride. Wouldn't they?

"It's because Camilla is half-price," said a maid across the table from him. "She's inexpensive because—"

Miss Winters flushed red and jabbed an elbow into the woman's side. "Kitty!"

"The rector came into a little money some years back," the cook said. "His aunt or some such? I hadn't the details, but he's able to do the household proud, far beyond a rector's means."

Maybe the answer was just that prosaic.

Adrian doubted it.

He probed a little deeper. "Certainly there's no need for apologies as to the fare. Why, the bishop received a telegram just yesterday and rushed here immediately. You must have had no notice to speak of."

"None," moaned the woman who had been called Kitty. She was willow-thin and white-capped, and half again as old as Miss Winters. "We had no idea you were coming until everyone arrived just after noon."

"I wonder what all the commotion could be about," Adrian said, hoping he sounded idly curious. "What could occasion such a swift arrival?"

"Well, if *anyone* knows, it's Camilla," Kitty said. "*She* brings the rector his tea because her soul is most in need of his prayers."

Miss Winters's eyes narrowed. She bit her lip, looked at Adrian, and blushed. Then she shook her head and applied herself to her potato. "In this instance, I know nothing."

He was getting quite the idea of Miss Winters. He could just imagine. She was young enough that she should have had a family to pray for her soul, not a rector who employed her at…half-price, had they said? Likely she was an orphan being taught a trade—so they would say—and she was told to be grateful for anything she could get. Her parents had no doubt been in debt or some such and her employment—at half-wages, good lord—had been presented to her as charity, not avarice. Adrian had seen it often enough.

Alas, this was business as usual, not a scandal—and even if it *had* been a scandal, it was the rector's, not Lassiter's. Adrian wasn't here to convince maids to demand a full salary.

"You may not know, Miss Winters," he said to her across the table, "but perhaps you would speculate. I imagine you're good at piecing together a story."

Their eyes met over the table and Miss Winters flushed again.

Adrian had pegged her about a minute after meeting her.

She was young enough to still have dreams, and lonely enough that she'd attach them to anyone who was kind to her. A smile, a slight hint of preference, and she'd tell him anything he asked.

Her eyes met his. There was a hopeless glow in them. She licked her lips, as if she had suddenly become aware of her mouth.

Adrian tried not to think of his in return. She seemed susceptible enough to kindness, and he didn't need complications. He was bad at lying, as it was—if he let himself think too much about how pretty she was, his preference would show. He didn't need to make her feel uncomfortable.

But Miss Winters, blush and all, just shook her head and looked away, smoothing her skirts. "No," she said quietly. "I *could* speculate, but I shouldn't. I have nothing interesting to add."

"Good for you," the cook said. "You don't want to be Half-Price Camilla forever, do you?"

Her eyes flashed. My God, that appellation. Half-Price Camilla? Adrian knew too well how unkind servants could be. Those who had little always wanted to shout to the rooftops that someone else had less.

He'd been put in his place often enough that he knew what it looked like.

He could track her rebellion by the pink splotches rising on her neck, the thinning of her lips, the way her shoulder blades drew up, tight and full of tension.

He almost thought she would burst with the effort of holding in her response.

But she didn't. That light in her eyes faltered; she looked down and took another bite.

Ah. Damn. Adrian had met people—men and women—who had had their hopes crushed right out of them. He'd known youths who still had their heads in the clouds.

This was the first time he'd seen someone in the process of getting crushed.

You know, he thought idly, *perhaps it would not hurt if I said a word to her...* But no. He had so much to do as it was. He needed to be back at Harvil within a week. Sooner would be better.

It rubbed him the wrong way to stay silent, but this entire endeavor rubbed him the wrong way. She couldn't be his concern. Either she had useful information or she didn't.

Miss Winters didn't look at him again during the meal. She didn't look at him so assiduously that he twice saw her on the brink of looking and coloring, before turning away again.

He shouldn't care.

But as he finished his potato, he wondered how long it took to crush a woman's spirit, and if there was anything to be done about it.

At the end of the meal, when she was standing up and clearing the table, he offered to help gather the plates.

She turned toward him, head down, hands full with the bread basket.

"You're kind." It sounded like an accusation when she spoke. She shook her head, as if dispelling a dream. "You're very kind," she said again, "and I don't need it. But thank you."

∼

The day had been long, and Camilla had tried so hard to be good.

She had not flirted over dinner, not even when Mr. Hunter had almost made her laugh four times.

It was unfair that she should run into him on the stairs after she'd finished the dishes and banked the fires for the night. Entirely unfair—and since he had undoubtedly dressed the bishop for the evening, extremely understandable.

"Miss Winters." He nodded at her.

It was an open stairway. She was a maid-of-all-work. There was nothing wrong with wishing him a good night. She did so to the other male servants all the time.

Nothing, except she'd have to look him in the eyes, and no matter what her single, overworked angel told her, she still *liked* him. She could feel the beat of her pulse in her wrist just because she stood close to him. She kept her head down, nodded in his direction, and turned to go into the room shared by the female servants.

"Oh, no," he said softly behind her. "It happened."

Before she could think, she turned to him.

Oh. A terrible idea, that. He was still handsome and a stranger, and with only the one guttering oil lamp standing at the head of the stairs, he seemed mysterious and enticing to boot. Golden shadows glittered across his skin. Camilla set one hand over her belly to quiet a sudden riot of butterflies.

"*What* happened?"

He smiled at her. "You perished after all."

It took her a moment to remember their earlier conversation, the one where she'd…flirted with him by claiming death? Oh, excellent work, Camilla.

She had only *felt* dead earlier; she came to life under his perusal, as if she were a parched plant drinking the first rain after a drought.

"I did," Camilla said slowly. "I am a walking corpse, shambling about the countryside."

Damn, damn, damn. She was doing it again. She was flirting—awkwardly, with talk of walking corpses—but no matter how badly she was doing it, she was still flirting.

"Does Kitty get your wire brooch, then?"

He recalled their conversation. He'd paid attention to her. She felt another burst of warmth.

No. She couldn't give in. Memory, she scolded herself, was not affection. She was not going to fall in love, not *again*. She was going to be good.

But he *had* remembered. Camilla exhaled and looked over her shoulder, at the servants' beds laid out in a row. Kitty was already under the covers. Cook would be up shortly.

"No." Camilla shook her head. "I am a jealous corpse. If she took it, I'd rise from the grave and do hateful things to her."

He smiled as if she'd made a joke. Probably because she had.

"Well." He nodded to the room behind him. "Rest in peace, then. I'm glad I got to meet you before you passed away." He tapped her arm, ever so slightly.

It was just a friendly gesture, but still her heart leapt. God. She wanted so much more than the brush of a finger. She felt absolutely starved for touch.

But Camilla knew how these things went, these little flirtations. One went from trading witticisms and smiles to trading…more. She was Half-Price Camilla because of that more.

She didn't fool herself, either.

She wasn't good; she never would be. But if she pretended hard enough, maybe she'd eventually fool everyone else.

She bit her cheeks to hide her smile.

"Good night," he said.

And because she wasn't good, she could feel her heart thump in reply. "Sleep well," she offered tentatively.

His eyes met hers one last time, and she thought of all

that sleep entailed—beds and removal of clothing and vulnerability...

Her cold covers awaited her, and for a moment, a thread of unadulterated loneliness rose up inside her, twining cold tendrils around her heart. "Sleep well," she said again, and retreated as best she could.

CHAPTER FOUR

Thankfully, Camilla didn't encounter him the next morning. She made plans—good plans, sober plans —to maintain a reasonable distance with no swearing or flirting or talk of shambling corpses at all.

Still, she felt sore and raw all day. That haunting feeling of loneliness from last night had not abandoned her; she was more aware than ever that her heart ached.

Maybe it was because she'd spent all yesterday tearing up and down stairs, carrying sheets and polishing silver until her arms ached. Maybe it was because of the way Mr. Hunter had looked at her the prior evening—with pity, as if he could see through Camilla's attempts to be good, and knew how little chance she had of succeeding.

For whatever reason, she felt particularly low when she slunk into the rector's study that afternoon with the tea things.

"There are rumors that Shoreham is stepping down," the bishop was saying, "and you've positioned yourself perfectly to…"

The conversation stopped as the plates on her tray

clinked, drawing the men's attention. They looked up at her as if irritated at the intrusion.

Camilla bowed her head and laid everything in place as quickly and silently as possible—toast points, tea, milk, sugar, lemon tarts. Her fingers lingered a second on the dish of tarts. She had loved lemon tarts once. No. She wasn't going to look back at a time when she'd had them regularly herself. She didn't think she could eat one any longer.

"Miss Winters," said the bishop.

Camilla jumped, yanking her hand away. "My apologies, my most abject apologies."

One moment. One moment, one little lapse of judgment, and there she was—straying into dangerous territory. Dreaming. *Remembering.*

His frown deepened at this. "What are you apologizing for?"

"For—taking so long?"

He blinked. "Well. Don't do that, then. I've been told that you are not, in fact, Miss Camilla Winters."

Camilla swallowed.

"That your name is Miss Camilla Worth."

It was, to be technical, *Lady* Camilla Worth, but after all that had happened to her, insisting on her title would do more harm than good. She couldn't get above herself. She didn't dare reveal the truth. She didn't answer this query with anything more than a nod. Her heart pounded heavily in her chest.

"That's an interesting family name."

She would not say a word.

"It's the family name of the late Earl of Linney," he said, examining his fingernails. "The one who was executed for treason a handful of years ago."

Nine years ago, it had been. Camilla tried not to think of the date, but she remembered it too perfectly. Almost half of

Camilla's life—if that barely remembered past really belonged to her. Her father was dead and a traitor; her brother was dead and transported. Next to them, Camilla's sins were merely banal.

Camilla knew she should hate her father for what he had done—to her, to her family, to the country. But the very thought of him—her brothers, her sisters—opened up that cavern of loneliness in her heart. She'd never been good at hating anyone.

No. Don't look back.

"Is that right?" She glanced at the rector who was watching her. "How very unfortunate that I should share a family name with them, then."

"So there's no relation?"

"I would hardly be setting out tea things if my father were an earl." Camilla ducked her head. "Now, if you'll excuse me…"

"So you don't know Lady Judith Worth."

Judith. A separate wash of forlorn desolation hit Camilla. Once, when she had been younger and even more stupid, her uncle had offered to take her in. Her and Judith and Benedict —and not their younger sister Theresa. She could scarcely recall why any longer—something about Theresa being difficult.

Camilla had said yes to the offer. He'd said she could have gowns, lemon tarts, and a come out, after all. Judith, her eldest sister, had tried to argue.

He doesn't love us, her sister had told her.

I won't starve, Camilla had responded, stupid at twelve.

It seemed a fitting punishment for Camilla, that she'd been granted none of her wishes—not the gowns nor the come out nor the lemon tarts. She'd spent every year since yearning more and more desperately for the love she'd dismissed out of hand.

She'd chosen to live without it; still, somehow, the demons on her shoulder whispered that she might still have it. Someday.

"Ah," the bishop said. "You *do* know her."

Camilla hadn't seen Judith once in the years since—Judith had made it clear she was unwelcome.

Camilla shook her head and spoke through the lump in her throat. "I don't. How would I know the Marchioness of Ashford?"

A pause. She could feel her longing, an almost tangible presence in her chest.

She'd heard the news about Judith's marriage shortly after Rector Miles had taken her in. He was the one who had impressed on her the seriousness of her misbehavior. He had told her that she should not long to be loved so, that it would drive her to destruction. He'd told her that she hadn't earned the right to such care, that the impulse that welled up inside her insisting that she might one day belong somewhere was the devil trying to seduce her.

Judith was married to a marquess, of all things. It was what Camilla had dreamed about when she'd abandoned her family. Rector Miles was right; Camilla didn't deserve what Judith had. Still, she could not stop herself from dreaming.

The bishop was watching her with a troubled air. "You seem to know her well enough to know of her wedding. Interesting, for someone who claims not to be related."

Camilla exhaled. "Well. Who *doesn't* follow the nobility? Particularly when one family—entirely coincidentally—shares one's name."

"Hmm." He didn't sound as if he believed her. Rector Miles must have disclosed something of Camilla's past if he knew her abandoned last name.

She hated admitting the truth. She hated even thinking it. "It really is the best that I'm no relation, don't you think?"

"Is it?"

"Well—what you've described. The treason." She swallowed. "Judith—I mean, *Lady* Judith's new marriage. The family's position in society must be terribly precarious." She could hear her own voice shaking as she spoke. She pressed her hands into her skirts to stop them trembling.

"Is that so?"

She felt speared by his eyes. "There was talk after the father and the brother had that incident, you know. People said the family was nothing but bad blood."

He examined his fingernails. "You do know quite a bit about them."

"If people thought someone like *me* was related to the likes of them?" Her whole being ached, just thinking of what it would mean. "I imagine it would ruin whatever progress they've managed to achieve in society."

"Someone like you. What are you, then?"

What are you. Not *who*. He looked at her like a thing, and under his gaze she felt like one.

The rector had made her say it—once—when she arrived here. She *knew* she was flawed to her core; she didn't want to have to say it again.

"Nobody," she whispered. "I'm nobody."

The rector must have told Bishop Lassiter the truth, for him to subject her to this interrogation. He must have told him how he found her eighteen months ago.

Kissing a footman she had no business kissing.

Miles had impressed on her the consequences of her conduct—*rumor is, your younger brother is going to Eton now. Maybe the family name can be rehabilitated. Maybe...*

Maybe would be *never*, if the truth about Camilla ever came out.

"That whole business has nothing to do with you, then?"

"No." She whispered the word hoarsely. "Nothing."

"Camilla," said the rector, "I'm filling out my logbook for yesterday. Do you remember who I discussed?"

The relief she felt at the change of subject was immense, a weight lifting from her shoulders. She *liked* being helpful; she had an excellent memory, and she'd often assisted him by providing names. "In the morning, before the bishop arrived? Mr. and Mrs. Watson. Miss Jones. Mrs. Landry. After the bishop, I wasn't about."

"Very well."

"Oh." She paused. "Wait—I do recall one name. Mrs. Martin—you discussed her while I was setting out the tea things."

He didn't smile at her. "That's very helpful. You should endeavor to be helpful, Camilla. That's the only way you'll make progress."

Even that tiny amount of guarded praise had her glowing. In the years since she'd left her sister, she'd had little enough praise. Deservedly so. Camilla had that chorus of devils on her shoulder and no matter how she sometimes felt about the rector, he'd made sure that any rumors of her would not harm her family. She had to remember that.

"That will be all, Camilla."

She escaped, feeling scraped raw.

Judas, it was said, betrayed Christ for thirty silver pieces. Camilla had sold her family for lemon tarts. It seemed fitting that she had nothing.

In a parable or a Greek myth, she would have been doomed to yearn for love hopelessly, forever. But this wasn't a parable or a myth, and that legion of devils on her shoulder still gave her more hope than her single angel.

It's been bad, they whispered, but just hold on. Don't look back; look forward, and it will all come out right. Any day now. Just hold on to your hope.

The rector had told her not to listen to that hope. It

48

sounded sweet, he told her, but it would lead her astray. *Foolishness,* said her angel, but its voice was small in comparison.

One day, said those devils. *It will all be better one day.*

Camilla took a deep breath, shut her eyes, and tried not to believe her devils. As always, she failed.

"Camilla!" The call came from below stairs. Camilla jumped. "Camilla? Where *are* you?"

She came back to herself again, and locked her bitter loneliness away. She tied it up with hope in the center of her heart. With any luck, it wouldn't escape again, not for a good long while.

CHAPTER FIVE

I t had been three days since Adrian arrived in Rector Miles's household, and he still hadn't discovered what he needed. A substantial part of the problem? Being a valet was hard work—particularly since Adrian did not know how to be a valet. Now, he had been told there was a red wine emergency.

Adrian didn't have time for emergencies, he thought, dashing up the servants' stair.

What he *wanted* to do was finish the task his uncle had set to him. But Miss Winters had avoided him the entire second day he'd been there, blushing when their eyes met, looking pensive and thoughtful, as if she'd been reprimanded. The cook knew nothing. Miss Shackleton, the other maid, shook her head and said to speak with Miss Winters. It was all dreadfully inconvenient.

The sooner he found evidence, the sooner he could quit, return to his uncle, and be back about his business.

More saliently, if he didn't find something *soon*, he was going to end up sacked.

Possibly, he thought, as he arrived at the room where

Lassiter was staying, he would get sacked today. He was absolute shite at being a valet, and his inexperience would be exposed at any moment.

When he'd interviewed for the position, he'd promised he was a veritable genius at removing stains. It had been a lie; he knew nothing about removing stains. He knew how to make extremely vibrant stains that would bond with the surface of bone china upon application of heat and not come off no matter what one did with the piece afterward. He had a wealth of expertise in dyes and metal oxides and glazes. Knowing about those processes had allowed him to construct realistic-sounding sentences that bore absolutely no relation to reality.

Luckily, there was one person who knew less about stain removal than Adrian, and it was Bishop Lassiter. The man had listened to Adrian make up some rubbish about vinegar and sunlight and... Adrian couldn't even remember what he had said. It had worked, though, which was a miracle. His lies rarely worked.

But it wouldn't last. He'd just been told that the bishop had spilled red wine down his front at lunch, and was waiting for him in his room.

Adrian opened the door.

A quick glance—nobody in the chair, nobody standing at the window, bed stripped of sheets....

Strange. Lassiter would be up shortly, no doubt.

Adrian crossed to the wardrobe, opened it, and started sorting through the clothing, looking for an appropriate change.

The shirt the bishop had worn two days ago should have done, except it had been stained with mustard. Adrian had tried to launder it, but...who knew mustard was so discoloring? Not Adrian. That yellow blotch would betray him.

Damn. That left—

His train of thought was interrupted by a noise on the other side of the room. He turned to see Miss Winters straightening, feather duster in hand.

Of course. He should have realized someone else was here, with the linen piled in a white heap in the corner.

Miss Winters had been avoiding him ever since that first night. She took a step back from him now, even though she stood on the other side of the room. They'd had almost thirty-six hours of monosyllabic exchanges, thirty-six hours of her almost looking at him before catching herself in the act and blushing.

"My apologies for the interruption," Adrian said, "but I've been told the bishop will be up momentarily. He spilled something on himself at lunch."

"No." Miss Winters frowned. "He didn't."

"But—"

"I cleared away the dishes an hour ago with him in the room. He didn't spill anything."

Adrian frowned. "But—I was told most specifically..." He trailed off. Maybe it hadn't been at lunch? But... Red wine at lunch. What a specific thing to say, if it hadn't happened.

From the back of his mind, intuition pushed a thought forward: Something was off. He'd also been told the bishop was already waiting in the room, and he wasn't.

Ridiculous. It was just a miscommunication.

"That's odd." He turned. "I'll go see what this is about, then, and leave you—"

He reached for the door handle, pressing down. It resisted movement. He tried once again, yanking harder, but to no avail.

That thought came back: Something was off.

He frowned. No. There had to be an explanation.

He turned back to Miss Winters. "The door is locked."

Her eyes widened; she shook her head. "Why ever did you lock the door?"

"I didn't lock the door."

"Well." She took another step away from him; her back hit the wall. "Open it. Open it immediately. It's one thing for two servants to speak in a room with the door wide open. It's another for us to be locked in a bedroom together. It doesn't look good." She shook her head. "It doesn't look good at all. What are you waiting for? *Open* the door."

"I can't," Adrian said. "I don't have a key."

She shook her head. "Open it, open the door."

He gave the door handle another frustrated wrench. "I can't. I don't know how to pick locks. Do you?"

"No, how on earth would I know that? You're the valet!"

Ha. "What does *that* have to do with it!?"

"Valets are supposed to have a wide and varied skill set!"

"Not that wide!" The door wasn't moving. "Not that varied!"

"Well," she gestured. "Climb out a window, then. Do you know how this is going to *look?*"

He gave her an incredulous stare. "We're on the third floor."

"They already call me Half-Price Camilla." She wrung her hands. Her breath was growing shallow. "If they catch me with a handsome man locked in a bedroom, do you *know* what they'll call me?"

"Quarter-Price Camilla?"

He'd been trying to lighten the mood. Apparently, that was not the way to do it. Her cheeks flushed crimson.

"No!" She sounded close to tears. "They won't call me anything at all, because I'll be *sacked*. I have nobody. No references. No family. No money."

Something's off, Adrian's instinct whispered again. But there was nothing to do except…

"Let's be calm," he suggested, "as the situation demands."

Her nostrils flared. "I am *precisely* as calm as the situation demands."

"You're not calm at all."

"*That* is what the situation demands!" She turned from him. "Very well—if you won't do it, I will. I'm going out the window."

She wrenched at the handle; it resisted.

"It's stuck." She looked over at him. "Help me, help me."

He couldn't let her go out the window. She was breathing shallowly, for one, and in skirts, for another. To make matters worse, there were no helpful climbing vines on the outer wall, no convenient trees.

She was going to break her neck. Damn it.

"All right," he said calmingly. "I'll help. But we should talk about a *real* strategy, don't you think?" He came up beside her. She was in the throes of panic. He wasn't entirely sure why—surely, if they were found together they could just tell the truth, and be believed?

"Stop *talking*," she said, "start *helping*."

She wouldn't let go of the little crank that opened the window, so he wrapped his hands around hers. "Breathe," he said. "On three. One—two—"

On two and a half, the door opened.

The other maid—Miss Kitty Shackleton, if Adrian recalled correctly—stood in front, a key ring in her hand. Behind her stood Albert, the footman, Rector Miles, and Bishop Lassiter.

A cold chill ran down Adrian's spine. Something was very much off, his instinct told him again, and this time he listened. Why were they all standing there? Why had so many people come up just to unlock a room?

"*There* they are," said the maid. "Holding hands."

Miss Winters jumped two feet away from him. "The door was locked! We were trying to open a window to escape."

"Really." The rector strode into the room. "Were you." It didn't sound like a question, not the way he said it.

Miss Winters answered anyway. "Nothing happened. We've only been here five minutes."

"You've been up here since you finished with the lunch things." Kitty folded her arms. "An *hour* ago."

"*I've* only been in here for five minutes," Adrian said.

"But, Hunter." It was Albert who spoke now. Albert who, a scant ten minutes ago, had claimed a red wine emergency. "Hunter, you told me you were coming up here to air out the bishop's wardrobe...an hour ago."

A sick feeling bloomed in Adrian's gut. Wrong, this was wrong. So wrong. He should have listened to his instincts the moment they whispered that something was off.

"It's not true," Camilla whispered. "It's just...not."

Miss Shackleton stepped into the room, crossing over to stand by Miss Winters.

"This looks bad, Camilla." The rector spoke in a low, soothing voice. "We all know your past. We know you have terrible impulses, that you often give into them."

Miss Winters turned crimson in ugly blotches.

"Is there some innocent explanation for why you've spent an hour behind a locked door with a man?"

"It wasn't an hour. And neither of us have a key." Miss Winters sounded on the verge of tears. "We couldn't have locked the door."

"You asked me for the spare key this morning," said Miss Shackleton.

"I didn't, I didn't!"

Miss Shackleton reached over, thrust her hand into Miss Winters's pocket, and pulled out a single key on a ring. "What is *this*, then?"

It was like watching a farce play out—and not the funny kind, either. Adrian could imagine how all this might seem, but...

He knew for a fact that she could not have locked the door. She had been here when he arrived—clear across the room from the entrance, feather duster in hand.

She had been standing four feet from the lock when he'd first tried it. Adrian wasn't sure who in this room was lying or why they were doing it, but he knew who *wasn't*. What the hell was happening?

"Camilla," the rector said in a sorrowful voice. "I trusted you when you said you would cease your immoral behavior. You've disappointed me."

Miss Winters started crying. Adrian just felt even more baffled. What was happening? Why?

"She's been flirting with Mr. Hunter since she first arrived," Miss Shackleton said, shaking her head.

"I haven't," Camilla sobbed. "I've been trying so hard to be good."

"The *truth*, Camilla." The rector's voice was calm.

"I flirted a little," she admitted. "The first day. But I did what you always told me to do. I noticed my behavior and I corrected it. Really, I did."

"The *real* truth, Camilla."

She swallowed. Her eyes, shimmering with tears, shivered shut. "I flirted a *lot* the first day."

For God's sake. It hadn't been *that* much.

But the rector shook his head. "Lying, deceit, licentiousness..."

She let out another sob, and something in Adrian's chest snapped.

He took a step forward. "This has been enough. I was here, too; it happened precisely as she said. She's in tears. Have a little human kindness."

A silence swirled through the room.

"So," the rector said. There was a pregnant expectancy in the way he drew out the syllables. "You're willing to make it right?"

"Your pardon?" Adrian said in further confusion. "Make what right?"

"We'll discuss this in my office," the rector said. "Kitty, conduct Camilla upstairs and lock her in the servants' quarters until her future is decided. As for you..."

He gestured at Adrian. None of this made sense. Everything was off. Adrian knew Camilla hadn't locked the door, that he hadn't been in this room for the hour that they claimed.

What on earth was happening?

Then, behind the rector, he saw Bishop Lassiter. Adrian had been sent here to spy on the man for his uncle; that small, self-satisfied smile that touched the bishop's lips froze Adrian's blood.

It was the only explanation he could think of: The bishop knew what Adrian was trying to do.

He had tried to be careful; he hadn't contacted his uncle at all. But Adrian *was* a terrible liar. Somehow, Lassiter must have found out that Adrian was working on his uncle's behalf. The two bishops hated one another. His uncle was willing to spy on Lassiter. Why had he not realized that Lassiter would retaliate?

It made perfect sense. Lassiter had planned this whole bloody thing just to discredit Adrian and any testimony he dredged up. Now, if necessary, he could provide witnesses showing that Adrian was an immoral fellow.

A second thought slotted into Adrian's head.

He should have listened to Miss Winters. She lived in this household; she *knew* what it was like. She had told him it was time to panic, and she had been right.

Unless…

It was *possible* that she was a part of this whole play. Somehow. Maybe not *likely*, but it was possible. She was either a very good actor, or he'd just watched them try to ruin her life simply to hurt him.

"Come," Rector Miles said, gesturing, and Adrian followed. Bishop Lassiter didn't quite smirk as Adrian went past. Maybe it was his imagination, but he still felt a certain self-satisfied air to the man.

Adrian had come here at his uncle's behest to try to bring Lassiter down. He'd hated the idea. He'd hated being in service. He'd hated the very underhandedness of the scheme. He'd been reluctant, to say the least.

Now?

Adrian knew he should be angry. Likely he would be, when he had a moment to think matters through.

But as he left Bishop Lassiter behind, what he actually felt was pity. If Lassiter thought a farce of *this* magnitude was necessary to cover up whatever it was he was hiding?

He'd done something wrong.

He was going to be ruined. Adrian felt sorry for the man.

CHAPTER SIX

The conversation that followed had played out precisely as Adrian had expected—farcically. He sat in the rector's office, in a high-backed wooden chair, bracketed between the bishop and the rector, refusing to perform the part they'd assigned to him.

His uncle *had* taught him how men like this thought. They expected him to be overawed by them.

The fact that he wasn't? It left them baffled and a little angry.

Of course he had been sacked. Good; hopefully the bishop would have all the joy of his mustard-stained linen without Adrian.

He'd just met the bishop's eyes. "Just as well." He had shrugged. "I could not work for you, knowing what you are."

The man had reacted in surprise. "What am I?"

Information was currency, and talking needlessly would erode any advantage Adrian held. Lassiter no doubt thought him some hired pawn. They had no idea who Adrian really was or what he wanted, and he'd best keep it that way.

"You're beneath me," Adrian said. "Both of you—you're liars and undeserving of your offices."

He watched the men color at the insult.

"You'll get no letter of reference from me," the bishop hissed.

"No harm in that." Adrian folded his arms. "A reference from a man with no character would be meaningless."

They gave up trying to make him feel ashamed.

"Of course you'll marry the girl," Rector Miles said.

"Of course I would, if I felt honor bound to do so. As I did nothing that requires such an act, I won't."

"Have you no thought for her reputation?"

They were trying to appeal to his emotion, to distract him from the logic of the situation. Adrian just gave the two men a scornful look. "Don't pretend that either of *you* care about that. If you did, you'd have believed her the moment the door opened. You'd have apologized already. If *you* had insisted there was no problem from the beginning, she wouldn't be facing repercussions. *My* actions haven't hurt her. *Yours* have."

Two hours of resistance on his part, and the men were flummoxed.

They had expected him to bow and scrape and apologize and give in, and his refusal to do so when he should have been begging for mercy was outside their comprehension.

Eventually, they withdrew to a corner of a room and held a whispered conference.

"We'll leave you to consider the ramifications of your decisions," they said, before conducting him to a basement cellar. The door was locked behind him; the high window was barred, preventing escape.

Adrian passed the time thinking of the sketches Mr. Alabi had sent from Harvil. Bears, ornate buildings, and bright designs. It was less than a week now until he had said he would be back. He had no time to be locked in basements. He thought of those sketches. He imagined possibilities for the plates that seemed impossibly far away and watched the shadows lengthen across the floor. The room was full dark by the time they came for him.

"Come along."

"Where are we going?"

"There's no more argument," Lassiter said. "We're going to your wedding."

Nothing fit together. If they had wanted an excuse to sack him because he was getting close, they could have just used the mustard.

Forcing him to marry served no purpose that he could see...except spite, perhaps?

Spite was a real purpose.

Or maybe...

"There will be no wedding," he said, because he insisted on being a person even if they didn't see him as one.

"On the contrary. There will be no more arguments," the rector replied, lifting a pistol.

Adrian's mouth went dry and rational thought fled. Looking down the barrel of a gun did something to his logical ability, choking it into nothing but the tarnished glint of moonlight on metal.

For a moment, he floundered.

"We can't marry," he finally remembered. "There were no banns read. We'd need a special license."

"We've had one sent up."

It didn't make sense. None of it made sense. But Adrian had never had a gun held on him before and it did something to his brain. All that he could think was that he couldn't die by pistol. Not now. His mother had lost three sons to war and gunshot. Grayson had watched at least one of his brothers die in his arms.

They could not lose Adrian, too. Not this way. He could not do this to his family.

Adrian tried to gather his thoughts on the way to the church. They didn't know who Adrian really was. They couldn't; they'd never treat him with such cavalier disregard if they knew his uncle was Bishop Denmore, that he was the grandson of a duke. They thought him a valet, a servant—ignorant of all proper church procedures. They no doubt thought him a hired mercenary.

But he'd served as his uncle's amanuensis on and off for years. He'd read ecclesiastical texts; he still had some in his library.

Lassiter and Miles didn't know the truth, but Adrian did. They could hold a pistol to his head and make him say yes, but it wouldn't be real. With a gun held on him, it wouldn't count as consent.

He was brought into the nave of the church, then conducted to the front. The way was lit only by flickering candlelight.

Miss Winters followed shortly. Her breathing was shallow and shaky. Her hands stretched and clenched, stretched and clenched. She seemed particularly pale, still in the gown she'd been wearing that afternoon.

It occurred to Adrian to wonder what Grayson would say of the affair.

You see? I told you're too trusting.

Well. With a pistol trained on him, now might be a good time to admit that was true.

He'd trusted that a bishop of the Church of England wouldn't force him to marry at gunpoint. That had seemed a perfectly reasonable supposition, honestly. He'd never heard of it happening before. And of course there was a first time for everything, he supposed, but why did he have to be the one to demonstrate the maxim?

He'd trusted that his uncle wouldn't let him get into such a situation.

Probably his uncle had not known what might result.

Even now, standing in a church with the bewildering events of the day behind him, Adrian was still trusting that Miss Winters wasn't a part of this plot.

He contemplated it now, eyeing her. If they suspected he was working with Bishop Denmore, maybe they'd thought to marry him off in order to have her report back what he knew, in which case...

The gun waved in her direction, and she gasped shallowly.

No. That was *too* untrusting. This wasn't her fault.

"I do not consent," he told them in place of his wedding vows. He needed that to be clear, for the sake of his own conscience. For the sake of his future.

The pistol waved in his direction.

He would give no wedding vows. He wasn't married; he refused to be. Still, he made promises as he stood there.

He was not the sort to take pleasure in anyone's downfall. This time, though? He refused to think of these wedding vows as binding, but he committed himself nonetheless. He promised his brother that there would be no cause to worry. He promised himself that he'd untangle himself from this ugly marriage.

As for Miss Winters... They'd judged her expendable, and they'd done their best to make her feel like she was worth nothing for one little mistake.

Adrian wouldn't be her husband. He wouldn't keep any of the promises they forced upon him—not in sickness, not in health, not for better, not for worse.

He made her his own promise, though, as they stood in the hall.

They thought we were expendable. They were wrong. Before we're done, they'll know that.

"Say it," the rector said.

They don't know who I am, but before I'm finished, they will.

"*Say* it."

"I do," Adrian said. And he would.

CHAPTER SEVEN

After the wedding, there was nothing to do but leave. Adrian and his new non-bride weren't offered so much as a room for the night—no surprise there, Adrian supposed—just directions to an inn and their things, already packed for them.

The inn was miles away and it was already dark.

The night air was cold, and Adrian fell into a rhythm, walking and thinking, trying to decide on his plan of attack.

When he had been young, he'd visited his father's family in Maine, where he'd met his great-great-uncle.

His great-great-uncle John had been born into slavery and had lived to see it undone. He lived still—or had the last time Adrian had heard.

He had sailed around the world. Nowadays, he stayed home, tending his garden, with great-great-uncle Henry.

There is no point getting angry at a bad hand, he had used to say. *Especially if the dealer cheated when distributing the cards. Anger leads to mistakes.*

Don't get angry; that's what they want. Get calm. They'll never expect you to do that.

Don't get angry; get creative. Take the hand you have and see whether you might not be holding something your enemy has overlooked.

Don't get angry at the cards; get the dealer out of the game.

Easy to say when it was something other than the entire rest of his life at stake. All the more important to remember it now, when calm, creative plans seemed as distant as his parents, back in Maine with John and Henry.

Adrian had always found walking calming; he focused on it now, one step after another claiming the road until he felt his fury bleeding into resolve. Until the anger clenching his heart slowly started to loosen and he could feel the cold of the wind against the back of his neck.

Then he remembered that he had to return to Harvil in five days, that the designs for the china plates were unfinished, and that he was now married and stuck in a tangle with no easy way out.

He stopped walking. "Fuck." That was when he became aware of something else—footsteps behind him. That noise, that swift scuffle and slide behind him, was Miss Winters. If he could call her that any longer.

He always walked fast; being angry had made him swifter still. He had a good eight inches on Miss Winters, and he had only a small satchel.

He'd been so angry he'd not really thought of her, scrambling after him with her luggage. She must have been half-jogging to keep up.

He stopped in the road and turned to the woman who had been forcibly joined to him in holy matrimony. In his anger, he'd allowed himself to look at her as a thing that had happened to him, but her eyes darted to his, then looked down the road. She wasn't a thing, and this was why he hated being angry.

She was breathing heavily, and he didn't think it was

from just the exertion. This couldn't be any easier for her than it was for him. In some ways, it might be worse. No matter how she felt, he seriously doubted she had wanted to be married at gunpoint.

Don't get mad at the cards, he reminded himself. Miss Winters was no doubt a card, one who hadn't wanted to be dealt in such a cavalier fashion.

"Mr. Hunter?" she asked. He could hear the query in her voice.

Well. He wasn't going to pretend he was happy. "I suppose this…is what it is. We'll have to figure this mess out."

She said nothing to that, but her jaw worked.

"Do you need any help carrying that?"

Her hands clutched tightly around the handle of her valise. "No, thank you. I can manage on my own."

Her shoulders were trembling.

"Are you certain?" he asked dubiously. "Because—"

"It's no trouble at all." She laughed unconvincingly. "Really, I'm very strong. I don't intend to be a burden on you, not ever, and certainly not right from the start. I promise."

"Not to contradict you," Adrian said slowly, "but you shouldn't make promises you can't keep. You are already a burden on me."

She winced. The moon overhead flirted with a ragged cloud; the dim light flickered patchily across her face. Her head bowed. "Of course you're right." Her voice trembled almost as much as her shoulders. "I'm sorry. I wasn't thinking when I spoke. I meant only that I didn't wish to be more of a burden on you. I'm sure you must be worrying about that."

He reached out and took the handle of her valise. "That's not what I meant. I had been thinking we were equally a burden on each other."

Their eyes met for an instant, and he wondered what she

was thinking. They were married—not really; he would have to explain—and he had no idea what she expected. Did she think they were going to become husband and wife immediately? Did she expect them to fall into bed? Did she think that she would have to pretend joy for such a consummation when they scarcely knew one another? When she'd been forced as well as him?

She was pretty and he'd liked talking to her, but that would be unthinkable. He felt sick for them both.

Miss Winters looked away first. "That's very kind of you, but we both know there is no equality here. You had a prestigious position as a valet with a highly respected member of society. I interrupted your employment."

He didn't think she was lying. He didn't think she wished him ill. Grayson would say he was being too trusting again, but the entire *point* of this exercise had been to demonstrate that trust was warranted. No. If Adrian had failed here, it was by not trusting enough. Just look at what he had thought to himself before—that it was no business of his if maids received full pay, that he'd finish his matters and move on, and never mind what that meant for Miss Winters.

He'd ignored the stirrings of his conscience. Look where that had brought him—to this moment on the road, the two of them not watching each other, not knowing what was going on.

This mess wasn't going to resolve itself in the next minute. "Have you eaten?"

"There's no need to worry about that. I'm not hungry."

"That's not an answer. I was locked in the basement after the events of this morning with nothing to eat. I'm utterly famished. Did they give you anything?"

A long pause.

"That's a no, then. Well." Adrian spoke with a cheeriness he did not feel. "That makes the next hour easy. You can't make battle plans on an empty stomach, not unless you want to end up attacking a bakery instead of your intended target."

Her lips twitched in a fleeting smile. "Battle plans? Are we at war, then?"

Too trusting?

No. Grayson had it wrong.

Adrian had not been trusting enough.

"Yes." He pulled her valise toward him. "I have been for a while, actually. Bishop Lassiter and Rector Miles are our enemies. I'll explain everything over supper. There's an inn not far from here."

She did not let go of the handle. "I—I can't. My funds are limited, to say the least. I have tried to be careful with my coin, but…"

"But Rector Miles has been underpaying you," Adrian finished for her, "and you're only human, and you need shoes and the occasional biscuit and hair ribbon."

She blinked, and in that moment her grip on the valise loosened.

"I told you he was the enemy." Adrian eased the luggage from her grasp. "Money is not our problem." He set her bag down long enough to dig in his waistcoat pocket. "Here."

He held out his hand; she took the coin from him almost without thinking, and then looked up in him in incredulity. "But—Mr. Hunter, I can't possibly take this."

"Yes, you can. In fact…" His mind was already racing ahead to the inn, to the evening, and how everything would have to play out. "In fact, you *must*. We haven't any choice, not if we're going to undo what just happened. I'll explain everything over supper tonight, but you'll need your own funds to pay for your dinner and a separate room. People will ask questions if I do it."

"But—"

"Whatever you do, you mustn't tell them we are married. We are not husband and wife, understand?"

Her eyes widened. "I—do—you—" She looked flummoxed. "Are you the sort of man who cannot bear to be contradicted? Because I can understand not wanting to think about what just happened, except... You do realize we *are* married?"

"Contradict me all you like," Adrian told her. "But that ceremony just now? It doesn't matter what words they said about us. We're not husband and wife, not if we don't want to be."

She licked her lips. "I don't think that is how reality works. It doesn't change because you wish it would. I should know; I've tried hard enough."

"They held a pistol on us, Miss Winters. They may have wanted us married; we don't have to be."

"I..." She looked down and sighed. "As you say. It's late. We haven't eaten."

"We have to agree in order to be married," he said. "Nobody else can agree on our behalf. I'm sure Lassiter and Miles think that we'll continue to agree after the pistols are no longer pointed at us, but their plan has done us enough harm. We don't have to continue."

"What does that mean?"

"It means," Adrian said, "that when we are finished, I'm going to feel sorry for everyone who helped this happen."

～

They arrived at the inn forty minutes later. It was late, but not so late that the place was unlit.

Adrian opened the door to find an entry alcove. A little table, empty but for a bell and a book, stood in front of them. In the room beyond, firelight cast a flickering glow. The rumble of conversation from the other room was distant enough so as not to resolve into actual words.

He set the valise down and gestured for Camilla to enter ahead of him. She did; he followed, and let the door shut behind them.

He hadn't had time to even ring the bell before the innkeeper came darting to the front.

"Welcome!" She had a smile on her face, one that faltered —slightly—when she caught sight of Adrian. She glanced at him, then at Camilla, then back at Adrian.

If this were America, she'd likely have thrown Adrian out in that first instant. Here in Britain, though, away from London, she probably saw black men seldom enough that she'd not had a chance yet to decide what to do if one threatened to do something so dastardly as to frequent her inn and give her money.

Adrian was used to this dilemma; he made it easy on the woman by making up his mind on her behalf.

"My good woman." It took a bit of a conscious effort to attempt to mimic his mother, but no more than he'd made to copy the lower-class speech he'd been using up until now.

He made a show of producing his wallet. It was made of fine leather, and he paused to let the innkeeper see the quality of it before withdrawing a coin slowly enough that she could also see that there was far more where that came from.

He flicked the coin to the innkeeper. "For your trouble. I know it's late to arrive, and we must have inconvenienced you and your staff."

"I—"

"I will need a room for the night," Adrian said. His mother would have said *require*, not *will need*, but haughtiness never worked for Adrian the way it did for a wealthy white woman.

The innkeeper's glance shifted to Camilla behind him. "Sir. I... I..." Her chin squared.

Adrian intercepted that thought before the woman could start nattering on about the usual nonsense—*respectable establishment* and so on.

"Ah, are you referring to Miss Winters? We met by chance on the road; she's on her way to serve as a governess to the Smiths in Lower Mackford. She had been given ill directions to an inn for the evening after being let off in the wrong town entirely. We've only arrived together because I knew where to go and she needed some help with her valise. She'll be getting her own room, I suppose."

Camilla's eyes widened at this speech, but she jolted forward. "Yes, please, if you will. I'm sorry to be a bother."

The innkeeper took her in—those wide, luminous eyes, the old valise of cracked leather, the cheapness of her dress coupled with the niceness of her speech. *Governess* was the best Adrian had been able to come up with. The position wouldn't command much respect, but it would hopefully command enough that she'd be treated as if she were a respectable woman.

"Please," Camilla said, her eyes fluttering shut, "please, I don't wish anyone to know. If the...um, Smiths find out I was lost, they'll wonder if I went astray on purpose, and..." She swallowed. "It's very late out."

The innkeeper nodded in decision. "Of course, you poor child. Of course. Let's get you in and warm you up. But if you don't want word to get out, maybe eat in the kitchen?" She glanced at Adrian. "As for you, sir..."

"Mr. Hunter."

The innkeeper bit her lip. "If I send either of you into the common room for dinner, there will be a bit of a ruckus."

"He can eat with me in the kitchen." Camilla looked down. "I would have been lost without him. Nobody else would help me—they saw a woman alone, and..." She looked up. "It doesn't seem fair, does it? If he can't have a bite."

The innkeeper let out a sigh. "It doesn't, does it? Well, I do suppose the Bible says something about kindness to Samaritans and foreigners."

Adrian did not point out that he had been born in England, or that in the Bible, it had been the Samaritan who was kind. Nobody ever liked facts in situations like this.

"If you don't mind eating in the kitchen, I'll serve you there. Cook's gone home for the evening, but we have soup and cold chicken and bread that she's left. It's open enough that there will be no worries for your reputation, Miss Winters, but it's late enough that you'll not be disturbed."

≈

It took half an hour to sit down to food. Camilla took her things up to the room the innkeeper provided for her—not large, she supposed, but anything was larger than the space she'd shared with Kitty and Cook for the last eighteen months.

There was a chipped yellow pitcher of water, a sliver of sweet-smelling soap, a basin, and a clean cloth atop a small table. Camilla wanted nothing more than to wash the day off her skin, as if all her heartbreak, fear, and indignation could be scrubbed into nothingness. Maybe she'd awake in her bed back at the rectory to discover it had all been a nightmare.

Instead, she soaked the cloth and set it against her face. The cold shock of water reminded her that she was *very* awake. Alas.

Her life had turned upside down. No, *upside down* could not describe what had just happened. Her shoulders trembled still, the way they did when she worked for hours without ceasing. She felt rubbed raw. She couldn't believe that it had been just this noon that she'd been sent up to change the bishop's sheets. None of it made sense. They'd been lying, of course. They had to have been lying.

But they'd all seemed so certain that she could not help but doubt her own mind. Maybe they were right. Maybe that legion of devils on her shoulder had pushed her to invent the whole thing with the sheets and the door, because she *was* the woman they feared, someone so brazen...

So brazen that what? That she'd locked the door from clear across the room and forgotten that she had a key in her pocket?

The entire affair was too painful to contemplate at the moment. She shook her head, abandoning the attempt, and finished her ablutions. Then she went down to dinner.

Mr. Hunter was already there. He had a plate of chicken and potatoes—both cold—and a bowl of soup, still steaming.

Camilla settled for just the soup and a bit of bread. He'd given her money, but who knew how long it would last?

Her first spoonful was heaven. Carrot and celery in a broth made from some indeterminate meat should not have been so good, but oh, God, it was warm and it was food.

"Ohhh." She could not help but let the syllable loose.

Mr. Hunter raised an eyebrow.

"The soup," she said. "It practically *melts* on one's tongue."

He blinked. "It's soup. It's not melting. It's already liquid."

She shut her eyes. Maybe the world would go away. Maybe there would be no ruin, no reputational damage, no *husbands* if she wished hard enough.

Maybe there would just be soup.

She opened her eyes to see him still watching her.

"I'm sorry." She had been apologizing to everyone the entire day; she felt as if she could not apologize enough. "But it's very good soup."

He prodded the congealing film on top of his cooling

bowl with a spoon. "It really isn't."

She dipped her own spoon again. Objectively, there was too much broth, too little salt, and almost no meaty bits.

"It's only edible because we're both famished," he told her. "You should eat more than the soup."

She didn't say anything. She took a bite of bread instead. It was excellent bread, delicious bread...

Well, technically, it was both dry and chewy all at the same time, as if the loaf had been forgotten in the cellar for a week after being baked. The crumb was almost impossible to tear with her teeth, and the loaf itself was dense as a board.

"Good thing I'm famished," Camilla said with a little nod of her head. "Or I'd finish the meal far too hungry."

He shook his head. They ate for a few minutes longer. Every bite she took chipped away at her hunger, bit by bit, and made the food less palatable.

She was still hungry when she gave up on the soup.

He set his spoon on the table and prodded the potato with his fork. It promptly fell into bits, as if it had been boiled into mush. "My brother says I'm too trusting, but..." He shrugged. "I am who I am. It's not changing. I could sit here and wonder whether I could tell you the truth. I could dance around the issue and keep silent, and you could wonder why I was behaving in a secretive and irrational manner. Or I could tell you everything all at once, hope for the best, and we could work together to get ourselves out of this situation."

Camilla felt her lips tilt up in a smile. "What an incredibly difficult decision you have before you. You could lock your-self in a cage of your own making. Or you could *not*. I suppose it's up to you."

He stared at her for a moment before his face crinkled into a warm smile. "I like you."

Well, that made one person. It was one person more than

the zero it had felt like an hour before. She took another sip of her soup. "Your voice sounds different." She wasn't sure when it had changed, or even how, the shift was so subtle.

"That's because I'm not trying to fit in with servants any longer. This is how I sound when I'm around family."

"Do you alter your speech much?"

"All the time. Most white Englishmen are nervous enough around me. The more familiar I sound, the more comfortable they are, and the less likely they are to have the constables come after me on some pretext. It's not even something I do on purpose most of the time. I'm just very good at fitting in, in every way that I can."

Camilla thought of her own speech. It, too, had shifted. Once, she'd had a governess who had drilled her on her vowels, slapping her palm with a ruler when Camilla spoke like—what had she called it? "Like a stable boy," the woman had said. "Speech makes a lady." Camilla had eaten it up, believing that if only her vowels were perfect enough, nothing bad could ever happen to her.

But no. She wasn't going to think of her family and the legacy she'd left behind. That version of Camilla was gone forever.

"That makes sense," she said instead.

"Let me get right to it, then. My name is Adrian Hunter. My mother was born Elizabeth Laurel Denmore, the daughter of the Duke of Castleford."

Camilla blinked.

"Which is why," Mr. Hunter said, straightening in his seat, and shifting *something* about his face, something so subtle she couldn't even identify it, "I can also talk like this. Do you see what I mean?"

Like her governess. Like the lady Camilla had once thought she would be. She swallowed and looked up at him. "That's...very good. Bravo!"

"My mother met my father when she was twenty-five and a widow at a meeting of abolitionists."

She looked over at him. "Before slavery was abolished throughout the British Empire? That was a while ago."

"I'm the youngest of..." His smile flickered momentarily; he looked away. "Two. I suppose it doesn't sound so impressive that way, does it? My father was a speaker for the abolitionist cause. Guess where he was born."

She swallowed. It felt rude to make assumptions, but he *had* asked. "Africa?"

"Close. Maine, in the United States of America."

"I didn't think the former colonies were close at all to Africa!"

His smile flashed out at her. "Not that close, no. I was just trying to make you feel better."

The conversation felt like it had the first time they'd met. Despite everything that had happened that day, he was easy to talk to. She found herself smiling in response.

"To make a long story short, when my parents married, her father disowned her entirely. If you'll believe it, my grandmother suggested she could take my father as a lover, but to marry him would be beyond the pall."

Camilla thought of her own uncle, shuffling her off to distant relations without a hint of embarrassment. "I'll believe anything of the gentry, really."

"After tonight? I should say so. In any event, her brother, my uncle on my mother's side, is the Bishop of Gainshire. He kept in contact with my mother. He's always been...shall we say, not entirely opposed to the causes my family cares about? We've always held out hope that maybe he'd come around. He asked me for a favor, and I thought..." Mr. Hunter looked up and let out a sigh. "Never mind the reasons, really. I am explaining how I came to be impersonating a valet. My uncle believes that Bishop Lassiter has done something wrong, and he asked me to help determine what it was."

Camilla's head hurt trying to follow this story. "I...see." She might, in a day or so, after she'd slept. But even on this, the longest day of her life, when she wanted nothing more than to retire to bed for a week... It wasn't the most believable story.

"That brings me to you. You seem like a perfectly nice girl, but I don't wish to be married to you."

That hurt not just her head, but somewhere just beneath her breastbone. Camilla bit her lip. It wasn't that she *wanted* him to swear his undying love. She wouldn't have believed him if he had. But it would have been nice if he'd been a little bit less blunt about not wanting her at all. It had been lovely earlier, when he had said he liked her.

"Of course you do not," she said instead.

"I imagine you don't wish to be married to me, either."

What was she to say to that? She wished the whole last day hadn't happened. She knew what she was—desperate, grasping, *wanting,* so much that maybe she'd hoped that he'd confess over terrible soup that he'd developed an affection for her, something that could blossom into more if they tended it properly.

What luck, that they'd married at gunpoint, she had perhaps hoped he would say.

God, it sounded stupid even admitting it in her head. And his story—she *still* didn't understand it. But of course he hadn't fallen in love at first sight. That didn't happen, not except in stories, and Camilla knew she wasn't any sort of heroine. There was nothing to do but pull her bravado about her like a cloak, and let none of her hurt show.

"I do prefer husbands I've known longer than a week."

He nodded, as if this was the answer he'd wanted. Good. She'd made the right choice.

"So, let us make a pact. I know a little bit about how annulments work."

"Annulments?"

"Yes, annulments." He leaned across the table to look at her. "You must consent to be married, and saying 'I do' at gunpoint is not consent."

Camilla swallowed. "But—the witnesses, *our* witnesses. One of them was a rector who knows me exceptionally well. The other was my particular friend."

She had used to hope Kitty was something like her friend, at any rate. After what she'd said? After the key ring that had appeared in her pocket as if by magic? Obviously, Camilla had been wrong again.

"And we were married by a bishop. Who will believe our version of events?"

"My uncle." He sounded almost uncertain, but as she watched, his jaw set. "My uncle," he repeated more definitely. "I told you I worked with my uncle, the Bishop of Gainshire? He cares for me and my family. I know it sounds ridiculous. I know you have no reason to believe that I would know a bishop on such intimate terms, but it is true. If I were lying, I'd come up with a better story. If I can swear to him truthfully that we qualify for an annulment, he will help us get one."

Camilla bit her lip. "So that's it, then? We just ask your uncle?"

What would happen to her after the marriage was annulled? She tried not to panic at the thought.

"It's a bit more complicated than that. There's this thing called consent after the fact."

Camilla was tired. The day had been interminable. But *that* made no sense, no matter how she turned it over in her head. Either one consented or one didn't. Her nose wrinkled. "That's a thing?"

"Law," he said in commiserating tones, making a face similar to hers. "Ecclesiastical law. But it's not that tricky. We must continue to show that we haven't started to consent to the marriage until it's properly annulled. That means we can't tell other people we're husband and wife."

That sounded very convenient for him.

"I see," she said suspiciously.

"And we cannot, um…" He looked away.

"I'm not a child," Camilla said. "You can say it. We cannot consummate the marriage."

He looked relieved not to have to voice the words. "The non-marriage."

She pulled her bravado about her again. "I have no wish to do either of those things."

"Lovely. We're in agreement."

There was no point wishing that he would say something appreciative at a time like this. It would do no good to idly hope that he would say *someone would be lucky* or *I'd be sorry not to be able to* or any of the polite locutions he could have employed to soften the blow of his not wanting her at all, not even in the slightest.

Camilla was used to harboring ridiculous hopes. She pushed these particular ones away and reminded herself of the truth. He didn't want anything to do with her; that made him like every other person on the face of the planet.

He took a bite of potato and made a face. "Dear God."

There was nothing to do but put on her bravest face. "You've given yourself away. Now I know you're just finicky. It's not possible to ruin a potato."

"On the contrary. Try it."

"That's the beauty of potatoes. They're good mashed, they're good in soup, they're good baked. They're practically a perfect food in and of themselves."

Wordlessly, he speared a pallid section and held out his fork. She took it, and tasted a bite of... Dear God.

"What did they do? Did they cook it in *vinegar?*"

"I think they might have tried to pickle it."

"Pickled potatoes?" Camilla made herself swallow the food. "At least it's alliterative." She frowned at the potato. "Wait. Give that here."

"Be my guest. If you can stomach it, by all means, do so."

She unceremoniously dumped the potato in her soup.

"What are you doing?"

"There." She took a bite of the concoction. "It's not bad. The vinegar of the potato balances the tastelessness of the soup."

When he raised an eyebrow, she reached across the table and filled his spoon. He took it from her, sipped, made a face, and shook his head.

"Well, I've learned something about you. You're one of those people who can find the good in anything, aren't you?"

She'd hoped and hoped and hoped for so long, and it had never done any good. Still, she kept on, hoping, tumbling into love for no reason.

She couldn't protect her heart; she had bruised it too many times to believe she would ever stop. She was going to do it with him, too. She already knew it.

He didn't want to marry her. He didn't want to have sexual relations with her. He didn't want to do anything but break their tepid connection as swiftly as his uncle could manage it.

And still she felt her hope flare, blossoming from the most tepid of compliments. He liked her, a little. That was something. It was a start.

"Yes," Camilla said, with a nod of her head. "I am. That's me."

CHAPTER EIGHT

Camilla's hope lasted until she reached her room and opened her tired valise.

She had not packed her things herself; she supposed Kitty must have done so.

On top of her worn gowns and threadbare stockings was one of her sole indulgences—a crochet hook and a half-finished scarf. She had learned to crochet years ago, and she enjoyed working with her hands on the rare evenings when she had time to relax.

But yarn was dear and she had no money to spare. This particular ball of yarn—half scarf now—had been crocheted and unraveled, crocheted and unraveled, again and again until the strands had begun to thin and fall to pieces.

Still, she'd kept on crocheting with it. She'd made thin scarves and very short stockings and part of something that could have been a jumper—one ball of yarn was hardly enough for more—for years and years.

She had learned to crochet, hoping that it would bring her close to the old woman who had sat at the fire, muttering and creating stitches. It hadn't.

Nothing she had tried had ever worked.

No point dwelling on the past. Camilla shook her head and slid under the covers. That didn't help. The mattress was lumpy and no matter how Camilla shifted, she could not make herself comfortable.

In the light of the kitchen, with Mr. Hunter sitting in front of her, it seemed the right thing to agree. *Let's work together. We'll get an annulment. Then we'll never have to see each other again.*

Even if she believed him—and the premise of his story was, *You should trust me, I've been lying to you all along*—all he'd told her was that he wanted to be free of her.

Free. She shut her eyes and tried to imagine what *free* would look like for her.

Free made sense for someone who could look her in the eyes and recite his family connections with a clear conscience. It was freedom for *him*. For her?

She'd be free to go…where, precisely? To whom? She'd be free to start all over with absolutely nothing to her name but two gowns on the verge of falling apart and shoes that were almost past the point of repair.

What if she'd done as he had, and recited her own family history? Looking back never did any good; she'd learned long ago that thinking of her past only hurt her in the present.

And yet—perhaps because nothing was crueler than a mind on the verge of panic—she found her mind slipping back anyway.

"Actually, *my* father was an earl." It would have sounded utterly ridiculous—like she was making up a story to match his, just to puff up her own badly battered consequence.

How would she have said it? "Actually, my father was an earl. But he was convicted of treason, and my family was ruined. My uncle offered to take me in—look, we've both got powerful uncles! He promised me pretty gowns, and I have no depth of character, so that was enough for me. My elder sister warned me that he didn't love me, but I didn't care. Ever since the day I decided that love was less important than pretty gowns, I've been doomed not to have it. So yes— marriage. Ha! It is definitely not to be expected for one like me."

God, she was pathetic even alone in her own mind— yearning for love after all this time. When was she going to learn? She could still hear her sister: *If you don't want love, we don't want to love you.*

Everything that had happened stemmed from that moment, year after loveless year.

She'd traded it away. She didn't deserve love any longer; she was never going to get it. The fact that she *knew* it, deep down, made her hope blaze all the more keenly in response. Mr. Hunter would want her, maybe, and she'd convince him to love her with…with…with?

With what?

In the darkness of the night, with the weight of years of experience, she knew the truth.

What did she have to offer, really? Her ability to work for half wages?

She exhaled, pressing the backs of her hands into her eyes. She was such an idiot.

It was stupid, stupid, stupid to feel the way she did. Rector Miles had tried to rid her of her worst tendencies. That chorus of devils on her shoulders kept pushing her to believe the most foolish things—that even now, after almost a decade of nobody loving her, someone would suddenly do so. If only she said the right things, Camilla kept thinking, someone would want her to stay.

Mr. Hunter thought of freedom. God, she wished she could care about something so abstract. What did she have?

A few hair ribbons and the money he'd given her. A vast emptiness inside her, the shame of knowing that even though she hadn't gone into that room with lascivious intent, her heart had still picked up a beat to see him there alone. She'd smiled to see him, and an electric current of want had swept through her.

She couldn't make sense of what had happened—of the door being locked, of the key in her pocket—except this way: Maybe it was as the rector always said—she had sinned in her heart, and that was why this had come upon her.

That was why she'd been married off to a man who didn't want her. That was why she was alone on her wedding night, with nobody to love her in even the most transient meaning of the word.

She wasn't sure when she started crying—she was just glad she'd managed *not* to do it around Mr. Hunter. She hated crying, and she hated that she cried so easily.

He was so strong, so calm, so *rational*, and she was nothing.

The pillow was made of hard, lumpy rags; her shoulders shook as it soaked up her tears. She hadn't had time to find a handkerchief in her valise, and the thought of getting out of bed to search for one was too daunting.

She cried until the moon sank low enough to shine through her curtains, cried for the family she'd left for such a stupid reason, cried for the uncle who had sent her off for bad behavior, cried for the friends she thought she'd made at every stop along the way.

She had spent years hoping and hoping and hoping. Three years ago, she'd hoped Larissa would swear lifelong devotion; instead Camilla had been sent on as a bad influence. Two years ago, James had told her she was pretty and sweet, and she'd made herself as pretty and sweet for him as she could, only to have him swear at her and call her names when they were discovered together.

She'd even hoped to impress Rector Miles with the way she'd changed.

Fat lot of good that had all done her.

Old Mrs. Marsdell had used to quote Shakespeare—*to thine own self be true*, she had used to say, usually as a justification for why she was such a harridan.

Camilla had been true to everyone *but* herself.

She'd made herself over and over into someone who might be wanted, turning herself again and again like an overused sheet. Now she felt threadbare.

And look—she was doing it again.

Mr. Hunter wanted her to be his ally, to help him break free of their marriage.

Why *should* she do as he wanted? A vision flitted through her head—of how she might resist. He'd told her himself how to not annul the marriage, trusting she wouldn't use it against him. After all these years, why *shouldn't* she try?

She might force him to stay. She didn't need love; she was just so, so tired of being left behind. She fell asleep, grimly imagining how she might force him to recognize their marriage.

When she awoke again, it was morning.

Sun peeked through the gap in the curtains. Birds were singing outside; she pulled the curtains back to see a cloudless sky on a perfect day. The air was crisp and sweet, scented with the smell of cut grass.

The ache in her shoulders from carrying her valise had matured into soreness; she stretched her arms overhead and felt her muscles protest. Her whole face hurt from last night's tears.

She was going to have to go downstairs and see Mr. Hunter.

She inhaled.

She remembered her strategy, formulated well past midnight. Wait. What had she thought? She'd imagined seducing him. Telling the world that he'd debauched her. Last night, exhausted and angry, it had seemed almost rational.

In the morning, these plans felt like odd, dark dreams.

He was going to rid himself of her, just as everyone else had done.

It was true: rationally, she *should* be angry at him.

To thine own self be true, Camilla thought ruefully.

There was no reason to avoid anger except this: She wasn't an angry person.

Camilla had been sent away over and over. Rector Miles had told her that the hope she carried was a legion of devils whispering from her shoulder, and despite his admonitions, she'd kept on hoping. She'd picked herself up and moved on time and time again.

It was time to face the truth about herself. If her hopes had not shattered for good by now, they weren't going to do so. She was the kind of person who, when dragged into hell, would hatch a plan to win the devil over with a well-cultivated garden of flame and sulfur. It wouldn't matter if it was impossible. She would still try. She just *would*.

Camilla took a deep breath and stretched her arms wide.

I like you, Mr. Hunter had said last night. *You're one of those people who can find the good in anything, aren't you?*

She looked out over the fields. They'd been picked over, some early summer crop plucked from the ground, and the remnants plowed over. They were now just long muddy furrows waiting to be planted with the eventual autumn harvest. She was the kind of person who could see all that ugly dirt and imagine the little seedlings that would poke bright green heads through the soil in a matter of weeks.

Everything she had thought about herself last night was true. She was worldly, idealistic, lascivious, flighty, and desperate. These were the foundations of her character, and no doubt they'd be her undoing, as they'd been at every step along the way.

Well. She'd tried doing what Miles wanted. She'd told herself her hope was a legion of demons leading her astray. She had tried to be good.

It hadn't worked. This was why she tried not to look back: Nothing she did ever worked, and it was best to forget that it had happened.

With sunlight kissing her face, she could feel her desperation fading.

You're one of those people who can find the good in anything, aren't you?

"Yes," she said. Her chin rose. "Yes, I am."

Maybe nobody would ever love her, but she'd hoped beyond reason for such an eternity that it appeared she no longer needed a reason for it. Hope made absolutely no sense under the circumstances, but it was the only thing that hadn't abandoned her.

She wasn't going to let it go.

~

"You don't look like you slept," Adrian said, looking across the table at Miss Winters.

Her eyes were red and puffy, her skin wan. Their rooms weren't on the same floor of the inn, but hers had been immediately below his.

He had suspected last night that he'd heard her sobbing. He could hardly blame her.

She gave him a dazzling smile that made him doubt what he had heard. "Of course I couldn't sleep. I was thinking."

He took a gulp of coffee. "I was, too. Our first course of action must be to contact my uncle."

She blinked. "Actually, I was thinking about what you said. That your uncle thought there was something not right with the rector. I have quite a good memory, you see, and I had an idea."

"I'm sure it's a good idea." The coffee scalded his throat. "And I absolutely want to hear it. I've inquired; it will take me an hour or so to go into Lackwich. That's the nearest town where there's a telegraph office. I can get everything taken care of in practically no time flat. Information and consultation really ought to be our first priority."

Her lips flattened, but only for a moment. "I see. Of course."

"You don't mind staying here until this afternoon?"

She stilled, looking at him. "You'll come back?"

For a moment, he felt a flicker of annoyance. Then he remembered that she didn't know him, and what she did know of him was that they'd met when he was pretending to be a valet. She didn't *have* to believe him.

"I'll come back," he said. "Before noon. Hopefully, my uncle will tell us to come down to Gainshire on the evening train, and we can get this all sorted out by tomorrow. You'll never have to see me again."

Her lips flattened once more. "Right," she said. "Lovely."

He wasn't sure why her teeth were gritting or why she'd stopped meeting his gaze, but in the long run, it really didn't matter.

"You'd best be on your way," she informed him, and after a long moment, he decided that he agreed.

∽

89

The telegraph was one of the most amazing inventions of modern society, Adrian reflected as he waited outside the office in Lackwich. Grayson had plans to lay telegraph wires everywhere in the world that was not yet connected—across the expanse of the Pacific Ocean, along the African coast. It was already a substantial domestic convenience.

Twenty years ago, there would have been no choice but to make his way back to Gainshire in order to discuss the matter with his uncle. He'd have arrived with a faux-wife in tow, raising questions that he didn't want answered. He would have been closeted with the bishop for an unconscionable amount of time.

Today, he merely sent a telegram. It traveled near instantaneously, racing over electric wires, repeated by operator after operator until the message arrived in his uncle's hometown a scant handful of minutes or so after having been sent. His uncle's office was a fifteen-minute jaunt from the telegraph office there, and so after the courier was dispatched, he could have an answer, yay or nay, within an hour.

His own message had been sent at nine in the morning, the moment the office opened.

ENCOUNTERED OBSTACLE
SUSPICIONS RAISED
EMERGENCY ANNULMENT REQUIRED
PLEASE ADVISE

He hoped that this terse explanation of the last dizzying day of his life would let his uncle know that circumstances had changed drastically for the worse. But no immediate response had been forthcoming. He took to pacing in front of the office as he waited.

"Come back," he imagined his uncle saying. "I'll take care

of everything." Or maybe: "Is all well? Tell me how I can be of service."

Over the last decade, he'd spent more time with his uncle than anyone else in his immediate family. True, he'd never been openly acknowledged, but there was real affection there. Even now, decades later, his uncle would speak of Adrian's mother, his favorite sister, with a forlorn look in his eyes.

Grayson might think the worst of Denmore, but his uncle was just not a particularly demonstrative man. At least he wasn't demonstrative in the way that the rest of Adrian's family had been when he was growing up, with hugs and laughter aplenty. Still, Adrian had seen him prove his compassion to hundreds of people who needed help.

Faith, he thought, was this—believing that the man he'd spent years visiting would say "I love you" in the language that he most often used: "That sounds horrible. Let me take care of this for you."

He was jolted from his reverie when the woman from the telegraph office approached him from behind.

"Excuse me, sir," said she. "I know you were waiting on a reply to your telegram. It's arrived."

Adrian took hold of the wax-paper envelope and yanked the sheer slip of paper from its container. He read, his heart pounding...

NO TIME FOR OBSTACLES
GET WHAT YOU PROMISED ME
AND QUICKLY

For a moment, his heart sank. Once again, not even an "if you please."

He stared at the paper, willing the dark ink to change. The letters remained firmly fixed in place.

GET WHAT YOU PROMISED ME
AND QUICKLY

Since the words wouldn't change, *Adrian* would. He took a deep breath, then another, thinking, imagining, putting things together.

He shouldn't make anything of the terse nature of the reply. Telegrams were no place for pleasantries. This wasn't a letter or a comfortable afternoon talk over tea. One didn't say "I love you" via telegram.

It also wasn't a useful answer. Not in the slightest. What was he to do with this?

Well. It was likely Adrian's fault. His original message had been unclear; he'd left doubt. "Emergency annulment" had seemed fairly straightforward in his own mind, but... Without knowing the circumstances, how would his uncle know he was talking about *himself*?

His mistake had been in trying to save space. He could be more clear.

"I'll need to send a response," Adrian said. The woman handed him a form, and he thought for a moment before scrawling his answer.

CANNOT EXPLAIN VIA TELEGRAM
TASK ABSOLUTELY IMPOSSIBLE
SITUATION DIRE

He looked at the clerk, who would have to convert this entire thing into dots and dashes. The woman no doubt heard far more entertaining stories.

Still... It was with grave hesitation that he committed the next lines to paper.

I HAVE BEEN FORCED INTO MARRIAGE AT GUNPOINT
I DESPERATELY NEED YOUR HELP

There. He could not make matters more clear than that. He handed the material to the clerk and slid over a coin. The woman made change, then read the telegram. Her brow furrowed.

She paused halfway through, frowning. She read it again. "Your pardon. I want to be sure that I have read this correctly. This does say…'forced into marriage at gunpoint'?"

"Forced into marriage at gunpoint," Adrian said. "Yes. That's exactly what it says."

The woman made a notation above Adrian's light pencil marks in dark slashes of ink. *FORCED INTO MARRIAGE AT GUNPOINT.*

"Gunpoint, sir? That word is gunpoint?" Her voice seemed incredibly loud and echoing in the small room. "Are you certain that you intend to say gunpoint?"

"Yes." Adrian felt his face heat. Good thing nobody else was about to overhear this. "I absolutely intend to say gunpoint."

"Gunpoint." She frowned at the page. "Well. Will you be waiting for a reply?"

For God's sake. His involuntary plunge into matrimony would be the talk of the town.

"Yes." He put one hand over his face. "Yes, I definitely need a reply."

She turned from him, a frown on her face, and tapped idly into the machine. She then took the sheet he'd written everything on and slipped it into a folder.

Adrian froze. "Do you have to keep those?"

"No," she said with a smile, "but sometimes someone bungles things upstream, and it's a terrible mess if I don't retain them. I know; I've tried. Besides, it does get quite boring in here."

Well. It was good to know the wreckage of Adrian's life was providing amusement to *someone.*

"I hate to be nosy, but…" She paused, raising an eyebrow.

Adrian met her gaze, doing his best to give her no invitation. *Hated* to be nosy? He suspected she lived for that very thing.

"But the woman you married at gunpoint," she continued, ignoring Adrian's distinct lack of interest, "was that Miss Camilla Winters?"

He frowned at her.

"Bishop Lassiter was here earlier," she said, "sending a telegram about her. I've been rather cut up about it, to be quite honest. I saw her a few times with the rector, when he came in, and...I know it's not right, to talk that way about the clergy, but the way he's treated her..."

"Mmm?" Adrian bit his lip.

"And the others in that household. He *does* go through servants. And he said he was paying her half wages right in front of me."

"I...see." He wasn't sure that he did. "It was her, yes."

"Well." The woman nodded. "Tell her for me, will you? If she needs anything, anything at all, please have her call on me. It's Beasley, Mrs. Susanna Rose Beasley, at her service. I wish I'd said something to her earlier." She sighed. "Too late for that now, I suppose. I'll fetch you if there's a reply, then?"

This reply took two hours. Mrs. Beasley took it upon herself to take it to him where he waited with a pint of ale at a nearby pub.

"Here," she said, handing the envelope over with a solemn look on her face. "Tell me if you need to respond."

NO REPEAT NO UNDER NO CIRCUMSTANCES

I BELIEVE IN YOU

YOU CAN DO IT

NOTHING IS TRULY IMPOSSIBLE

ALSO COMPLETELY UNABLE TO HELP WITH ANNUL-MENT UNTIL CURRENT MATTER RESOLVED

CHURCH POLITICS

AM SURE YOU UNDERSTAND

"Son of a bishop," Adrian muttered.

"What sort of church politics?"

Mrs. Beasley was still standing there, peering over his shoulder. For God's sake. Adrian looked up at her, considered his ale, and gave up.

"The political kind," he said. "The kind you keep secret."

She clapped her hands together. "Ooh, those are my favorite! Here, now. What kind of secret? Perhaps I can help!"

She continued to look at him in slowly dissipating delight before she realized that he didn't intend to explain.

Adrian thought long and hard on his reply to his uncle. He could try to explain further—but once his uncle claimed it was a matter of church politics, he was unlikely to budge. And when he thought of it...

Well, the response did make sense. In a horrible way. Denmore would have to push Adrian's case through personally. He'd need to vouch for Adrian's character. If his uncle wouldn't reveal the truth of his relationship with Adrian at this moment, he *couldn't* actually do much about the annulment. Not yet.

He wouldn't do anything until Adrian found the evidence of wrongdoing that they both now suspected.

Except now that Adrian was in desperate need of an annulment, he was unable to obtain that evidence.

Damn, damn, damn.

He hated that his uncle had a point. He also hated being stuck in impossible situations.

He hated that "I believe in you, you can do it" was the way that his uncle said "no, no, under no circumstances will I come to your aid." He hated it.

He hated that if Grayson saw this exchange, he'd raise his eyebrow, and Adrian would *know* that he was thinking that he had told him so.

Adrian exhaled.

No. No. If he believed just a little longer—if he did the impossible—it would all work out.

Still, he tried one last time. He had to try, even though he knew that pushing the matter was already futile.

YOU PROMISED, he sent to his uncle.

He drank beer while he waited for one last response—not so much that he lost his senses, of course, but enough that he felt his thinking beginning to fog at the edges. Enough that the connections his mind made started to loosen. Enough that he stared at Alabi's sketches that he'd put in his notebook and actually tried to make something of them with his own pencil. He couldn't draw at all. He made nothing but a mess.

It was afternoon by the time the response came. Adrian had nothing to show for his time but sketches of lopsided bears, alongside some ideas he had about his uncle's problems.

I ALWAYS KEEP MY PROMISES, his uncle's final telegram said.

BUT SO DO YOU

AM COUNTING ON YOU

Damn it. Somehow, somewhere, Adrian had to find a way to obtain the proof of wrongdoing that he needed. He was going to get it—there were no two ways about it. But until then...

He glanced at his notebook.

Disguise? he had written. The word stood next to a giant dark misshapen lump that was supposed to be a hibernating bear. *Household informants? Illegal entry?*

Nothing sounded right. In lieu of a plan, he sent his brother a telegram full of lies.

EVERYTHING GOING ACCORDING TO PLAN

JUST A LITTLE WHILE LONGER

WILL RETURN TO HARVIL TO FINISH DESIGNS SOON

AND TELL YOU ALL AFTER

There. Now he was committed.

He'd figure this puzzle out. He had to do so.

There was a more immediate question that he needed to address. It would have been easy if he had been returning to the inn to simply tell Miss Winters that they'd be off to Gain-shire the next day, and they'd have an annulment by the end of the week.

Now?

Now Adrian had to figure out how to tell the woman who wasn't his wife that she was going to have to continue not being his wife for a while longer.

CHAPTER NINE

"**Y**ou know, dear. You must face the truth. He's left and he isn't coming back."

Camilla was in the kitchen at the inn where she'd spent the night.

It had taken two hours for the truth to come out. In the first hour, the innkeeper's wife, one Mrs. Lawson, had made helpful suggestions for further conveyances to take Camilla on to her destination in Lower...where had Mr. Hunter claimed she was heading again? She couldn't recall.

Mrs. Lawson had mentioned guides, helpful farmers going to market, even directions to follow on foot. That was back when she'd believed the story about Camilla being a governess who had become lost.

Then the truth had arrived in the form of gossip.

Mrs. Lawson had come out to where Camilla was sitting, waiting and watching the road for Mr. Hunter's return.

"Miss Winters?" she had asked. "Lately of Rector Miles's employ?"

That was it; the truth was known. Camilla had sighed.

Mrs. Lawson sat beside her. "I know what's happened to you."

If she had been cruel, Camilla could have held up. Instead, the sheer weight of her unwanted kindness, the sincere depths of sympathy she showed at Camilla's fall from half-grace, nearly undid her.

"I should have known," Mrs. Lawson said. "He did seem to have a bit of a golden tongue. Knew precisely what to say and when to say it, didn't he?"

"That's just what he is like," Camilla replied, a little too earnestly. "It doesn't make him dishonest."

"And how long have you known him?"

Four days, Camilla did not say. She didn't have to; the woman had heard the gossip.

"We are women, dear." She said it gently. "And I know you're still almost a child—"

"I've just turned twenty. I'm hardly a child."

Mrs. Lawson just clucked her tongue. "If you insist, of course. We're women, dear. It's not an easy world for us, if we lie to ourselves. Your Mr. Hunter said he'd be back before noon, and it's almost four. He's gone. He's not coming back. You must face reality."

No, Camilla wanted to say. *He's coming back. He said he would.*

The alternative—that he had lied and already joined the crowd of people who had abandoned her—was too cruel.

Deep down, rationally, she was sure that Mrs. Lawson was right. The story he'd told last night…it should have beggared belief.

His uncle was a bishop? His grandfather, a duke? He was pretending to be a valet? She'd believed him because he gave her kind words and enough coin to pay her shot at the inn.

Logically, she knew that half a pound was a low price for ridding oneself of a wife.

"You can't stay," Mrs. Lawson said, ever so kindly, "not for long. One more night's stay may be seen as charity on my part. But I'm known for running a respectable establishment. Have you no family you could go to?"

Camilla had gone through all the family that would have her and then some. They'd all wanted to be rid of her. Camilla just shook her head.

"There, there." The woman patted her head. "You're pretty enough, you know. If you could make it to London, I'm sure you could find some man or such who would be willing to help with your living expenses. And you do seem to be the sort who might thrive in that environment. Take a day and think it over, dear, and you'll see I'm right. I know it's not what you had imagined for yourself, but many a woman has done worse, and it *is* the best you can expect, under the circumstances. For the time being, would you mind staying in the kitchen? I can't have people seeing you."

Being told that she'd ruined herself so thoroughly that prostitution was her best option would not have been Camilla's conversation of choice on the day after her wedding.

Still, she stayed in the kitchen and cut vegetables when asked, and slipped salt in the soup when the cook wasn't looking.

All the while she dreamed.

Mr. Hunter would come back. He'd been delayed by...a telegraph malfunction? Oh, why not. She'd hoped for far dumber things.

Hope, she had been told, was the devil whispering on her shoulder. But if she listened to the thread of doubt that she'd been told was her angelic nature... She would decide to become a prostitute. She was no expert on such matters, but she was pretty sure that theology just did not line up. To hell with Miles and his entire pack of devils. She was done feeling guilty about wanting good things.

Mr. Hunter would come back, and she would have words for him. It lifted her spirits just to imagine them.

She would be brave and tell him to have some consideration for her feelings. By the time dusk had come around, she'd figured out precisely what she would say to him and how he would react.

He was planning to get rid of her by means of an annulment—that made her daydream excessively awkward—but he'd be kind about it, and he'd apologize, and—

"Miss Winters," Mrs. Lawson said, appearing in the doorway. "You'll never imagine who has arrived."

Camilla didn't have to imagine. Mr. Hunter was standing right behind Mrs. Lawson, a head taller than her. He wasn't smiling—*that* was different; in her daydream, he'd smiled when he saw her. His clothing was rumpled and dusty from the road.

What the *hell*. He'd come back? He had *actually* come back?

Camilla was used to daydreaming; she wasn't used to her daydreams coming true. Dear merciful heavens.

"Let me guess," she said slowly. "Telegraph malfunction?"

He sighed. "I could only wish for such luck."

"I was here all day." She had planned out the speech so perfectly in her fantasy that it seemed a shame not to use it. "It didn't take long for the gossip to arrive. I've had to spend the remaining hours listening to advice on the best way to go about starting my new, exciting career as a prostitute."

At least he winced. That was good.

It was a good thing she'd had *hours* to imagine going over this speech; she'd never have been able to deliver it off the top of her head.

"You should have sent word that you were delayed."

"I should have."

"I know I said I didn't wish to be a burden on you, but in

101

retrospect, for as long as we are…whatever we are? I should like you to remember that I am a fellow human being. With *feelings.* And I don't—"

I don't like to feel abandoned, Camilla almost said, but it was so close to her real feelings that it crossed the line, pulling her sharply from her practiced fantasy into reality. Reality was the ache of her chest, the throb of her heart.

She dropped her voice instead. "Do you know, they all believed you'd left me. Forever. For good. They believed we were lawfully wed and I'd been ruined and then abandoned. I had to wait for you here, smothered by the weight of their belief, the entire day. It wasn't pleasant."

He sighed. "I can see how it must have looked. You must have believed that I'd left for good."

"Not entirely." Camilla didn't want to explain that she was all too good at hoping for the best. "You said you would come back."

He seemed puzzled by this. "*I* knew I would. *You* know nothing about my character."

"Well, that's not true," Camilla heard herself say. "I don't know *everything* about your character, but I do know *something*. I know you told me a ridiculous story last night."

He made a face. "I know it sounds ridiculous, but—"

"Let me finish, please. You told me that your uncle is a bishop in the Church of England, that your grandfather was a duke, and that our marriage can be annulled."

"All of those things are true, and—"

She held up a hand.

"You said we would work together, but you gave me the barest description of the situation and disappeared without listening to me this morning, when your supposed mission— finding out about Bishop Lassiter and Rector Miles— requires you to know about the inner workings of a household where I have lived for eighteen months."

"I *will* listen to you—in fact, as it turns out, I—"

"Let me *finish*," Camilla said. "I also know that whatever it was that happened in the bishop's bedchamber? You were the only person who spoke up in my defense. I know you have never called me a name just because others did. You were a little thoughtless today."

"I'm not sure where you're leading right now." Mr. Hunter rubbed his head.

"I have spent the entire day being told that I was an idiot for believing one word of your cockamamie story."

He didn't scream at her for doubting him.

He exhaled slowly. "You're right. From your point of view, it makes not one lick of sense. What can I say or do to convince you?"

She lifted her head. "There's no need." Her eyes bored into him. "I told you, I have spent the entire day in contemplation. I will receive no references from the rector. I have almost nothing. Honest labor in places where I will not be disturbed will be nigh impossible to come by. Rationally, intelligently, I have come to the conclusion that my best hope for continued prosperity is to become a prostitute."

His eyes widened. "That's—that's—"

"That's logic," she told him. "That's the cold hard truth I have had to face while you have been off doing whatever you have been doing. I have no idea how to *be* a proper prostitute, mind. I don't mean the trading money for favors part—that, I assume, is simple enough. But I have enough experience to know that prostitution is a business like any other business. There are ways to do it well and ways to do it badly. I haven't even the option to take an apprenticeship. But I'm not stupid. I imagine I could figure it out. Eventually."

She had rendered him dumbfounded.

"There." She stood up and offered him her hand. "There is nothing you need say to convince me of your story. I believe you, even though it's idiocy to do so. I believe you because you were kind. I believe you because you *did* come back. I believe you because holding onto my hopes, however irrational they are, is better than the alternative, which is horrid. You don't need to convince me. Just—please. Don't disappoint me."

He looked into her eyes, and very slowly, he smiled. "You're a bit of a tiger, aren't you?"

It was her turn to blink at him in confusion. "A what?"

"A tiger," he said. "Large-ish cat? Orange and black stripes? Occasionally eats people?"

Nobody had ever called Camilla a tiger before. Likely nobody had ever thought it. She stared at him a moment before shaking her head.

"I'm really not," she said slowly. "I only knew what to say just now because I had an entire day to plan it out."

"There, you see?" He dusted his hands together. "That settles it. Tigers are planners."

"What do you know about tigers anyway?"

"Well, I know you now," he said unhelpfully.

Well. Then. She wasn't going to hurt her head trying to figure that out. "Enough about me. Tell me about your uncle and the...telegram malfunction that delayed you, or whatever it was."

Mr. Hunter rolled his eyes. She didn't think he was rolling them at her this time.

"You *did* say he'd be able to help us with an annulment, didn't you? Were you wrong?"

He licked his lips and looked off into the distance. "You... are not the only one here who tries to see the best in people, it turns out."

"Ah. He disappointed you, then."

His eyes shivered shut. "A little. It's...not the first time he's done it. I really shouldn't be surprised. Grayson—my older brother—he says I'm too trusting. But…"

"But?"

"But my uncle does need my help," Mr. Hunter said. "And —I've thought it over—if we are to annul our marriage, we'll *have* to offer some reason why Lassiter and Miles, two men of the church, acted as they did. My uncle is not *wrong* to insist that I find proof of Lassiter's wrongdoing. I just don't know how to get it."

"Oh." Camilla found herself smiling. "How *sad*. If only you knew someone who had spent eighteen months in Miles's household. If only you had talked to her this morning."

He looked at her. "Do you know something?"

She bit her lip. "I know someone who might know something. There's only one small problem."

"What's that?"

"We'll need to stay somewhere in the vicinity while we ask questions," Camilla said. "It's late. And I would vastly prefer not to stay one more night in a place where I am expected to start the exciting profession of walking the streets at any minute."

He just looked at her for a moment before nodding. "I can find somewhere in town for me—there's a rooming house there. For you…this may sound odd, but I know just the place for you."

∾

"Here, here, sit down," said Mrs. Beasley. Camilla had met the woman a few times before, when she'd been sent to the telegraph office in town, but they'd never said much to one another—certainly not enough for the woman to be bustling about and fetching her tea. "Poor dear. You've been through quite the ordeal, haven't you? I'm sorry I haven't much better to offer than a space in the back."

Camilla and Adrian had been ushered in and seated at a table near the mantel, in a room that appeared to be composed almost entirely of doilies. Doilies on the wall. Doilies under the plates. Doilies hanging off the table. Little decorative doilies had been bound together into pink covers that adorned the poker, shovel, and tongs that stood by the fireplace. The room was a veritable museum to the doily.

Camilla inched a doily to the side and set her spoon down.

Her head was spinning, and not just from a superabundance of doilies. Poor dear? She felt her ears heating with embarrassment at the moniker. It was bad enough that she had to accept this kind of charity; having pity thrown atop it was too much. She didn't know how she'd ever repay the kindness.

But she was too hungry to object to bread and stew being offered to her, especially when it smelled the way it did. *This* stew, unlike last night's soup, was actually good—thick and warming with real chunks of beef.

"My husband is out at the pub," Mrs. Beasley said as she settled near Camilla in a rocking chair. "And the children are grown, so it leaves me with little to do of an evening but knit and plot the demise of my neighbors."

Mr. Hunter, sitting on the other side of the table, looked up at that in something like consternation.

"A little joke!" She laughed. "I don't knit! Obviously, I crochet. Also, I don't wish to destroy *all* my neighbors. Only Ruford Shamwell and his uncontainable goats."

"Of course," Mr. Hunter said. "I see."

"Hm." Mrs. Beasley rocked in her chair. "Now that I'm making a list, I must add Bertrand Gapwood. He keeps throwing his chamber pot in the alley. I tell him over and over, no, we mustn't do that, haven't you read the newspaper, that's how we all get cholera and die. But he never listens."

"Two neighbors seems quite reasonable," Camilla said around a spoonful of beef.

"Mm. Then there's Stephen Wade. He yells at his wife. I've told him a thousand times that if they can't get along, he should go spend his evenings in the pub like my Bobby, but he never listens. And he always yells about the *same* things. I enjoy hearing a bit of good gossip, but for heaven's sake, have some imagination. Variety is the spice of life." The woman frowned. "Well, that's it—that's all my neighbors, and they're all on the list."

Camilla took another bite of stew.

"Yes," Mrs. Beasley said, in response to a twitch of an eyebrow from Mr. Hunter. "I must admit I'm a terrible intermeddler. But I'm not a gossip—at least, I only *accept* gossip. I don't give it out. So don't mind me. I'm sure the two of you have much to talk about, so go ahead, go ahead. Mr. Hunter won't be staying here past eight, so you mustn't waste any time. Pay me no mind."

Mr. Hunter took a bite of his own stew and glanced over at Mrs. Beasley. She was, in fact, crocheting. She concentrated on her yarn with an intensity that fooled neither of them.

"Do you need anything?" Mr. Hunter finally asked Camilla in a low voice. "I've had occasion to carry your valise twice now, and while it's very heavy, it doesn't feel like a lot to contain all your worldly possessions."

Camilla shrugged. "I'm used to moving about. I don't even bother acquiring things any longer. It's much more convenient to not have to move them." She let out a little laugh, because it felt like the thing one ought to do at a time like this.

If she laughed, maybe he would be fooled into not feeling sorry for her.

Mrs. Beasley, across the room, poked herself with her crochet hook and made a muffled sound.

"About…that thing we talked about earlier." Camilla dropped her voice. "I have an excellent memory, and if I were to guess, I would say that we should visit Mrs. Martin over in Highham. She's angry at the rector about *something* involving money and a charitable donation. It would be a good place to start, don't you think?"

"Better than anything I could guess at." He spoke even lower than her. "And we can converse further on the way there and back. Away from prying eyes."

"It's my *ears* you should worry about," Mrs. Beasley said, as if she were a part of the conversation. "Not my eyes. But never you mind, I'm just here crocheting. Paying no mind to anything you say."

"Highham is eleven miles away." Camilla thought of her shoe-leather, already painfully thin, and the mud, and her stockings, and then put those thoughts away as pointless and smiled instead. "That'll be a nice walk, don't you think? Especially since I won't be carrying a valise for it."

He looked at her. "I can well afford to rent a carriage from someone."

She did not know what to say to that. Instead, she just licked her lips.

"I know you're only believing me out of necessity," he said. "I know my story sounds ridiculous, and I can't blame you for having doubts. But it really is true. I won't even blink at the cost."

She took another sip of her tea. "Of *course* I believe you. If you say it's so, it must be true."

He sighed. "I'll see you tomorrow, then."

CHAPTER TEN

"**F**ollow my lead," Mr. Hunter said in the carriage on the way over. "Just go along with what I say, and it will all work out."

Camilla considered—for a moment—not saying anything. Then she remembered that this was her life, too. She sighed. "Mr. Hunter, you said that when we were going to the inn. You told everyone I was a governess who had become lost, and then everyone discovered it was a lie. I was humiliated."

Mr. Hunter glanced at his reins. He looked over at her. His nostrils flared. "That was then," he explained. "This is *now*. I've had more time to think of a story. This one will be better."

"Oh," Camilla said, "I suppose...maybe...it will?" She'd tried to keep the doubt out of her voice, but apparently she failed. His nose twitched in annoyance.

"Look here," he said, "I pretended to be a valet for an entire week and nobody suspected a thing."

"Didn't they?"

"Well, not much. I didn't pretend to be a *competent* valet. That helped a great deal."

"Well, in that case." Camilla gave up. It was *his* idea to get the annulment, after all. "I'll leave it to you and your particular brand of incompetence."

When they arrived a half-hour later, though, she regretted not pushing the matter.

"No." The elderly woman who swept into the room did not bother to introduce herself, nor to inquire after their purpose. She just stood in the doorway of the parlor, leaning on her cane, glaring at them from underneath a white frilly cap. "Under no circumstances. No. Good-bye."

It took Camilla a moment to recover from the surprise. She'd thought, after Mrs. Martin's slightly less elderly servant had shown them into the parlor and allowed them to sit down, that they might perhaps be received. Apparently not.

"Might we not put the question to you before you decide to reject it?" Mr. Hunter asked.

Mrs. Martin—at least, Camilla supposed it was her—rolled her eyes. Her shoulders drew up, shortening what was otherwise a ridiculously long neck.

The pause was of short duration. She tilted her head. "No need. I know what you want—my donation to some charitable cause that will benefit the least fortunate among us, et cetera and so forth. My thank-God-now-deceased husband crassly trumpeted the size of his fortune to all and sundry. You have heard, no doubt, my proclamation of a year past, that my disgrace of a nephew would receive not one penny from my hand, and you have thought that you, too, would try your luck." She turned back to them. "Go. Shoo. Tell all the gossipmongers. It's too late; I've learned my lesson."

Camilla blinked. "Oh. But we aren't here to—"

"I will never give another pound to anyone's supposed charity project. I tried; it was no good. I plan to spend every last penny on myself in ways that will send me straight to hell, before I kick off this mortal coil. If I have to spend it on pretty young things to keep me company, so be it. Bring on the pretty youths."

Camilla couldn't help herself. She almost smiled.

The woman glanced at the two of them—dismissively, at first, and then, as if taken aback, giving them both a longer, more searching gaze. "*You're* pretty enough. I don't know why you're here."

Mr. Hunter coughed into his glove. "Mrs. Martin, you've utterly mistaken our purpose." When he spoke, there was yet another difference to his voice—a change in his vowels, an alteration in the rhythm of his speech. Camilla tried not to startle.

"We are not here to ask you for charity or to solicit any other sort of favors. Let me introduce myself. I am acquainted with a wealthy, prominent family from the old Yoruba kingdom." As he spoke, his eyes slid away from them, finding an unoccupied corner of the room.

Mrs. Martin blinked rapidly. So did Camilla.

"Mrs. Winters here," he said, gesturing to Camilla, "is a woman of good family who has been advising me on the necessary social etiquette of Britain. I fear that her kind lessons are falling on deaf ears; please do not hold her in low esteem for my failings. I wish you very well, of course, in all your endeavors. Including your spending habits."

"Oh." Mrs. Martin tilted her head and looked at him. "You are likely lying, and I'm too old to be taken in. But it *is* a nice story." She glanced at Camilla, and her eyes softened. "You're too pretty to fall into this sort of scheme, dear. You should know—men who lie never change. If you're looking for work after this man cheats you, too, do consider coming to see me."

Camilla choked.

"But *do* go on," Mrs. Martin said. "It's a new lie, at least, and at my age, you don't often see new things."

Mr. Hunter seemed taken aback, but he continued. "I have been in Britain for the last four months, and I am astonished by the depths of poverty that I have seen in your country. I had thought to make some donation to a cause, to alleviate the situation of your unfortunates. I heard that you had given money to the parish, and thought it sounded like as good a way as any to offer my assistance."

Mrs. Martin clapped her hands. "Oh, that's good, that's good!"

Camilla stared at her. "It…is?"

"I know how this one goes now! You have access to princely funds, but you just need someone to make the donation on your behalf. You'll give me a bank draft for my troubles or some such. *Right?*"

"No!" Mr. Hunter shook his head. "No, we were just going to ask you about your experience donating to the charity fund Rector Miles set up in your name."

Mrs. Martin recoiled as if from a spider. No, Camilla realized, not that. In this scenario, Mrs. Martin likely *was* the spider; she was just recoiling. Her lips curled in a gesture of extreme distaste.

"Urgh," she said. "That's a *terrible* deception. I don't see how you make money at *all* that way."

"We don't!" Mr. Hunter threw his hands up in exasperation.

"Well, you are the worst pair of fraudsters ever to grace my doorstep," Mrs. Martin said. "You need to practice your swindle—this one is *dreadful*. The absolute *worst* I've ever heard, and I've encountered a lot of them. Dear God, I have never *heard* such a pair of rank amateurs."

Mr. Hunter sighed. "Of *course* we sound like incompetent fraudsters. It is because we are not fraudsters at all."

"Well, you are not telling the truth."

"Yes," Adrian said, "technically, I am—that is, I do know someone who has ties to Yoruba, I suppose, broadly speaking? And also, I *do* donate money to charity."

He trailed off as Mrs. Martin shook her head, clucking her tongue. "You really *are* bad at this. If you have to put the word 'technically' in front of 'the truth,' you are not telling the truth. I don't know what you're after, but you won't be getting it from me."

Camilla sighed. Well, she'd left the matter to him. That hadn't worked. Should she…?

Yes, she decided. It was time to intervene.

"Mrs. Martin," Camilla said, "you're right. We haven't been honest with you."

"Utterly shocking." Mrs. Martin shook her head, singularly unshocked.

"Rector Miles found me eighteen months ago," Camilla said. "I was in another household, and I had developed the unfortunate habit of kissing a footman named James."

"Kissing." Mrs. Martin scoffed. "Is *that* what they're calling it these days?"

"I, um—"

"Just call it what it is. Fucking. The word is *fucking*."

Camilla felt herself turn bright red. She hid her face in her hands.

"I can hear it without combusting," Mrs. Martin informed her. "I'm old. If my ears were going to fall off, they'd have done so years ago."

"Rector Miles was worried about…the state of sin I was potentially dealing with."

"By fu—"

"By *kissing*," Camilla said, hurriedly. "Among *other things* that do *not* need to be detailed at length at this moment."

"Have it your way." Mrs. Martin sighed. "Children these

days. So circumspect about everything."

"Rector Miles offered to take me in. To provide me with spiritual instruction. He kindly offered me half wages for his trouble."

"Hmm. And *did* he provide spiritual instruction?"

Camilla shut her eyes. "Yes." Her voice shook. "He reminded me at regular intervals that I had very little hope at redemption. He told me I was a disgrace and an embarrassment and that I should consider myself lucky to have my half pay."

"Hmm," said Mrs. Martin. "Sounds like him. Go on."

"And I *tried*," Camilla said. "I tried, I did, but every week I did something wrong. I was too friendly or not friendly enough, or maybe my gaze lingered somewhere too long or I looked away too quickly—*nothing* I did was ever right. And *then* Mr. Hunter visited—serving as a valet to a guest—and we became stuck in a room together, and the rector tossed me out and told *everyone* I'd been—" She cut herself off. "Kissing. Among *other* things."

"Hmm," said Mrs. Martin again. "And you hadn't?"

"No!" And then, because the woman was watching her with narrowed eyes, she added, "Not that time. Not with him."

"Go on, then."

"So I thought of you. I know you'd talked to the rector months ago about a charity donation. And he had mentioned that you were angry about something earlier when I was in his presence. Did he misuse funds you donated? We want to know because we despise him and wish to expose him as a fraud."

"My goodness." Mrs. Martin shut her eyes. "That was an *excellent* effort. I feel myself wanting to give you money just for that. Dear *God*, that was good. Sir, you need to let this young lady conduct your fraud. She's much better at it."

"We're not after your money," Mr. Hunter said in aggrieved tones.

"Speak for yourself," Camilla snapped. "I've been working for half-wages for eighteen months. I'll take anything."

Mrs. Martin cackled.

"But technically, we're really *not* after your money. We just want to know what happened. Will you tell us about your experience? Did Rector Miles convince you to donate money?"

Mrs. Martin sighed and shut her eyes. "To my great dismay. Worst experience of my life—excepting, of course, my marriage."

Camilla leaned forward.

"Tell me more."

"So *here* I am, imagine." Mrs. Martin threw her arms out. "I have one living relation in the world—my nephew. Like all men of his ilk—which is to say, men in general—he had lived upon the expectation of an inheritance from me, his aunt. I cannot begrudge him that, I do not think." She looked dubious, as if her grudges were growing lonely and she would not mind giving them company.

"Mmm," Mr. Hunter said, and Mrs. Martin sighed.

"But he came to visit me, as he does, to flatter me and try to convince me to part with a portion of my money before I kicked off this mortal coil. And would you believe what he did?"

"I..." Camilla swallowed. "Um, the way you said 'men in general' just now, it suggests...?"

"Precisely. He kissed my maid, and I do mean *kissed,* and not anything more, because I happened upon them in time. She hadn't wanted it, and thank god I interrupted. I told *everyone* he did it, and not one person listened—not the constable, not *anyone.* They all just said 'boys will be boys,' but Susan—she was the girl who did for me, and she'd done for me ever since her mam became too ill to continue, and I thought of her as close to my own daughter as could be—"

Mrs. Martin looked around the room, sat down, and, after carefully setting her cane to the side of her chair, pulled out a handkerchief. She didn't dab her eyes with it; she waved it angrily, as if she were gesturing some unseen bull to charge.

"In any event, I am *not* here to tell Susan's story. In a fit of rage, I gave her as much of my money as I could make her take, but she told me she didn't want anyone to think she was greedy. And after what he did to her!"

"Your nephew sounds like a cad."

"So, of course," the woman continued, "I *had* to get rid of the rest of my money. *He* isn't getting a half-pence from me. I went to the rectory, and I specifically asked if I could make a donation to assist women who were down on their luck in *that* particular way, if you catch my drift. Before I'd handed over my money, they assured me that they'd use it as I directed. It was only after I'd given them two thousand pounds that the excuses began."

"Excuses?"

"The explanations. The lies. The money had gone into the parish purse in general without being specifically marked, Miles said. He had to do so, as there were no wronged women needing help from the parish—as if *that* could be believed! Are there men in this parish? Yes? Then there are women who need help. It's that simple. Eventually, he claimed they'd used the money for renovations for the church, but absolutely nothing has changed. What renovations?"

"How dreadful, that you could not rely on their representations," Mr. Hunter intoned.

"Stop trying to say agreeable things," Mrs. Martin snapped. "I utterly despise it. In any event, I have realized that nobody will listen to what I want. I'm too old and too female. If I can't do any good with my money, I might as well have fun. Send some pretty young things my way, that's what I say."

"I..." Camilla choked. "I will do so, if...I see any? Mr. Hunter may have more expertise in the matter."

Mr. Hunter looked appalled. "That's honestly not my forte. I think I'd make a better fraudster, and we all know how that turned out. I wouldn't know how to obtain men."

"Men." Mrs. Martin rolled her eyes. "Did you not just *hear* my thoughts on men? I buried one man and took his money, and let me just say that the money was the best thing he ever wanted to give me, and it wasn't worth what I had to put up with. I suppose I shouldn't say such things aloud, but I'm so old that nobody takes me seriously. I *vastly* prefer women. Pretty *men* are nothing but pains all around."

"I...see," Mr. Hunter said.

"I wasn't talking to *you*." Mrs. Martin tilted her head in Camilla's direction. "You," she said, pointing, "on the other hand—you would do."

Camilla jumped. "Me? I—I am—"

"No, not *you*, specifically, not like that. I want a young thing, and you're, what, nineteen?"

"Twenty."

"I thought as much. For myself, I have more a young lady of forty or so in mind—not an actual *child*. Good God. I'm not a *man;* I have standards. If you're at all so inclined, you should find yourself a rich woman. Better work than bumbling about the countryside with *this* fraudster."

"I..." Camilla swallowed. She could feel her face heating. "I will have to take it under consideration?"

The woman nodded at her sagely. "I thought as much. You had that look about you. We can always find each other, you know. Women can be terrible, too. But here's a bit of wisdom I've acquired over the years: However terrible women are, they're usually better than men."

"Thank you." Mr. Hunter folded his arms in annoyance.

"You're welcome." Mrs. Martin smiled beautifully. "You're entirely welcome. Come back if you ever need to hear it again."

❧

M iss Winters shifted uncomfortably on the seat of the hired carriage on their way back to Lackwich. They had a long drive ahead of them—eleven miles passing through several towns—but she did not try to make polite conversation.

She did not look at Adrian. Instead, her hands gripped the seat, knuckles white—and it could not have been the speed of travel that bothered her, as Adrian was scarcely holding the horses above a trot.

It took him five minutes to realize that she was nervous. It took him even longer to guess why. And it took him the longest while yet to figure out what to do about it.

"I shouldn't be surprised that I'm a bad liar," he finally said.

She turned to look at him. Her eyebrows rose in something that could have been encouragement. He decided to take it as such.

"Too trusting," he told her. "That's what my brother Grayson tells me, and maybe he's right. When we were children, he convinced me once that chocolate was made with mud."

That won a tentative smile. "You didn't *believe* that, did you?"

"I'm not *that* gullible." He turned to her as much as he could without losing sight of the road. "Um. Not any longer, at least. I learned my lesson. But here's the thing about being too trusting—I don't know what to look for when people are lying to me, and that means I don't know how to evaluate my own lies."

"Your eyes," she told him. "They give it all away."

"My eyes?"

"Yes. You look up and to the right. As if you're so disgusted with yourself that you can't help but roll your eyes at your own words."

He couldn't help but laugh. "I do not!"

"You do. You really do."

"You see?" Adrian bit back a smile. "I *told* you that you were a tiger."

"Oh, am I?"

"You see, tigers are patient. Some predators, if they are discovered, give up and go on to new prey. Tigers *pretend* to give up and then circle back and try again and again and again. You could have let Mrs. Martin throw us out. You saved everything."

She made a face. "Where are you getting these tiger facts?"

"Did you see my eyes go up and to the right?" he countered.

"Well, no. But—"

"Then it's true."

"I don't think it works like that." But she was biting back a smile for now.

They lapsed into silence once more, the only sound that of the carriage wheels rattling over rutted roads. This quiet felt slightly more comfortable than the preceding one. Still, Adrian waited another mile before speaking again.

"You know, tigress. I keep expecting you to tell me that I'm not trusting enough."

"Why would I say such a thing?"

"I've told you to leave matters to me twice, and twice you've had to rescue yourself from the tangle my lies made," he said simply. "I should have trusted you *more,* not less. I will endeavor to do so in the future."

She looked down. A blush painted her cheeks—small, but completely crimson. Her eyes squeezed shut. "Mr. Hunter." She sounded pained. "I hate to be the one to bring this to your attention, but...you are wrong. You should trust me *less.*"

"Why?"

"You keep talking about an annulment." Miss Winters wrapped her arms about herself. "I don't know much about those. But isn't a physical examination of the woman a part of it? To see if she's...?"

There was no Mrs. Martin present to fill in the indelicate word the moment required.

"Yes," Adrian said. "Technically, there is."

"'If you have to put the word *technically* in front of the truth...'" Miss Winters quoted at him. "You should be angrier. I'm telling you, I won't pass that examination."

"You *do* know they can't actually tell, right?"

She looked over at him. "But—"

"Some women have a hymen until they lose their virginity. Some do not. Some have theirs torn by intercourse; others don't. Sometimes tears repair themselves; sometimes they don't."

She stared at him.

"I'm serious," he said. "You've seen me when I lie. Do I look like I'm lying to you? I told you, I served as my uncle's amanuensis for a while. He talked to a doctor about this very thing in my presence. They don't *actually* know if anyone's a virgin. They just guess. And if we both swear we haven't had intercourse, if we have witnesses to our character—"

Her face fell once more. Ah. Right.

"In any event," he said, "it won't matter. Have you been worrying about that?"

"I've scarcely had time to worry about anything, to be honest. It's all happened so fast." She bit her lip and looked away to the passing fields. "Talking to Mrs. Martin about what happened was hard enough. I don't want to have to *think* of it again, not now. Everything's over and done with. Can we focus instead on what lies ahead?"

"Of course."

She inhaled, and it was as if the breath gave her sustenance. She turned to him with a smile.

"Well, then. I have an excellent memory—it is one of my few talents. We now know that Mrs. Martin donated money to the parish for a purpose. She does not believe that purpose was fulfilled."

"That's not wrongdoing."

"No." She tapped her lip with a single gloved finger, thinking. "But if they absconded with the money altogether it would be, yes? Maybe...we could prove that there are no funds available for the purposes Mrs. Martin intended."

"How?" he started to ask, and then realized. "Of course. We need to have someone apply for assistance—a woman who has been...ah, harmed by a man? We could find someone to pretend—"

She made a disbelieving noise. "Mr. Hunter." There was a tone of amusement in her voice. "Haven't we learned that lesson already? Enough with the pretending."

"But—"

"But we already *have* such a woman at our disposal. Gossip has entirely ruined her. She exists, and she's willing to help." She spread her arms. "Behold. Here she is—in the flesh."

"Oh." Well. That was entirely logical. "Do you intend to go apply to Rector Miles for assistance yourself?"

"No." Her hands clenched. "I don't think I want to look at his face, not right yet. But the groundskeeper is kept appraised of any such programs, so he knows where to send people."

"You'll talk to him?"

"He likes me." A smile flashed on her face quickly, then vanished. "He used to, at any rate. Or I thought he did. I'm not the best judge."

Adrian was silent for a moment. "It's quite a lot to ask of you."

She shook her head. "I don't want to be a burden on you. I want to do my part. Really, I do."

"Well. I will keep that in mind the next time I need to draft someone to participate in one of my schemes." He'd meant it as a joke, but she gave her head a vigorous shake.

"Lying would be hard for me. I don't think I could lie well. I'm pretty near the end of my resources." She stopped speaking, and pressed her hands into her skirts. "I have next to no money. Nobody I can go to. I have no home, and those I could call friends are…" She laughed. "*Kitty*, I thought, was my friend, and she lied about me and ruined me." Another laugh, this more shaky. "I'm *not* going to be a burden on you. I promise, I won't. But I'm desperate and it shows. You're trying to be kind by calling me a tiger to bolster my confidence. I'm sorry. I can't hide the truth."

Somehow, he had not thought her side of things through. He had realized—intellectually—that she couldn't have much. He'd held her valise. He'd seen her shoes.

"Haven't you got anywhere to go?"

"I have been everywhere already." She shut her eyes. A slight breeze caught a little tendril of her hair; it flapped in the wind, and she leaned her head back. "This last time? It's not the first time I've been sent off in disgrace. It's happened before. Multiple times."

He didn't know what to say to that.

"I lost my family when I was twelve." She didn't open her eyes. "I was sent first to my uncle, who found me too talkative, then a bit later, to his cousin. From there on I have passed through what feels like scores of homes. I have yet to inspire any sort of lasting affection." A faint smile touched her lips. "It's been half my life. I suppose I should really accept that I'm not the sort of person that people actually like, but I am pigheaded stubborn. I never do learn."

The wind picked up a touch, ruffling the fraying edges of her hat. God. Even her *hat* was frayed.

"I grew older. The incidents grew worse. There was a girl my age named Larissa who became my particular friend. Her parents didn't like how particular the friendship was. I told you I'm too desperate to lie—Mrs. Martin was right about *that*, too. Larissa and I practiced kissing together. Then we... weren't practicing, and... They didn't like that, not when they found out. So on I went. At the next house, a son wanted—never mind. After that came James, the footman." Camilla shrugged. "I was sent on so many times. I regret my memory is good enough to count them all. James is when Rector Miles found me. He told me that I was destined for hell, that I should change my name and try my hardest to reform. If I was good for two years, he promised to help set me up in a place where I was unknown. For the sake of my soul."

She had started rubbing her hands together as she spoke. He noticed now that there was a hole in her gloves.

"So you see," she said, "it's not that I *wasn't* guilty of what they accused me of with you—I *was*. Not at that moment, but I was. I have nowhere to go. I *am* desperate. So desperate that —" She paused, then shook her head. "I am so desperate that I've contemplated trying to force you into this, you know. We *were* joined in matrimony. It would take so little for me to make an annulment impossible, and you already told me the rules."

He must have made a sound, because she turned to him.

"I'm sorry. I don't mean to alarm you. I won't—I promise I won't. I'm naïve and hopeful, and some part of me just wants someone, anyone, to care that I exist. I *won't*. But you should know—I'm desperate enough to *think* of it. Even though I am not yet desperate enough to do it."

She was trembling.

She talked when she was nervous, he realized. She also talked when she was happy, but they were two different kinds of talking.

"You know," he said, "if I were a different person, one who *expected* less, I would count myself lucky over the events of the last day."

"You wouldn't. No one would."

"On the contrary. You're pretty and capable and clever. You're honest enough to tell me the truth instead of hiding it. And you undervalue yourself immensely—enough that you seem grateful for receiving the normal human kindness that should be everyone's right."

She looked over at him. Her eyes were alight with liquid hope, and he almost felt sorry for what he had to say next.

"If I were a different person," he said. "I'd be happy to have you for a wife."

"But." She said the word for him, yet her eyes watched his with an almost avid hunger.

"But I want what my parents have," he said simply.

She sighed and dropped her eyes. "It sounded like a lovely story, when you mentioned it earlier. It must have been something like love at first sight."

"Nothing like that. It took them three years to marry. My mother was an ardent abolitionist, and she said that she worked with my father at events for ages before she realized what was happening. She looked up one day after eighteen months of hearing his lectures and realized that she had slowly, sweetly, fallen in love. She waited another six months for my father to realize the same. They waited another year, just to be sure."

Miss Winters exhaled. Her eyes squeezed shut.

"That's what I want," he told her. "A long, slow falling in love. When I say 'I do,' I want to mean it—*really* mean it, more than I've ever meant anything in my life."

"That's sweet. Extremely sweet. I hope you have that." Sorrow—that's what he was hearing in her voice.

"Miss Winters," Adrian said. "It's not sweet. Anyone who wants love should have it. You can hope for the same. Really. Truly. You deserve someone who *chooses* you. Who you *know* loves you. Who believes that out of all the women in the world, you are the one who should share the rest of his life." He paused, thought of Mrs. Martin and what she had said about Larissa, and he added: "Or hers."

Her lips parted. She looked almost in pain. "You know," she said, "it is almost self-serving of you to say so."

"Maybe. But I promise that if you help me get what I want, I will not abandon you to your desperation. Money isn't a problem for me. We'll find you a place, a position. Whatever it is you want. And someday, somebody will choose you. For yourself."

She touched one hand to her head, sitting in silence for a moment. Finally, she looked back at him. "I have spent so many years wanting. Refusing to give up on hope. I didn't know why it got further and further away with every step. Still, I didn't give up. *I couldn't.*"

"You shouldn't."

"Good." Miss Winters looked away. "Thank you for reminding me that I could still hold on, even now."

The conveyance rattled on. "You know," Adrian finally

said, "you're the best woman I've ever had to marry at gunpoint."

"Oh? Has it happened often, then?" She smiled slightly.

"Just the once," he said, "but I have a phenomenal imagination. I've considered everyone else in that household, and would you know, since I had to be locked in a bedroom and forced to marry *someone,* I'm glad that it was you. Just think—it could have been Bishop Lassiter himself."

She laughed aloud at that.

"*That* would have made him a bigamist," he said. "It's a shame. We would have had proof of his wrongdoing already."

"Well." She squared her shoulders. He could almost see her folding up her self-pity like so much laundry. "I suppose in lieu of such an easy solution, we'll have to do this the hard way. When shall we visit the groundskeeper? Will tomorrow do?"

Adrian thought of Harvil, and his promise to be back for the final china design. He only had a few days before it really *would* be too late to put in the effort needed.

Maybe he should suggest that they go tonight? It was summer, and the light was still lingering. Still, he thought of the hole in her glove, and the six miles they still had to transverse. He thought of her saying that she was desperate. Maybe…

She made an almost incoherent noise, an unintelligible mumble, and he looked over at her. Her head tilted at an awkward angle; her hair was spilling from its messy bun. She had fallen asleep, he realized.

Tomorrow, then.

CHAPTER ELEVEN

Camilla wasn't aware that she had fallen asleep in the carriage until she awoke with a crick in her neck and the jingle of the harness in her ears.

She blinked, straightening, her eyes focusing on... Three shops, all next to each other, with a bit of a park across from them. It was late afternoon.

They weren't in Lackwich. They were in the town they'd passed through on their way to see Mrs. Martin—Cranfield? Something like that.

Here was a green-grocer. There was a baker. And there, on the corner, stood a little shop advertising ready-to-wear clothing. Mr. Hunter was tying the horses.

Camilla blinked and rubbed her eyes. Every muscle in her body felt stiff.

"Why are we stopping?"

"Because you need to purchase some things," he said.

She looked over at him. She felt as if she must be missing something. "Things." She frowned dubiously. "What sort of things?"

He reached into a pocket and removed a fine leather wallet. "Well, that's what we need to discuss. I ought to have thought of it before—when you had only the one valise—but I didn't. You need a new pair of shoes and gloves—that much is obvious. You could probably do with another gown or two." He looked away, as if embarrassed. "And...I cannot know without inspection, which would be awkward, but possibly some..."

Underthings. She didn't want to disclose the sordid, threadbare state of her underthings. "Things?" She waved her hand gravely.

"Yes. Things." He fished around in his wallet and found a bill—more money than she had seen since... She couldn't remember. He held it out to her. "For obvious reasons, I shan't go into the store with you, and you'll have to make do with ready-to-wear..."

She stared at him. Make do with ready-to-wear? Ridiculous. It had been ages since she'd thought of having anything personally made to fit her. For heaven's sake, it had been years since she'd purchased anything new.

He gestured with the bill. "You should buy some clothing, don't you think?"

"It's..." She swallowed. "It would be improper to allow a man to...buy me clothing?" She didn't mean for the end of her sentence to tip precariously upward into a question; she already knew she should say no.

But she *did* need shoes. And gloves. And if her second-best gown wore through again...

He let out a little bark of laughter. "What do you think will happen if word gets out, Miss Winters? Do you think your reputation will be ruined?"

"Oh, you're very amusing." Still, she couldn't bring herself to reach over and take the bill.

"I've been thinking," he said. "While we were en route. I've been trying to make sense of what happened to us and what it all means. My best guess is that Lassiter figured out that I had some connection to my uncle. He wanted to discredit any information I managed to unearth by painting me a scoundrel. You became caught up in this because you were there and you were convenient. It's *my* fault you are in this desperate predicament. And it's easy enough for me to make your situation less desperate. Allow me to do so."

She could scarcely think. "But I can't pay you back."

"I've never found that keeping score is a good way to maintain a friendship. See here, this is all in my best interest. Mrs. Martin was losing her eyesight; if we ever had to fool anyone else, you'd never be able to bamboozle them into thinking you a respectable lady. Not dressed like that."

Camilla colored. "I thought we had decided that there was to be no more lying."

Mr. Hunter shrugged, opened his wallet, and took out a smaller bill. He added this to the one in his hand. "I hadn't imagined it would be so hard to do something nice for you. Get a new hat as well."

"But—"

He simply added another bill. "Every time you try to politely protest, I am going to tell you to buy something else. What else do you suppose you need? A scarf, for sure."

"My scarf is in acceptable condition!"

"Ha, unlike the rest of your things." He smiled at her.

She could not stop her own smile from peeking out. "You're being ridiculous!"

"Counterpoint: You're exhausted. You're terrified of the future. It is hard to find a respectable position when you look like you're threadbare. These are perfectly reasonable feelings on your part, and I can do something about it. Doing so will improve my own quality of life by making you less anxious." He nodded. "So go. I'll be in the bookshop."

$\sim$

It was substantially later in the afternoon when Camilla found her way back to the carriage, laden with parcels. Shifts that had not been mended fifteen times over! Gowns where the print had not faded! Shoes where the seams did not leak! She'd left her family hoping for pretty gowns; it was the first time since her uncle had sent her away that she'd had anything like them.

Gowns weren't love, but they were at least, gowns.

Her fingers were warm in blue knit gloves that had not been darned again and again using three separate shades of gray yarn.

"Here," Mr. Hunter said as she clambered into the carriage. He handed her a paper sack.

"My God." She stared at it. "What *more* could I possibly need?"

"Lunch?"

The sun was dipping down toward the horizon, and her stomach chose that moment to growl. Camilla laughed. "Oh, very well."

The sack contained a meat pasty.

"There's a bottle of soda water at your feet," he said as he started the carriage. It took her a moment to free the cork stopper, but the water was cold and fizzy.

She couldn't remember the last time she had indulged in soda water. Not since she was a child, surely. The bubbles went up her nose, tasting of something almost tart. It made a perfect complement to the savory beef and gravy in the pasty. She devoured the whole thing in minutes—before they were even out of the tiny hamlet.

"Mr. Hunter," she said. "I am beginning to suspect that you are very kind."

"Oh, I don't know about *very*. Maybe a *little*."

"Very," Camilla said assuredly. "You forget—I have moved about a great deal, and have experience with a vast multitude of people. You are *very* kind."

"Or you have been uncommonly unlucky. I've been blessed with family circumstances that allow me to be kind. That's no great accomplishment."

"On the contrary," Camilla said. "Most people I know who are so blessed are usually convinced that they deserve what they have—and that those who *don't* have it, don't deserve it. You will have to take my word for it—you are *very* kind. Thank you, Mr. Hunter."

"What, for being a reasonable human being?" He looked taken aback. "There's no thanks owed for that. That should be the bare minimum expectation."

Camilla wiggled her fingers, now free of crumbs, back into her new gloves. "I am entirely certain that you are at least three marks above the minimum."

He glanced at her sidelong and smiled. "No more than two."

In the days since their abrupt marriage, Camilla had been doing her best to avoid thinking of what had caused the trouble in the first place—she and her flirtations. Mr. Hunter and his handsome countenance, his easy disposition, made every conversation feel like sunlight.

But she'd liked him at first glance, and liked him more after they'd spoken. Now he'd fed her. He'd bought her gowns. His smile…God, it did things to her insides. She felt her stomach give a little betraying flip and her heart kicked in her chest. He had become even more handsome than when they first met.

"Three marks above minimum," she said, "at *least*. For

heaven's sake, Mr. Hunter, let a girl give a compliment every now and then."

There it was—she could almost feel the pink rising in her complexion. She was doing it again. She was *flirting*, and oh, she shouldn't, she *shouldn't...*

"I'm terribly sorry," he said, "but my friends all call me Adrian, not Mr. Hunter. You've exceeded the compliment level for bare acquaintances. I must send your compliment back with my sincerest regrets."

She pulled away, feeling a little stung. "I'm sorry." She *had* been flirting. A little. She shouldn't have done it. Their situation was fraught enough as it was; she was just making it worse. "I didn't mean to impose. I'll stop—"

He looked at her for a long moment before shaking his head. "Silly. I wasn't telling you to stop complimenting me. I was telling you to stop calling me Mr. Hunter. That's my father. You can call me Adrian."

"Oh." She was so used to being called forward. She blinked at him. "Are we friends, then?"

"I don't know; do you want to be?"

He was going to leave her. The entire *point* of this exercise was for them *not* to be bound to each other. The flare of hope that lit inside her should not be there, Camilla knew. He'd asked if she wanted to be friends, not if she wanted to stay with him forever and have his babies.

She felt like a pile of dry leaves in autumn—the slightest hint of fire, and she'd combust immediately. She knew she should hold herself back.

She had never successfully held herself back from anything.

"Yes," she said. The world seemed to explode with color about them. "Yes, I should like that very much."

"Good."

She glanced at him next to her and flushed again.

"You should call me Camilla," she said. "Or Camille. Or just Cam." She felt as if she were glowing with delight. "Call me anything you like. I don't mind."

~

The small back room where Mrs. Beasley had allowed Camilla to stay wasn't much, but there were clothes-hooks and a little chest of drawers, and now she had things to put on them.

And! And! Mr. Hunter—no, *Adrian*—had called her a friend. He'd said she was clever and brave and—well—*technically* they were only working together because he wanted to never see her again, but there was no point in dwelling on the unpleasant.

She smiled, brought the new linen shift up to her face, and inhaled.

Ah. The scent of new clothing. It was the *best*. She smelled starch and something crisp and fresh. She did a little spin of joy in the room, grinning with delight.

"Ah—Miss Winters?"

Camilla stopped mid-twirl, turning to Mrs. Beasley. *Oh, no.* She imagined herself saying, *I wasn't actually dancing. By myself. That would be odd, ha ha ha.*

She managed to keep herself to a bare: "Why hello, Mrs. Beasley. Can I be of service?"

"Mr. Hunter is here to speak with you."

"Of course." Camilla nodded. "We have to speak to the groundskeeper tomorrow morning, and we must talk about the schedule."

"Yes, of course." Mrs. Beasley shifted in place, her jaw working, before she squared it and faced Camilla head on. "But before I send you out, may I ask a question? Are you well?"

"Do I look ill?" Oh *no*. And she was going to see him soon, too. If she appeared sickly or wan—

"No, dear. You *look* physically healthy. I meant in other ways. This has been a difficult time for you, and unscrupulous people might choose to impose on you and make the time more difficult, not less. I just wanted to ask. To be certain."

"Oh." Camilla felt touched by her concern. "Please don't worry. I am better than I have a right to be."

"There's no such thing. You have a right to be extremely well, you know." Mrs. Beasley gave her a half-hearted smile. "Just be aware that you can tell me anything, yes? It's not difficult work, running a telegraph office, but it is troubling. I hear portions of everyone's story and never the full thing. I pretend not to know half of what I hear." She took one of Camilla's hands and gave it a squeeze.

"I'm well," Camilla said. "The situation is hard, but…I'm well. Thank you for caring."

Mrs. Beasley shook her head. "The hardest part of my work is staying silent. Most of the time, it's all just fodder for my amusement. But sometimes I hear and I must sit in silence and pretend I don't notice. My biggest regrets come from that—the not asking. You *will* let me know if there's anything I can do?"

"I will."

"Good." Mrs. Beasley gave her fingers another squeeze. "Then go have your chat."

❧

Adrian had been waiting for ten minutes in the front room before Camilla appeared. Mrs. Beasley very obviously did not close the door to give them privacy. Adrian sighed. Well, so be it.

"I had been thinking eleven in the morning for when you talk to the groundskeeper," Adrian said. "The church is a few miles away, so I should come by at ten thirty or so, to drive you out."

Camilla sat in a chair across from him. She'd changed into one of her new gowns, pink stripes with yellow cuffs. The colors suited her—bright and cheery in the diffuse light from the gas lamp.

"Better be early," Camilla said. "Mr. Graves gets hungry for his lunch around then. We want him in his best mood."

"Nine thirty?"

"More like eight thirty."

"Gah." Adrian felt his nose wrinkle in disgust. "So early. I detest waking early."

Camilla just laughed. "How did you *ever* pretend to be a valet? Really, Adrian."

She said his name almost shyly, and then glanced at him through dark lashes, as if wondering if the familiarity that he'd specifically asked for was too much.

"Badly," Adrian said. "So badly. I was a terrible valet."

She leaned forward, smiling. "What do you do when you're not pretending to be a valet?"

"Oh." He shrugged. "This and that. My family has some business interests here, and I'm the one who spends the most time in England. So I see to them. I'm a little better at that than I am at being a valet."

She let out a little gurgling laugh. "I suspect you are. You have an air of competence about you; you had to earn it somehow."

If he had thought she was putting him on or flattering him on purpose, he would have pulled back. But she said it so matter-of-factly, and with such a smile, that it made him feel a little dishonest.

He thought about telling her about the china designs. But

he really had almost nothing to do with them—he had excellent artists who did amazing things with almost no direction on his part—and she'd laugh at the story. But…he liked the way she looked at him. He shouldn't have, but he did.

"Oh," Adrian said, suddenly. "That reminds me. I brought you a treat? It's a celebration for a successful day. Here." He reached down and found the paper bag at his feet, opening it up. "I hope you like lemon tarts. They were all that was left at the bakery."

She froze in place, her eyes fixing on the little pastries. Her hands flew behind her back.

"Oh." He felt a strange sense of disappointment. When he'd stopped in front of the bakery, he'd thought of her smile earlier when he'd bought her a meat pie. She'd had little enough reason to smile lately; that was the only reason he had wanted to see her face light up. Not because he'd enjoy looking.

Nothing like that at all.

"Oh," he repeated sadly. "You don't like lemon tarts."

"No." She shook her head. "It's not that. I love lemon tarts. Or at least, I used to do so."

"Then you should have them both."

She actually sat on her hands and shook her head. "I'm sorry, I can't."

"Of course you can. Don't worry about me. I never want for lemon tarts."

That smile he had hoped for did not materialize. Instead, she looked even more perturbed.

"It's not that. Or—it's not just that." She swallowed. "I said earlier I lost my family. Actually…" She stopped again, then glanced at the open door behind them. She dropped her voice even further. "Actually, I left them."

He waited for her to continue.

"I was twelve. My uncle was wealthy; my father had

just…" She paused, her lips pursing as if she were searching for the right word. "Died," she settled on. "My family was in shambles. We were utterly ruined. My uncle offered to take me in. My sister told me not to go, but *he* told me I would have gowns and lemon tarts. So I gave in."

He didn't know what to say to that.

She looked down. "I gave up everyone who cared about me for lemon tarts. Fat lot of good *that* did me."

"Well." Adrian wasn't quite sure what to say to that. "But…you still like lemon tarts, don't you?"

Her eyes dropped to the floor. "I tried to eat one again when I was fourteen and staying with Mrs. Heilford? Back then, she had only just started asking me to do little tasks around the house. It was a special treat and I put it in my mouth, and…"

"And?"

"And I couldn't taste anything," she whispered. "It reminded me too much of things I couldn't have any longer. It might have been sawdust, for all I knew. It has seemed like a waste to try one ever since."

"Well." Adrian held out the tarts to her. "Time to try again, don't you think?"

She stared at the pastry. "What if I don't taste it?"

"Then you'll try again." He moved his hand even closer.

"What do I do?"

"Touch it," he said. "There's no rush. If your mind goes blank, just fill it with details. Remind yourself what it feels like first."

She reached out a tentative finger, running it over the golden-brown ridges of the crust. "It looks smooth," she said quietly. "But it's rough. It feels…crisp? Can something *feel* crisp?"

"Break off a piece."

She snapped off a small section. Little crumbs scattered on the sack where he held the pastry.

She raised it to her lips, then stopped.

"Smell it first."

She inhaled. "Oh, it smells so sweet. And lemony."

"Does the crust smell different?"

She turned the piece in her fingers. "Buttery," she said, "with a hint of salt."

"Go ahead. Taste it."

Her lips parted, pink and inviting, and he was transfixed by the sight of her tongue darting out. She bit off a dainty piece and closed her lips. Her eyes shut.

"Oh." Just one syllable, somewhere between pleasure and pain. "Ohhh." She chewed slowly. "I *can* taste it. It's—oh, so good. The lemon is so tart, and yet so perfectly sweet. And the crust? It's rich and buttery and salty all at once. I can taste it again." She opened her eyes and looked at him. "I can't believe it. Adrian, it's back. I can *taste* again."

And there was that smile he'd seen before—brilliant, sparkling, and so utterly beautiful that he felt as if he'd been knocked back a pace.

Oh. No. He had known that he liked her. He had known he thought she was pretty. He hadn't realized that he *liked* her. Bad idea. Very bad idea.

"Of course it's back," he heard himself say. "You deserve lemon tarts—all the lemon tarts that exist in the world."

Her eyes shone. "No, no, that's too many lemon tarts. I will be smothered."

His throat felt hoarse. "You deserve lemon tarts in reasonable quantities, then." And because he needed to remind himself, he added: "You deserve someone who chooses you, someone who wants you for who you are. Someone who doesn't let you slip away."

She just looked at him, her eyes shining, and oh, this was

not a good idea. Why had he thought making her smile was a good idea?

"I promise you," Adrian said. "We'll get you everything after the lemon tarts, too. It will all be yours—just as soon as we can end this thing that entangles us."

CHAPTER TWELVE

"I had thought that you might be able to be of assistance." Camilla tried her best to look at the church groundskeeper with a friendly smile. The morning sun was bright, and she had been full of hope all day since she woke. The sun was golden, and it had driven off the morning mist entirely. During the drive out, green leaves had rustled on the trees. "I had heard that there were resources available for women who were in need of help, and I...well. You may have heard..." She trailed off invitingly and gave him another hopeful smile. There was still dew on the grass, and she could feel it, cool and comfortable, against her ankles.

After the lemon tarts last night and the drive this morning, she'd thought she would never be unhappy again. But Mr. Graves was peering over her head as if she didn't exist. His eyes focused on a point far away from her.

A disappointment, to be sure. Well. It just went to show—not everyone would be as kind as Adrian. She'd never expected more. She had just hoped for it.

"Ayep." Still he didn't look at her. "I heard what you did.

We all did." His nose twitched, as if he smelled something bad—and it was her.

"*Are* such resources available?" She was proud of herself for asking without a hint of a quaver in her voice.

"No." He didn't look at her. "Why would there be?"

"I just thought, I had thought…" She trailed off, trying to figure out how to ask about charity without using the words *Mrs. Martin gave money for a charity gift and I want to know if it was used properly.*

"What?" Mr. Graves sounded scornful. "You thought that you didn't deserve what you got?"

That started a slow, nervous fluttering in her stomach. She didn't want to think, didn't want to get distracted. As long as she didn't think of it…

"Could you—I don't know, have you asked? Is there not some sort of fund set up for women in need, that one could inquire after?"

"Not a chance. I have specific orders from the rector himself to make sure the likes of you move on swiftly. Don't want you being a burden on the parish, we don't."

"But." She swallowed. "Are those *recent* orders? Might something not have changed?"

For the first time, he looked at her. She almost wished he hadn't. "He told me himself. In person. This morning."

She couldn't back down. In this circumstance, her very helplessness made her a weapon that could be used. Camilla balled her hands and returned his gaze. "Is there perhaps some evidence that he told you that? Did he say so in writing? Or is there a circular on the matter?"

She realized her mistake when his eyes flared in anger. Oh. He thought she was accusing him of deception.

He took a step toward her. "Be gone!"

He was taller than her by a foot. It took all her strength not to turn tail and dash away. "I didn't mean to imply you were lying. Just—it would give me some comfort to know...? If there were some official pronouncement on the matter?"

"I'm not a perambulating stack of documents," he said, and this time he did reach for his shovel. "Get *off*. Nobody wants you. Nobody wants you here at all."

No doubt he meant nothing by it; men reached for shovels all the time. He was a groundskeeper; shovels were a tool of his business. But for a moment, Camilla stood in frozen horror, her lungs aching inside her.

"Get out of here." He actually raised the shovel.

In the end, she broke and ran.

~

The walk back to the carriage, which Adrian had tied up out of sight, afforded Camilla an opportunity to calm down. Trees, she reminded herself. Trees with leaves on them. Leaves rustling in the summer wind. Green grass. Sun.

No shovels, not anywhere. Her pulse had mostly stopped racing by the time she found him around two bends of the road. She felt chilled through, though, and she couldn't explain it. It was a warm day, and she had her cloak. There was no reason to be shivering.

Adrian jumped down to meet her as she turned the bend in the road. "And how did it go?"

Camilla could be calm. She wasn't the sort of woman to panic simply because a man told her no and picked up a shovel.

"It went well." Her voice was even, so even. She was proud of herself. Why should she feel anything? There was nothing to feel. "Precisely as we had expected. I asked if there were any resources for women in my position. He told me to take myself off." Another shudder ran through her; she wrapped her arms about herself.

He didn't notice her involuntary tremor. He met her by the carriage. The horses were tied, and the sun crept higher in the sky. "Well, that's as we suspected. That's good."

It hadn't been good.

"I asked if there were not recently changed circumstances; he said there were none. I asked if there were any proof of this—circulars or a letter or such-like—and he..."

For a second, it felt as if Mr. Graves were still standing over her with the shovel; she felt his presence like a flash of cold lightning and recoiled.

"He told me it was rude to question him." That was the problem, Camilla realized. Mr. Graves was too closely connected to her old life, the one she'd had at Rector Miles's home. She'd learned early on that forward was the only possible direction. If she looked back, she'd yearn. She'd remember. She would think of all her carefully tended hopes and how they had come to nothing.

If she looked back, she would have to face the truth, and if she faced the truth, how could she ever go on? There was her mistake just now; she'd looked back.

She shouldn't have looked back.

"Hmm." Mr. Hunter was frowning and looking upward.

Which meant that he hadn't noticed her mood. Good. She'd learned her lesson. She'd keep her eyes forward, her hope buoyant, unweighed down by the reality of her past.

"Well." He sighed. "I suppose that's to be expected. It's not like they would commit to flouting the terms of the gift in print, would they?"

"Do you...do you think my word on the matter alone would be enough to prove it? For your uncle?"

He turned to look at her. *No,* he did not say. He did not need to say it.

"What we need," he said, "is the rector's private records. His books of account, if we could get our hands on them. I wish…" He trailed off, his mouth twisting. "I wish you and I had formed this alliance before our current situation. You would have had access back then, and…"

She couldn't think of being employed in the rector's house. That was looking back. It felt like a shovel held over her head. It felt like the resistance of a locked door. She couldn't look back. Not now, not when she needed to hope.

He tapped his fingers against his chin.

"You know," he said, looking at her, "if you would be willing, do you know what you could do?"

She knew what he was going to say. God, she was thinking it herself. She didn't want him to say it. She wanted it out of her mind. She wanted her past gone forever.

"You could go back to the rectory," he said. "Ask Miles to give you another chance, another trial. You wouldn't have to mean it; you could make an offer he could not refuse—less money, perhaps no money? Ask for a trial period for a week. A day, even. You only need a few hours."

Her chest hurt. She couldn't go back. That wasn't how this worked. It wasn't how it ever worked. Miles had locked her in a room and told her she was going to hell. He'd said her hopes were devils. If she went back to him, she'd have to tell him—believably—that he was right, and she was so close to desperate that she feared if she said the words, they'd become true.

She'd stayed with him for eighteen months. It had never felt terrible, not while she was going through it.

But now Adrian was here. He noticed if there were holes in her gowns and told her that she deserved lemon tarts. Mrs. Martin had told her to care for herself. Mrs. Beasley had asked after her well-being, and told her she deserved to be happy. Even Mrs. Martin had given her advice.

Camilla had not realized that Rector Miles had made her feel small and unwanted for every one of those eighteen months until she had experienced kindness again.

She had to keep looking forward—not back. *Be reasonable,* her mind whispered. *It would just be for a day. Half a day.* But her stomach churned. Miles had never hurt her, so why did she feel so utterly harmed by the prospect of seeing him again?

Adrian looked over at her.

"What did we decide about lies?" Camilla heard herself say.

"True. I'm terrible at them." He gave her a warming smile. "That's why I'm sure you will come up with a far better story than I ever would. Especially if we work together."

She didn't want a story. She just didn't want to do it.

"Camilla?" He looked at her—really looked at her, this time with a searching glance that ran over her trembling hands, then traveled up the length of her arms to her tense, tight shoulders. "Is something the matter?"

She opened her mouth to say that everything was lovely, fine, no problem…

Nothing came out.

"Camilla?" He took a step toward her. "Whatever is the matter?"

Nothing was the matter. Everything he was asking for was logical. All he was asking her to do was…

…Was to go back into a place she could no longer bear to see, with someone who had claimed to care about her soul, but had made her desperation the object of laughter.

Adrian was asking her to look back, and every time she looked back, she thought of her family. She thought of the people who had never loved her. She remembered all the hope that had never come to fruition. She didn't want to look back.

Camilla drew in a deep breath, then another, then all she could concentrate on was trying to breathe through the iron fist that gripped her chest.

"Camilla?" He took a step toward her. "Are you crying?"

"No." She wrapped her arms around herself. "I *hate* crying. My eyes are just easily bothered, and it's windy out."

He stopped a pace from her. "Camilla. We're in this together, remember? We're allies. We're friends. If something is the matter, you can tell me."

She hadn't meant to say it; even though he'd told her to speak, she hadn't meant to really do it.

But when her mouth opened to say once more that nothing was the matter, something else came out.

"I can't go back," she said. "I can't. I can't look back."

He stood in place. Through the haze of her tears, she could see him shaking his head in confusion.

"I *want* to. I *want* to be useful. I am trying so hard, but I can't, I can't. I don't want to have to remember. Nobody wants me. Nobody ever, *ever* wants me to stay."

Now grief and anger twined together, rising up inside her. It was one thing for her eyes to get misty. It was another thing entirely to sob. She wouldn't. It would be weak and ugly and—damn.

She had always felt her emotions so keenly, and this time was no different. She swiped at her eyes.

He looked totally taken aback.

"I left my family," she told him. "I didn't tell you the full truth before. Do you know what happened to them? My father was convicted of treason. I tried to walk away from it. My uncle took me in. I told you that."

This was why she couldn't look back—because the past hurt too much.

Camilla could recall what happened as clear as day—that conversation with Judith when she'd decided to go to her uncle. "Camilla," Judith had said, "he's stuffy. He doesn't love you."

And Camilla, stupid child that she had been, hadn't *wanted* to understand the truth. She'd just wanted to forget the people who pointed at them in the streets and called them names. She had wanted her life not to change.

Camilla felt her fists clench. She looked over at Adrian and told him the devastating truth. "My eldest sister said our family should stay together because we loved each other. I told her that I wouldn't starve."

Judith had looked at her and said, "If you don't want to be loved, we don't want to love you."

She remembered that feeling of foolish surety she had harbored that could only belong to a child. She remembered how upset Judith had been. They'd had an all-out row.

Judith had always had something of a temper, and it had ignited at that. At the very end, Judith had stalked out of the room, pausing only in the doorway to deliver this: "Have it your way. I hope you *never* have love again. I hope you don't get to wear it or eat it or experience it. When you're crying yourself to sleep at night because nobody cares about you, don't come crawling to me and expect me to make it better. You made your choice. You don't *get* love anymore."

Judith had been right. Camilla hadn't had love—not ever again. Not after that.

Camilla had asked her uncle to post letters for months after she'd arrived. She had tried writing for years—even though she hadn't known her sister's direction, she'd sent the letters to her uncle to send on for her.

There had been nothing from Judith but resounding silence. That silence had swallowed all her hope.

When she was sixteen, after four years of silence, Camilla had vowed to look forward, not back.

Now, if the news was to be believed, Judith had found

love. Her husband was wealthy and respected; she had gowns and lemon tarts. She had everything.

Camilla had nothing.

"That is how I lost my family," Camilla said. "I threw them away. I chose to go to my uncle instead of staying with them. And he sent me to his cousin. And so on and so on, until I found myself here. I traded away my right to ever have anyone love me when I was twelve, and I..." Her voice faltered. "I *know* it deep down. I *do*. But I am not strong enough to face the truth. I have to keep hoping or I'll fall to pieces."

"Camilla." Adrian's voice was low. "That's not how it works. You can't give up your right to be loved. And you were twelve."

"I'm twenty now. I have amassed close to nine years of proof. Do you know what it's like to hope for years and years that someone will like you enough to marry you, and to know that the only reason you said 'I do' is because time in my company is marginally preferable to death?"

"Camilla." He bit his lip. "That's—look, this isn't about you at all."

"I *know*." She swiped angrily at her cheeks. "Of course I know! Even my own wedding wasn't about me, for God's sake!"

"Camilla, I'm sure *somebody* will want you."

"*You* don't."

Even now, even at her worst, she couldn't keep from hoping that he would deny it. That he'd tell her he'd fallen stupidly, deeply in love over the course of five days.

But he didn't say that. Instead, he let out a long breath. "That's not fair. I want what my parents have—decades of happiness, a partnership that has withstood the test of time, a long, slow chance to really fall in love. I am not going to apologize to you because I want that for myself."

Of course. Camilla's sobs had progressed to the ugly stage of hiccupping. "And I *will* apologize for being as weak as I am. I just have to keep hoping."

There was a long pause. He took another step toward her and set his hand on her shoulder. There was nothing importuning about it; just comfort given in small measure.

"Cam," he said quietly. "There you are, little tiger."

"Tigers are strong. I am *not* a tiger."

"Tigers never stop hoping," he said. "Hope is not weak. It takes courage to hope and hope and hope, when nothing comes out right. It takes strength to continue to believe that *this* time everything will come out right when it's always gone wrong before. You are not weak."

He was going to break her, giving her just this much kindness and not one iota more.

"See here," he said, and the hand he had on her shoulder gave her an awkward pat. "I can't know what it's like, but I can tell you this. You deserve to be loved. You have always known it; that is why you keep hoping. But look at you, little tiger. You look on the bright side of things—most of the time, if not always. You rarely complain; you are willing to work hard to achieve a result. You have an excellent memory. You're witty and charming and pretty. You deserve more than someone who has been tied to you by the caprices of fate."

She shook her head. Her heart felt so stupidly empty and so ridiculously full, all at the same time.

"I promise you," he whispered into her hair, "it's not impossible. Someday, somebody is going to adore you for how wonderful you are."

He put one arm around her. It wasn't an embrace; it was a gesture of comfort. She *knew* it for precisely that, and still she couldn't help but feel her heart beat just a little faster.

"You deserve that," he whispered in her ear. "You deserve

to *truly* fall in love and to be loved in return. You deserve to be worshipped for the person you are, and not just tolerated for existing."

It had never happened yet. If she looked back at everything that had ever happened to her, she'd conclude from all available evidence that love would never find her at all—not in any way, not in any form.

Her heart was too fragile to take that crushing a blow.

So Camilla did what she had done a dozen or more times over the course of her life—she looked forward and pushed the darkness of her past back into hiding.

She let herself hope through the twinge of her bruises and the sting of her tears. She let herself believe despite all the evidence.

Someone would love her. Just because it had never happened yet, didn't mean it wouldn't. Hope stung like an old ache, but it was better than the alternative.

"There," Adrian said, one arm still around her. "There, there. That's better. You're feeling better, aren't you?"

Camilla sniffled and opened her eyes. Her forehead rested against the skin of his neck; he smelled clean and bright, full of promise. She pulled away an inch.

She had thought he was handsome when first she met him. Here he was, telling her that she deserved to have her long-held wish granted. Telling her that she was pretty and charming and…and…

And, oh God, he had ceased to be merely *handsome*. It felt like the darkness of her mood lifted when she looked at him, like every sunbeam in the sky reflected off his skin.

He must have mistaken the shy smile she gave him, because he nodded and smiled back at her.

"There we are," he said softly. "That's not a fake smile is it?"

Oh, no, no, *no*. She *wasn't* feeling better. Her hands felt clammy; her whole body prickled with the awareness of his proximity.

"Maybe I can do it," she said slowly. "Maybe. I can go back, if you want me too."

He looked off over her shoulder, as if seeing something she could not, and then nodded once. "No." He sighed. "My uncle asked me to pose as valet. I didn't want to, but... Never mind my reasons. He shouldn't have asked me, not after I said no the first time. And look what happened. I'm not going to be him. You said no; that should be enough. We just need a different plan, that's all."

He should be yelling at her, calling her a stupid girl. Anything but kindness. Camilla was horribly susceptible to kindness, and every inch of her soul was responding to him in silent entreaty.

"This affects the rest of our lives," he pronounced. "We don't need to fix it in five minutes." He sighed, then shrugged. "Or even, I suppose, in five days."

She exhaled.

He was almost talking to himself now. "No matter how swiftly we proceed, there are still elements of this business that will necessarily take time. We'll need to obtain an affidavit from Mrs. Martin as evidence. Besides, I have some things I must attend to; I have already put them off for far too long. I need to go back to Harvil. We're not resolving this tomorrow or even the next day, no matter what you do; it was foolish to think we could."

Oh. *No.* A thread of panic reasserted itself. "You're leaving."

"Well, you do get a vote." He smiled faintly. "I'd like to go to Harvil—I have business there. You may come along, if you wish; now that I think of it, this will be good for our case. We can introduce you to everyone there as someone who is not my wife. The more witnesses who say that we have not held ourselves out as married, the better it will be for us. And it will give us a chance to think of some possible avenues for proceeding that don't leave you devastated."

She didn't say anything for a moment; she could hardly speak.

"We can always arrange for you to go somewhere else," he said when the silence lingered. "This is difficult enough for both of us. I understand if you don't want to spend more time in my vicinity."

It was an all-too familiar feeling. Camilla, fool that she was, recognized the emotion that flared in her chest far too well. She'd always wanted to *get* love, and so she gave it too easily. At the proverbial drop of a hat.

She could almost laugh at herself. *For God's sake, Camilla.* He hadn't even needed to drop his.

He didn't love her. He didn't intend to love her; he didn't want to love her.

It didn't matter.

She inhaled, long and shuddering. "Yes," she said. "I mean, no. No, your family property is perfectly acceptable. We're not married, but we are tied to each other in a way, and what if I recalled something that might help us? We should be close enough to consult."

He smiled.

"I'd have to send telegrams if we were apart." She was joking, and it almost hurt to joke when her heart felt so fragile. "And somewhere along the way there'd be a Mrs. Beasley, and she might remember the whole thing. How embarrassing for us both."

"I know you don't want to look back," he said more quietly. "I arrived at the tail end of your stay with Rector Miles. What I saw was dreadful. I can't blame you for not wanting to look back."

She shook her head.

"Sometimes you look back and it's a wedding at gunpoint. Sometimes it's lemon tarts. You're a generous person, Camilla. You give a great deal. Give yourself time, and look back a little when it's possible and maybe you'll see that you've gotten more than you thought."

He was just saying it out of self-preservation. He wanted her to get the account books; he was telling her to wait a few weeks until she felt better. She *knew* this was true.

And still, that praise made her heart thump. Generous. He thought her generous.

His smile flashed out, bright and merry, and Camilla gave up on herself. Hopeless; she was utterly hopeless.

She had fallen in love before, and it always hurt. This would be no different.

She'd come through worse. She'd survived the loss of her father, her brothers, her sisters...

Her sisters. She had mentioned her family twice, but hadn't told him who her sisters were. She'd changed her name so she wouldn't embarrass them.

Judith was a marchioness. Her youngest sister was fifteen now, and would likely be coming out soon.

Lady Theresa Worth had stayed with her family. She was getting all the gowns, all the love, that Camilla had not had. And Camilla loved the sister she hadn't seen—the sister she could not let herself look back on—enough that she would leave her to those gowns and never disturb that.

If Camilla could survive not knowing the woman her sister had grown into, she could survive anything. She could even survive Adrian Hunter.

Camilla took a deep breath and did what she did best. She smiled and looked forward.

CHAPTER THIRTEEN

Lady Theresa Worth was not the sort of young lady who left anything to chance. The Dowager Marchioness of Ashford had told her that an acceptable gift for her sister's birthday would be a commemorative embroidered cushion.

The dowager was her sister's husband's mother, a woman who had taken Theresa under her wing the moment Judith's marriage had been announced. She had declared that she'd always wanted a daughter, and after a few uneasy months together, they'd actually become friendly.

So Theresa had planned to do exactly as the dowager suggested. She had made a plan, stitch by stitch, obtained the appropriate silks, then sat down to wage war on the fabric.

The main problem with this plan was that Theresa's embroidery was utter shite.

She'd given herself a full three months to produce something within the bounds of acceptability—something that her oldest sister could put on, say, a divan in a rarely used room, instead of quietly sending up to the attic. Or burning it to stay warm in the winter.

Alas. After two months, Theresa stared down at her current attempt—try nine—and the lopsided things that were supposed to represent the ravens of the Ashford crest.

Instead of sleek, feathered things, Theresa had managed to produce something that looked more like a withered, blackened cauliflower. Or maybe, a diseased octopus?

A shame. She liked octopodes.

She imagined herself presenting this cushion to her sister.

"What are these?" Judith would ask, her lip quirking in dismay.

Oh, just some rotting vegetables, Theresa would reply. *My love for you is like a field of rotting vegetables—like rot, my love grows to encompass the entire crop. It's rather hard on the vegetables, but if you would just look at it from the rot's point of view—*

That explanation would go over *so* well.

The other idea that the dowager marchioness had come up with was that Theresa could compose a poem. Perhaps Theresa could combine the two? At least she'd get a laugh.

She glared out the glass window.

"Theresa?"

Theresa turned at the sound. Her younger brother, Benedict, stood in the doorway.

She raised a single eyebrow, set her cushion of rotted splendor aside, and folded her arms, waiting for her brother to realize his mistake.

His legs came together; he straightened. His hand rose in a salute. "My pardon, your Excellency. General Worth, I mean. I beg a moment of your attention."

Theresa considered whether she should punish her brother. On the one hand, insubordination needed to be extracted from the root. Besides, nobody told *Benedict* that he had to produce a cushion or a verse for his sister's birthday. He was a *boy. He* was allowed to do all sorts of non-labor-intensive things, like purchasing flowers as a gift on the morning of Judith's birthday.

On the other hand, thus far, nobody in her family had noticed that she had dragooned her younger brother into her own private army, and Theresa intended to keep it that way.

Today, she could be magnanimous. "Proceed, Corporal Benedict."

"You promised we would deal with my little problem."

Benedict's *little problem* was not so little. Over a year ago, he'd refused to return to Eton. She could hardly blame him; he'd been badly treated. Since then, Judith and Christian had attempted to find him a place in the world. He'd been made to sit in a lawyer's office for the last three months.

He hated it with a passion that burned hotter than…than a field of withered cauliflower, put to the flame?

"Give it some time," Judith had told him comfortingly. "A year may feel like forever to you at this age, but it's nothing. You can't know if you like the work if you don't take time to get good at it."

"You'll grow into it," Christian had promised Benedict. "You like talking with people and being right. You should love the practice of law."

Theresa, who knew her brother far better than either Judith or Christian, had promised to come up with a plan to free her brother from the tyranny of the law office. Which—admittedly—was not so tyrannical, as the man was incredibly kind to Benedict and his wife brought him biscuits. But all professions that one did not wish to have were a tyranny.

"I've been thinking about the matter." Theresa slid her embroidery underneath a cushion. "What you need is to show an aptitude for some other profession. They'll never agree to pull you from this law thing if you haven't provided an alternative."

"Yes, but I don't *know* an alternative."

"I do," Theresa said. This was *probably* not a lie. She technically *didn't* have an alternative in mind at the moment the words came out of her mouth. She was just certain that by the time she finished speaking, she would have figured one out.

"Excellent! What is it?"

"Let us come at it another way," Theresa said. "What were your thoughts on Judith's birthday present?"

"Flowers," Benedict said glumly.

"Ask yourself: Does Judith really want flowers?"

"Well…"

"No," Theresa decided. "She does not, any more than she wants terribly embroidered cushions depicting the last century's worst farming tragedies. She'll *appreciate* them, because they come from us, but she doesn't *want* them."

"True."

Theresa folded her arms and tried to look like a wiser older sister. She was fifteen to Benedict's fourteen; it shouldn't be hard. "Let us ask ourselves this: What does Judith want? What does she *really* want?"

What an excellent question. If only she knew the answer.

Benedict considered. "A new hat?"

"No," Theresa said, realizing the answer as she spoke. Judith had stopped speaking of the matter six months ago; that didn't mean she didn't care.

Years ago, their family had been separated. Her eldest brother had been transported as punishment for doing things that really ought not to have been crimes, but which were *technically* treasonous. Her father had been…could you call it separation, if he was separated from his life? And Camilla, their middle sister, had gone to live with an uncle.

Judith had tried to find her, but their uncle had passed her on to someone else, and so on and so on. Letters had not been forwarded. The whole matter was something of a disaster.

They hadn't found her yet, and Judith was in mourning. She hadn't said anything; she was much too *Judith* to do so. But after more than a year of searching with no response, Theresa knew precisely what her sister thought about the matter of Camilla.

Judith had started wearing black ribbons, the only outward show of grief that she allowed herself.

"Judith wants to find Camilla. *That* is what we are going to accomplish for her birthday, you and I. We are going to find Camilla."

Benedict glanced over at Theresa. His lips pressed together. "Uh. Well. Um." He fell silent after this proclamation, shifting uneasily from foot to foot.

Theresa tilted her head. "Permission to speak more precisely is granted, Corporal Benedict."

"I mean to say…we have less than a month. And perhaps investigations should be left to professionals? And also…this is precisely how you *always* get me in trouble."

Ha. Benedict *never* got in trouble, not the way she did. Not even when he was *deeply* at fault. It wasn't fair that only men were put to studying law; men were *never* held accountable for practically anything they did. It was always *Theresa, why did you* and *Theresa, what is going on?*

"Think on it, Benedict," Theresa said. "You would enjoy being an investigator. Very little sitting around in an office reading boring pages. A great deal of talking to people and walking about and looking at clues and such."

Benedict's nose wrinkled.

"Besides, who better to find Camilla than family? Nobody knows her the way we do."

"I was five when she left," Benedict offered. "I don't remember her at all."

Theresa had been six, and she scarcely remembered Camilla, either, but there was no point in admitting to a weakness.

"Dream large or don't dream at all," Theresa said with a toss of her head. "Besides, think of what it would mean to Judith. Nothing means more to her than family. Finding Anthony is...not an option." She wasn't going to think of Anthony. "Neither of us remember Camilla the way Judith does. We were both too young. But *I* can understand the pain of losing a well-loved sister. *I* lost a sister I loved once."

"Your sister was not real," Benedict put in. "You invented her when you were three. She did not exist."

"Insubordination," Theresa snapped. "What is experience and memory, if not a product of the mind? The fact that my sister may have been imaginary does not make her loss any less painful."

Benedict just stared at her.

"In fact, it makes it a hundred times worse for me than Judith," Theresa tossed off. "At least *her* sister might someday be recovered. *Mine* is lost forever."

Benedict let out a sigh and sat on the divan. "I'm guessing you have a plan."

"However did you know?"

He didn't say anything. Instead, he reached his hand under the cushion where she'd stashed her misadventure in embroidery. He withdrew it and squinted at her scene.

"Let's assume Camilla is alive," Theresa said. "It may not be true, but it would be a horrid present if she's dead. If she still lives, then the following must be true. First, she is not reading the newspapers. If she were, she would have seen one of the advertisements Judith and Christian have taken out."

Benedict nodded. "Also, she cannot be using her maiden

159

name—or someone *else* would have seen the advertisements and sent word in. Perhaps she is married?"

"Good!" Theresa grinned at her brother. "You *are* good at this."

He flushed in pleasure. "That would make her difficult to find. How do you reach the unreachable, General Worth?"

Theresa couldn't remember precisely *when* she'd made her younger brother into her personal, private army, or how she'd become general of it. But it helped to have someone relying on her, someone who didn't judge her for her terrible embroidery.

If she'd been left to her own devices, she wouldn't have felt any need to deliver. But the sheer pressure of being called General Worth made her think that she had something to offer. She was going to… She was going to…

Yes! She had it. Or at least, she knew where to start.

Theresa met her brother's eyes. "As it turns out," she said, "I have an idea about that."

～

"Well," Adrian said, as the barouche pulled up in front of a two-story building. The sun was hanging low on the horizon, lighting the windows in orange. "We're here. The family country cottage."

It had only been this morning when Camilla met with the groundskeeper. In the intervening hours, they'd changed trains twice before arriving at the station in Bristol. They'd been met there by a Mr. Singh, an Indian gentleman who had greeted Adrian with a handshake and brought him out to the waiting conveyance. The weather had been fine enough that the top had been left down.

Adrian had taken the seat closest to the driver, leaving

Camilla to face forward. They'd wound their way out of Bristol proper into the countryside.

Her whole body ached; she'd been swaying back and forth all day. She was glad to have arrived.

Still…

"Cottage," Camilla said weakly, looking at the edifice that stood before her. The word 'cottage' made her think of a cozy little space, maybe three rooms large. Not this monstrosity of gray stones and thatched roofs set on acres of land. Not so far off, a blue thread of a river wound down and about; a more modern building stood near the banks, all red brick with chimneys pointing to the sky. A faint clatter could be heard even from here.

"Right," Adrian told her. "That's the china-works; the whistle should be sounding soon for the end of the day, and then it will quiet down a bit. My family owns it. I do some work there sometimes."

Beside him, Mr. Singh, his hands full of luggage, made a little noise of protest.

"A *little* work," Adrian said. "*Sometimes.*"

"He is completely in charge of the design process, the sales, the advertisements, and the exhibitions," Mr. Singh said. "He fools himself. Don't let him fool you."

Camilla cast Adrian an inquiring glance.

"The property's been in the family for almost a century."

Camilla wasn't entirely sure what to say to that. "Your… mother's family?"

"My father's. It comes…from uncle Henry? My brother is named for him."

"I thought your brother's name was Grayson."

Adrian's smile froze. "Ah. I mean…my brother was named for him. Henry passed away. Not uncle Henry—he's really great-great uncle Henry—and technically not an uncle. But an uncle."

"I...see." She didn't.

Adrian turned away from her. "Enough of my family. The china-works was built maybe thirty years ago by my uncles John and Henry. They really started the family enterprise."

"The family being you and your brother and...?"

"Far more complicated than that. It starts with John and Henry. Henry was my great-great-uncle John's business partner. He inherited this land from *his* aunt. They had thought first to sell it off, but..." He trailed off. "But you don't need to hear my family history, do you?"

She wanted to hear it all. She could listen to him speak for hours. But she was trying not to betray her stupid, stupid heart. Camilla just smiled. "Don't worry, tell me all you wish."

"I will. First things first. This is Mrs. Singh. She and her husband keep the cottage."

The woman who had come out to greet them took a step forward, waving her hand. She was heavy and blond, and she smiled brightly. "Mr. Hunter. We're so glad you've returned. Was your business successful? Mr. Alabi has been ranting about your absence for weeks."

"Mr. Alabi is an artist," Adrian said in an aside to Camilla. "He is *very much* an artist. Outsized personality and all."

"Don't let him fool you; so is our Adrian," Mrs. Singh said, and Camilla felt dizzy when Adrian ducked his head almost shyly. How had she not *known* that about him? How had she not known any of this?

"Mrs. Singh, this is Camilla Winters. I am sorry to have to condense so much history into so little space, but..." Adrian glanced at Camilla, and she gave him a nod to proceed. "To make a very long story short, I was doing Bishop Denmore a favor. Things went awry, and Camilla and I were forced to marry one another at gunpoint."

Camilla winced at this bare recital of the last week.

But Adrian sounded positively cheery. "She's had quite a

time of it. We're *not* married. Neither of us consented, and we are in the process of perfecting a petition to have that marriage annulled. I would count it a particular favor if you could take care of Miss Camilla for me, Mrs. Singh."

"And what does Captain Hunter think of that?"

"Nothing," Adrian said with a grimace. "Please, God, let him not be aware of any of this at all. Is Mr. Alabi in the study?"

"Yes, and he's been waiting for you."

"Then I'd better see him."

Confident, she thought, watching him stride away. That's what he was—he was confident in a way she'd not yet seen him be. It was as if the moment he set foot on his own territory, with his own people, he grew an extra inch.

She watched him go almost wistfully.

If only *she* had that sort of confidence...

"Come, Miss," Mrs. Singh was saying. "You've been traveling. You'll want to wash and have something to eat, won't you?" Camilla couldn't quite place her accent. Nothing English.

Camilla swallowed, then nodded. "Yes, please. I would be so grateful."

The woman just smiled. "Well, you have nice manners, don't you? I could never be so polite, not if I'd been through such an ordeal. Why, when I first came from Russia..."

She chattered on, as if recognizing that Camilla was too shocked to speak, nicely filling the silence until she brought Camilla up to a room.

"I'll be back in thirty minutes, then, to show you where we'll be dining tonight. You must be starving."

"Oh, food." Camilla smiled wistfully at the thought. "I will love you forever," she promised.

The door shut; she was left alone. She set her things down on a chair.

Adrian had put on confidence as if it were a coat from the moment he arrived. She wished she could do that, too. If she were confident like Adrian, then...

No. She squeezed her eyes shut. No looking back.

She took off her gown; it was dusty from travel. There was a basin and a washcloth; the water slowly turned brown as she rinsed her face.

She had stayed in dozens of rooms over the years—some for months, some for weeks. This was another room just like those. It was larger, though. More room for her hopes.

Every time she had moved, she had let herself love, reaching out despite every one of her last failures—yearning for connections with grandmothers, daughters, women who could have been her sisters, men.

Look forward, Camilla thought. She had been thinking it all day, and every time it happened, she remembered Adrian telling her that sometimes, looking back meant lemon tarts. Camilla was exhausted; she had been weary since she spoke to Mr. Graves that morning. Look forward, she thought, trying to banish the image—but Adrian had been right. She'd been running headlong into the future for so long that she felt off balance.

She'd yearned and yearned and yearned, and she'd never looked back. But if she didn't learn now, once Adrian left her, she couldn't allow herself to remember *him.* Not his smile, not his kindness. She'd have to leave behind all memory of a time when she was happy.

She didn't want that. Camilla knew herself well enough to know that the love she felt now was the love she always gave —easily earned, tossed at anyone who paid her attention. It didn't *mean* anything that she yearned for him. It was just Camilla being Camilla.

It didn't mean anything that she liked him. It meant everything that he liked her.

Camilla drew in a deep breath.

She opened her valise and there, sitting on top, was that half-scarf she never had finished and her crochet hook. For a second, she thought of the time when she'd learned to crochet. Adrian was right; she would have to look back.

But... Not today. It didn't need to be today.

She set aside the crochet hook and found one of her new gowns instead. It was serviceable, made of thick cloth, and it fit her as well as could be expected for ready-made clothing. She had thrown her whole heart into love as if she were fishing, tossing her hook out into waters and hoping for a bite. Again and again.

After the storm of this morning, she felt almost calm.

She was contemplating the day, lacing up a clean gown, when there was a knock on the door.

"Ready?" Mrs. Singh's tones were muted through the door.

She was ready.

In the dining room, a sideboard contained a feast—roast chicken and turnips and greens and oranges. How long had it been since Camilla had an orange?

"We don't stand much on ceremony," Mrs. Singh told her. "I hope you don't mind. Fix yourself a plate."

"Of course I don't mind."

"Good—I've given up on these two lunks."

These two lunks were Adrian and another man. They sat at the table, engrossed in the work before them—the table was filled with dozens of papers, each decorated with patterns. Some were colorful, vibrant reds and golds and greens in stripes on one square, vermilion chevrons on another. Next to those was an interlocking design of green and pink cranes.

"Gentlemen." Mrs. Singh spoke loudly. "*Dinner* is served."

The men looked up.

Adrian blinked. His eyes focused on Camilla; he looked back at the table, then at Mrs. Singh.

"Oh." He blinked again, then shook his head. "*Oh*. The time. I had not noticed it at all. My apologies." He pushed a few squares to the side, making scant room. "We didn't mean to take up the whole table—we just didn't notice."

"Oh." Mrs. Singh rolled her eyes affectionately. "To be sure."

"Before I forget." Adrian gestured at the man to his right. Like Adrian, the other man was black. His skin was darker than Adrian's, a rich, deep brown. He looked up at Camilla, then over at Adrian. His lip quirked up.

"Could have been worse," he remarked.

Camilla had no idea what that meant.

Adrian apparently did. He made a face, but pretended nothing had happened. "Camilla, this is Mr. Alabi. He's our lead artist."

"Pleased to meet you," she said.

The plates set out for dinner were a riotous mix of mismatched color. The one Camilla picked up depicted a tree in blossom. The nearest flowers were limned in gold, but the entire thing was marred by an inexplicable red slash.

"Ah," said Mr. Alabi. "You've noticed."

Camilla looked up. "What have I noticed?"

"The plates," he said. "After the underglaze, all the plates we produce at Harvil are hand-painted. The rejects get used here. That one's not the best."

"Oh?"

"Where's the one with the two-headed peacock?"

"In London," Adrian said, turning to Camilla. He served her lamb and potatoes and peas, covering up the tree. "I just hate wasting anything, is all."

They settled around the table with their food.

"Is there anything I can get for you?" Adrian asked as he took a bite of lamb. "I'll be busy the next few days."

Camilla glanced at the designs. She wanted to ask more about them—where they came from, who painted them by hand. "I want something to do. Idleness doesn't suit me."

Adrian glanced at Mrs. Singh, then over at Mr. Alabi. "Of course. But—"

"We could use her," Mr. Alabi said, "For the test audience. We don't have enough white people here in any event."

Camilla's eyes widened. "What's involved in that?"

"It's not hard," he told her. "We show you china designs. We get your reaction. We refine our designs."

"But you don't know if I have any taste."

Mr. Alabi shrugged. "Most white people don't, and yet they still buy china. That's why your input is invaluable."

Adrian let out a snorting laugh, and Camilla found herself smiling alongside them. "That will be nice. Is there not anything else I could do?"

"You've been traveling all day," Adrian said. "Have a rest. Don't worry about anything; I'll finish the questions for Mrs. Martin's affidavit when I've returned tonight. It's just one more thing to do, after all. One more thing can't hurt."

He'd been traveling all day, too, and he was leaving to go do more work. Once he was finished, he'd do more work still.

"But—" she started to protest, and then realized that demanding that he help her figure out how to spend her time would only be more of a burden. She subsided.

"But?"

"But I hope you have a productive time," she told him. "Best of luck."

CHAPTER FOURTEEN

It felt only natural to assist Mrs. Singh in clearing the table. If the woman thought anything of it, she didn't say. But she accepted the help, and afterward, the two of them made tea.

"It sounds," Mrs. Singh finally said, as she drew two chairs close to the small table, "that you've had quite the time of it recently."

Camilla shut her eyes. God. A week ago, she had not suspected what awaited her. "You could say that." She shrugged. "I try not to complain."

"Well. *That* makes you one of a kind."

"Oh. I *want* to complain sometimes. I have just never found it to do any good."

"Then you aren't doing it right," Mrs. Singh said briskly. "You need a sympathetic ear and a real conversation. Sometimes the only way to find the route forward is to grumble about all the paths that have closed."

Camilla looked up at the woman. That lift of hope she felt was familiar—too familiar. For a second, a warm little fantasy filled her heart. They would talk, share secrets, become friends…

Mrs. Singh sighed. "It will be hard for you here, then," she said. "I'll warn you—when it comes to Adrian, we are all more than a little protective. This world is a hard place, and for most people, it hardens them or it breaks them or it rots them." She shook her head. "Adrian, however…"

"He has always been kind to me."

"Kind." Mrs. Singh sighed. "Yes—that's him. Kind to a fault. I surely don't know where he gets it, because it's not as if nothing bad has ever happened to him."

Camilla could listen to Adrian being discussed for hours. She made a sympathetic noise and leaned forward.

"There was that eternally wretched business with his uncle. His middle three brothers were killed in the American conflict. I've been with him in London, and I've watched what men say to him. It takes a certain gentleness of spirit to not be all scars after that." Mrs. Singh looked off.

Gentleness of spirit. Camilla let these words wash over her.

"You know," Mrs. Singh said, "he took over here first when he was fifteen. Harvil…well, for historical reasons, the china-works here has offered employment to every sort of person, regardless of race. Sailors who were left in port, Chinamen who hoped to do business but fell on hard times… Harvil gave them all a chance."

"That sounds very hospitable."

Mrs. Singh's lip curled up. "It does, doesn't it? In reality, when Adrian arrived, the community was divided five ways. Nobody took him seriously. He was a fifteen-year-old boy and his family owned the place. It should have been a disaster. But he didn't issue orders. He didn't take charge. He didn't tell us all what to do. He just…listened, and then somehow…?"

She shrugged. "I can't quite explain it myself. There are some people who are popular because they tell you you're allowed to be the worst version of yourself. And then there's Adrian."

"He makes you want to be your best."

"Yes." Mrs. Singh shrugged. "And when you aren't, he makes you want to be better without telling you how you've failed. As I said. We're very protective of him."

≈

B y the time Adrian arrived, the meeting was in full swing—which was to say, the artists were all arguing. As usual.

Tea stood on a sideboard; he made himself a cup and listened.

"I know you are *capable* of delicacy of principle," Mrs. Song was saying, "but here—look at this abysmal glut of color! No spareness of design. No sense of balance! There must be room to *breathe* in art. I would honestly rather gouge my own eyes out with a pitchfork than look at what you've done!"

"Well," Mr. Alabi shot back. "We can't all design perfectly white plates with dots on them, can we?"

"It is a *bear cub*, not a dot!"

Beside them, Mr. Namdak chuckled. The two artists froze as one, turned to him, and frowned.

"What are *you* laughing about?"

"Yes, really," Mrs. Song put in, one hand drifting to her hip, "what are those…things you've rendered? Are they stars? Are they flowers? Are they fish? Are they cat paws?"

"Actually, they're stylized representations of—"

"Stylized?" Mrs. Song made a face. "You call *that* style?"

When Adrian had been fifteen and newly alone in

England, he had tried to do his part by taking over his father's work at Harvil Industries.

"You have a good eye," his father had said. "And we have excellent artists. Just pick the design that is most eye-catching."

He had walked into a room of adults arguing, yelling at each other about whose work was better. Back then, the artist picked to design that year's china would receive a bonus; the others would stew and vow vengeance for the next season.

Adrian really *hadn't* intended to change everything. It had just happened. By the time the war was over, the damage had been done. Which was to say, Harvil Industries had tripled its yearly profits, the system of choosing one artist's designs had been tossed like so much rubbish, and for some inexplicable reason, the men and women he worked with treated Adrian like an equal, even though he couldn't even draw.

"Thank God you're here," Mr. Namdak said, rolling his eyes. "We've been at this for *weeks*. We're desperate for you."

"One of these days, you will all realize I don't do anything at all, and you'll be rid of me entirely."

"You do own the company," Mr. Alabi muttered.

"Well, my family does, at any rate." They only listened to him because they had to. "If it weren't for that, you'd not rely on me for anything."

Mr. Alabi rolled his eyes. "*I* know what I am good at. I have a better eye for color than any man on this planet."

"More humility, too." Mrs. Song snickered into a fist.

"I can't do what you do."

"True," Mrs. Song said. "Only *you* can change Mr. Alabi's designs and make him think it's his idea."

"How many times must I tell you? You can't *change* the design! It's telling a *story*. Adrian, tell her—"

"A story nobody will understand." That was Mr. Namdak.

"All the better! It's about *us*—all of us here in Harvil, wanderers dispersed far from homes that no longer exist, coming together, forming new friendships."

"It's messy." Mrs. Song shook her head.

"I'm trying to compliment you, you foo—" He stopped, glanced at Adrian, and cleared his throat. "You fine woman."

"So what is Mrs. Song in your story?" Mr. Namdak asked. "Is she the angry zig-zaggy pattern?"

"Boo. Don't be rude, not unless *you* want to be the squiggly green lines."

Adrian stood. "Well, that's the problem. If the design is about coming together, then really, Mr. Alabi, you shouldn't be speaking for everyone."

"Why not? I'm so good at it."

Adrian ignored this posturing. "What if we used just a ribbon of the design, superimposed over the bear cub?"

His artists exchanged dubious looks.

"A larger version of the bear cub."

"Like..." Mrs. Song sketched her bear cub swiftly in pencil; Mr. Alabi followed with a few strokes of water color.

"No." Everyone spoke at once, almost in horror, at the result.

"What about..."

It went on for another hour, then two. Adrian was almost ready to end the session in disgust, when his exhausted brain offered up one last idea. "The silhouette of the cub," he said. "But...more stylized. And fill it with Alabi's design."

It took another five minutes to sketch this out. Adrian stood, stretching.

The final result was... No. Not quite right. Maybe it was because a bear's silhouette was too bulky, but it lacked a certain something. He wasn't sure what.

"Like that," Adrian said, "but maybe with more sense of movement. Maybe if it's hunting?"

"Do bears hunt?" asked Mrs. Song.

"Well, I'm sure they must. How else do they eat?"

Silence reigned for a handful of seconds. Then Mr. Namdak shrugged. "We're artists, not...animal behavior experts. I don't even go outside unless I have no choice in the matter. How should I know?"

Adrian sighed. "Let's pretend bears hunt. It's probably true. Mr. Namdak, maybe it's trying to catch your dream-star-fish thing?"

He could feel the excitement growing in the room as they worked, sketching over each other.

"That's it." Mr. Namdak smiled, stepping back. "That's it. We've done it."

There were handshakes all around. Adrian stood back and looked, and thought, and...

"No," he said, to everyone's groans. "We haven't. Not quite. First, we've promised an eight plate series. What we have here is one plate at best. And it's not even fully fleshed out."

"An utter tyrant," Mrs. Song said. "We are employed by a tyrant. And here it is, ten at night."

"Second," Adrian said, "I don't love the sketch of the bear cub. I'm not sure what's wrong, but I want more of a sense of play here. This is a cub, not a full-grown animal."

"Hmm."

"And third, we have this cub catching the—dream-star, whatever it is—on the first plate. That can't be right. It's an eight plate series; it ought to tell a full story. You don't catch your dreams on the first try, after all."

"Lots of people do." Mrs. Song rubbed her eyes. "But I suppose I see your point."

"Still, we have a direction." Adrian smiled. "We have something that is almost a preliminary design. And this is going to be amazing once we've finished. Enough for the night."

"We couldn't have done it without you."

Adrian just stared at Mr. Namdak and shook his head. "You literally could have done exactly that. You're the ones drawing."

"Oh, stop being modest and go home," Mr. Namdak said. "Don't you have something about an annulment to think about, too?"

All thought of bears and designs dropped from Adrian's head. Home. God, home. He had a thousand things to do. The designs needed more work tomorrow, and he still had his uncle to please and an annulment to plan.

Well.

He sighed. Good thing there was the rest of the night.

~

A drian had expected to find his cottage dark when he returned, and from the outside, it appeared that way. But as he was hanging up his hat and coat, he noticed a dim glow from the study.

Bemused, he drifted down the hall.

Camilla sat at a table, a book in front of her. Her hair was loose around her shoulders. She bit her lip and found a strand, worrying it between two fingers as she frowned at the book in front of her. The lamp painted her face in gold and brown—a tiger's palette, he thought.

"Hello, tigress," he said aloud.

She jumped; her hands flew in the air. The pen she'd been holding landed halfway across the table, splattering ink.

"My God." She glared at him. "You scared me."

"*I* scared you?" He couldn't help but smile. "*You're* the tiger. Why should *I* scare *you?*"

Her eyes narrowed at him. "Clearly you need to sleep."

"Clearly," he replied, "I need to do nothing of the kind. Why are you still awake?"

Their eyes met again. He was tired, tired enough that he couldn't quite summon the willpower to politely look away, as he should. Tired enough that he let his gaze wander down the swell of her breasts to her waist, down past the smooth curve of her hips. She wasn't wearing shoes, and he could see her ankles. They looked like bronze in the dim light of the lamp.

"Your feet must be freezing," he said, and *that* made him think of kneeling on the floor in front of her, taking her foot in his hand…

To warm them, of course. Nothing more.

"Oh, my feet rarely get cold."

Ah. Maybe he was not purely selfless, then, because that image didn't go away.

She gave him a smile. "It's one of my best traits."

He couldn't touch her. It wouldn't be fair to her, dependent on him for everything. It wouldn't be fair to *him*, because if he touched her, he would have to stop. He'd known up until now that he thought her attractive. He'd known that he liked her. She was pretty and kind and clever, but she was also legally married to him and no matter how lovely she was, he didn't want that state to persist.

He couldn't touch her. But he wanted to. He wanted it with an ache that was…probably just weariness?

Right. That was it. Weariness. He'd sleep it off and it would all be better in the morning.

Except he had too much to do to sleep.

"Camilla." He said her name just to say her name.

"Mmm?"

Question. He needed to ask her a question. "You didn't tell me why you were still awake."

She blinked at him. "Well, that's obvious, isn't it? You said we'd have to write questions for Mrs. Martin, to send out tomorrow morning?" She gestured to the paper. "I've been doing them."

He frowned. He looked at the paper, then at her, then back at the paper. He was tired, and…

"I should do that."

"Too late." She smiled. "I'm almost finished."

"You don't really care about the annulment the way I do," he told her, "and it doesn't seem fair that you should have to, under the circumstances… It's not really a bother. I can handle one more thing."

She stood. She took a step toward him, and his breath froze in his chest. "You tell yourself that a lot, don't you? That you can take on one more thing?"

"Well." He swallowed as she took a step forward. "I've been very lucky in my life. I've been given a lot. It seems only fair that I try to do something with what I have, doesn't it?"

She took another step toward him. Lit from behind, her expression was impossible to make out.

"One more thing," Camilla told him softly. "One more thing. One more thing. Of all the men in the world I could have been forced to marry, it ended up being you. I, too, count myself lucky. This time, let *me* do one more thing for *you*."

She was close enough to touch now, and he couldn't. He couldn't touch her. It wasn't right, it wasn't fair.

She touched him. She reached out and put her hands on his shoulders. It was only strength of will that kept him from pulling her to him. His hands clenched into fists at his side.

But it wasn't *that* sort of touch she gave him. She pushed him, turning him around so he faced the door away from her. He could feel the palms of her hands in the small of his back.

"Go to bed," she said. "I'm almost done. And *I* don't have to be up at seven in the morning."

She pushed him, and what could he do?

He couldn't touch her, so he went. He was almost up to his room, half-exhausted with weariness, when the thought came to him.

"Oh," he said, looking into the darkness, feeling as if he had been struck by lightning. "Tigers. Of course it's tigers."

CHAPTER FIFTEEN

Camilla had left the draft of the questions she'd written for Mrs. Martin on Adrian's desk; by the time she came downstairs the next morning, it was gone.

In its place was a note: *Thanks. These were excellent; have sent on. See you tonight?*

There were no other instructions. That left her with nothing to do all day but think—always a dangerous prospect—or walk or read. It was raining; that didn't bode well for walking.

Adrian was not much for fiction, she discovered upon perusing his shelves, and he—or rather, his family—had the strangest collection of books. A multi-volume set on the production of pig iron. Seven separate tracts on ecclesiastical law that were well marked. And an entire shelf of books on the chemical composition of various dyes.

One of the ecclesiastical law books turned out to be a collection of accounts of trials in the ecclesiastical courts. She leafed through them, thoroughly confused by a multitude of words she didn't know. Another book ended up being a legal dictionary. It proved only slightly helpful, as she didn't know half the words used in the definitions.

There were two accounts of annulment proceedings in the first book. The rain was not letting up; she was supposed to be getting an annulment. Why not read through them?

"How are you getting on?" Adrian asked her that night over dinner.

"By and by. You?"

He shrugged, much the same as she had. "Passably. Things are taking shape, I suppose."

He didn't say anything about wanting her input—of course, she realized, they'd need to develop something before she could have an opinion on it—and he seemed sufficiently harried that she did not want to ask.

Well. She had reading and she had crocheting.

The days slipped by. She read through the two annulment proceedings in their entirety, once, and then again, and a third time.

The confusing legalistic language slowly started to feel comprehensible after the fifth read. The outcome of the cases, once she understood them, began to bother her more.

Miss Jane Leland, an heiress, had been drugged with opium before saying "I do" to a man she had before refused; the courts had refused to grant her an annulment on the grounds that she had insufficiently proven that she did not consent to the opium.

By contrast, Sir William Tannsy had agreed to marry Lady Catherine Dubois; he had been so nervous at his wedding (or so he claimed) that he had not noticed that her maid, Miss Laney Tabbott, had taken her place and so (he claimed) a fraud had been done on him.

It didn't look like fraud to Camilla, not unless Sir William had gravel in place of brains. Sir William was supposed to have married Lady Catherine six weeks later, with the banns already having been read the first time before he left.

Sir William had claimed that Miss Tabbott, purporting to be her mistress, had sent him a letter begging him for an immediate Fleet Marriage to calm her nerves.

There followed pages of text— "legal reasoning," it was apparently called—that purported to explain that somehow Miss Tabbott had cheated Sir William. Even though her actual real name had been used on the register. Even though he had spent four hours in her company before the ceremony, and not once noticed she was a different person than her mistress. Even though Miss Tabbott stated that Sir William himself had courted her and asked to marry her.

Tabbott claimed the marriage was consummated, which Sir William denied. The medical examiners claimed that the fact of consummation could not be established.

Miss Tabbott's testimony was deemed unbelievable. She had committed fraud, the court said. Annulment granted.

"What is this utter nonsense?" Camilla found herself demanding at dinner-time, pointing to the book.

"Oh," was Mr. Hunter's bemused reply. He had been frowning at a notebook of sketches as he ate. "You're reading *that?* Why?"

"I am attempting to. I don't understand it."

He glanced over, swiftly scanning the pages in question. "Well, the court is saying that—"

"Oh, that's not what I meant. I *comprehend* the words perfectly now. I just don't see how any person in their right mind could possibly have come to the conclusion that Sir William was tricked into marriage."

"I don't recall what happened."

Camilla was warming to her subject. "As best as I can tell, this absolute rapscallion obtained a *marriage license* with her *actual name on it,* told this poor maid that he loved her, had his way with her, and then claimed the marriage wasn't real and she had tricked him into it! And the ecclesiastical courts agreed!"

"Mmm." He nodded.

"I want to get a stick and beat him."

"I support you in your desire for justice, but the case was decided in 1721. He's probably dead."

"Then I want to beat his grave," Camilla declared. "And it's worse than that. *This* is the sort of court that decides if we can have our marriage annulled? They have no sense of justice, no principles. What are we doing, going before them?"

"Be fair," Adrian said. "The men who decided this are all dead, too. It'll be a different set of men."

Camilla looked up at him. Her eyes narrowed. She *wasn't* going to laugh. "Is this amusing to you?"

"No," he said. "It's not. It's why my uncle's help is of the utmost importance. If they think we are upstanding people, they'll be more likely to treat our story, outrageous as it is, with belief and kindness. If they don't..." He shrugged. "Well, you've seen it. This all would be dead easy if you were a lady; we could play the lady and the utter blackguard for the court, and the annulment would come too swiftly for us to blink. They'd find a way to make sure you weren't tied to the likes of me."

"The likes of you." Camilla blazed out. "If they say anything about the likes of you, I'll beat them, too. As if these idiots could judge anyone's character. I hope *she* hit him."

"You hope who hit whom?"

"Miss Tabbott." She gestured. "Sir William. Of course."

And then the words he'd spoken came back to her—*if you were a lady*—and she remembered. She tried to think of her past so little that it no longer registered as a truth about her, not even when he said it aloud. *This all would be dead easy if you were a lady.*

Of course. He didn't know.

How could he know? She hadn't told him. She hadn't *wanted* to look back.

They might be able to end this tomorrow, without any of this rigmarole. All she had to do was tell him the one thing that she no longer wanted to recall.

He would thank her; she could let him go without letting him see how much she hurt.

Or…she could keep silent and have him for a little longer. For company. For tea.

She looked over at him across the table. For a moment, she wavered on the edge of indecision. Was it even a lie, if she simply chose not to tell him the truth?

No. It *wasn't* a lie. Camilla shut her eyes.

"Camilla? Is everything all right?"

It hurt to remember it. She could not be anything except a scandal to her family. The truth of her birth had no relevance here. She didn't *have* to tell him.

It wasn't a lie.

But it wasn't right, either.

She exhaled slowly. "There's something I should tell you." Her eyes opened. "I didn't mention it earlier; I didn't know it would be of use. But… You should know that I used a false name on the registry."

He blinked. "That doesn't invalidate the marriage, you know."

"My family name is not Winters. I was born Camilla Worth." She kept her eyes down. "My father was the Earl of Linney, and he was hanged for treason, so my family name has no real value. Rector Miles convinced me to use a different name, so that the shame of who I had become would not further damn the rest of my family. *They've* made it out of this mess. I don't... Even if they don't want me, I don't want to hurt them. But you said we could use it, so..." She shrugged. Her throat felt hoarse. "Here you are."

"The shame of who you are?" he repeated. He said the words slower, enunciating them, grinding them into her soul.

"Please don't make me say it. I don't even like *thinking* it."

For a long moment, he didn't speak. She could hear the tick of a clock behind them. She shifted uncomfortably.

"I know you don't believe me. But...I thought I should tell you." She lifted her head to look at him.

He was watching her, his eyes dark and intense. "It likely wouldn't help, you know," he said slowly. "Your sister hasn't talked to you in years, and you'd need her to vouch for her."

"Well. Then."

"But you didn't have to tell me. Why did you?"

She shrugged one shoulder. She could not speak, not with that lump in her throat.

"I..." He shook his head and leaned forward and set his hand atop hers. "Camilla, I know how hard this has been for you. At this point, you have seen where I come from, what I have. I have several homes, horses, and ready funds. You have nothing. All you would have to do was lie, once, to the examiners, you realize, and there would be no annulment. I would be legally obligated to supply your needs for the rest of your life."

"Please don't point it out." Camilla didn't want to be tempted.

"And I know what you want. You want permanence. A place to stay."

She couldn't meet his eyes. "Someone to care about me, just a little."

"And yet here you are, helping me win an annulment that leaves you worse off."

"I know," she whispered. "I can't help but know it."

"Why, then?"

Because she *didn't* want to hurt him. Because she made bad choices. Because... "You told me the other day, that someday someone would love me for who I was?" The room felt large around her. Or maybe she felt unbearably small. "I shouldn't believe it. There is no evidence it can be true. If it *could* happen, would it not have done so, once?"

"Camilla."

"I should not believe it, but I do. I have no reason for hope, so I hope beyond reason. I keep hoping, that someday, someone *will* care. I believe that I deserve it, even though I know I cannot. I have known for *years* that it cannot be, and yet I refuse to stop hoping. You are the only person in the world who has ever told me that I should keep on hoping. I'm not going to repay that kindness with cruelty."

He was watching her so intently, some fierce emotion in his eyes that she couldn't quite interpret.

Now that she'd given voice to that hope, it rose within her, strong and indomitable. She was going to be loved, damn it. Someday. She was *going* to.

It wouldn't be him. She knew that, the way she knew that she wished it would be.

"You can't steal love," she told him. "You can only earn it. And I want to be the kind of person who can still believe, after all this time, that I will deserve it."

"That's it." He stood straight up and closed his notebook of sketches. "That's what I've been missing—the last three plates, of course—we've been trying to tell the wrong story."

"Your pardon? Adrian—we should talk about whether we use this—"

He almost ran to the door. "Sorry—I have to fix this *now*. It's—ah, sorry!"

He was putting on a coat and hat, and Camilla was utterly bewildered.

"I'll tell you when it's done." The smile he gave her was painful and brilliant and so warm that it felt like it could burn her. "I'm sorry," he apologized one last time. "I have to go."

~

A drian barely saw her for days once he understood what to do with the plates. It didn't matter.

He gradually came to realize that he had a problem over the course of those days.

He spent most of his time at Harvil Industries, working with his artists. Refining, looking for everything that was wrong, shaping the china designs again and again until the story meant more and more to each of them.

He came home for late repasts.

Camilla was always there. She'd tell him about something new she'd read in the ecclesiastical reports or another idea for when he had time again. They would talk, and he would *like* it, and he didn't have time to think about how *much* he was liking it. He really didn't.

He'd go to sleep and he'd think about china designs— about tigers chasing dreams, and...

And the plates weren't about her. Really, they weren't. Every one of the artists involved had a different opinion of what they meant. Mrs. Song didn't precisely *cry* when they decided on that first plate, a tiger cub chasing that stylized dream over a waterfall into new and strange terrain, but it was close. Adrian felt a strange compression in his chest when they planned out the last one.

The plates weren't *about* Camilla. They were about everyone.

Yet somehow, Adrian had started thinking of her as part of that everyone.

That yearning just got worse with every passing day.

Adrian had a problem, he realized after he'd been working on the design for so long his head was spinning with lack of sleep.

Truth be told, he'd had one for a while, but he admitted it to himself for the first time on a long night, while they were on the verge of finishing their designs.

He realized it at night, in bed, when he was alone.

It wasn't cold, and he wasn't lonely. Not in any traditional sense of the word. He wasn't one of those sordid creatures who claimed that it was impossible to go for any length of time without having intercourse: any man who claimed such a need was hardly a man.

Adrian had nobody to blame for his problem but himself, and he should have seen it coming.

His problem was this: Adrian liked Camilla.

He more than liked her; he'd noticed that first dizzying swirl of sexual interest the first day they'd met. She was pretty and so easy to talk to. She listened to him and had her own thoughts. She'd adjusted to the whirlwind that they'd embarked on with a grace that few would have managed.

He knew what she'd gone through; he'd watched Rector Miles and the others she had worked with for only a handful of days, and even that alone had been mildly painful to watch.

She'd told him everything she had experienced, and as bare as her recital had been, he'd heard her loneliness, her worry. He knew how much she yearned.

And still, she'd looked him in the face and told him that she believed she would be loved.

It had sunk into his skin. Every moment he spent with her, he found himself wanting—just a little. Every minute in her company, his heart seized with an almost painful gladness. Tonight, she had talked about something else she had found in that book of ecclesiastical law that she had started carrying about. He'd found himself leaning forward, smiling, wanting that future happiness for her, so much that...

That he'd gripped the arms of his chair to keep from reaching out and touching her himself.

He let out a sigh.

Oh, he had a problem. If they weren't semi-legally married, it might be different. He might have moved his hand to touch her tonight. He might have asked if he could kiss her, just so he could taste the determination in her voice. If they hadn't been married, he could have explored this—slowly, sweetly.

But they *were* something like married, and he didn't want to be. They had to not consummate the marriage. And if they started kissing and touching... No. A bad idea all around. He knew it was a bad idea.

More importantly, he knew how much Camilla wanted affection; it would be the cruelest thing he could do—to give that affection she wanted to her, when he didn't want anything aside from that momentary affirmation. That footman she mentioned had done just that to her—used her and then discarded her.

He wasn't cruel; he just didn't want to be married to her. He wouldn't want to be married to anyone like this.

He *liked* her. And he wanted her. He shut his eyes and let himself imagine a different conclusion to their talk this evening—or *any* of the evenings they'd spent together. He imagined her eyes, sparkling in the lamp light, the fierce determination on her face as she looked across the room and said that she wasn't going to steal love, that she was going to earn it.

He imagined that they weren't semi-goddamn-why-me-legally married, or whatever this was, and he could tell her the truth: *You deserve the world at your feet.*

She would look at him with the confidence that had begun to creep up on her, a look that suited her as if it had been perfectly tailored for her. She'd tilt her chin up.

"Oh?" He could just see how she would say it. "Why don't you show me?"

Now he was veering into fantasy territory, but—he knew this for a rationalization—it was better to get the fantasies out of his blood than to indulge in more of this foolishness while watching her over supper.

God, he wanted to show her what it was like to be desired. Camilla wasn't the sort to lie there passively, not if she were interested as well. He'd do his best to listen to her, to watch her awakening desire and to stoke it until she was gasping beneath him.

He gave up on pretending. He took hold of his hardening cock and imagined her hand on his, the warmth of her exhaled breath in his ear. He imagined her kissing down his neck, her body brushing his lightly at first, and then with more certainty.

She'd slide down on him so wetly, so perfectly.

His hand was an imperfect substitute, but it would do. He strained up into it, thinking of her, of the little noises she would make as her hips met his. She would smile as he found every sensitive spot with his tongue—ears, breasts, everywhere he could reach. She wouldn't play coy; she'd give herself to him with all abandon. She wasn't the sort to hold back.

His hand moved faster; his whole body seemed afire. God, he was an idiot; he couldn't be thinking about her this way. He was going to have to see her tomorrow; he couldn't be wondering what it would be like if she—if *they*—

And then he wasn't thinking at all. His body tipped over

the edge, filled with heat and desire. He painfully swallowed his own grunt of pleasure before it came out sounding like her name.

He lay in bed afterward, far too warm and more than a little embarrassed. Not that there was anything wrong with masturbation. If it were actually possible to go blind from it, he'd have lost his sight long before he turned eighteen.

It was a bad idea, thinking about her like this. It was possibly the worst idea he could have had.

She'd had enough done to her. She'd been hurt too much. She *trusted* him. He wasn't going to be the person who took her confidence, not when she had so little of anything in this world.

And the fact that she might, possibly, be willing to give…

…That was unthinkable. Because with her, with the way things were, there could be no idle kissing, no mere enjoyment to be found together. If he came to her wanting *this*, he was married to her for life. He had a problem, but that's what real men did—they had problems on their own, where the solution required a hand towel to clean up afterwards, and not an apology to someone for ruining her life.

Well.

On the bright side, masturbation was limited only by his refractory period. And it made less of a mess.

~

Camilla didn't realize she was changing until she was almost at the end of her transformation.

It started with Miss Laney Tabbott, the woman who was seduced and abandoned by the horrid, lying Sir William.

She read the court's account again and again—first, she thought, to learn what was happening and how she could do better. Then she started reading it with her crochet hook in hand, thinking and wondering and crocheting without truly knowing her own thoughts.

She imagined that she was Miss Laney Tabbott, born a century and a half before, betrayed by the man she loved. It was easier to imagine herself angry on behalf of someone else than to think of her own situation. The anger she felt for Miss Tabbott was almost unbearable.

So she crocheted and she imagined.

She imagined herself facing the ecclesiastical court and giving testimony as Miss Tabbott had undoubtedly done.

Camilla wouldn't beg for them to not annul her marriage with a man who clearly didn't want her. No; Camilla as Miss Tabbott would wreak maximum embarrassment.

"No," she imagined herself saying with confidence, tilting her wrist just so. "Of *course* we didn't consummate the marriage. He wanted to, but I took one look at his private parts, and... Syphilis, you understand. Poor thing."

They said that hell had no fury like a woman scorned, but they were wrong. Women were scorned again and again and again. It was only after the seventieth scorning that they let loose a fraction of their righteous anger. Frankly, men had no idea how lucky they were that any woman was rational at all.

Day after day, Camilla honed Miss Tabbott's speech, muttering it to herself as she paced in the library or as she walked through the little clumps of trees along the riverbank. She honed it as she crocheted, finished her scarf, and ripped it apart again for yarn.

She wasn't sure when she started delivering her own words—when, instead of the sordid details of Miss Tabbott's unwelcome ruination, she started talking about what had happened to her instead.

"I just wanted to do what was right," she told a stand of

willows. "I was *trying* to do what was right, and they ruined me." She thought of the look on the rector's face. "They made me feel shame for my friendliness, for my willingness to trust others. They made weaknesses of my strength." Her eyes stung with hot tears, and she clenched her hands together.

"I won't let them," she said blindly, through the hot veil of her tears. "I won't let them have me. I won't let them make me weaker or stupider. I'm *not* going to let them take me away."

She imagined Miss Tabbott standing at her side as she spoke.

Three days in, she looked at her crocheting and thought of old Mrs. Marsdell—the woman who she'd tried to impress by learning to crochet.

Adrian had told her that she should try to look back eventually. Every time Camilla thought of Mrs. Marsdell, she remembered those sniffs and suspicious looks. Camilla had opened her heart, and...

And she'd learned to crochet. The feel of yarn beneath her fingers gave her strength; the activity let her think in ways that simply sitting did not.

She had tried to give, and giving had made its own form of return. Once she started thinking of it that way, she could look back a little more. Camilla had read a book of fairy tales to Baby Angela; when times were hard, she still thought of women who kept on going, even when there was no reason to do so. Camilla had learned to kiss from Larissa. She had learned to put a square sheet on a bed from Kitty.

Camilla was a collection of things she had learned from the people she had loved. They hadn't loved her back, but she'd taken everything she learned with her any way.

All this time, she thought she'd found nothing all those years.

She looked up from the chair in her room, crochet hook

in hand. A mirror stood on the wall; she eyed her pink-flushed cheeks. Love hurt, but… Love had shaped her, too.

It would this time as well.

Adrian was going to walk away one day. But if the past were any sort of guide, she wouldn't leave him empty-handed.

What would she take from him?

If she could choose…

If she could choose anything, it would be that confidence she had seen so often seen on him. Could she learn that? She considered it, and she watched him, wondering where that wellspring of braveness came from.

∾

I t took Camilla five days to make friends—across the span of a hundred years—with Jane Leland, opium drugged heiress and Miss Laney Tabbott.

It had taken her seven to read their accounts so often that she knew what she and Adrian needed for this annulment—proof, absolute proof, indisputable proof.

They didn't yet have it.

It had taken her ten days to think about going back—about *really* going back. She pushed the thought away the first time it intruded, then the second. If it had been just her own future at risk, she wasn't sure she could manage it.

But for Laney Tabbott, for Jane Leland… For the women who had not had a chance for justice, she thought she might be able to try. The men who had hurt them were long gone, but if she did nothing, Bishop Lassiter would one day maybe sit over a question of annulment. Rector Miles would hear from women who had been injured by men on a near-weekly basis. There was no justice for the dead, but there were too many women still living in need of kindness.

For Laney and Jane, Camilla allowed herself to imagine that she had the courage to act. She imagined herself walking into the household. The long-dead women would walk invisibly by her side, present only in her imagination.

The first time Camilla imagined going back, she cried by the riverbank; she didn't let herself consider it for another two days.

But she could not let them down, not like this. Not anymore.

She returned to the prospect again and again, imagining the words she would say. Imagining the precise turn of her neck. Imagining how someone in the household might respond, and what she would do if they asked her *this* question or *that*.

The second time, she didn't cry. The third, her hands scarcely shook. By the time she had done it fifty times, her determination had become a bonfire.

That evening, three weeks after they'd come to Adrian's house, she sat with Adrian at dinner one night.

"We'd like to see what you say about designs," he said. "They're almost finished."

"Good." She looked down at her plate, then over at him. He was watching her with an intensity that prickled the palms of her hands, the soles of her feet.

"Tomorrow morning?" he asked.

"If you wish." She inhaled, almost afraid to commit herself. But she'd promised herself—and him—and she'd promised Jane and Laney, so she swallowed her worries and moved forward.

"I know what we need to get our annulment," she told him. "I know how to get it, and I'm prepared to do it."

CHAPTER SIXTEEN

"Centralization, you said." Theresa's brother folded his arms and kicked his legs out impatiently from the seat where he had spent the last handful of weeks. "Less time in an office sitting around, you said." He looked at the heavy volume in front of him. "We'll do better than the man Christian paid a vast sum to, who does this for a living. Really, Tee?"

Admittedly, their quest had not run as smoothly as Theresa had imagined. In her mind, they would have arrived at the General Register Office on a Monday and discovered what they needed halfway through that afternoon, before they even had a chance to get hungry for tea.

In reality, it had been weeks. Theresa herself would have been bitterly indignant, except she had to pretend serenity for her brother's sake.

Instead, she sniffed. "Have some patience, Corporal. Rome wasn't built in a day."

Her brother frowned mulishly. "Everyone always says that, but it's never because someone is complaining about *an entire city* not being constructed over the space of twenty-four hours! It's always about something utterly stupid that should not take longer than fifteen seconds. And we *asked* last night at dinner and it turns out that *of course* the people who Christian hired *did* go through the General Register Office. Because they're not idiots, that's why. Your assumptions were wrong and you were wrong and I'm *tired* of sitting here."

Theresa shot him a quelling look. "*How* am I supposed to be addressed again?"

A long sigh. "I'm tired of sitting here, *sir*," he muttered.

"Well." It was time to bring out her most fearsome weapon. Theresa fixed her brother with a look. "You are younger than me, after all. And everyone knows men haven't the patience of women; they never have the chance to develop it. I suppose I have been remiss in not making allowances for your incapacity."

"That's—" Benedict bit off his complaint and glared at her. "That's *not fair.*"

She waved a hand. "You're free to go at any time."

Theresa, on the other hand, was going to sit here and go through these damned records for the rest of her natural life if she needed to. The alternative would be that she would be *wrong*, and she refused to let that happen.

"Have it your way!" Benedict picked up a book. "I'm staying."

She shot him another look. "Corporal Benedict."

He let out a groan. "I'm staying, *sir*."

"Your choice not to desert is commendable." She flipped a page of her record book. "And you're right—we *did* find out last night that Judith's people had looked through the records. That was valuable information; it helps us expand our search, if we must. *They* were looking for a Camilla Worth. We're looking for anything abnormal involving something that looks a little like her name. Let's start by assuming that she'd make only a minimal change. She's still called Camilla. If I were constructing a false identity, I would use a last name that starts with a W. Or maybe a Y."

"Right." Benedict just looked disgusted. "Do you know how many people there are named Camilla in Britain? How are we to pay attention to them all?"

Theresa set down her book, stood, and strode confidently down the hall, not waiting to see if her brother would follow. Luckily, he scampered after her. There was no point being anything other than confident.

"We should finish up the marriage registries today," she said as he caught up to her. "If we don't find anything there, we'll get to look into birth records, and won't that be a delightful change of pace?"

In all honesty, they should have started there. A child born out of wedlock was the most likely reason why Camilla would have changed her name. She wasn't about to spring the notion on Benedict's young, innocent ears unless she had no choice.

After that, there were penal records and death certificates —but those both sounded terrible, and she hoped it wouldn't come to that.

Theresa marched up to the clerk at the marriage records desk as if she were not fifteen years of age. She hoped the hat she was wearing made her look older; it was ugly enough.

"My good man," she greeted him. That was how the dowager marchioness spoke, and it always seemed to get results.

He straightened and turned to her. "Yes? How can I help you, miss?"

Theresa tilted her head up and attempted to look down her own nose. It didn't work, because he was a good six inches taller than she was, and also, her nose was somewhat lacking. She felt herself blushing. "I should like to see the marriage registers for 1864 and 1865, if you please. And if you have a folio for recent marriages, we should like to see that."

"If you could fill out the request form…" He indicated to her right.

"But of course. I should be delighted to."

"Why are you talking like that?" Benedict asked loudly. "All stodgy-like? Have you had a stick inserted up your—"

"Shut up," she responded in a quiet hiss.

A bit of lead pencil, two minutes, and her terrible scratchy handwriting later was all it took to produce the form. The man took it, bowed, and disappeared into the ranks of shelves behind him.

"I'm always amazed," Benedict whispered at her side, "that they're willing to give us whatever we ask for just because we fill out some stupid form. Do they have any idea who you are and what you do with things that make you angry?"

Theresa rolled her eyes at him. "Stop being so dramatic. We're just asking to look at some ruddy pieces of paper. Nobody cares about them, so nobody's going to make off with them. It's not as if we're filing a request to steal the Crown Jewels."

"Mmm. You'd find a way."

The man came back with two books under his arm and a sheaf of bound papers.

"Here you are, Miss. You mayn't take them from the room, of course."

"Thank you. You've been most helpful."

She and Benedict divided the work between them. Theresa had become almost familiar with the ebb and flow of the reading. The records were divided into books listing name after name after name, alphabetically set forth, with numbers following after that indicating where the full record was kept.

There were no Camilla Worths married in 1865, Theresa found, nor anyone with a last name starting with a W. She tried a few other combinations—Camilla Cassandra, for her middle name, and Camilla Weston, for her mother's name.

Nothing, and they had gone through weeks of nothing. Boring. Her fingers tapped the table in irritation as she read. She hoped she wouldn't have to go all the way to death records. That would be inconvenient, tragic, and also? A terrible birthday present for Judith. Even her diseased embroidered crows would be preferable to unveiling Camilla's tragic, early grave.

"Nothing," Benedict said, closing his own book. "God, I'm weary."

Theresa had never been one to give up. Instead, she started on the recent folios. These were easier—pieces of freshly printed bound materials, much thinner since they contained a few weeks' worth of material each instead of an entire year. There were only a handful of Ws in each sheaf, and she amused herself making stories about some of the people whose names she saw.

Ann Edelbert Wumbler, for instance. She seemed like a solid sort. She owned her own bakery, Theresa decided, but it was actually a sham. Instead, she housed a printing press in the basement, one that produced lewd woodcuts...

"What about this?" Benedict, who had started on his own folio, and who had not been distracted by Ann Edelbert Wumbler, pointed to a record.

The registry index was sparse at best, listing names, parishes, and the location of where the final record was. Theresa followed her brother's finger and felt her heart begin to hammer.

Winters
—Camilla Cassandra, Surrey, Lackwich, 1b 902.
Oh, God. It...

It *could* be a coincidence. There was no reason there could not be two Camilla Cassandras in the entirety of England. But… But… She swallowed. She looked over at her brother.

"It's her." He said it as guardedly as she did. "At least, it *could* be? It's the closest we've come."

It *could* be their sister.

The moment should have felt more portentous. Drums should have sounded or a raven could have got into the building and cawed in dismay. Instead, the office whirred about them as if they had not just succeeded.

Theresa scarcely remembered her sister.

If that person on the registry was Camilla, it left so many questions unanswered. Why had Camilla changed her last name? Why had she not told her own family that she was marrying? Who had she married?

This last question they could answer on their own. She smiled at her brother. "Here, you've seen me do it. You're the one who found this. You fill out the request for the full record."

He did. They waited, holding hands so hard that they squeezed each other's fingers to numbness.

Theresa scarcely knew her sister Camilla. She had a vague memory of a dark-haired laughing girl, swiping Theresa's face clean and patting her on the head. That was it—one single memory, compared with the millions she had for Judith.

Or the dozens she had for Pri.

Maybe Theresa had been afraid to think too much of Camilla. When Theresa had been young—very young—she had accompanied her father and brother to China. She remembered the trip dimly through the gauze of distance that made all her early childhood memories seem impossibly far away. She remembered standing on the deck of the ship.

Anthony used to have to keep dragging her away from the edge.

She'd been the only child on the trip, and so apparently, she'd invented a playmate for the journey—a sister to take the place of the ones she'd left behind. Priya—that was the name she remembered, Pri for short—had been older. Dark-haired, brown-skinned, with laughing brown eyes. She had been maybe Camilla's age, although at three, Theresa had been unable to judge such things with any degree of certainty. She'd been sweet. She had played games with Theresa, pulling her away from the edge of the ship when Anthony wasn't around...and occasionally, sneaking there to stand next to her, watching the waves pass far below.

Don't worry, Tee. I'll keep you safe.

Theresa could remember her imaginary sister better than she could Camilla, and it was frightening that her mind could fool itself so well. Perhaps she never let herself think of Camilla because she was afraid that she'd invent something out of nothing.

Look at her; she'd invented an entire story, ending in lewd woodcuts, around Ann Edelbert Wumbler, and the poor woman had done nothing but get married.

Theresa knew that she worried Judith.

In truth, sometimes Theresa thought she worried Judith on purpose. She never wanted to forget that she was different, that her mind did things that other people's minds did not. And maybe she wanted to remind Judith, because she never knew when she would...

"It's arrived," Benedict said, breaking Theresa out of this depressing reverie. Thank God. There was nothing more annoying than reflecting on reality.

The records from the parish were just sheaves of paper sewn together, so new that Theresa could still smell a hint of pungent ink.

Her brother's fingers fumbled to the right page, spreading it open.

Camilla Cassandra Winters, age 19. Her parents were listed as George Winters and Anne Marie Weston. Her occupation was servant.

"It's the right age," Benedict breathed. "And...isn't that's her mother's name?"

Camilla had a different mother than Benedict and Theresa. She stared at the name in question. "I think so."

"George was father's given name."

"True," Theresa said slowly. "But everybody's named George. That doesn't necessarily mean anything."

Still. It seemed increasingly possible that they'd found their sister. Now all they had to do was...*find* her.

A handful of weeks ago, she had married a man named Adrian Hunter. *His* parents were listed as a John Hunter the IIIrd and an Elizabeth Denmore. His occupation: valet.

Benedict exhaled. "This will be...interesting. Do we tell Judith now?"

"Tell Judith what?" asked a voice behind them.

Benedict jumped. Theresa was too well-disciplined to do so; inwardly, though, she winced.

It was the Dowager Marchioness of Ashford—her sister's mother-in-law. She was a sweet, sweet lady who loved Theresa dearly.

Theresa still couldn't figure out why. She looked at the black ink smeared on her gloves from examining freshly printed records and scrunched her hands into fists.

"Lady Ashford." Theresa turned. She curtsied. "How lovely to see you. We were just getting ready to go home?"

The woman raised a single eyebrow. "Theresa, I taught you that trick. You can't go all mannerly on me in an attempt to get out of an explanation. Whatever are you two doing here?"

Benedict looked at Theresa. "We were going to tell them anyway."

"No, we weren't," Theresa contradicted. She turned to the dowager. "It's a surprise. For Judith's birthday. We're planning it."

The dowager looked around the General Register Office with a dubious air. Theresa could imagine how the place looked to her—an ugly, dusty building, inhabited by men in dour brown suits. They sat at a table, surrounded by volumes. It smelled of must.

Yes, she imagined herself saying, *we are obtaining these lovely records requests for Judith's birthday. Who doesn't want to request records?*

The dowager shook her head and sighed. "I knew you were up to something when Judith said you were shopping for hats. You never like shopping. You hate hats. You've been shopping for three weeks. Is this a *good* surprise for Judith?"

"It's the best surprise," Theresa said earnestly.

The dowager looked unconvinced. "Would Judith think so? Or will this be like the mice?"

"Judith will be overjoyed," Theresa said. "I promise. With everything I have in me."

Assuming that Camilla wasn't dead, that was.

The woman looked around. "Very well, then. Are you almost finished?"

"We've just a few notes to make," Theresa said. "Then we'll be off home."

"Off to get a hat," the dowager told her. And when Theresa's nose wrinkled, she gave her a stern look. "It won't be much of a surprise if Judith suspects you of anything. Finish your...whatever it is you are doing. Then, for the sin of telling your sister a lie, I sentence you to hat yourself."

"But—"

"You know how it is," the dowager said. "You can be as

odd as you like if you're wearing the right hat. And you, my dear, need to watch yourself on that count."

"Very well." Theresa frowned. "If I must."

Benedict waited until the other woman had retreated to the hall. "You're so nice to her," he murmured. "You're getting soft, General."

Theresa glanced at him. "Am not."

But she was. She wasn't sure entirely how it had happened. The dowager hadn't done anything, really, except try to teach Theresa manners and put her in pretty gowns… and then, when she'd realized that both of these things were going extremely badly, she had shifted tacks.

Theresa loved Judith and Judith loved Theresa.

But you harbored a different love for someone who had known you since you were a child—a love tempered by the tantrums that you had once thrown. Judith's affection felt so conditional—given only when Theresa behaved. Somehow, that made Theresa not want to behave at all.

The dowager liked Theresa—General Register Office visits, terrible embroidery, and all.

"She's just got good ideas," Theresa said instead. "She understands me. Judith wants me to be a lady. The dowager wants me to be happy."

And she likes me, just as I am.

The dowager had told her that once, and Theresa had never realized she wanted to hear it until it had been said.

But Theresa didn't say that. It made her seem vulnerable, and the one thing she knew for certain was that she could never let her brother see her vulnerability.

~

Adrian had made plans to leave with Camilla tomorrow.

Mr. Singh checked the schedules to Lackwich for Adrian. Tomorrow he and Camilla would need to be up before dawn; that meant this was the last morning here before...

His thoughts wandered, and he pulled them back to the land of rationality. No point in feeling odd about the matter —they would go to Lackwich, hopefully find proof of Bishop Lassiter's wrongdoing, head immediately to his uncle, and file the paperwork for annulment with his assistance. It was what he wanted.

Definitely that.

And if they had one more day together? He had a great deal to do. He'd show Camilla the plates and ask her opinion. They'd talk; he would go to work. It would be just like every other day.

At that thought, he heard the tap of footsteps and he looked up.

She stood at the top of the staircase, smiling down at him, and...

It took him a moment to remember that she wasn't his.

She could not be. The early morning sunlight cascaded through the east-facing window, catching on motes of sunlight. It danced across her face, as if the daybreak itself were smiling along with her. Oh, no. What was he *doing*, thinking those thoughts about her?

And then she skipped down the stairs and his heart squeezed in his chest. Oh, damn. What *was* he doing?

Right. The china. He was showing her the first run of the china plates that Harvil was bringing to the exhibition this year.

He should offer her his arm for the walk, but even that

seemed too much. Instead he gave her a smile that he hoped was friendly and not stupid with the pent-up desires that he could not indulge in. Not here. Not about her.

"You don't have to come." His voice felt rough.

"Of course I don't have to." She smiled up at him. "But I *want* to. How else will I know what you've been doing all day, every day?"

"Well." It was a good thing she couldn't see him blush like a schoolboy. "Let's be off, then."

He didn't offer her his arm, and she didn't try to take it. Still, he felt the phantom pressure where her hand ought to have rested on the crook of his elbow as they walked.

You know, he could have said. *I like you. I think you're lovely. I think you're brave. I think I want you.*

He hadn't said the words, and she hadn't said them back. But he felt them on the tip of his tongue. He could see them in the way she tipped her head back to catch his expression, in the way her eyes followed him, bright with happiness.

It wasn't love. It was attraction, and there was no place for attraction between them now. He wanted to choose someone, not to give in to lust and physical ardor, trapping himself for the rest of his life.

"They're really just review pieces," he told her as they approached the building. "You'll see. We have a lot to do. Once we've settled on the design, we have to make a copper-plate for transfer printing the underglaze."

He shuffled the keys into his hand and opened the door.

"None of those words made sense to me," Camilla said at his side.

"Well... I'll explain it if you want. Probably in greater detail than you want. Most people don't want to hear. In any event, after it's been glaze fired, we enamel it." Their steps echoed in the corridor. He stopped at the door to the studio.

"That was last night. I haven't seen the review plates since they were fired."

"Does firing change it?"

"Um...yes. The overglaze colors, see, are made of flux, minerals, and—" He stopped, catching himself. "Right. You don't need to know."

Her eyes glowed at him. "Oh, you can tell me anything. I don't mind." That shy little dip of her head, the splay of pink across her cheeks. She was so damned lovely, the way she blushed so easily. "I'd like to hear anything you find interesting, really."

And he wanted to tell her.

He pulled away. "Well, I should show you the plates. I would go on forever, and it would make more sense if you were looking at something first, don't you think?"

They had been laid out in a row on the sideboard.

"Here," he said, gesturing her forward. "They tell a story. We'll start from the beginning."

She didn't need to tell him how she felt—not when she already proclaimed it with every smile, with every little blush.

He didn't need to tell her, either. Not when there were the plates, after all.

She came to stand beside him.

His heart beat heavily.

"Here," he said, pointing. "This is the first one. You'll notice that faint green patterned background, redolent of leaves and bamboo? That's the underglaze painting."

She had frozen in place, her eyes trained on the plate. "Adrian."

"The way we get that light green underglaze is a family secret." He smiled. "As is the orange in the enamel—that's these colors here, you see, the stripes—"

"Adrian. It's a tiger and her cubs."

He felt a lump in his throat. "Well. So. It is."

"What's she chasing, that one cub? Is she headed to the river?"

He didn't object to her pronoun. Now that the plate had been glazed, that little stylized dream looked like a glistening star. They'd specially made a paint for it, a mix of blues and greens so light that you could only see the color when the plate tilted into the light. Gold flecks—real gold—gave it a luminous look.

"I don't know," Adrian said. "Maybe it's a star. Maybe it's a dream. You decide."

"It's lovely. What's the next one?"

He gestured her on.

On this plate, the underglaze was the cobalt blue of traditional china pottery, painted in waves and roils depicting a raging river.

The tiger kitten, caught in the current, tossed and turned, one paw still outstretched to that stylized star as if to catch it even in the midst of drowning.

Alongside the riverbank, her mother ran, desperate to catch her.

"Adrian, is that a *waterfall* ahead?"

"Um...yes?"

"You're sending a kitten into a waterfall?"

"Maybe?"

She turned to the next plate. The tiger cub stood on a riverbank, looking up a sheer cliff down which the waterfall thundered. At the very top, small in the distance, were the faces of the mother tiger and her other cubs.

"You *separated* them?" Camilla stood in place, looking at the scene. She set a hand over her heart. "That's not right."

A fourth plate showed the cub sitting at the base of the cliff. Claw marks marked her attempt to climb back up, futilely. The kitten looked almost despondent—but just to the side, leading away from the cliff, that dream glittered.

In the fifth plate, the cub, slightly older, traversed a swamp, nervously avoiding being caught by some ugly sharp-toothed reptile.

In the sixth, the cub, now juvenile, padded through a dark forest inhabited by fantastical looking birds—drawn forward, forever in pursuit of that glittering dream.

In the seventh, the tiger stalked the stars themselves, a thousand dreams flashing around her paws.

In the final plate, fully grown, she descended a mountain, crowned in stars, to the valley where her mother awaited.

Camilla set the final plate down and looked at Adrian. "I don't know a thing about art. I couldn't give you any advice at all." Her eyes shimmered.

"Did you like it?"

"It gave me feelings." She tapped her chest. "*Here.*"

"That's always a good sign."

She swallowed and turned to him. "It's…it's about a tiger."

"Yes?"

Her eyes found his. "You tell me I'm a tiger sometimes."

"Well." He put his hands in his pockets, the better not to touch her with them. "Yes. I do."

Her eyes were so wide, so bright with hope. "Are these about me? The tiger cub, lost from home so young? Searching for years as she grows, going from place to place?"

"Never giving up?" he added. "Looking forward, always forward?"

She made a little sound in her throat.

"Really," he said, "I don't want to give you the wrong idea. It's about all of us. Mr. Alabi left his home at twelve, when war came to his home city. Mrs. Song came to Britain in search of a child who had been impressed in the pig trade."

She looked away. "Oh."

"As for me," Adrian said, "my family left me in England during the rebellion. We were reunited afterward, but I lost three of my brothers. That's why at the end, some tigers are missing."

She turned to him. "Oh, I'm so sorry. I didn't know. And here I've been complaining to you. I should never have done it."

He looked away. "I don't talk much about it. I'm the lucky one. I didn't die. I didn't even have to go to war. There are untold millions who will never have what I have. There's no point asking for sympathy for me when so many have less."

"Adrian. You don't need to ask for sympathy. You *deserve* it."

God. If he looked down on her now, he would take every inch of comfort she was offering—the liquid warmth of her eyes. She almost reached for him, then pulled back.

"In any event, the plates." He cleared his throat. "I just help my lead artists put things together. All the feelings you saw in there—they weren't all mine. The tiger's journey wasn't entirely about you. It was about all of us. But…"

Her breath caught on that word, *entirely,* betraying as it was. She looked up at him.

"But." His voice was low. "It was partially about you."

Because I think you could belong. He didn't say it, though. They were going to Lackwich tomorrow, and—and—

And the sound of a door opening echoed down the corridor. Camilla jumped away from him, blushing, and Adrian exhaled.

"I thought," Adrian said in the moments before whoever it was arrived, "that even if you moved on, after…this, that… this way you might stay here a little, too?"

Even if. There—he'd said it, put the possibility out in the world. Her eyes widened.

Behind them, the door to the studio opened. Mr. Alabi strode in.

"Ah," he said. "Miss Winters! What do you think of my plates?"

Camilla straightened, smiling at Mr. Alabi as if, a moment ago, she hadn't looked as if Adrian had handed her the stars.

"Your plates?" She shook her head. "And here I thought they were *everyone's* plates."

"But *I* am a part of everyone."

"I *hate* your plates," Camilla said.

Alabi's face fell.

"They almost made me cry, they were so perfect." She gestured to him. "Here. I'll tell you what I thought. Let's start from the beginning."

⁓

By the time Adrian returned that night, he had made all the arrangements to start final production in earnest.

Their train left early the next morning; he had already tasked Mr. Singh to pick them up at the break of dawn. A valise sat by the door—Camilla's. It did not escape his notice that she had, once again, packed everything she owned into her one piece of luggage. She'd leave nothing behind.

She wasn't wrong to do so; if she simply walked into Rector Miles's house and walked off with a record book, showing everything that had been done, then they'd go off to his uncle, present him with the evidence, have their annulment, and...what?

Never see each other again.

God.

This might be the last evening they had together. He made his way into the parlor.

Camilla sat on the edge of her chair, biting her lip. She had a ball of yarn in her hands; she was crocheting...something? He didn't know what that misshapen lump could be. They greeted each other; they always did. She asked about his day; he inquired as to hers. Then silence fell.

It was a silence stalked by the memory of tigers and plates.

After ten minutes of glancing her way, he gave up on pretending.

"Nervous?" he asked.

"I keep thinking," she said. "I'm thinking of what to say when I arrive at the rectory. There's part of me that says that they lied first, and so I shouldn't let myself be bothered by it. But I *am*."

"They did lie," he said, with as much authority as he—someone who had once spent a few months acting as page for a bishop—could provide. "You shouldn't feel badly at all."

She bit her lip again. "What if they don't believe me?"

"Don't worry. I'm sending a telegram before hand, remember, purporting to be from Bishop Lassiter. Miles will be out of the house to respond; nobody there will know the truth in his absence. They'll respond positively if you sound certain. It's human nature."

She nodded slowly.

"Go through it, then," he said gently. "Tell me what you are going to do. The more you think it through, the more real it will be, the easier it will be to execute in the moment. Let's practice now."

She nodded, this time less slowly. "I will come in shortly after he has left."

"Not looking like that," he said, smiling at her. "If you come in looking like *that*, all nervous, they'll doubt you. Look at them the way you looked at Alabi this morning. When you were sassing him."

She shut her eyes and looked away. One inhalation, then another, and she stood. When she opened her eyes, there was a light smile on her face and a sparkle in her eyes.

He felt a knot form in his chest. God, she was lovely. "Like that." His throat felt dry as he spoke. "Do it just like that. What will you say to them?"

She spun around, her skirt flaring briefly around her ankles, before smiling at him. "I've just realized." Her smile broadened. "I'm definitely going to tell them the truth. Two lies don't right a wrong, now, do they? And the more truth I tell, the stronger I will feel."

He didn't want to contradict her, not when her confidence seemed so shaky. But he had to say it. "I'm not precisely sure the truth will be effective."

Camilla just licked her lips and took a step toward him. "Oh, for goodness' sake, Albert," she said, and her voice had an almost amused quality to it. "You didn't actually *believe* all that, did you? That was a stage drama."

He swallowed.

She sashayed toward Adrian, one step at a time. "The whole thing was a ruse. Half-Price Camilla? The rector simply didn't want anyone to take me seriously."

"Well." He tried to get into his role as—who was Albert again? It didn't help that he knew almost nothing of the man, save a vague memory of brown hair. "Why would he do that?"

"Did you not *notice* that he called me into his office to consult, occasionally, on serious matters? I've been in communication with other members of the church, of course."

She came next to Adrian and sat on the arm of his chair. She seemed so absolutely in control, so utterly *right* and perfect in the role. Adrian could hardly bring himself to breathe.

"Don't tell me you actually believed any of that. I thought you smarter than that." She reached out and set a finger on the top button of his coat.

"Camilla." His voice came out hoarse.

"He wanted the bishop to think me discredited so I could go assist with some other matters. But here I am." She tilted her head in an inch, so close that he could almost taste her. "I've returned. Did you miss me?"

And in that moment, he did. It made no rational sense; he'd talked to her every day for weeks; he could not *possibly* miss her. But he felt the distance between them, that bare inch, so keenly that he almost vibrated with it.

"Cam..." Her name came out almost a groan. She swayed toward him, not quite completing what he wanted, and he reached out. Maybe it was to steady her in place. Maybe it was just to touch her. His hand found her waist.

She exhaled, and he could feel her breath—on his lips, in his heart.

"One of my favorite duties," she whispered, "used to be starting the morning fires. Our room was cold, coal being too dear to waste on servants who would warm themselves in labor. So I'd dress in the morning, my hands too numb to do my buttons, and rush downstairs. There was pride to be had in adding kindling, bit by bit. Blowing on the banked coals. Encouraging them to catch flame in a blast of heat."

He could almost taste her words. He could feel the picture she painted, that warmth of the fire.

His hand was on her waist. She leaned in a little more, so her forehead touched his.

"I always dawdled as much as I could about the job, letting my hands grow warm. I'd find some excuse—I needed to make sure the fire caught everywhere, so that it burned evenly. I wouldn't leave, even if I threatened to bake through."

"Cam." He felt almost hoarse.

"I have always been susceptible to flame," she told him.

He wasn't sure if his lips found hers first, or if hers found his.

God. Oh, God. He couldn't think; he couldn't let himself. If he *thought*, this couldn't happen, and it *had* to happen. He could not have let himself stop, not for a thousand rational arguments. The gentle pressure of her mouth on his felt like a promise. Her lips whispered against his, wiping away his concerns one by one.

It will all work out. You have nothing to fear from me. We are in this together.

He had thought at first that he could simply get the annulment and walk away, unchanged. Then she'd worked her way inside him, with her smiles and her impulses and her strength. Now she was fire itself, and he wanted to be burned.

Her lips stroked his in tiny little kisses—almost chaste, despite the heat in them. His other hand slipped around her waist, bracketing her in place.

He felt full, so full. His mouth devoured hers, and she opened another inch to him, blooming in the incandescent heat of his kiss. Her lips burned him, and oh, he desired. He wanted more—her on top of him, not sitting to the side; her opening to him fully, not this chaste embrace.

But he couldn't take anything else, not after what had been done to her. All he could do was stand here and wait, wait for her to give.

Their lips touched briefly, parted for a second, then came back together in a symphony of perfection. It was too much. He wanted her too much. He wanted to take hold of her and pull her down onto his lap. He wanted to lick her lips and slide his tongue inside, if she'd let him. He wanted to take her upstairs to his bed, no questions asked, not a moment of hesitation, and damn the fact that it would doom any chance of annulling the marriage.

He wanted her and nothing but her, her forever.

She brought one hand up tentatively, setting her fingers against the fabric of his shirt. For one moment, she didn't move; then, ever so slightly, she stroked downward, sending a spiral of electric want through his nerves. Her hand slid down his ribs, a delicate brush against his flesh. *I want you. I care for you. I see you.*

He let out a gasp, and encouraged, she shifted her hand farther down, letting it catch on the waistband of his trousers.

Yes, he thought wildly. *Yes. Don't stop. Don't—*

She pulled away first. Her eyes were suspiciously bright; she jumped to her feet, leaving him feeling cold and alone.

"Oh, look at that!" She did her best to come up with a smile. "It worked, I can't believe it worked! You knew it was an act, and *still* I fooled you!"

It took a moment for reality to set in. Right. They'd been play-acting. He almost reached for her; his protest almost came out. What was that he felt?

Disappointment? Surely he could not be disappointed. He'd been on the verge of letting go of the entirety of his future; he should be *delighted* that she had called a halt to the endeavor.

He was not delighted. He wanted to keep her.

It felt so selfish, so desperate, so wrong. He wanted to keep her, and he couldn't.

He put his head in his hands. Truth, eh? He'd never been good at lying.

"Cam," he muttered. "I wasn't acting."

He could hear her stillness, the lack of motion. He could almost envision the look on her face.

She let out a long, slow breath, and when she spoke, her

voice was low. "I know. I'm sorry; that was cruel of me. I thought you would come to your senses at any moment, and figured…it would hurt less if I did it first?"

He lifted his head and their eyes met. Hers were dark and…no, not unreadable. She was watching him with an intensity that he understood all too well. She'd looked at him that way often enough.

"And what," he said slowly, "if I didn't want to come to my senses?"

She folded her arms and looked away. "Then it would hurt even more when you finally did."

Oh, Cam. Brave Cam, clever Cam, vastly unloved Cam. Cam who chased stars and deserved to wear her dreams like a crown. He wanted to punch the entire world for what it had done to her. She should not have felt that way.

She should not have been right.

He stood and took a step toward her.

"Please." She sniffed. "We shouldn't."

"I won't," he promised. "Not that. But would it hurt so much if I gave you a hug?"

"Yes." Her voice cracked. "But it will hurt more if you don't."

He wrapped her in his arms and held on as tightly as he could. It was just for now, but he wanted to enfold her in all the comfort he could send. And she burrowed into him, melting as if she were meant to be molded to him. Her chest shook, just a little, and when he brushed her cheek, there was a little wetness to it.

God. How long had it been since someone touched her in affection?

He realized he'd asked the question aloud when she answered.

"It feels as if I've been nine years starving."

He stroked her hair. This was unfair, so unfair, most of all to her. "And here you are—not allowed to eat."

She shook her head. "I'm allowed, but I'll pay the price. If we let ourselves do any more, we *will* be married. In truth."

It was madness to think they should contemplate that possibility. He didn't want it. If he gave in like this...what if he regretted it later?

What he said was this: "Am I so horrible, then?"

She looked up at him. "You know you're not. Of course you're not. But you told me so yourself. You don't want a wife who will choose you because you're not 'so horrible' and she felt she didn't have a choice. You want..." She inhaled. "You want a long, slow falling in love." She said those words precisely, as if she'd memorized what he'd told her those weeks ago. "A partnership, built over time. Certainty and sureness. You want a choice, and you want to be chosen. You don't want this—not like this."

"Cam."

She looked up at him. She reached out and slowly, slowly touched his cheek. "Adrian. I like you well enough that I promise I am going to give that to you. Don't give it up, not like this."

He exhaled.

She pulled herself from his embrace and wrapped her own arms about herself. "Tell me about your parents again. What you said the last time... It was lovely. I want to hear it again."

I need to hear it again, he heard, *and so do you.*

He nodded. He sat back down, because if he didn't, he might reach for her once more. His hands made fists on the arms of the chair, as if holding onto it would somehow substitute for her. "My mother married young, once. She never speaks of that. After her first husband died and left her a wealthy widow, she defied her family to join the abolitionist movement. She devoted her fortune to the cause. Worked with my father for years. My parents fell in love slowly and surely."

"That sounds lovely."

"They were comrades-in-arms before they were ever married."

Cam had become his comrade. His ally in truth, not just in name. Even now, she protected him. She was the one who was reminding him what he wanted, no matter what it cost her.

He trailed off, searching for the right words.

"You're right," he finally said, "I want a choice." He looked up at her. "And I want you to have one, too. You've had so little of it; I want whoever ends up loving you to know that you could have had anyone in the world, and you chose him. I want him to think that he has had a gift bestowed upon him, not that he was sentenced to your company by circumstance. You deserve better than this."

Funny, how she'd faced everything that happened to her in the rector's household with nothing but resolve, but this could bring tears to her eyes.

"You deserve to have no doubts," he told her. "You deserve to believe that you were wanted above all others."

His heart hurt in his chest.

"You deserve everything I want," he told her. "You deserve a partner, a comrade-in-arms, a slow falling in love. You don't deserve to be stuck with a man simply because he's got a hankering for his own pleasure."

"Is that what you're after?"

He didn't answer. He'd made a set of plates for her—partially, at least. It wasn't as if he could *hide* the fact that he had some finer feelings.

"We can't give each other anything else," she said quietly. "But I can give you that. If that's what you want—if you want a slow falling in love, if you want joy, if you want not to be stuck with a woman simply because she'll do and you've a hankering for pleasure—then I will make sure you have it."

His throat almost closed.

"I'm sorry for what I did earlier." She gave him a firm nod. "Teasing you, when we were practicing. I will not let myself forget. We have too many enemies in this world to be at odds with each other on the question of how we feel."

"And what if we decide we want to choose each other?"

She didn't speak for a long time. She bit her lip. She looked away.

"I've been alone a long time," she finally said. "I've wanted someone. *Anyone.* Rector Miles made me believe that when I told myself I would be loved, it was a legion of devils driving me into sin. He told me the tiny voice of doubt I always heard was my sole hold on righteousness." Her voice shook. "But I refuse. I cannot believe it is evil to hope somebody will love me someday."

"Cam."

"I never needed that person to be a husband. I imagined being a faithful companion to an elderly woman. A bright spot in the day of a shopkeeper. And yes, sometimes a wife." She looked over at him. "I don't have to be your wife, Adrian. But can I be your friend? No matter what, even after all this is over? It would be more than I have ever had."

There was nothing for it. He stood. He walked to her again. His arms came around her once more, this time in friendship. His head leaned against hers.

"Yes," he said. "Please. I think we could both use a friend."

CHAPTER SEVENTEEN

Camilla lay alone in her bed that night, knowing that she should sleep. Tomorrow they would embark on a long journey. If they were successful, Adrian would disappear from her life.

In her heart, she knew she was susceptible to praise. That she was practically starved for affection. Even the offer of a scrap of goodwill would have had her heart in a tangle. But he'd given her a veritable feast. Actual respect? Friendship? Encouragement? Eight plates of tigers?

Of *course* she had fallen in love with him. It didn't mean anything—she would have fallen in love with anyone who gave her as much.

No matter how much her brain told her this, her heart still hurt.

Part of her wanted to go back to their time together in that room. To that moment when he'd looked at her and he'd desired her, when their lips had come together in heat and fire. She wanted to throw her inconvenient sense of right and wrong in the dustbin.

She didn't want her stupid conscience. She just wanted his hands on her.

It would take so little to get it back and if she did, she could have him forever. All she had to do was stand. Go down the corridor to his room at the end of the hall. If she were to show up in nothing but a nightgown...

If they consummated this thing between them, there would be no annulment.

She put her hands over her face.

God. She was a horrible person to even think such a grasping, calculating thing. To trap another person for the rest of their lives?

That wasn't love. She knew it wasn't love.

Still, she shut her eyes and let her imagination run wild.

She didn't want to trap him. She'd spent enough time with people who didn't like her; she could hardly hope to spend the rest of her life with someone who felt the same. She couldn't even find joy in imagining it.

Her breath hissed out.

But what if he wanted you?

What if he was in his room, thinking the things she was thinking? What if he was thinking not of his imminent freedom, but of his loss? What if he decided he wanted her?

He might stand up in his night things. She didn't know what he wore to bed, but her imagination stuttered, and she imagined...nothing. Nothing at all. He'd feel the way she did. He'd find a robe, or perhaps a spare sheet, for modesty's sake.

She shut her eyes, thinking of what he'd look in the moonlight, his skin showing like midnight through almost translucent bedsheets.

He'd stand. Pace his room, thinking of what to do. He'd make his decision after an hour of deliberation—that he didn't want an annulment, that he wanted *her* instead.

Adrian did not strike her as the sort of person to put off acting on decisions, once they were made. He'd take off down the hall. He would tap lightly on her door.

She would never tell him no, not in a million years. He'd tell her that he had chosen, that he didn't want to be without her.

And Camilla would reach out and pull the ends of that sheet—in her imagination, it was a strip of almost sheer gossamer—from his grasp.

They'd kiss the way they had wanted to kiss tonight—skin to skin, his hands holding her in place as if she were precious, as if he didn't want to let go.

She could imagine him trailing kisses down her neck. She could imagine herself giving in. The heat of his breath against her throat; the slide of his body against hers. His hardness.

She wasn't a virgin. She knew what would happen. She wanted it to happen; she wanted it rather desperately.

Her hands slipped between her thighs. It wasn't helping matters at all to think this way about him, to touch herself and imagine his fingers instead of her own, to bite back her own response.

She had told him that she wanted to earn love, not steal it. She had hoped he would see through her words, to understand that she wanted *his* adoration, *his* attention. She wanted it now.

It was madness to do what she was doing—imagining him pressing on top of her, his lips finding hers. She did it anyway. She shivered as she imagined him inside her, thick and hot, his hands tangled in her hair. She thought of him whispering that he wanted her, only her, for the rest of their lives. It was madness to feel this kind of desire, something that was so deep, her fingers could not palpate it.

She wanted him to want her. It was madness to wonder if he was in his room, feeling the things she did—that flutter of desire deep in her abdomen, flames fanning with every brush of her own fingers.

In her imagination, she could have him. She could dig her nails into his back, encouraging him to take everything from her and give it back.

It was too easy to imagine their joining. Too easy, and yet so impossible, when it was just her lonely hands bringing out her own response.

Even the orgasm that came felt imperfect. Unfulfilling. She could hear her own breath panting out in the night, the only sound present in the stillness.

She shut her eyes.

God, she was such a fool. He was asleep. He was grateful she'd called a halt to their activities earlier.

She wasn't going to have his love. She'd take his gratitude, and it would be...

Not enough. It would never be enough.

She stood, washing herself off, wiping away the stupid tears that insisted on coming now that she was alone, demonstrably alone. Her skin felt hungry, almost desperately so, for another person's touch. That tiny taste earlier had only whetted her appetite.

Camilla exhaled slowly and nodded at the darkness in front of her.

So be it. She'd built fantasies in her imagination before, and she'd survived the wreckage of them, when they crashed against the unforgiving shoals of reality. She was good at that—surviving the inevitable destruction of her hopes. She would do it again.

In the corridor, a board squeaked.

She straightened, turning. Her heart beat double time. It

was him. He was coming. He was *here;* he cared. She waited, breathless, time drawing out until hope fell into discouragement.

There was nothing. She let out a long breath. That creak was merely the sort of sound that a house made at night.

She'd always been good at reconstructing shattered hopes. She did it now, building the truth out of the ruins of her desire.

He didn't love her. She had survived not being loved this long; she would survive it longer.

He didn't love her, but he did like her, and it was more than she'd been given in ages. He liked her, and he wanted well for her. It wasn't enough—not forever—but that?

That would be enough for *now.* For giving her that much, she would give him anything he wanted. The thing he wanted was for her to shatter her own heart, true, but her heart had been broken before. Now she knew the truth of heartbreak—that morning would come, and she would stand up and move on.

She stared at the ceiling, listening to the faint ticking of the clock in the hallway until all sense of sound finally dissolved into the nothingness of sleep.

∾

The train ride east to Surrey, then down to Lackwich, was one of awkward silences. Every time Camilla thought of how brazen she'd been the night before—seating herself on the arm of his chair, leaning in, practically taunting him until she was unsure of who had actually closed the gap between them—

She felt herself coloring.

He hadn't said anything about their tryst that morning.

He'd only looked at her, and the way he'd looked... She had to hold herself back from hoping.

She had no space for hope, no space for worry, not when she had this final duty to perform.

He did not say anything as he had the telegram sent. He did not say anything as he walked with her halfway down the all-too-familiar road. He stopped a half-mile out, with the house where she had spent eighteen months on the horizon.

Don't look back, she thought, but she finally could.

Her hands felt cold. He reached out and took hold of them. "Camilla," he said.

It was a friendly gesture, she reminded herself, because they were friends. It was a gesture of comfort and...and maybe a little more, but Camilla had been desired before, and she wouldn't let it change what she had to do.

She loved him, but it would end. She loved him, and she'd learned to pull her confidence about her like a cloak. She loved him, and he had brought her to Jane and Laney, her sisters in marriage annulment, and it was for them that she did this—for all the women who had been given no choice.

She patted his hand. "Don't worry," she said cheerily. "I won't fail us."

His fingers convulsed around hers. She made herself smile at him as brightly as she could, and he almost flinched at the sight.

She'd misjudged it, unfortunately. Too bright, then.

She pulled away and started off down the road.

Miles wasn't there; *he* was the one who had made it all go to hell. Miles wasn't there, and she had discovered that she was stronger than he'd thought. Miles wasn't there, and...

And Camilla was walking up the path. She felt a little out of sorts, almost as if she were observing herself from a distance. The brick-and-ivy walls of the rectory seemed impossibly far away, even when she was standing on the stoop.

She didn't knock; only someone who did not belong would knock. She opened the door to the rectory and walked in. She kept walking, down the hall, past the parlor and into the rector's office. She knew what she was looking for; she knew where the record books were kept. She kept going forward, reading spine after spine. Her heart beat heavily in her chest; her fingers tapped in time with that rhythm as she went. Not this one, not this next one—

"Camilla?" The voice came from behind her.

She whirled around. *Damn it.* Why? Why did she have to jump like a scolded child? She reached for her rationality, her confidence.

"Kitty?" Her voice trembled. *God* damn it; she had practiced. Why hadn't it been easy, the way she had practiced?

It was something in the air, something in the place where she stood. It sapped all pretense at confidence.

Kitty took a step forward, frowning at Camilla. "Camilla." She, too, was trembling. "Camilla, Camilla. You're back. You're back. I thought I'd never see you again."

"Here I am." Camilla managed to sound bright and cheery, which was a good first start. She reached for some useful truths that would form a false impression. "It's funny. You seem to be upset. The rector—"

"I had to," Kitty said, bursting into tears. "I'm sorry, I'm sorry I ever called you Half-Price anything. But he did it to me before you arrived and I was just so grateful that it wasn't me anymore that..." She choked. "That I went along with it? And once I did, there was no turning back. He ordered me to lock you in, to put the keys in your pocket. And he offered to give me money, and my girl, my girl, she needs it so much, my sister has her—" Kitty wiped away tears. "My sister has her, and she's kind enough, but you know how it is—she's going to think of herself as Half-Price Ellie if I don't do something about it, and she's only three."

Camilla should be angry. Kitty had just admitted to lying, to creating that horrific scene that had trapped her. Camilla would have been enraged a few weeks ago.

Instead, she reached out and took Kitty's hands impulsively. "None of us have to be Half-Price anything anymore, you hear?"

Kitty just shook her head.

"I didn't know you had a daughter."

"He said—if I didn't tell anyone—" Kitty hiccuped.

"Oh, Kitty. What happened to me here was terrible. I doubted myself. I doubted reality—there were nights I wondered if I had maybe put the keys in my own pocket. I doubted my own senses."

"You can't forgive me." Kitty bowed her head. "I didn't expect it, honestly. Truly. I didn't."

Camilla squeezed her hand. "No, that's not what I'm saying. I am telling you that more than anyone in the world, I know what you've been through. You're not the one in need of forgiveness."

"I prayed to God for the chance to make things right with you," Kitty whispered. "But what can I do?"

"You can change everything now," Camilla told her. "Come with me. If you want to make things right, come with me and we'll tell the truth. We'll find you work."

Kitty sniffled. "Who is we?"

"Me and Adrian. I mean, Mr. Hunter." Camilla's hand landed on the book of records that she needed; she opened it and looked through it, flipping until she came to the right date. *There.* She had it. Now she just needed his personal accounts. "You want to make it right. Would you be willing to swear that he had you lock us in? That he asked you to tell untruths?"

There was a moment's pause. Then… "Yes," Kitty said.

Camilla nodded.

"Come. Pack your things and meet me across the way. There isn't a lot of time."

Kitty smiled ruefully. "Don't worry. I haven't many things."

CHAPTER EIGHTEEN

Over the last few days, Theresa had learned a great deal that she hadn't ever expected to know.

She and Benedict had pooled their allowances and managed to hire an investigator of dubious origins who had gone to the place where Camilla had been married in order to obtain information about the couple. He'd come back with a description of a woman who could have been their sister—"plump, dark-haired, eager to smile, chatty"— and the man she'd married—"a valet of African ancestry."

They had wed under circumstances that the man had been unable to determine precisely, but which sounded extremely suspicious.

After that success, Theresa had run into problems. Where the newly married couple had gone, nobody had been able to say.

Maybe south. Maybe north. But after the first night— when a Camilla Winters had taken rooms in a nearby inn— the man they'd hired had been unable to find hide nor hair of her in inn registries in all directions. The trail had disappeared.

That was, up until yesterday, when by chance, Benedict had spotted a note in a newspaper about trading, of all things.

Contact Captain G. Hunter, in his office by the Catherine docks with regards to sale of good quality telegraph cable, or make inquiry with Mr. A. Hunter in Harvil, Bristol county.

Hunter was a common name. There was no reason that a valet should be associated with these Hunters, but it was *something* to do while they waited for their investigator to widen his search of inns. They'd scrambled to make an appointment; here they were.

The office they'd been directed to was small, the sort taken temporarily by traders who arrived in town for a few weeks in order to sell their wares. They waited in the hall, listening to two men argue, then laugh, then agree to terms.

Captain G. Hunter was, by the sounds of it, an American. Well. Theresa supposed there were worse things in the world.

The door opened; one man left. A woman ushered them in.

The man who sat at the desk watched as they entered, then frowned at the two of them. He had brown, piercing eyes. His skin was a dark brown; his hair was short and curly.

Theresa shoved her hands deeper into her muff.

"Captain Grayson Hunter." He didn't stand. "You're Mr. and Mrs. Worth?" He sounded dubious.

She would need all of her dignity for this. Theresa raised her chin. "I am Lady Theresa Worth. This is my younger brother, Benedict Worth."

Captain Hunter's eyes touched on Theresa's hat, then her muff, as if sizing up her wealth. He glanced at Benedict's cuffs. Then he leaned back in his chair, one arm over the edge. Piercing eyes indeed. "*You're* here to answer my advertisement about telegraph cable?" His accent was definitely American.

"Um." Benedict looked at Theresa, a clear sign that meant *I'm bad at lying, you go ahead.*

Captain Hunter looked up at the ceiling in entreaty and shook his head before looking at the two of them. "I'm sorry, I know that actual adults look younger and younger to me every year—but are the two of you even of age?"

Theresa's hands clenched together in her muff. "We're not children. I'm—"

"Old enough to sign a contract?"

"That's not my fault! I'm older than I appear."

"You must be all of thirteen years old, then."

He was mocking her. Theresa felt her cheeks heat. "I'm *fifteen.* Two months ago. And I don't wish to sign a contract. I wish to speak to you about one Adrian Hunter."

"Oh." He let out an amused huff. "Has my brother offended you somehow?" He leaned forward, and his voice seemed almost a mockery. "Was it by existing?"

"I don't know if he's offended me!" Theresa shot back. "He could have! That's why I'm here. Do you have any idea what he's been doing these last few weeks?"

Something in her voice made him stop. He glanced to his side, at a stack of papers, and then pressed his lips together. "And here I thought he was back at Harvil, seeing to the china plates. Suppose you tell me."

His tone was mild—too mild, really. Theresa stared at him in something like awe. He was even better than the dowager, refusing to give away any information until he'd gotten it himself.

"I don't know," she heard herself mutter. "We're just *children,* how could we know anything of importance?"

He shrugged. "Don't mind me. I'm a bit prickly these days; England does that to me. And I don't dislike children.

It's hardly your fault you were born a short time ago. Can you tell me something I don't know about my brother?"

She suspected he was still mocking her. She didn't care. She took a deep breath and bulled ahead. "I think your brother married my sister."

He picked up a series of interlocked iron rings that sat on his desk and turned them over in his hands. He did not react to this, not for a moment, just turning them over and over. "You think. You...*think*. Do you not *know* who your sister married?"

This was where matters became delicate. Theresa was trying to figure out how to explain the tangled knot of their family, wondering whether to start with the treason. In her experience, it never turned out well when she started with the treason, but no story ever made sense without it. Drat.

"We lost her," Benedict said simply.

Captain Hunter blew out his breath. "You...lost. Your sister. That seems careless."

"Well, the fact that you haven't immediately denied the claim suggests that you lost your brother, too." Theresa shot back.

"Point." Captain Hunter looked up at the ceiling. "I *told* him so."

"Do you really trade ambergris?" Benedict asked, picking up a piece of paper off his desk. "Why ambergris? Why not tea or rum or cotton? Isn't that what traders into London normally trade?"

"Benedict!" Theresa grimaced. "This is no time to get excited by trade!"

Captain Hunter did not seem even slightly disturbed by this rapid change in subjects. "Yes, I trade ambergris. Among other things. And no, I have not *lost* my brother. He has just been unusually evasive for the last month, and given what he was supposed to be doing… He would not want to admit to me if things went amiss. How he could imagine he would hide something like a marriage… In my defense, I spent four years fighting off privateers and blockading Charleston. I have to work hard not to order my family around. Apparently, I didn't work hard enough. But you don't want to hear my family history."

God, she wished *she* could do that. That insouciant look up at the ceiling as if he didn't care about either of them. Theresa did her best to copy him. "A convenient excuse to lose track of family."

His lips twitched. "*I* was fighting for the freedom of millions. What was *your* excuse, little girl?"

Benedict took an eager step forward. "You fought privateers? You were in a blockade?! What was that like?"

Oh, God. Benedict had latched on to the man. Theresa tried not to groan aloud.

Captain Hunter glanced at Benedict. "Not as exciting as it sounds, unfortunately. The most fun I had the entire time was getting struck by lightning thrice, which tells you precisely how entertaining the endeavor was. Now, as to my brother—"

"You were struck by lightning? And you *lived?*"

"There's a trick to it, but—"

"I want to be struck by lightning!"

For a moment, Captain Hunter seemed to be struggling with laughter. He set a hand over his face and shut his eyes before looking up. "I don't endorse it. Now as to my brother—"

"What's the trick?"

Captain Hunter sighed. "Little boy. I'm an incredibly inconvenient case for your hero worship. Choose someone else, if you please. My brother, Adrian—"

"How does one become a person who fights privateers in

the first place? I want to fight privateers! It sounds loads better than going into law."

Captain Hunter turned to spear her brother with another gaze. When he spoke, his words seemed excessively dry. "You make laws that starve them of income, that's how you fight privateers. If you have to do it with guns, you've done it wrong. Stick with law."

Benedict subsided into confused rejection.

"Every so often, some spoiled child decides he wants to learn about trading from me. His parents pay a vast sum of money for him to come along on a journey, and the only reason I ever allow it is the child inevitably gives up because he doesn't want to actually do *work*. If I wanted to answer a thousand irrelevant questions about what I do, I'd have an apprentice. Right now, I want to know about my brother."

"And I want to find my sister," Theresa said. "I have some information. You have more. If we pool what we both have, we'll achieve greater success, don't you think?"

Captain Hunter considered her. "That depends. How did you lose your sister?"

There was nothing for it. She was going to have to start with... *Drat*. "It all happened when my father committed treason," Theresa said. "Our family was split apart. We haven't seen Camilla for more than nine years. Our family fortunes have improved, and we are searching for her. We know she was married less than a month ago, in Surrey. And we know where they aren't. Which is Surrey."

"Plus," Benedict added, "it's Judith's birthday coming up exceedingly soon, and we should hate to disappoint Judith."

The man—to his credit—ignored the treason and the birthday and asked an even more irrelevant question. "Who solemnized the marriage?"

"What?"

"Who solemnized the marriage?" he asked. "It's not so hard a question, is it?"

Theresa fumbled for her book and withdrew her copy of the record. "It was...a Bishop Lassiter? Witnessed by a Rector Miles and a Catherine Shackleton."

Captain Hunter shut his eyes. "Fucking Denmore. Left him in the lurch once again. I told him—" He looked over at them. "Pardon my language. Small children. Ugh."

"No pardon necessary," Theresa said brightly. "I'm not that small. I've used that word before myself. Twice!"

"All of twice. My, my." He didn't look impressed by her ability to flout social stricture. "Very well, then. Your information is useful. Trading seems fair. Bishop Denmore is our uncle on our mother's side. Adrian told me that he had hopes to bring Denmore around to recognizing our branch of the family. Denmore and Lassiter are at odds with each other. If Adrian has got himself in trouble with Lassiter, and if my gods-be-damned uncle didn't officiate at his own nephew's wedding, I know precisely what's happening. I was right, Adrian was wrong, and he's trying to work everything out so he doesn't have to admit it."

"Your pardon?"

Captain Hunter sighed. "I don't know where Adrian and your sister are at present, but I know where they will be."

❧

Camilla had returned to Lackwich by means of Adrian's cart. Kitty sat next to her, clutching her valise and not speaking much.

Adrian had glanced at the two of them with curiosity, but hadn't said anything, not until they'd gone to Mrs. Beasley's home and asked if they might use her front room for a moment.

She had agreed, and then—with one look at Kitty's trembling hands—clucked her tongue and disappeared to fetch tea. Camilla had finally turned to Adrian.

"We didn't have much time," Camilla explained as she handed the rectory's account book over. "I haven't had a chance to truly look through it. I took this and his personal accounts. I verified that it was the proper dates, but... I hope they're enough. Tell me they're enough."

She felt her fists clench and tried to tamp down that horrible feeling that felt something like hope, something like betrayal. Deep down, she *didn't* hope it was enough. She hoped it wasn't.

He took the book, looking at her, and then at the woman who stood five paces behind her, head down. Adrian's eyes narrowed. "Isn't she—?"

"You may remember Kitty," Camilla put in hastily, "from the time she perjuriously witnessed that we were legally wed? We found each other and spoke."

"I recall everything about that evening in vivid and excruciating detail."

Kitty winced and turned away; Camilla reached out and took her hand.

"She also put the room key in my pocket," Camilla said. "And we have an affidavit from Mrs. Martin about the funds, right? I thought it could not hurt to have testimony from someone who would explain that she had an active role in the circumstances. Kitty will say that she had been coerced by threats to expose the truth of her three-year-old child, born out of wedlock."

"Oh." Adrian took a step forward. One of his hands drew up an inch—as if he was reaching out to touch Camilla—and then fell, slowly, as if he'd remembered not to do so. "Well done, you."

His voice was warm with praise, and Camilla blushed as if he *had* lifted that hand and run it along her lips.

"Will it be enough, then?"

Let it not be enough. She hushed that selfish desire and held onto her conscience with both hands, willing herself to do the right thing, the best thing. But oh, part of her wanted. Part of her wanted their quest to be hopeless, wanted him to look at her and say, "We've done all we can, let's try to make this marriage work."

He flipped through the parish account book instead.

She had thought he was handsome the moment she met him, but now, now that she knew his moods, now that she could read the intense concentration as he scanned down the pages...

Now, her whole being swayed toward him. That firm set of his eyebrows, the press of his lips...

Part of her wanted their quest to be hopeless.

But it was no longer just conscience. There was another part of her, something that had always been there. A part of her that had yearned and wanted and desired, year after year.

I want to be loved.

Not just picked as a default. Not just accepted as fate.

She wanted to be loved. She wanted him to devote that intense concentration to her not because he had no choice, but because she'd earned it.

I want to be loved.

It was no longer enough to win for the sake of her conscience. Now, it felt almost imperative—that she should prove it to herself. That he should care for her by choice, not by necessity.

I want to be loved by him, Camilla thought.

His finger halted on the page, tapping. "Here," he said. "This is where the entry ought to have been. But there is very distinctly nothing in the parish accounts."

"That's good. But...have you checked? Perhaps he recorded it earlier? Or later?"

"Did he often do so?"

Camilla shook her head. "I don't think so. But—we can compare." The second book—the book of Rector Miles's private accounts—was taken out.

There it was—a thousand pounds entered into the ledger. *Income from investment,* it read.

"But Mrs. Martin gave two thousand pounds."

"Lassiter must have received half. Somehow. But... There's no record. At least not here."

"Well, then." He exhaled. "We have them. Proof of wrong-doing. Mrs. Martin can prove she gave the rector money; we can prove they never sent that money on to the church or used it for its intended purpose. And Miss..."

"Shackleton," Kitty provided.

"Miss Shackleton," Adrian said, "I must ask you—did Bishop Lassiter speak to you about this scheme? Did he threaten you?"

"No."

"Ah." Adrian shut his eyes.

"Is it enough?"

Still, Adrian hesitated.

Her mind raced through the possibilities. She'd read the reports after all.

"It might be enough if all we needed was to prove facts for our annulment." She knew how it worked, unfortunately. "It would be enough if facts were enough. There is motive. There is explanation. There are witnesses."

"But." He gave her a sad smile.

"But." She shut her eyes. "But facts are what people believe them to be. And with nobody powerful on our side, the truth will not be enough. Your uncle..."

"My uncle," Adrian said, "wants Bishop Lassiter. And all of this points to Miles alone."

"You don't think your uncle will help anyway?"

He looked over at her. "I want to," he said slowly. "I *want* to think he will lend his voice. But…"

She watched him.

"But," he said, "I've known him too long. I suspect he won't."

Another silence fell. Camilla bit her lip and considered. She *was* technically Lady Camilla. Judith had no desire to see her, but… Maybe, if Camilla asked nicely?

"They must have corresponded," Camilla said. "The bishop arrived on almost no notice."

"If they did, it was not in my presence."

Camilla shut her eyes and thought about that morning again. She could see it, plain as day. She'd been harried, running around. They'd had no notice of the bishop's arrival, not until lunchtime. Her memory was good; she returned to it now, trying to recall any helpful detail.

There had been someone at the door. Camilla had run through Rector Miles's office in haste. She had had so much to do, and…

Right. She could see the fireplace in his office, the gray ash that she'd had to clean out, mixed with little curling bits of paper… It had all gone in the dust bin.

Damn.

"They must have corresponded," Camilla said, her nose twitching. "But he burned the correspondence. After eighteen months of cleaning, I know what a burned telegram looks like."

Adrian lifted his head. "*What* sort of correspondence did you say it was?"

"A telegram. Several, I would imagine. He burned them. I had to clean out the fireplace; I would know."

He was staring at her, his eyes broad and wide.

"Drat." Camilla squeezed her eyes shut. "Drat, drat, drat. We're so close. There has to be *something*."

"You said it was a telegram?"

She turned to him. "Why?"

"Oh my God." Adrian didn't stand. He didn't move an inch. Still, that broad smile took over his face. "There's still a chance, then." And then, in his regular voice, he spoke. "Mrs. Beasley," he said, "are you listening?"

CHAPTER NINETEEN

I t took Mrs. Beasley approximately five seconds after being hailed to appear, tea-tray in both her hands. "Well, dearies," she said brightly, "who would like some tea?"

"Um." Camilla looked at Kitty, then back at Adrian. "I've got some questions, I think, about a telegram that might or might not have been sent through your office."

"Oh, I heard you the whole time." Mrs. Beasley smiled and set the tea-tray down. "All the more reason to serve tea." She began pouring the brown liquid into cups. "Never gossip on a dry throat. It doesn't turn out well."

"So were telegrams sent between Lassiter and Miles?" Adrian cut in.

Mrs. Beasley brandished the sugar tongs. "One lump or two?"

"One, but—"

"You know how I am," Mrs. Beasley said. "Gossip only goes in, not out. I could *never* tell you what another person sent via telegram. That would violate a sacred trust reposed in me, and I'm not the sort to do that."

"But—then—"

"I would never speak of the telegrams I sent or received," Mrs. Beasley said, adding sugar diligently to a cup and handing it to Kitty, "but I would *love* to tell you about the procedures of the telegraph office."

"Ah." Adrian nodded and took his own cup of tea. Camilla wondered what procedures she meant, and how it would help. But Adrian seemed almost comfortable.

"How long do you keep the telegrams that are sent?" he asked.

"I don't keep them. I send them on."

"No. I mean, when someone fills out a form, or when you're taking notes on a telegram that comes for someone in the area. How long do you keep those notes?"

Mrs. Beasley tilted her head and looked at Adrian. A little smile played over her face. "Well, dearie. You know I'm supposed to burn them all at the end of every day."

"But in reality?"

"Well." Mrs. Beasley shrugged. "Every day is quite often, you know. In reality, I sometimes take a little longer."

Camilla felt her heart thump. "How much longer?"

"Ah." A flicker of a smile passed over the woman's face. "Well. It may have been…a bit since my last burning."

"A week? Two weeks?"

"Oh, less than that," Mrs. Beasley said. "Three days. But… How shall I say this? Operating a teletype machine is not interesting work, Miss Winters. Sometimes, we keep things around for our own amusement."

"Do we?"

"I could *never* show them to anyone, you understand," Mrs. Beasley said kindly, "but they're all in the attic, organized by date. And speaking of the office—my husband has finished his time there, and he'll be expecting me to take my turn there for a few hours while he heads to the pub."

"Is that so?"

By way of an answer, Mrs. Beasley withdrew a keyring from her pocket. "It *is* locked, the attic, but this..." She fished one key out from the lot and jiggled it. "This, that'll undo the attic door. I would never let these keys out of my sight." She set them on the table. "Never, at least not on *purpose*. But I am old-ish and forgetful-ish." She smiled brilliantly. "What a shame. I've misplaced them. Do let me know if you see them."

~

K itty offered to help, but the attic wasn't large, and in any event, Camilla knew what it was like to walk away from a place of employment with nothing but a valise.

"Send your sister a telegram," Adrian told her. "And tell us what you'd need. I'm sure we can find a position where you can have your daughter with you. If I can't think of something in my family's holdings, I'll find somewhere else."

It took Camilla and Adrian several hours to sort through the sheaves of paper in the attic. There had been hundreds of telegrams exchanged over the years; few of them were relevant. They retreated downstairs with a stack of papers.

"Here," Camilla said. "This one—what do you think?"

TO: LASSITER

ANOTHER PACKAGE HAS ARRIVED

DISPOSAL IN THE USUAL MANNER

Adrian read it. "I have actually seen quite a few of those. And here's this—the date seems right."

TO: MILES

PACKAGE RECEIVED

MY THANKS FOR ANOTHER SUCCESSFUL DISPOSITION

A few more minutes found this:

TO: LASSITER

AN ISSUE HAS ARISEN IN RE PRIOR PACKAGE.

~~*ORIGINAL OWNER IS RAISING A FUSS*~~

ASKING FOR PACKAGE WHEREABOUTS

ADVICE IS NECESSARY

CANNOT COMMIT MORE TO TELEGRAM

Camilla stopped. "This is the day before you arrived."

"It is."

"This is it. I know it's not perfect, but… This shows they were working together, yes? And that they had an agenda that they could not discuss in public."

"I think it is enough," Adrian said slowly. "Given the dates, Lassiter's arrival, the fact that they discussed Mrs. Martin in your presence…it might be enough." Adrian tapped his finger against the page. "And these are the last telegrams we have. But for this. It's the one sending for a special license. No surprise there."

Camilla took the form.

It was hard to see her future written out in India ink like that. Lassiter had made the request, issuing the order with all the authority of his position.

NEED EMERGENCY SPECIAL LICENSE.

The details followed. To think so much had changed since the Wednesday weeks ago when this has all transpired…

Except.

Camilla pushed the page forward. "Adrian, this telegram was sent on a Tuesday."

"Yes?"

Her voice shook. "Look at the *date*. He requested a special license the day *before* we were put in the bedchamber together."

He blinked, then looked up at her. "So he did. And that's our story—it all fits together now. Rector Miles receives his package—two thousand pounds. He pockets half, and shares the remainder with the bishop who is helping him cover the crime."

"Yes."

"The bishop comes to consult on the matter. I start asking questions about the rector's household, and the two of them get wind of this and decide to discredit me. But Lassiter sends for a special license the day *before* their scheme goes into operation—and that pins the blame squarely on him."

"Yes," Camilla agreed again.

And then, across the room, Kitty, who had been sitting and reading said, "No."

They turned as one.

"No?"

Kitty smoothed her skirts and looked away. "When the rector approached me, he said it was about Camilla. That she'd done something wrong and he couldn't prove it, so he needed to catch her in the act. The only thing he said about you, Mr. Hunter, was that you were nobody."

Camilla felt a strange sensation—an almost dizziness. "Me? But—that had to be an excuse, of course. What would I—"

"You knew about Mrs. Martin," Adrian said. "You're the one who told me."

She had, technically. She'd overheard it, and remembered —even if they hadn't mentioned the words. "But—who would I have *told*? I don't know anyone. *I'm* nobody."

"No," Adrian said. "You're not."

"Maybe not in the *general* sense of things," Camilla said, "but to the rest of the world—"

"No." Adrian said, and Camilla felt her chest contract as she remembered. "No, even then you're not. You're the daughter of the Earl of Linney."

She felt sick. "And Bishop Lassiter *asked* me about my

sister. But she doesn't want anything to do with me. I *know* she doesn't. Why would that matter?"

"*Do* you know that they want nothing to do with you?"

"Of course I do. Judith said—she said—" She *had* said, years and years ago. And she hadn't written, and Camilla had taken all the hope she could not contain and pushed it into the future—hoping, hoping, hoping, and never looking back.

Adrian looked at her. "Do you know?" he asked once more.

Yes. Of *course* Camilla knew it. She *knew* it, knew it the way she knew everything she had told herself over and over at night, knew it the way she knew that it was likely hopeless to love, knew it the way that she knew that she'd do it anyway. She knew that nobody wanted her, that nobody remembered her, that nobody cared about her. She knew she'd hope for it forever.

She knew it with a heart that had been bruised too often, with hopes that she'd held onto and lost too many times. She knew it with every fiber of her being.

She just didn't know it with her head any longer.

"No," she whispered. "I don't know."

Her finger reached out and touched the dark letters asking for a special license—and pulled her hand away, feeling stung.

"It makes a sort of sense," he said. "I should have considered it the moment you told me. They *didn't* know who I was. It wasn't me they were trying to discredit. It was you all along."

"Oh, God." She inhaled. "Of course. It's all my fault. I should have known."

"Camilla." His hand pressed against hers, warm and comforting. Her heart was beating fast and impossibly loud in her ears. "It was not your fault. It was never your fault. It was always theirs."

She bowed her head.

"And we've won," he told her. "Look at this. They thought they could make you into nobody, and they couldn't. We're going to bring them to justice—you and I together."

She inhaled. She didn't know what to think, what to say. *Look forward,* she thought, don't look back, don't look back, don't look back.

If she looked back and they *didn't* want her, it would hurt too much. Even for her.

It was too much to comprehend.

"Not me." She shut her eyes and turned her palm over so that their fingertips could glide against each other. His breath hissed out. "Us," she told him. "It has always been us." She was saying too much; she wasn't saying enough. "From the moment when you stopped me in the road and told me Miles and Lassiter were our enemies," she confessed. "From the moment I chose to believe you without proof."

He leaned into her. "Camilla," he whispered.

She held her breath, hoping. The heat of his body warmed hers. His arm, not quite around her waist, braced her in place. His breath whispered against her ear. But Kitty sat half a room away, and hope was all they could do.

She tilted her head and looked up at him.

He smiled at her. Oh, God, that smile. She could feel it break across her like sunlight. She had never felt so precious, so *wanted.*

His hand twitched at his side, but it did not come up to brush her cheek. She felt it only in her imagination—the brush of his hand, like the caress of his gaze, stroking her.

All the want she couldn't let herself feel rose up in her. All this time, she'd hoped and hoped and hoped.

Maybe it wasn't all the hope that had been the problem. Maybe it was that she had not let herself hope enough.

Adrian's smile felt almost sad.

"I could not have been more lucky in my choice of women to not be married to," he said.

And maybe she could hope for more with him, too.

Her heart wasn't breaking. It was too full to break. She wanted him, and he wanted a choice, and she wanted to be chosen. It hurt, the best kind of pain, this holding back. But this prickle of hope, of sheer desire... It was nothing to the sea of loneliness and want she'd swum in for too long. To know that she *might* be loved, that she *might* be respected? To know that her family *might* want her?

It was more than she'd had in years, and still, now that she gave free rein to her hope, she hoped for more.

She had not come this far, holding onto all this hope for this long, just to give it up. She wanted him, too. She wanted him to choose her, freely. She wanted it all, and her entire being ached with the wanting.

And so she just nodded.

"It's the same for me," she whispered. "Not being lawfully wed to you has been a singular honor."

CHAPTER TWENTY

Weeks ago, standing in the road with the bad taste of the marriage still in his mouth, Adrian would have been delighted to know that this moment would come—that he would be sitting on a train with the woman he had been forcibly wed to, his satchel packed with affidavits and accounts. They were ready to annul the legal flimflammery that bound them together.

The problem was that it was *only* the legal flimflammery that bound them together. When they were finished... What then?

Camilla sat looking out the window. She'd taken off her gloves, but held them still. She did not seem to notice that she was turning them around over and over again, as if she could direct all her nerves into the cloth.

"Have you thought of trying to find your family afterward?" he finally asked. "I know you haven't wanted to speak of them. But they're still there."

"I don't know." She blinked, looking at her gloves, then set them aside. "Nothing's changed. Judith didn't write to me. And maybe she's changed her mind—I suppose there's no reason to imagine she's tracked my whereabouts all these years—but if I go to her and she throws me out..." Camilla trailed off, shaking her head.

"Would you like me to accompany you to visit them?"

She turned to look at him for a long moment. A faint flush spread across her cheeks.

He wondered what she was thinking. Then he wondered what *he* was thinking. Her sister was a marchioness. The woman he was thinking of as simply 'Camilla' was the daughter of an earl. And yes; his mother had been the daughter of a duke.

That only meant that he knew the set. He knew his own uncle, refusing to acknowledge his nephews, not even speaking his own sister's name in polite company, no matter how he professed his love in private.

He'd met Camilla after she'd been out of that milieu for years.

They'd been in his domain these last weeks. He hadn't forgotten the reality of the matter; he never let himself forget reality. But he was used to the notion of Camilla not having a family.

"Never mind." He looked away. "I only just now realized how that would look."

"I was just trying to imagine how I would introduce you," she told him. "'Judith, this is Mr. Adrian Hunter; we used to be married.'"

"It does sound absurd."

"'Now,'" Camilla said, "'we are friends.'"

He looked over at her.

"That is what I would say," Camilla said. "Maybe I would add something like this: 'There are very few people I trust in the world; he is one of them.' I do not know what she would say to that."

Adrian looked over at her. He licked his lips. "Cam. You do realize that I'm black?"

"I had noticed." She swallowed and looked at him. "I cannot pretend I know how my sister will react. I have not spoken with her once in the last nine years. I do know that she…" Her voice faltered. "I know that the last time we talked, she told me that I'd made my choice. That I deserved to never be loved, if I was willing to give it up for the chance at pretty gowns."

"Camilla."

Camilla looked away. "And *you* told me I deserved it. That I *deserved* to be chosen. That someone would love me for who I was. I do not know what my sister will say, but I won't stand for her telling me that *you* don't deserve love. She is clearly not an expert in who is deserving." Camilla shook her head.

They were sitting so close and yet so far away. The space between them seemed like a vast cavern. Her skirts were eight inches from his shoes. Adrian leaned forward a little, and—he didn't know if it was the movement of the train, or the sway of her body—but she mirrored him, coming closer.

"If we can't get an annulment, Cam…"

He could see the smooth column of her throat contract.

He wanted to give her freedom first. "I wouldn't impose on you, Cam. We could live separately. I wouldn't have expectations. It wouldn't be fair under the circumstances."

Her cheeks flushed even pinker. Her eyes dipped to the floor, but only for a second. Then she looked up, her eyes liquid.

"You could…" Her voice trailed off. She bit her lip and inhaled. "You could expect, if you wanted."

"Could I?" He leaned in another inch, lowered his voice. "What could I expect?"

That flush painted her cheeks a dark red. "Must I say it?

251

I'd give you anything you wanted, Adrian. You would just have to want it. The more you wanted from me, the happier I would be."

He could not help himself. He reached out and took hold of her hands.

Her breath hissed out, but she didn't pull away. Instead, she ran one fingertip around the edge of his glove, brushing his wrist. Her eyes, when she looked at him, glowed like stars.

"And if I already wanted?" he asked.

She didn't say anything. Her fingers traced a circle around his wrist. She bent her head, just enough to press a kiss into his palm.

He leaned forward, even further, reaching—

"Adrian," she said in a soft voice. "We shouldn't. If we're seen like this, you know what they'll say. We have one chance to obtain an annulment. We mustn't ruin it."

Mustn't we? He didn't say that aloud, and she didn't let go of his hand. Instead, she shut her eyes, turned his hand over, and pressed a kiss to the top of his wrist.

"Well." He didn't pull away. "Let's talk about what our ruin should look like when we know what our options are."

❧

Let's talk about what our ruin should look like.

Camilla could not get his words out of her mind, not as he brought her to a home on a side-street near their destination, not after he introduced her to the housekeeper who had aired the sheets and removed the covers from the furniture in preparation for their arrival.

A maid showed Camilla to her room.

Let's talk about what our ruin should look like. She could still feel the warmth of his wrist against her fingertips even though they were no longer touching.

She washed and changed, then came down to find Adrian sitting before a plate of cold cheeses and meats.

"Make yourself at home," Adrian said. "The place is my mother's. I believe she inherited it from a great-aunt. It was leased for years, but the tenants went back to America, and we haven't found new ones yet."

Camilla nodded.

"There's no point delaying," Adrian said. "I'm going to bring our evidence to my uncle. I'm going to hold him to his promise—that he would help us with the annulment once I found evidence incriminating Lassiter."

She looked over at him.

His eyes met hers. "It's precisely as I said. Once we know that we *can* make a choice, we can decide what the choice will be. Annulment or..."

There was an *or*. He was considering an *or*. Her heart beat too swiftly in her chest and she could not contain her joy.

But he didn't specify what that *or* would be. He left to go speak to his uncle.

She was left in the house with nothing to do but wander the rooms and imagine the *or* that might await.

The space here had none of the warmth of his cottage back in Harvil; there were fancy carpets underfoot and elegant tables of stained mahogany. The plates were matched china—no amusing mistakes here. Her stomach knotted in nervous tension.

She had never met Adrian's uncle; she couldn't even imagine what the room they would meet in would look like. For his sake, she wanted it to go well.

And for hers.

She wanted. She *wanted*—not the annulment, but *him.* She

wanted to be chosen. She wanted someone to want her. She wanted—

The sound of the front door opening interrupted her reverie. She almost dropped the book she'd unthinkingly taken from the library shelf. It took a moment to set it on the table with unsure hands. Another moment to take a deep breath.

Her nerves mounted to a flutter in her belly. She reached for her composure and did her level best to walk to him, rather than run.

She failed.

She came to a skidding halt in the front room. A man stood there, handing off his coat and hat to the housekeeper with a, "Thanks, Genevieve."

He was black like Adrian. He was maybe a few inches taller than her not-really husband. His hair was in short curls; he wore spectacles. He was adjusting his cuffs as she came skittering into the room.

He looked over at her.

Camilla felt her heart hammering in her chest, nerves and tension reasserting themselves as she stopped short in front of him.

He didn't seem surprised to see her, and the housekeeper seemed to recognize him, too. He took a step closer.

"Miss Camilla Worth, I take it?"

It had been years since she had been called by that name. It brought back memories—strange, tangled memories. Laughing with Judith and trying on bracelets far beyond their ages. Judith saying, *if you don't want to be loved, we don't want to love you.*

Her breath stopped, then skipped, then stopped again.

"Yes?" Her heart seemed to not function properly. Her head felt far too light.

The corner of his mouth ticked up. "A pleasure to meet you," he said. "I'm Captain Grayson Hunter."

Oh, for God's sake. Adrian's brother. Of *course* she had to meet him under these dreadful circumstances, when she was nervous and scared and full of hope.

She struggled and somehow found the power of speech. "Mr. Hunter," she managed. "How...nice to meet you. I am..." No, what was she doing, introducing herself? He already knew who she was. He'd said it.

"Ah, that's right." He considered her. "I shouldn't have called you Worth, should I? It's Camilla Hunter, now. Welcome to the family." He wasn't exactly asking a question.

"No," she heard herself say. "Adrian has been most insistent on that point. If we are to get an annulment, we must not hold ourselves out as married."

"Ah." He touched his fingers together. "How interesting. So you're getting an annulment, then?"

"It is generally considered the accepted practice when one is forced to marry at gunpoint."

His eyes flashed, but all he said was: "Is it, then? I hadn't realized that gunpoint weddings *were* an accepted practice."

"They're a rare enough occurrence that they are not usually covered in the etiquette books." Camilla's hands fluttered uselessly by her side.

"Well, by all means. Amend the etiquette books." He looked around. "Is my little brother around, by any chance?"

"He's gone—" She gestured, her hand waving in the direction of the cathedral. "To, um... Speak. With his uncle. Your uncle, I mean. About the annulment and other things."

Captain Hunter looked heavenward, as if beseeching some unknown power.

"So. Let me guess. Adrian found himself married at gunpoint—God, I have *no* idea how that happens to a man—and rather than tell his older brother about it, which would involve admitting that he was wrong, he asked Denmore for help. Denmore, of course, didn't give two sweeps of a broom about what had happened, and demanded some sort of quid pro quo. Have I got that right?"

Camilla bit her lip.

"That goddamned man. I *told* him so—but never mind. Here I am, forgetting my manners, and this *is* in the etiquette books. I'm Adrian's brother, and captain of *The Pursuit*. I was informed that my brother had wed, and suspected it was part and parcel of this entire mess, which meant he'd come back to Denmore eventually."

He must have heard about it from…someone at Harvil? No, not that. He'd called her Camilla *Worth*. "But how did you know my real name?"

"Ah!" His face cleared. "As to that. I've something for you." He reached into his pocket and withdrew a piece of paper. "Here." He held it out.

She took it. It was sealed with a bit of wax, stamped with the initials *TLW*.

TLW? She had no idea who…

The wax snapped under her trembling fingers. She unfolded the paper.

Dear Camilla, the note read. *This is your sister, Theresa.*

Theresa. Good *God.* She almost dropped the letter. She'd just allowed herself to hope that her family might receive her if she tried one last time, but she'd only considered Judith— no one else. The last time she had seen Theresa, she had been a little girl tracing her ABCs.

Obviously time had passed, but Camilla had no image of her youngest sister at all.

We—and by "we", I mean Benedict and I, but also Judith and Christian—Christian is Judith's husband; you may remember him from the time he had our father convicted of treason—which is probably not the best introduction—and bother, I've used too many dashes and I have no idea where this sentence is going.

Dash it all!

A little punctuation humor to lighten the moment. Ha ha.

Camilla stared at the page. Oh, dear. The first thing she had learned about her youngest sister in almost a decade was that she had a dreadful sense of humor.

We have been looking for you. Judith misses you dreadfully. She wants nothing more than for you to come join us.

Camilla felt her vision blurring. No, she couldn't cry—it mustn't mean what it said, it *couldn't.*

The next paragraph was taken over by a different handwriting—the letters darker and less blocky.

Benedict here. That sentence seems to imply that Theresa and I are indifferent. We are not indifferent. I have little memory of you, but I have heard stories. You would be a ripping great addition to the family, thank you.

Theresa had apparently wrestled the paper back to add:

You did grow up with Judith and, quite frankly, we need someone to commiserate with us.

She is an absolute tyrant and I do not doubt you were right to stay away for so long.

The handwriting for the next line changed once again.

Theresa has no call to refer to anyone as a tyrant. The only hope the world has is that she is a girl and girls are very rarely allowed to take over everything. Judith is not a tyrant.

She is by far the least tyrannical of the two sisters I am acquainted with.

The letter resumed in Theresa's handwriting.

Since I must be honest: Judith is a perfectly good sister who would be improved only by being a little less perfect, but also, she favors Benedict over me and I refuse to turn a blind eye to injustice. You have been gone so long that she will no doubt favor you above us both, which will finally put us younger ones on equal footing.

Camilla felt overwhelmed in the best way possible.

Benedict took over again.

Please do not listen to Theresa. She will give you an ill opinion of us all, and you should only have one of her.

Back to Theresa's writing again:

We have become distracted from our mission, and I refuse to get distracted for longer than five minutes. It is Judith's birthday very, very soon, and we had hoped you might be willing to come for a visit.

Our direction is...

Camilla read this all in absolute bafflement. The last she'd seen Benedict, he'd been a child. When he was a toddler, she had used to carry him around the house and call him her sweet boy.

Theresa had been bossy even at six, but Camilla knew very little of her. She'd gone to China with their father while she was practically an infant, and most of what Camilla remembered was her absence, and then her return.

She had used to throw tantrums back then—loud, angry ones, ones that wouldn't stop until Anthony wrapped her up in his arms and held her so tightly she couldn't move. Theresa had *liked* that.

Of course, Theresa had grown out of the tantrums—children often did. It should have been impossible to imagine the friendly, familial bickering that the two engaged in, but...

She remembered it.

Not from Theresa and Benedict; they'd been too young to bicker properly. But Judith and Anthony had done it, and reading it now... Her heart ached.

She read the letter again.

She had no idea what Theresa and Benedict sounded like; the childish voices she could dimly recall no longer fit these two people who used words like 'tyrannical' and 'injustice.' But between the taunts, there was something there that made her yearn.

It hurt, to imagine being so comfortable in another person's presence that you could call them a tyrant to their face and not fear being tossed out. It hurt, and it felt good, and…

Camilla had been sent all over England. She had tried to make herself into half of what she could be just so she'd have the barest chance of acceptance. And all the while, they'd stayed together. They loved each other, just as Judith had said they would.

Camilla had given up *this* for gowns. She'd given up *this.*

She read the letter a third time. *Judith misses you dreadfully.* How? How could Judith miss her? How could it be that *anyone* remembered her enough to miss her? And if she missed her, why hadn't she written?

Camilla had spent her entire life hoping that *one* person would care for her. It was too much to discover that someone already did.

She burst into tears. Her whole heart hurt in the best possible way. She didn't have room in her soul to understand how this could have happened, but it was here.

"Oh, God," Captain Grayson said. "You're crying." He said it the way another man might have said, "Oh, God, I'm being eaten by wolves."

"I'm sorry." Camilla sniffled and tried to hold back her tears. "I hate crying, and I cry so easily. I haven't seen my sisters in years. I thought they didn't want me. I could barely even let myself think of their existence. This is…"

A gift, she wanted to say. But if she said those words, she'd start sobbing in earnest. "It's been a while since I saw my siblings. I have no idea what they're doing. You can't imagine."

The captain sighed. "I can imagine discovering that my brother was married because two hellions showed up in my office waving a duplicate from the General Register Office."

Camilla sniffled. "Very well. You win the competition. Have a biscuit."

"You're right. That was an unnecessary comment. You're here in our family home; I should endeavor to be polite. Have a handkerchief." He removed a square of beige linen from his pocket and held it out.

She took it. "I'm here in your family home. I should be the one who endeavors to be polite."

"That's true," he said. "Well, then. Don't get tears on the family carpets. Those could stain, and I would have to throw you out to defend the family honor."

She looked up at him. There wasn't so much as a single telltale flicker of amusement on his face to suggest that he was joking. If he were Adrian, he'd have been smiling at that remark.

Camilla blew her nose messily on the handkerchief he had given her and then looked up. "Oh dear. I hope that wasn't a family handkerchief."

"Yes." His voice was very dry. "It was. Non-Hunters who use it perish."

She looked over at him.

He held up his hands. "Adrian is going to kill me. I'm bad with tears. And comforting. I don't even know if I'm supposed to comfort you. Why isn't Adrian here?"

"He's getting us our annulment."

"You sound *so* excited." He practically rolled his eyes.

Camilla shook her head.

"Ah. *You* don't want an annulment."

"'Want' is a complicated word, Captain Hunter." Her voice was steady now. She folded the handkerchief and placed it on the side-table. "It's not that simple. What I want is to have not been forced into marriage at gunpoint in the first place."

"Oh." He considered this. "Shit." He winced. "Goddamnit, pardon my—I mean—"

"Don't worry." The very crassness of the word emboldened her. She looked over at him and met his eyes. "I am standing in excrement, and I want to not stand in excrement. We have an opportunity to clean the shit off our shoes. What we choose afterward…is complicated. And what I want…? I don't truly know. But you don't end up working with someone for a common goal for weeks on end without becoming friends. And when that person is Adrian…" She trailed off.

"Adrian is related to me," Captain Hunter said matter-of-factly. "You don't need to tell me how attractive he is. We are similar in countenance, and I have a mirror."

Camilla glared at him. "I'm beginning to think you are a terrible person."

That brought out a smile—the first one she had seen. "Oh, absolutely. I am. I gather that when Adrian returns, the two of you will have much to discuss."

That was an understatement. Camilla's hands wrung together. "Yes."

"Well, then. I won't complicate matters by waiting here with you. My questions are less urgent than the rest of your lives. I'll leave a note. When he has a chance, tell him I want to speak with him, will you? Don't tell him I said 'I told you so.' He already knows."

CHAPTER TWENTY-ONE

The papers were spread across Adrian's uncle's desk. Bishop Denmore nodded as he looked through them. Occasionally, he asked for explanation. Sometimes, he shuffled back through them.

Denmore waved one of the affidavits. "And could you get this Mrs. Martin to testify in person?"

Adrian thought of the angry elderly lady. "I gather she would love nothing more."

"Hmm." Another pause as his uncle once again re-read the telegrams. "My God. This is extraordinary." He looked up and smiled at Adrian. "This is truly extraordinary, Adrian. It's complete, and taken as a whole, it is utterly damning. You've done an amazing job."

Adrian could not help but feel a flutter of pride in his chest at that. He smiled shyly.

"I knew I was right to believe in you, to leave this in your hands," his uncle continued. "Thank you, thank you so much. This is wonderful. Lassiter will *have* to step down now."

"I'm glad to have helped." Adrian was going to have to mention the annulment himself, he supposed.

"I don't know how ever I will thank you for your assistance," his uncle said.

"Well." He could not have found a better entry to the subject. "As it turns out—you may recall—a very good way to thank me already exists. You promised to assist me in the matter of the annulment of the marriage that was forced upon me in this matter?"

His uncle looked down at the papers on his desk, not meeting Adrian's eyes, and Adrian's heart fell.

Denmore smoothed the papers over, once and then again, before he spoke. "We mustn't rush into this."

Adrian wasn't sure who *we* was supposed to be.

But his uncle gave a nod, as if he had just convinced himself. "That's precisely it; we mustn't rush ourselves. We must consider it very carefully. Mustn't we?"

"I was forced to join myself for life to a woman I barely knew," Adrian said, "with a gun pointing at me. I personally feel that rushing is an appropriate response in such circumstances."

"Quite, quite!" The bishop looked up. "My dear boy! That's an excellent point. If we had wanted to take action on this front, we should have done so immediately. Now, weeks later…"

Adrian stared at him. "You're joking. You were the one who counseled me to wait."

"I would not call it 'counsel,'" his uncle said thoughtfully. "Via telegram? More a suggestion. Think of what a mess this is. I couldn't support your bringing a claim. There would be public scrutiny. I should have to admit that you were a relation of mine, and how would that appear? My own nephew, serving as valet to another bishop, to obtain information on his wrongdoing? That would make me seem underhanded."

"That would be the truth," Adrian said, even more disturbed than before. "You *told* me to do it, and I didn't want to. If you knew it would be a barrier to your acknowledging me, why did—"

"I didn't expect you to get caught!"

"You *told* me to act as his valet. You obtained references. You told me to obtain information on his wrongdoing. All of this happened because *you* wanted it. You say you didn't expect me to get caught, but what did you think would happen when the entire world discovered that the man that Bishop Lassiter thought of as his one-time valet was actually your nephew?"

Denmore stared unblinking in front of him for a few moments. "Oh. I hadn't thought that far ahead."

He hadn't, Adrian realized, thought of it at all. He hadn't imagined how any of this would take place. Maybe he might have vaguely intended to acknowledge Adrian if he could figure out how to do so without consequence. But he had not given it any real consideration.

Adrian just shook his head. "Of course it makes you look underhanded. That's because your behavior in this entire affair *has* been underhanded."

"That's...technically the truth. But..."

"It's *actually* the truth. Not technically so."

"Well, perhaps, but how was I to know that you were going to insert yourself in the story in this manner? If you'd only—"

"No," Adrian said, standing up. "You will not pin the blame for this on me. *You* asked me to act in this manner; I had doubts. You directed me to continue the investigation after it had gone awry. Against my misgivings, because I believed you actually cared for my future, I went along with it. I did everything you asked. All I want is one thing and you *owe* it to me."

His uncle looked at him. "Is she so terrible, then? The woman you've been married to?"

"That's not the point." Adrian glared at him.

"Who is it?"

"Her name is Camilla Worth. She's a lovely woman, and she doesn't deserve to be forced into marriage either."

"Well!" His uncle brightened. "To my mind, it sounds like you've managed to find a better woman than someone like you could expect. What are you complaining about again?"

Someone like you.

Someone like you.

Adrian hadn't wanted to believe it.

Oh, that was stupidity. He had known it all his life. He had known it from the moment his uncle refused to acknowledge his own sister. He had known it from the moment he had been introduced as his uncle's page instead of his nephew. He had lied to himself, telling himself that if he was kind enough, if he was understanding enough, he would show his uncle the truth—that he and his mother deserved love, deserved recognition, deserved everything that Adrian had wanted to believe him capable of.

All that time. All that effort. All that putting his heart into it, for this moment.

Someone like you.

He tried anyway, one last time. "Please," he said. "For the love you bear for me. For the love you bear for your sister. Help me."

"Oh, Adrian." His uncle just smiled. "Now that I hear what you've said, I really *do* believe this is all for the best. This can't come out in public. Lassiter will step down, once I let him know what I know. We'll keep it all silent, as it should be. And one day—when this has all blown over—one day, then, I'll acknowledge you."

There was no one day. There was only a string of todays, a string of empty promises.

"I have quite a lot to do with everything you've done for

me," Denmore said. "Do you think you could show yourself out?"

～

The wait for Adrian to return seemed almost interminable to Camilla. She didn't know what to do; she had a family, and they...wanted her? If that were true, might it not be possible that Adrian could want her, too?

He'd implied as much. He'd looked at her as if she were precious. He'd told her that she deserved a choice of her own —that she deserved to be *chosen,* not just accepted.

Was it so wrong that she was beginning to believe him?

She had never known that joy felt almost the same as despair. Her heart was so full that it strained its boundaries, overflowing to the point that it might burst.

Good that she was used to heartbreak; she suspected if he wanted her upon his return, she would break into pieces. Every sound that filtered into the room from the street below brought her to a height of dizzying fear, mixed with hope.

Hope. Hope, the thing that had always ripped her heart in two. Hope, the thing she had held onto despite—perhaps *because* of—the pain.

Hope that he would come back. Hope that Adrian would return and look at her and say, *I wanted a choice. Now I have one. I choose you.*

It was growing dark when she heard footsteps outside— determined footsteps, slowing before the door.

It might not be him.

Camilla's pulse picked up nonetheless. She made herself breathe—slowly, surely, as if she were awaiting news no more dire than what she would have for breakfast or whether Parliament had decided to change some law on foreign importation that would no doubt one day affect the price of whiskey.

She could not fool her body; her heart raced faster and faster.

The footsteps outside stopped; the door opened. She could imagine him in the hall below. The lamps were lit. In that golden splendor, his skin would glow.

She could hear the muffled sound of his voice, addressing the housekeeper, his footsteps as he ascended the stair.

Her hands clenched on the arms of her chair.

His footsteps stopped outside the door of her bedchamber.

There he was, rapping for entry.

"Yes?" She managed not to sound nervous.

Her whole chest burned, as if it were she being opened wide instead of the door.

He stood in the doorway.

She had no idea what he was thinking. She couldn't tell; her own imagination was going so wild that he would have to tell her.

Their eyes met, his that dark, rich brown she had come to…what was the word? Ah. Yes. Love. She had come to love him. She had thought she loved him before, and every time she decided she did, she found new depths of emotion that made her see how shallowly she'd cared.

She knew how sweet he could be. How gentle. How clever. How… *Everything.*

It wouldn't break her to lose him any more than any of her other losses had broken her. He'd helped her see that she was strong enough to withstand anything, even the loss of him. Still, she hoped that tonight, she wouldn't need strength any longer.

"Camilla." His voice was a low whisper. Slowly, he shut

the door behind him. That was intent in his voice. He came to stand in front of her.

She ought to stand, but she wasn't sure her knees could bear her weight.

Then he smiled at her, and her world broke into sunshine.

"Will you be mine?" he asked.

That painful ache in her chest squeezed more painfully. She was all too aware of her surroundings. Of the creak of the floor as he shifted toward her. Of the sound her breath made as it left her lips.

She could feel her mouth cracking into the most absurd smile she had ever worn. All the hope she had been nurturing —she had carried it this far, and she had finally been rewarded.

"*Yes.*" The word burst out of her. "Yes, yes. Yes, I will."

His smile tilted; it felt almost tender.

They had found each other, and they would belong to each other.

He sat on the arm of the chair next to her. Slid his arm around her. "Will you be mine now?"

"In every way."

His lips touched hers. There was a sweetness to his kiss, one she hadn't expected.

"Horehound?" she murmured against his lips.

"Guilty." He wrapped his arm around her, pulling her closer. "I bought a sack in town. I'm sorry it took me so long to return. I wanted to think things over, to be sure of what I wanted."

She was what he wanted. She realized it with a sense of wonder. *She* was who this brilliant, wonderful man desired.

"I brought back most of it for you. I thought you might…"

"Like something to suck on?" Camilla said sweetly. "Why, yes. I suppose I would."

He laughed and leaned to touch his forehead against hers. "My Camilla. I…"

"I'm going to make you happy," she told him. "I want nothing more."

He touched his fingers to her cheek. "I have every hope you'll succeed."

And then he kissed her. His lips were soft and gentle, and the touch of his hand, grounding her in place, made all those years of misery seem almost worth it. He had chosen her. He had *chosen* her.

They were married in name; they would be married in truth when they were finished.

He pulled her close, close enough that she could feel the strength in his arms, the planes of his chest. "God," he said, "I've been wanting to do this for so long."

Another kiss, this one long and lingering. He tasted sweet, like her future, and she could see it spread before them. She would take to being his wife with alacrity. She would introduce him to her family, and stand by him if they were rude; she would learn her duties and do whatever was required. She would have his children and make jokes with his brother and have a life filled with sunshine and joy.

She could hardly bear to believe that she had somehow earned this joy.

His hands slid to her ribs, and slowly he stood. She stood with him. It felt natural to touch him like this, natural for their bodies to wind around each other. He pulled her to the bed. They sank down against the covers together. His weight was solid on top of her, solid and real and here, and…

And, oh God, she still wasn't prepared. She'd bolstered herself for heartbreak, but she'd wanted *this*. She'd wanted it so much.

He had chosen her. He had actually chosen her.

"I am going to make you so happy," she whispered again.

It was a promise; it was more. She had so much joy in her now that she could not possibly keep it all to herself.

His mouth levered hers open. He tasted of something that was dark and caramelly. She opened to him and to the unbearable sweetness of the moment.

"Camilla, sweetheart." He slid to the side. She almost protested the loss of him, but he didn't take his hands off her. Instead, he undid her sash. Camilla worked the laces of her gown, until they were loosened, and the whole thing could come off.

His eyes lingered on her ankle. His gaze shifted up…

"You lovely woman," he breathed. He took off his own coat and laid it next to her gown.

He undid her corset; she fumbled with the buttons of his shirt. Every so often, their eyes would meet and their fingers would slip. She would stroke his satiny skin, or his knuckles would brush the tip of her nipple through her corset…

She was on fire for him when he got her down to her shift. When he had on nothing but trousers, and a bulge in them, too.

He stood and undid the buttons slowly, stripping his trousers away to reveal lean hips meeting a sculpted stomach in a perfect cursive V. At the apex…

She slid her hand along that perfect line between thigh and torso, following it from hip to majestic point. God, he was perfect there, too. Dark skin, edging darker still at the tip of his penis. Erect and so lovely.

He let her play her hand along the length of him, exploring the entirety of the organ that would enter her, from root to end. Her body clenched in liquid anticipation.

She looked up at him. He knelt on the bed below her.

"Adrian?"

He set his hands on the hem of her shift. "Camilla?"

"Please."

He took her shift off. For a moment, they looked at each other. The air was cold against her skin; her nipples pebbled in response. Then, ever so slowly, he set his hands on her knees and slid them apart. He inched forward, and set his mouth...

Oh, God. She'd imagined that sort of a kiss before in her wickedest dreams, and had been shocked at herself even then. Reality was even more delightfully shocking. His tongue swirled against her thigh, then up, until the tip slid inside her. She let out a little gasp.

He glanced up at her with a smile that could not have been more self-assured. As if he knew exactly what sort of pleasure shot through her at that lick. And the next one. His hand came up; his mouth shifted, clasping onto a point higher, and Camilla let out a squeak.

"Sweetheart. It does get even better."

She nodded. "Of...course it does."

He set his lips back against hers, and... And it got even better. Lick by lick. Swirl by swirl, until she shut her eyes and saw a spiraling pattern against her vision. Her fists clasped against the bedsheets, squeezing. Her thighs clamped around his shoulders.

"There."

"Yes." She felt breathless, even though she was scarcely moving. So little—just the shift of her hips in time to the thrust of his tongue. She was on the verge of something powerful, something bigger than she'd ever experienced. She was on the verge of...

Of Adrian pulling away. Cool air touched her thighs. She looked up at him, and for one second, dark doubts assailed her.

No.

He didn't really want her. He'd done this to prove he could have her. He meant to leave her here and—

And no. No. She stopped before her fear of the past caught up with her.

Adrian could never be cruel. Her doubts were unworthy of him.

She let herself frown a little. "You stopped."

A little smile touched his lips. "I didn't realize you'd warm so easily. And there's much I haven't done to you yet."

"Do it all."

He set his hands on her hips and came up off his knees until he was over her. "Don't you worry, my lady Camilla. I will." His fingers whispered up her sides. He leaned down, and his mouth caught her nipple.

She made a choking sound.

"Ah, you like that." He licked around her areola, then gave her a determined suck. Her eyes fluttered shut again. She'd been on the brink of desperation when he'd stopped before; he drove her back to that brink now, desperate and needing. Wanting him. Wanting all of him.

And then she had it. A pressure—welcome, at this point needed—between her thighs. Pushing. Her body opened to him. He entered her slowly, masterfully. She felt herself stretching around him. She needed him so much.

He wasn't holding back any longer. It was too late for an annulment now. It was too late to say no, and she never wanted to do it.

Now they were one.

He let out a sigh. She opened her eyes again to see him watching her tenderly. Perfectly.

He had *chosen* her. She would never stop grinning. He had chosen *this*, between them and nobody else, for ever and ever, for the rest of their days. She gave everything up to him.

He moved inside her. There was a delicious feel where they joined. She could drown in the sensation of his hands moving on her, of her body accepting his, over and over. The sound of their bodies made delightful music.

His mouth found hers once more. The sweetness she'd tasted before mixed with her own musk. His kiss lingered and possessed. His thrusts turned harder. Faster. He claimed her all over, and she gave herself up to him.

All of her.

She let go all at once, in a spill of perfection. She felt her body squeezing, catching fire...

And he did, too. She could feel the heat of him. His hands clenched into her hips. He let out a noise, a perfect little growl, as he came.

"Adrian." She ran her fingers along his brow. It was damp with exertion. She looked up at him. "Adrian, sweetheart."

"Camilla." His eyes met hers. "God, I have wanted to do that for an age."

"And now we can."

They lay in each other's arms. His hand stroked down her hair. It felt almost like perfection.

It took a moment to remember. "Your brother came by."

He shut his eyes. "Oh, God. Grayson. He is going to be an absolute wretch. I have no idea what to tell him."

"He had—of all things—a letter from my sister and brother. They..." She smiled shyly. "They asked us to visit? And—" It occurred to her suddenly, and another jolt of happiness raced through her. "They've met Grayson, and they want us to visit?"

"That's lovely." He stroked his hand down the side of her face. A flicker of a smile touched his lips again. "Family is lovely. Even if Grayson is a wretch."

She smiled back. "So. Do I get to meet this uncle of yours while we're here?"

He tensed beside her. "Camilla."

Just that one word and the doubts she had thought

banished rose to the surface of her consciousness, like gold-fish rising in a pond to be fed.

She was imagining things. She was so used to unhappiness that she could not let herself believe…

But no. She *wasn't* imagining it. Adrian had pulled away. Just an inch, but it was there between them.

"Do you not want me to meet your family?"

He sat. Put his hands over his eyes. "Family." The word sounded so bitter. How could he be so bitter about a word like that at a time like this? "I won't call him that anymore. I asked him for one thing. One thing. And I was fed…that astonishing pack of self-serving lies."

Camilla felt her whole body go cold. "What happened?"

He scowled up at the ceiling. "It's too late, he said. We waited too long. If his colleagues find out that his own nephew posed as a valet, it will make him seem under-handed. He can't stick his neck out for me, no. Not even after all that I've done. And I should be happy that you are not a complete wretch."

Oh.

It was all she could think at first. Her happiness felt cold and out of place.

Oh. Oh. Of course he hadn't chosen her.

He turned to her. "Oh—no, Camilla. I didn't mean it like that. The one thing he was right about was that I am unstintingly lucky that it was *you* I was tied to. I went for a long walk afterwards. I didn't know what to think; I felt numb all over. The only thing that made it bearable was knowing that it was you. I promise you, the thought of you was like a ray of light amidst all the darkness."

He hadn't chosen her.

"I'm not upset about you at all. It's about him. About my own expectations." His voice shifted—higher, more quavering—as if he were imitating his uncle. "'My dear boy, it's better than someone like you could have expected.' I'm such a damned idiot."

It wasn't about her at all. This last hour, when he'd brought her to bed? It hadn't been about her.

She ought to have burst into tears at that. It hurt enough. But she'd cried too much today already.

Camilla shrank back. She didn't want her mind to work, but it did. It was working all too well. "He…was not willing to assist you in obtaining an annulment?" She should have asked outright, but she had been so happy that she hadn't questioned.

"No. Grayson was right." Adrian turned around. "And I'll have to tell him so. I've come to realize that I doubt my uncle actually thinks of me as a blood relationship. I'm a convenient tool, and his only surprise is that I expected him to care about me in return for the care I gave him. Tools shouldn't ask for a response."

She shouldn't focus on what this meant for herself. He'd just had his heart ripped out. He'd lost something—something enormous—and she knew she should comfort him. She had promised to make him happy, after all.

Nonetheless, the next quavering words out of her mouth were these: "You didn't choose me?" She had thought…

After how he'd held her. After what he'd said on the train. After everything that had just happened…

Camilla was all too good at inventing encouragement; she'd done it often enough.

She was sure that if she went through it all, she could find all the ways she had misstepped, the ways that she had imagined appreciation where there was none.

She had invented it all, a tale of love and forever out of lustful looks and a weeks-long friendship. She'd put her heart on her sleeve once again. She'd imagined that he would choose her, that he'd *want* her.

She'd prepared to have her heart shredded. She hadn't prepared for this—to have it taken from her, treated with gentleness, and then burnt to a crisp in a blast furnace.

Adrian turned to her. The harsh, unforgiving lines of his face melted. "Oh, Cam." He came to sit next to her. His arm went around her. "I won't lie to you. No, I didn't choose you. But you have been everything to me these last weeks. I didn't choose you, but I do choose this: I choose to make the most of what we have."

Before she'd come to know Adrian, she would have accepted that. Second best was still a form of best, after all.

But she hadn't just wanted him to want her. She wanted everything he had painted in that idyllic picture weeks ago, when he'd told her why he wanted an annulment. She wanted a slow falling in love. She wanted a merging of friendship and adoration. She wanted a promise of mutual joy. She thought she had found it.

He hadn't found any of that with her. She would always be his forced bride. She would always know that they were joined with a pistol and a deception first, and his uncle's betrayal second. She would never know what it was like to be chosen.

She leaned her head against his shoulder. "Adrian. I'm so sorry."

She was. For both of them, she was sorry.

He brushed his lips against her forehead. "Don't be sorry," he said lightly. "We'll make do. We're remarkably good at that."

CHAPTER TWENTY-TWO

C amilla made herself retain her composure through the dinner and the bath that followed. She made herself laugh when he said something funny; she reminded him to contact his brother, and she nodded when he sighed and promised to do it in the morning. She made herself act as if her heart was still intact.

He joined her in bed that night. She would have given him anything, but he just held her tightly, the clench of his muscles saying all the things he did not speak aloud.

He hadn't chosen her.

She felt the moment when he drifted off to sleep, his arm around her loosening.

The lamps were out. She was in his arms. All she had to do was forget what she knew, forget what she wanted, and this could be her everything.

He held her for comfort, and it *was* comforting. He was the farthest thing from a monster; Adrian had suffered a horrific blow delivered by a man who ought to have cared about his welfare.

He'd brushed it off as best as he could, but…

She knew what he had done for his uncle. He didn't deserve this.

And yet, that also meant…

It meant, quite simply, that he didn't deserve to be saddled with her. That he deserved the choice he wanted.

Once, she might have thought that in sorrow. But with his arm around her, in the dark of the night, it felt like simple, rational truth.

He'd wanted a choice. He'd wanted a slow falling in love. He'd wanted a family and joy. Instead, he'd found betrayal and tears. No matter how Camilla valued herself, she could not take that away. She would always be inextricably tied with his uncle's treachery.

And she? Gently, she pulled his arm off her. She turned to face the wall.

She hadn't said it to him. The fact that his uncle's betrayal hurt her, too, was not something he needed to grapple with at the moment.

But it had wounded her deeply.

He didn't deserve to be saddled with her, and *she* didn't deserve to be a saddle. She deserved to know that the man she spent the rest of her life with wanted her. Valued her. Believed in her. *She* deserved a choice, and a family, and joy, and a slow falling in love…

If she did nothing, he wouldn't have that. Neither would she.

She slipped out from under the covers. Her feet found the cold planks beneath.

She'd always paced when she thought, and she did it now, hopping around the parts of the floor that squeaked under her passage so as not to wake him.

One turn of the room, and her mind was boiling.

She didn't deserve this. She didn't deserve to spend the rest of her life wondering if he was regretting her at the moment. When they argued—and she was sure they'd find cause to disagree, as all people did—she *deserved* to know that he would strive to listen because he wanted her above all others. Not because he *needed* to.

She did not deserve to wonder if he was envisioning someone else or if he mourned the woman he had not had the chance to choose.

She didn't deserve a lifetime of not knowing.

A second turn about the room. She watched his slumbering form, a dark lump under the blankets. One arm was poised over the empty shell of covers she'd left on the bed, as if he were still trying to comfort her, even in his sleep.

Camilla gave her head a shake. She was being dreadfully unfair. Adrian wouldn't do that to her. He'd never let her know that he had doubts. He wasn't the sort to hold her worries over her head.

But she *would* wonder. As much as she would tell herself not to, she would.

She made a third circuit. There were worse things than a marriage where she wondered, were there not? He wouldn't beat her. They had a firm friendship and a physical rapport. She loved him, and she had no doubt he would deserve that love every day of her life.

She had almost completed her fourth circle of the room, had almost convinced herself that she would grow used to this new reality. Her feet had warmed with her exertion. She loved him; was that not enough?

What did it matter, when there was nothing to be done about it? It would be enough. It had to be.

But deep inside her, Camilla had always had a dream. She had spent so long wanting someone to love her. She'd wanted to be chosen, to be wanted. She'd made bargains walking back from the store in the snow—"please, if she will just love me, I'll never complain about anything again."

She was no longer the woman who made desperate bargains for distant dreams.

She didn't deserve to be loved as second place. She deserved to be loved without reservation or condition.

She deserved more. *He* deserved more. And just because the thing she wanted was impossible...

That didn't mean she needed to give up hope.

She stopped walking. She stared straight ahead, thinking. They would have to get an annulment. They'd consummated the marriage, true, but she'd never been a virgin in the first place, and she'd read the reports. Others had lied about the matter; why couldn't she?

She wanted a choice.

She imagined the world where she had that choice. In order to get there, she would have to obtain an annulment. An annulment in this circumstance meant power, and power meant...

She had not thought of the letter from Theresa, not since Adrian returned.

Judith missed her.

Judith wanted her.

Judith was married to a marquess and living in Mayfair. Maybe, once she heard the whole story, she'd reject Camilla as unfit.

But even if Judith wanted nothing to do with Camilla, that too was useful. She could make a fuss until Judith gave in.

Camilla exhaled.

Camilla didn't need anyone to love her—she'd done without it long enough that she knew she could make do. Hope had given rise to certainty—someday, some way, she *would* have it.

Camilla needed someone powerful.

She *had* someone powerful.

She crept out of the room before she even quite knew what she was thinking, down the stairs, and found paper and a pen in an office on the ground floor.

My dear Adrian, she wrote.

I refuse to accept the outcome that we have been given. I refuse to accept that we have no choice.

I am going to get our choice back by the means available to us. You can find me at my sister's, if you wish; your brother will have the direction.

Your friendship has been the greatest gift that I could have known. I hope that even after we are separated, we are able to continue our acquaintance.

If I had been given the chance to choose your friendship from the start, I would choose you again—and again—and again. I would choose everything about you except the one thing I have been given, which is a you who did not choose me.

Yours, most truly,

Cam

She couldn't find the blotting paper in the dark—not without upending the desk drawer and risking detection. Instead, she watched the extra ink bead, then dissipate into dark, spidery stains on her letter. She sat at the desk and watched the letter, making excuse after excuse why she should forget this all.

She sat thinking until the clock struck four in the morning.

There would be an early train to London; there was no more time to delay. She knew what she wanted; she just had to go get it before she lost her nerve. Camilla found her cloak on the hook in the wardrobe by the hall. She still had some coins left from the money he had once given her in her pocket.

But now, now that she was pulling the fabric about her, now that she had written the letter, now...

She didn't want to leave. She wanted to stay here, to pretend that she'd never had the idea. She wanted to choose him in truth. She loved him; she didn't want to leave.

Her eyes stung.

But no. There were things she wanted more.

Her chin went up. It was time to go, before he awoke. Before she lost her nerve.

She slipped out the front door, closing it gently behind her.

The moment her feet touched the cold cobblestones, she realized her mistake—in her haste, she'd left her shoes behind.

Or maybe, perhaps, she hadn't truly forgotten.

Maybe she'd wanted to go back. Maybe she'd left them behind as a sign of cowardice, forcing herself to let go of a choice she knew she had to make.

Camilla was not going to be a coward.

Her chin went in the air, and she took another step forward. Thousands went without shoes every day. She could make do.

Another step, and another, and with every step, the cold bit into the soles of her feet.

It didn't matter. None of it mattered. She'd be in London by morning, and she didn't need shoes for what she was going to do.

CHAPTER TWENTY-THREE

The speed of modern transport meant that it was just past seven in the morning, with the sun already beating down oppressively overhead, when Camilla arrived in London. The price of the ticket had taken most of her reserve funds; what remained was not enough to hire transportation of any stripe to the Mayfair direction given in Theresa's letter.

Or, for that matter, to purchase a pair of shoes.

She'd walked only to the train station, and then off the train—not so far to go, even without shoes, she had thought. A mere half-mile. She'd walked a hundred times that with shoes that were falling apart. Her feet almost never got cold; how bad could it be?

It turned out that even the least successful shoe was a vast improvement over pavement on bare skin.

After quick consultation with three people—one of whom refused to speak to her, with a pointed sniff at her bare feet, and one of whom propositioned her rather than answer her questions—she finally was told how best to proceed to her sister's home.

It was several miles more.

Her bare feet didn't draw quite as much attention in the near vicinity of Paddington. Still, she made the acquaintance of every sharp stone between Paddington Station and Mayfair. None of it hurt as much as the deep, bruising ache in her heart. *He hadn't chosen her.*

The further she went, the more her feet hurt, and the more people glanced down and then up, a sneer on their faces. She really didn't belong here. She wanted nothing more than to stop, to sit down, to give her soles the rest they screamed to have.

But the houses around her grew nice, then comfortable, until finally they were downright imposing. There could be no stopping. She'd be told to leave the minute she looked like she didn't know where she was going.

It took her hours to traverse the distance. By the time she arrived, she was half-limping. Still, when she finally stood in front of the white stone building where Theresa had directed her—large and imposing, four stories high, flowers in the windows—she stopped and almost wished she could go back.

Her heart was beating fast, so fast. What if Theresa had been wrong? What if it was a lie? Reality had played cruel tricks on her over the years. Her whole body ached with the cruelty of the last one.

It was almost impossible to believe that this was not yet another cruel trick.

What if they didn't want her?

Her hand crept to her pocket; she checked the direction on the letter one last time, just to be sure.

Hope was a choice. It had always been a choice, from the first moment she decided to hold on to it. It had been hope that pushed her from bed this last night, and hope that put one bare foot in front of the other all the way here. Camilla inhaled, made fists of her hands, and chose—foolishly, despite all possible evidence—to trust in it one more time.

Her chin went up; she climbed the stone stairs to the entrance. The door did not open for her. Of course; she wasn't expected. On the other side, she could imagine a footman glaring at her barefoot form.

She rapped the knocker and waited.

No response came. She rapped again.

Finally, the door opened an inch. The man who blocked that narrow gap glared down at her. "The servant's entrance is round the back. If you have business, apply there."

Camilla straightened her spine. "I'm not a servant."

"Then shoo altogether."

She wouldn't start this way. She wouldn't act as if she were begging for scraps.

Deep down inside her, she remembered the child she had once been—the one who might have been entitled to enter here. That girl had been disabused of most of her finer notions, but Camilla would do her best to remember.

"You have to let me in." She refused to speak quietly or demurely. She refused to let any hint of a quaver show. "I don't need to go 'round the back. I wish to have a word with Lady Judith. I *must.*"

The man grimaced and attempted to shut the door. Camilla stuck her foot—her bare foot—in the way, and winced as the wood struck her abused flesh.

"Move," the man hissed, "or be moved. And you will refer to the lady of the house as Lady Ashford. Don't speak of her in such familiar tones."

"I shall speak of her any way I wish," Camilla said, "because—"

There was a great clamor in the hall behind the butler. He turned, and Camilla took advantage of his temporary inattention to shove her way into the entry. She looked up.

Judith stood at the end of the hall. *Judith.*

God. It had been almost a decade since Camilla had seen her sister. Last time she'd seen her, Judith had been selling all her frocks. She'd been dressed in ugly wincey, and she'd looked pale and wan with grief.

This was an older Judith. She was rosy-cheeked and plump once more, dressed in a fine blue day gown and silk slippers. There were pearls at her ears.

Camilla didn't look down at herself. She knew how dingy her gown was. She hadn't had a traveling cloak to keep dust off her, and her clothing was stained with soot and smoke from the journey. She was all too aware that she had no shoes, that her feet were black with dirt and…well, she didn't really want to know what else.

The butler turned back to her.

She looked like a servant. Honestly, that was unfair to servants. At the moment, she looked far worse than one.

Judith's hands went to her mouth. Her eyes shone. "Camilla?" Her voice was low.

A man came to stand behind her sister. Camilla knew him, too—he'd visited their family often as a child. Christian.

Another woman joined them—tall and blonde and willowy, dressed in a pink gown with frothy lace at the edges. She was—inexplicably—holding a fork in one hand.

"Camilla?" that woman asked.

Camilla didn't know if she was welcome or not. She didn't know how to ask. But then Judith ran to her—slipping, barely catching herself on an ornate side-table in an attempt to stay upright. She didn't hesitate, not for one instant. She wrapped her arms around Camilla, soot and all.

She was warm and clean and—

"Oh, God, Camilla. Where have you been?"

Yet another woman appeared—this one, an elderly lady dressed in a dark purple gown. And another man—no, not a man, despite the height, not with that new fuzz on his cheeks. He was a boy.

That was *Benedict,* Camilla realized, the chubby five-year-old child she'd loved so well. He had grown taller than her.

That made that blonde, willowy lady who was watching her... Theresa?

Camilla could hear her heart hammering in her chest.

"Never mind," Judith was saying, taking her arm. "Listen to me. Come in. We have food and towels."

Camilla felt as if she'd faced down a wall, as if she'd pulled her fist back to punch it to pieces until she broke her hand—and as if the stone barrier that had reached impossibly far above her head had crumpled like paper. She was going to break down, right here. Right now.

She couldn't lose her nerve. "Judith," she said. "I need your help."

Judith was still clinging to her, and Camilla found she could not let go. All for the best; her sister hadn't noticed that Camilla's soot had transferred to her gown.

Camilla reserved a silent prayer of apology for whichever servant would have to remove it. She knew from bitter, personal experience precisely how long it would take.

"Anything," Judith said.

Camilla had to marshal her thoughts. There were years of explanation to give, and so much to hear in return. Right now, though, all of that distance boiled down to the last hours of her life.

"I'm married," Camilla said.

Her sister stared at her. "What?"

The elderly woman tilted her head. "To whom?"

Christian frowned, glancing at her bare feet. His question came out a little more of a growl, almost a warning. "When?"

Judith shook her head, brushing all that aside. "Do you love him?"

Adrian would be awakening just now. She could imagine him blinking in the sunshine. Reaching for her across the mattress. Not finding her.

Her breath seemed hot inside her, burning her lungs.

Adrian would look around the room. He'd wonder if she had gone to get something to eat. He'd find her note in the study...

She hoped he found the note soon. She hoped he understood. She didn't know if he would read it with relief or sorrow. She wouldn't know if he would understand the difference between fleeing him and fleeing the situation.

"It hardly matters," she said. "You see, I want—no, I *need*—an annulment. And you're the only one who can help me."

After all these years, her sister should have hesitated. She should have frowned, perhaps, or asked for more information. After all these years...

"Of course," Judith said. And she held her close.

~

A whirlwind descended before Camilla could understand what was happening.

Judith sent for a solicitor, and then—before she did anything else—she sent Camilla off for a bath in her private room. Because apparently that was the sort of thing her sister had now—an entire private bath.

The water was deliciously warm; the Marquess of Ashford ("Christian," he had said, "we knew each other when we were children, and you're not about to start calling me by my title now.") had plumbing and taps in the house, and there was as much hot water as Camilla could ever want.

The soap smelled of roses; a jar of bath oil released the scent of vanilla. Camilla changed the water twice, until it was almost clear when she rinsed.

A towel had been placed on a marble-topped table next to a dizzying array of glass jars. They were all labeled—skin cream that smelled of cherries, hand cream that smelled of oranges, foot cream that smelled of peppermint, eye cream that smelled of lavender.

Who knew there could be so much cream in the world?

She dipped her finger in each one. Aside from the scents and faint hints of color, she could not detect a difference between any of the creams. They all felt equally creamy.

Her feet hurt; tiny little cuts had broken the surface. She had bled and bruised. It was nothing that wouldn't heal in short order.

In an act of defiance, Camilla applied the hand cream to the soles of her feet. It was probably a dreadful faux pas; they would know her for the imposter she was the instant she set her orange-smelling feet outside of the bathroom.

It felt appropriate.

The towel had a sachet of lilac folded inside; the soft, fluffy robe hanging on a hook smelled of cinnamon and cedar.

She'd forgotten how the wealthy could surround themselves with scent, so much scent. They hardly had to smell the real world at all.

When Camilla finally opened the door to her sister's dressing room, she found Judith and Theresa awaiting her with two maids—Beth and Jenny, she was told upon inquiry.

Camilla had more in common with Beth and Jenny than Judith. If they'd worked in the same house, they would have thought themselves above her.

Camilla tried to protest that she didn't need help dressing, but Beth looked hurt and Jenny looked worried. She gave in.

One of the maids combed her hair, then vanished to

obtain hair pins. The other brought in gowns that were too long.

"You're so short," Judith said. "When did that happen? Goodness."

But between the two maids, they pinned the hem in mere minutes.

A third maid arrived with a tray; she deposited a teapot, then a plate of sandwiches, and finally, biscuits.

"The biscuits are currant," Judith said. "The sandwiches are beef, pickled onion, Wensleydale, and a bit of horse-radish. One of my creations."

Camilla stared at them for a moment. "I had forgotten about you and sandwiches."

"Yes, well. If one is going to grow plump, it had best be on sandwiches." Judith offered her the plate.

Camilla picked one up and took a bite. Her stomach growled as she did, and oh, God, how had she not known how hungry she was? She hadn't eaten since the night before.

The sandwich was divine—the savory flavor of the beef mingling with the sharpness of the pickled onion, finishing with that little kick of horseradish.

"So," Judith said, as one of the maids came back into the room armed with a curling iron and sparkling pins. "Tell me about this marriage that must be annulled."

She didn't know how she managed to get through the entire story without sobbing, but she did it without a tear.

The last weeks sounded utterly unreal. Working for Rector Miles. The wedding at gunpoint. Adrian telling her they mustn't consummate their marriage. Their friendship; then working together. Telegrams, Mrs. Martin, then Kitty and finally, Adrian's uncle. That last betrayal was where she ended her story.

As Camilla spoke, she began to feel something besides heartbreak—something she'd been feeling ever since she wrote her letter in the middle of the night. She was beginning to be…angry. Actually angry. How dare Adrian's uncle treat his loyalty in so cavalier a fashion?

And for Adrian himself…

She loved him, but God, now that she'd had a moment to breathe, she wanted to scream at him.

Obviously, he'd been upset when he had come to her last night. She could hardly blame him. But he'd made a decision that he'd suffer through marriage with her, and he hadn't consulted her about whether she wished to be suffered with. After everything they'd been through? After he'd promised that they were allies and friends?

It was too much. Far too much. She had deserved better than to discover that she was his second-place prize after she opened her body to his. She had deserved better than to kiss him with her entire heart, only to discover that she'd only had half of his. She had deserved better, damn it.

She finished her sandwich and her story—skipping the parts about kisses and consummations because really, it wasn't any of Judith's business—and looked at her sister.

Judith had taken her hand about two sentences in and had not let go.

Judith didn't speak, not for a full minute. "All those years." Her voice shuddered. "All those years, every time you moved. Why didn't you *find* me?"

Camilla had managed to avoid tears all this time. But those years of loneliness choked around her now. Those years of hoping, dreaming, wanting, and never being fulfilled. She had to look away.

"You told me you never wanted to see me again."

Judith sniffled. "I didn't mean it. I was young. I was scared. I thought you'd go away forever unless I convinced you to stay."

"You told me I had to *choose.* You told me that it was either luxury or love, and I chose luxury."

"No, no."

"I thought I had bargained away all right to your love. I threw it all away. Willingly. How could I demand what I'd discarded?"

"Easily," Judith said. "Always."

"And how was I to find you? I wrote and you *never* answered."

Judith looked haunted. "It's a long story. I should have tried harder, but... I did write. I did not realize you were not in your uncle's care until a little over a year ago. That's when we discovered he wasn't passing on letters. He thought you were better off not hearing from us; I assume it must have gone both ways."

Camilla shut her eyes. "Dear God."

"As for the rest, we tried to find you. We traced you from place to place, until we finally heard that you'd left with some person—a rector whose name started with P? I suppose you must have gone from him to this Rector Miles."

Camilla shut her eyes. "That *was* Miles. He knew who I was; he knew that Benedict was going to Eton. He convinced me to change my name so nobody would use me to embarrass you."

"And you agreed to that?"

Camilla looked up. "Of course I did. I wanted you to have all the chances in the world to reclaim what we'd lost. Why wouldn't I?"

Judith stared at her. "Cam." She reached out and touched Camilla's face. "Wait here."

She stood. Camilla could hardly have moved. Beth was curling her hair, putting it up in little wisps. She couldn't remember the last time someone had made up her hair.

Judith came back a few minutes later, holding a packet of papers tied up in string.

"Here." She held it out to Cam. "Here they are. It's not all the letters I wrote you. But when you didn't respond, after a while I started saving them instead of sending them."

Camilla stared at the stack.

"There's letters from Benedict and Theresa mixed in there, too," Judith said. "Every Christmas. Every birthday. Every month, for years. I have a terrible temper. It's one of my worst qualities, and I try to rein it in. But when it breaks, I indulge in it spectacularly. I hold the worst grudges, I do. You know that about me."

Camilla nodded.

"But my sisters are my heart. How could I hold a grudge against my own self? What can I say, except that I'm sorry? You should never have felt that you didn't deserve love. That you had to hide who you were to keep us safe. I'm so sorry."

Camilla couldn't help it. All the emotion that she'd kept tightly wadded inside herself started to leak. Her eyes stung, then her nose ran, until she was crying in earnest, sobbing against her sister's shoulder.

"I kept imagining what would happen if I showed up and you didn't want me. This is like a dream," Camilla admitted, "one I will wake from at any moment."

"I can't imagine what you've experienced," Judith said. "I can't even try. But I love you. I love you, I love you. There is no alternative. There has been no waking world in which I did anything but miss you. You deserve to be loved, and I'll make up for every last year we've missed together."

They didn't speak for long minutes. They just held each other. Camilla felt her sister's hands on hers, her shoulder against hers. She leaned her forehead against her and breathed in all of her scents—rose, orange, cinnamon.

She deserved love. She *did.* And she wasn't going to miss

out on it simply because the man she'd fallen in love with had made a mistake.

After a while, there was a rap on the door.

"Judith." It was Christian. "The solicitor has arrived. Shall we speak with him?"

Camilla dried her tears. A maid wiped away all evidence of them with a rosewater wash and dabbed at her eyes with one of Judith's fancy creams.

"Yes," Camilla said. "Yes. I'll be ready."

CHAPTER TWENTY-FOUR

Camilla had known Adrian would come. The only question had been how long it would take him.

Adrian Hunter had arrived at four in the afternoon, after the solicitor had left, right in the middle of the appointment that Judith had made with a seamstress to take Camilla's measurements.

"Mr. Adrian Hunter is here to see Lady Camilla," a servant announced, as Camilla stood in her underthings, patiently allowing the woman to measure every inch of her body.

Judith—who had stayed in the room with her, as if she feared Camilla would disappear—frowned at this. "Do you know a Mr. Hunter?"

Biblically, Camilla did not say. *Just last night.*

"Technically speaking, we have been married for almost a month." Camilla looked upward. "Although you heard what the solicitor said—we're not supposed to hold ourselves out as married. But yes. I suppose you could say we are acquainted."

Judith's face hardened. "Cam, you don't have to speak to

him if you don't wish to. You heard the solicitor. It was one thing to stay with him when you had no choice. But your chances at an annulment will be best if you keep yourselves as separate as possible from this point onward."

Eventually, she would have to tell her sister what Adrian meant to her and what she truly wanted from him.

For now, she settled for a shake of her head. "Don't talk of him that way. You cannot understand how vulnerable I was when we were wed. There is not a better man in the entirety of England."

Judith just looked at her. "If you want to get an annulment, you shouldn't say things like that. People will take it amiss."

Now was not the point where she wanted to explain. "Just this once won't hurt. We've worked together this long; he deserves to have me personally explain what is happening. Please convey to him that I'll be there as soon as I'm able."

It was torture to finish the fitting; she was scolded three times for not being able to stand still. She could hardly help it; her heart was beating so. She could scarcely control the hopeful, involuntary clench of her hand. Her entire being wavered between delight that he'd arrived, and anger that he hadn't told her about his uncle.

He'd made her believe he'd chosen her. He'd told her that she deserved better and then not given it to her.

"Are you sure?" Judith said as the maids bundled Camilla into a day gown at the end of the fitting. "I'll come sit with you. You shouldn't be alone with a man. Your reputation—"

"Oh, for God's sake." Camilla rolled her eyes. "What reputation? I've spent the last nine years of my life having no reputation to speak of. I am about to get a marriage annulled publicly."

"I'm just trying to help."

Camilla reached over and patted her sister's shoulder. "I

appreciate it. Really, I do. You can help by telling me if my hair looks presentable."

"It's lovely, but Camilla—"

There was nothing for it. She'd been too long without an older sister; she couldn't let Judith smother her, not already.

"You can help," Camilla said, "by believing that in the years that have passed, I really have learned what's best for myself. I'm going to talk to Adrian alone, and you're going to let me do it."

Judith looked at her a long moment, then sighed and looked away. "Yes," she finally said. "I'm sorry. I just have so many years of care I've wanted to give you. It's hard not to give it all at once."

From the other side of the room, Camilla was aware of Theresa watching her intently. She hadn't spoken much beyond greetings. She'd actually seemed a little shy, which was odd, given how forward her letter was.

Camilla nodded. "I'll introduce you after we've spoken." She paused, tapping her lips. "One last thing about Mr. Hunter. I don't know if Theresa has mentioned it."

Theresa straightened, her eyes widening.

"What has Theresa to do with Mr. Hunter?"

Camilla looked in her sister's eyes. "Adrian is of African descent. If you in any way treat him as inferior because of that, I will walk out of this house and never speak to you again. I mean it. I may be annulling my marriage, but I know what it's like to be looked down upon. Don't do it."

Judith blinked. She did not speak for a moment. She looked down at her hands and then over at Camilla. "Well, I suppose it's best that we've all come down this path. I have not lived here all the time you've been gone. We used to live near the docks; I knew a great many people then that I'd never have been introduced to otherwise." She shrugged. "I'll still fight him if he hurts you."

Camilla exhaled. "I'm going to see him."

"This isn't what I assumed, is it?"

Camilla didn't answer. Instead, she let the maid guide her to the parlor where her quasi-husband waited. She found him pacing in front of the mantel, hands on his hips. He turned to her.

The last time they'd spoken, they'd been in the same bed. They hadn't had so much as a sheet between them. They'd been bare and naked and... And, oh, God, how had she forgotten?

He'd healed her and hurt her, all in the same moment. She could feel that hurt inside her like bruises in her chest, aching every time she drew breath.

Maybe he was remembering the same thing, because he didn't approach her. He just stopped next to the mantel, watching her with an unreadable expression on his face.

"Hullo, Cam," he finally said. "How are you?"

"Is that a polite 'how are you,' or a legitimate inquiry into my feelings?" She felt as if she were made of ice. "It's lovely that you remembered that I have them. A bit tardy, but lovely."

"Ah," he said in an annoyingly steady tone of voice. "You're a little angry. It's simply smashing that you can express your feelings aloud, clearly, in words face-to-face. I find that communication works best when we use words to say precisely what we mean, instead of leaving in the middle of the night with nothing to say where you'd gone except a note that might not be found for hours."

"I also believe in communication." She took a step toward him. "For instance, here are some words you might have said yesterday: 'My uncle won't grant us an annulment, so let's have sexual intercourse out of desperation.'"

"It wasn't like that. You know it wasn't like that."

"You're right." Her hands went to her hips. "I'm sure you

could have chosen other words in the moment. I would have accepted any words from you, in fact, except using no words at all."

"This is not all my fault. You didn't seem to be in a terrible hurry to stop and talk in the moment."

"No," Camilla said. "I admit as much. I was stupid with hope. I thought you had actually chosen to love me of your own free will. Don't worry; I blame myself for not asking as much as I blame you for not telling."

She could see the moment he understood how she must have felt.

His mouth slowly opened. The annoyance dropped from his stance. He took a step toward her. "Oh, Cam."

She hated that they were friends. She hated that she loved him. She hated that he could say those two words, just like that, and all she wanted was to sit next to him and weep on his shoulder.

He reached a hand out tentatively in her direction, but when she didn't lean toward him in response, he let it drop. "I'm so sorry. At the time I was thinking that if I didn't tell you, it wouldn't hurt you. You've been through so much. It was just one more thing for me to bear."

She shook her head. "I never want to be that one more thing for you to endure. Do you understand me?"

"Yes."

She hated most of all that the feelings she had been trying to ignore—the anger, the hope, the heartbreak, the joy turned to ash—bubbled over in that moment, stinging her eyes. She'd been holding the pieces of herself together through the night, through her journey, through a bath and her sister and a solicitor.

Her life had changed irrevocably, and there wasn't a person in it who she knew well enough to share her vulnerability. No one but Adrian.

She hated that she cried so easily. She hated that her eyes stung now. "I'm sorry I left the way I did, with only a note. I just thought that if I waited for you to wake up, I would never be able to leave you."

He took another step toward her, then another, and then she was in his arms, her head pressed against his chest, his arms around her.

His hand stroked her hair. He leaned down and whispered in her ear.

"Cam. I'm sorry."

She hated that he absorbed her tears. That he was the wall she could lean against, that he didn't think her weak or stupid. She hated that he understood every bitter tear that she shed.

"What were you thinking?" she sobbed.

"Not very much," he admitted. "I was hurt. I felt betrayed by my uncle. I…" His voice trailed off. "You know I've… wanted you for a while now. I wasn't thinking of you as one more burden. After the conversation with my uncle, I thought of you as something close to salvation, and I didn't want to delay any longer."

She couldn't keep the affection out of her voice. "We are rather lucky that out of all the millions of people in England, chance forced the two of us together."

He continued to pet her hair. "You're the best wife I've ever married at gunpoint."

"Shut up," Camilla said through her tears. "We cannot hold ourselves out as married. You know that."

"So…your sister thinks she can still do something about that annulment? After last night?"

Camilla nodded. "I haven't told her about last night. And you did say that the doctors can't really tell if I'm a virgin."

He just pulled her closer. "Do you want this? Do you really want this?"

He should have asked her that last night. Camilla wrinkled her nose. "You have undoubtedly put my hair in disarray. It was curled before."

"It looks pretty to me."

"I need to blow my nose."

He handed her a handkerchief.

"Still pretty," he told her, after she'd made an embarrassing noise. "So, I assume that if your sister is willing to help you, that she cares about you, then."

Camilla nodded again.

"Good," he said. "You deserve it."

Another breath; his arms were still around her. Camilla smiled. "I do, don't I? I deserve this." She looked up at him. "I deserve this. I deserve to know that I was chosen. That the man who married me adored me above all others. I deserve a slow falling in love."

He let out a little huff of laughter. "You know, the first time I told you that... I have to admit it may have been entirely self-serving on my part. I wanted you to believe it so that I wouldn't have to fight you about getting an annulment."

He was still holding her, and she couldn't help but smile. "I know. I realized it at the time."

"I wish I had been a little less self-serving then. That I'd thought a little more about you."

She shook her head. It took her a moment to collect her thoughts. "*I* don't. It never mattered to me that you were being self-serving. Most other men in your position wouldn't have told me I deserved *more* than I had received. They would have told me I deserved less. That I was unmarriageable. Unwantable, even." She inhaled and pulled away far enough to look him in the eye. "It says a lot about you, that your way of serving yourself was to tell me I was worthwhile."

"That sounds like a compliment."

"We're all self-serving." Camilla shrugged. "It's just a matter of what we do to others in service of ourselves."

"So." Adrian's hand stroked her hair. "You want an annulment?"

"I want a *choice*," she clarified. "I want to choose and be chosen."

"They'll interview us," Adrian said. "They'll ask if we've ever had intercourse. And if either of us say that we did… that will most likely be the end of it. No annulment. You understand that?"

"I do."

He tipped her chin up. "Are you asking me to lie under oath?"

Her heart was breaking. Her voice quivered. She looked up at him and told him the truth. "Yes?"

"If you want it, then I'll do it. You know how bad I am at lying. I'll practice. Grayson will have to help. But…" He hadn't looked away from her. His finger was still on her chin. His thumb came up, brushing her lips.

"But what?"

"But nothing." His arm tightened around her, and then he kissed her.

Her mind had not expected it. It went blank. Her body, though… Oh, her body had known. It had been wanting his lips against hers ever since he'd put his arms around her. No; ever since she'd seen him standing next to the mantel.

Her stupid body believed they belonged together, and before her mind could take the reins and demand that he give up this idiocy, her body rushed forward. Her hands crept around his neck. Her mouth opened to him. She pressed herself against him, giving herself into his kiss. Their tongues touched, gently at first, then with desperation.

The last remnants of anger faded into something softer. She was still stupid with hope.

This might be the last time they would kiss.

But he pulled away first, and when she brushed up on tiptoe to continue, he set his finger against her nose, stopping her. "That was also self-serving."

She found herself blushing. "Your self-serving nature suits me."

They stared at each other. His finger was still on her nose. He looked down at her, his eyes sparkling, and then…

Then he smiled.

"Lie about that, Cam," he said. "Lie about the times I touched you. Lie about the night we shared together."

His finger dragged down her nose and tapped her lips. He leaned down an inch until his nose brushed hers. She could feel the heat of him. Her heart beat heavily.

"Lie to whomever you want," he said quietly. "Just don't forget that it happened."

No. His skin was imprinted on hers. She'd never be able to step into the morning sunlight without thinking of his smile. She let out a shaky breath and found herself grinning.

"I see how it is now. 'I'm so sorry, Cam' didn't last very long, did it?"

His mouth tilted into a smile. "Well." He sounded just a little too self-satisfied. "I am incredibly sorry about hurting you. I'm not in the least bit sorry about the rest of it. I would do all of the rest of that again as often as you wanted it."

"I'll keep that in mind." She pulled away from him. "I still want the annulment. I still want to be chosen." Her heart pounded, and she hoped he understood.

"Well." He exhaled. "You know what would be helpful if we were to obtain an annulment?"

Ah. Here it came. "The solicitor said that it would probably be best if we did not see each other until after the proceedings." She didn't want to. She had grown so used to seeing him every day. "He told me to tell you that if you had something to tell me, you should send it to him. We don't want to make it look like…"

"Like we're friends?" he asked.

"They'll call it collusion. That's what the solicitor said. I hate it. I hate it. I know your uncle wouldn't acknowledge you, and if it will bother you too much, I'll tell them no—"

"Hush." He set a finger on her lips. "I asked you to do far more distasteful things for this damned annulment. I can manage silence. And that wasn't what I was going to say. I was going to say that it would be very useful for us to have all that paperwork we obtained. The affidavits. The accounts. Everything that sets forth the motive in question." Adrian gave her an easy smile.

"But you gave it all to your uncle, didn't you?"

"Well." He shrugged. "The affidavits will be easy enough to have redone. But it wouldn't be hard for me to get the rest. I could walk into his office and take it."

She stared at him. "Your uncle—you'd just walk into his office and steal the materials? I can't ask you do that for me."

He smiled. "You don't have to ask." He reached out and took hold of her hand. "You want us to have a choice, don't you? Let me go get us one."

~

Theresa was seated on her divan when Judith walked in.

There had been no time to explain what had happened since Camilla's arrival; Judith had sent for solicitors and seamstresses. It wasn't until now, with supper almost upon them, that she'd had a spare moment.

Theresa managed a little smile. "Happy birthday, Judith."

Judith sat next to her. Her expression was… Very hard to read. Her eyes were narrowed; her eyebrows made angry dark lines.

"Camilla mentioned that you knew about Mr. Hunter just now. She seemed to think that we had been expecting her. Theresa, what is going on? How did you get her direction? Why didn't you tell me you were in contact with her?"

Oh. Theresa's heart hurt just a little bit. She hadn't managed to do it right after all. She was going to get scolded again. Everyone was always telling her to think before she did something rash, and she *had* thought this time. She had thought a great deal.

If by *think before you act,* people meant *think what we want you to think,* Theresa wished they would just say so. It would make everything so much easier.

Only now that she knew Judith was going to be angry could she see how she'd misunderstood. It was entirely one thing to obtain a present like gloves in secret. It was another to hunt down a missing sister, to withhold what she had learned when she knew Judith was so desperate for information.

Sisters were not gloves; she ought to have known.

In her defense, at the time it had all made complete sense to her.

"I didn't have her direction," Theresa said. "I wasn't in contact with her. It was Mr. Hunter's brother who delivered the letter."

Judith just frowned at this. "But how did you know of Mr. Hunter?"

Theresa looked away. It hurt too much to try and look in Judith's eyes, and never mind that it made her look guilty not to meet her eyes. She *felt* guilty.

"Because we found her wedding in the marriage registry?" The *we* slipped out before she had a chance to think it through, and then she really was in a tearing panic. She really *hadn't* meant to get Benedict in trouble, too.

"The marriage registry?"

"The one at the General Register Office," Theresa admitted. "I...may have lied to you about the whereabouts of... Benedict and myself...for the last handful of weeks?" She scrunched in on herself, feeling like one of her cats. She'd dragged in a mouse and had expected praise for her prowess as a hunter.

"And so you found Mr. Hunter at the General Register Office?" Judith's voice was shaking. "I don't understand."

It was like they spoke two separate languages. No matter how hard Theresa tried to make herself understood, she always failed.

She glanced up. Judith was still staring at her; Theresa looked away.

"Theresa, how..." Judith did not seem to know how to complete her sentence. "When..." Another shake of her head. "What..."

"It was an accident," Theresa said, on the verge of panic. "Pure accident! Benedict and I happened to be looking at the folio of marriage registries at the exact right time. Had we tried a week before, we'd never have seen the entry, it was that new."

"I don't understand why you were looking at marriage registries in the first place."

"Well, it's because of the Births and Deaths Registration Act of 1836..."

Judith looked even more baffled at that.

Theresa would never know why people asked questions when they really didn't to know the answer. She shook her head and tried a different tack. "We utilized the process of elimination. *You* couldn't find Lady Camilla Worth anywhere, so either she was dead or she was using a different name. I eliminated the possibility that she was dead because it was inconvenient, and the most likely reason for her to change her name was marriage. So we looked through the registry of marriages. All of them."

Judith just shook her head. "You didn't *tell* me you were doing any of this."

Now that she'd done it, it was so horrifically obvious that she'd made a mistake. Again.

Theresa knew she was difficult; she'd been told it all her life. She'd been told, over and over, that she was impossible, horrible, awful, unladylike, selfish. And it wasn't just Judith who was doing the telling. Just about everyone who came into her life told her that.

She didn't *want* to be any of those things. She didn't particularly *want* to be good and ladylike, either, but it seemed that there should have been space for the person she was in this world without having to make her over into someone else entirely.

Maybe, deep down, she'd hoped that if she got this right, doing it *her* way, her sister would hug her. That Judith would say, *I see who you are, and you are a good, loving person.*

Apparently, she hadn't yet earned the right to that praise. Theresa's eyes stung, but she hadn't given up. Not yet.

"Well." Theresa's hands wrung. "It was supposed to be a present for your birthday. If you don't like it, I have about nine dreadful cushion covers that lie abandoned on the floor of my wardrobe. You can have any of them that you like. All of them, in fact. If you ever want to decorate a room with unnerving embroidery, they should prove useful."

Judith didn't say anything and Theresa huddled in misery.

She would plan better next year. With a full year to practice, maybe she could manage that damned embroidery. She'd give Judith the best raven that anyone had ever embroidered, and when she did—

Judith made a pained sound, and Theresa finally looked up. Judith was *crying*.

"You are impossible," Judith whispered. "You don't know what you can and can't do."

"It was…really, it wasn't even my first choice?" Theresa sniffed. "I really tried to do the cushions first. They're so terrible. I don't know what I was thinking."

"What *were* you thinking?"

"I was thinking that my love for you is…" She thought of those cushions and the diseased produce. "My love is like the rot on the fields. It grows with no bounds, even if you don't want it to, and you probably have to burn it with fire to stop the spread of disease."

Judith emitted something like a choking noise. She buried her face in her hands.

Theresa jumped off her bed. "I'm sorry!" Somewhere, she had a handkerchief. It was probably even clean. She crossed to her dresser, flinging open drawers. "I'm sorry. I'm so, so sorry. I was only trying to help." She found a piece of linen, shook it out, sniffed it—definitely clean—and waved it in her sister's direction. "I'll do better next time. I'm learning every day, even if it doesn't seem like it, and—"

Judith crossed the room to Theresa, plucked the fabric from her hand, and dropped it on the floor. "Shut up, Teespoon," she said. "I love you. This is the best birthday present I have ever had. And just because I don't have the words to say it…"

She wrapped her arms around her, squeezing Theresa so hard that she could scarcely take a breath.

"You are impossible," Judith said again. "You don't know what you can and can't do. I wouldn't take any other sister, ever, in your place."

Crying was a weakness. Theresa didn't believe in it. But somehow, the kind of tears that made her angry—the ones that crept out when she felt small and inconsequential and incapable—were nothing like the ones that pricked her eyes now. Funny, how tears could encompass both frustration and accomplishment.

"I know I'm hard on you," Judith said. "I just worry so much. You're...you, and the world is...so..."

"Ugly?"

"Ugly is a good word. You're fearless, and sometimes I think you're like a kitten trotting into a lion's den, meowing a defiant challenge. You're going to get eaten."

"The way I see it," Theresa said matter-of-factly, "if I'm a kitten and they're all lions, they're going to eat me no matter how I act. I might as well enjoy myself before I'm dinner."

Judith laughed. "That's worse. You have no sense of self-preservation."

"There are more kittens than lions," Theresa replied. "They can't eat us all."

"There are a great many lions, and most of the kittens hide in caves."

"But if we all descended into the lion's den, we could mew them to death."

"What are we even talking about any longer?"

Judith looked at Theresa and shook her head. "I don't know."

Theresa looked at the wall. "I am impossible. Maybe, deep down, I thought... If I could find Camilla *this* time, I could find Anthony...later."

"Oh, sweetheart."

"And..."

Judith hugged her. They didn't move for a few minutes. Finally, Judith spoke.

"You know," she said, "he sends letters."

Theresa's heart stopped. "*You* are in *contact* with Anthony? You have his direction?"

Judith shook her head. "Not entirely. We don't know where he is or what he's doing. We can put coded messages in the advertisements section, and sometimes, fourteen months later, he'll provide an answer. He doesn't really tell me anything. And—I need to warn you—he says things that are...of the sort that used to tend to set you off when you were younger, you know? I didn't want to tell you."

Theresa sat up straight. "You are telling me that I can send *my older brother* a message." She felt her fingers curl. "That he is *aware of my continued existence* and has not come for me?!"

"Honestly." Judith shut her eyes. "I think it would be easier for all of us except Anthony if he *were* dead. It makes a mess of everything."

"It sounds fine to me," Theresa said. "This way, I'm not the worst of your siblings."

Judith laughed. "You never have been. Theresa, I think... I've been unfair to you. You're fifteen. You may not go about being yourself the way others would, but you're old enough to make your own decisions. Would you want to see what he's written?"

Theresa exhaled. "Yes."

Judith patted her knee. "Later," she said. "It's been a long day, and the solicitor keeps them. It's time for dinner now."

~

Adrian wasted no time. He went back to Gainshire on the evening train. Walter Evans, the footman, conducted him to the office to wait. He was accustomed to Adrian waiting for Bishop Denmore, and—as he considered Adrian a servant—thought nothing of it.

He was allowed into his uncle's study without a blink of

an eye. Adrian took his time, making sure he got every last affidavit, every last note.

The documents they had told most of the story—why Bishop Lassiter had acted as he had, why the rector had chosen to discredit Camilla, where the money had come from, and whose pockets it had eventually lined.

But there was one point that might be questioned, one that Denmore himself had raised: why had it taken them so long to file for an annulment?

Before he went back to London, he took the train back up to Lackwich.

Mrs. Beasley, it turned out, had saved more than Bishop Lassiter's telegrams.

She had saved his uncle's, too—all of them, the ones saying that Adrian needed to stay the course, that he believed Adrian would succeed, and that he could do nothing to help.

Whether Denmore wanted to acknowledge Adrian was no longer relevant. If the truth came out, it would come out.

CHAPTER TWENTY-FIVE

A drian had left a note informing his uncle that he was taking possession of his own papers in preparation for the annulment proceedings. That note must have been magic. Up until that moment, his uncle had always been too busy to visit Adrian. Now, he suddenly found the time to come to London.

Adrian received him in the home he shared with his brother. He let Denmore slog through the hell of polite conversation as the tea things were brought out, let him look away and sigh uncomfortably and rub his hands together.

Adrian told him about the china that was in production.

His uncle nodded and bit his lip, until finally, he could keep silent no longer.

"Adrian," Denmore finally said. "What are you doing?"

Adrian could have been obnoxious. He could have answered with a false innocence that he was drinking tea.

Instead, he answered as simply as possible. "I'm having my marriage annulled. This cannot be a surprise to you; it has been my stated goal from the moment I was trapped into it at gunpoint."

The fact that his goals and desires had shifted? Not relevant any longer. Camilla wanted a choice; he'd give her one.

His uncle shut his eyes. "You must understand, Adrian. Those papers you acquired... They are not entirely convenient for me. Not if they are made public."

"Are they as inconvenient as being married at pistol point?"

"Dash it." His uncle set his tea cup down firmly. "I don't see the point in comparing such things. I ask you to reconsider. You owe me that much."

Adrian could have quibbled about who owed whom. But when all was said and done, it didn't hurt to try. Instead, he just nodded. "Very well."

His uncle looked almost startled. "Oh. Really? You'll give it up?"

"I didn't say that. I'll reconsider. Give me a moment."

And he did—Adrian reconsidered.

On the one hand, he was fairly certain that what he felt for Camilla was more than passing fancy. They got along well together. When she smiled, something in his chest lifted. She had asked him to have a choice, and he had promised her she could have it because he knew it would make her happy, and he loved the idea of making her happy.

On the other hand, if he granted his uncle's wish, his uncle's promise of reconciliation *someday* might still be a possibility. There was something to be said for family harmony. Adrian had been taking on one more burden for so long that maybe...

He realized the real reason he was giving the notion such consideration the moment the thought popped into his head unbidden. *You could stay married,* his mind whispered. *You could keep her and allay your uncle's worries all at once. You could have everything you want. And you want it, don't you?*

He did. He wasn't sure when he had started wanting it, wanting her.

But she had asked for a choice, and he wanted her to have it. And—most importantly—for coming up on four decades, Denmore had chosen to pretend that his family didn't exist. That was his choice. He'd had all these years to choose otherwise, and he never had.

Adrian wanted to be chosen. Even if he had been selfish enough to defy all Camilla's wishes in the matter, he was too selfish to give up that chance for himself.

"There we are," Adrian said. "I've considered once more. The answer is that I will still be seeking an annulment."

His uncle let out a long sigh. "How disappointing. A bare moment's thought is all I get? After all that I've done for you."

Adrian still felt raw from their last conversation. More; he had looked over the telegrams he'd exchanged with Denmore the day after the wedding. They'd firmed his resolve. He'd given his uncle the benefit of too many doubts.

The hell of it was that Adrian suspected that his uncle was being honest. He sincerely believed he *had* done everything for Adrian, because in his mind, Adrian deserved nothing and anything more than that exceeded his allotment. Likewise, he didn't notice anything Adrian had done for him. He expected everything, and anything less than that was too little. All Adrian's risk, all his worries? They didn't count one whit, not in Denmore's estimation.

His uncle had taught Adrian to rely on argument, not emotion. It was a shame he had never been able to take his own advice.

"You know," Adrian said slowly, "I think you really believe that. You really believe that you care about me."

"Of course I do." His uncle pulled back. "You're my own flesh and blood. How could I not care?"

"There are a number of ways that one shows what caring

looks like." Adrian closed his eyes. "For some people, caring takes the form of little gifts. Of looking out for your future. Or perhaps it's saying the right words when it's necessary, or maybe even being present when times are difficult. Caring is a mutual exchange of support in a thousand different ways." He thought of Camilla telling him to stop shouldering all her burdens.

"Yes, of course."

"When I think of the way you care for me," Adrian said, "it looks like this: When you need something from me, you are willing to say you love me in private. Never in public." He met his uncle's eyes. "You may think that that is love. But what you expect of yourself is so much smaller than what you expect of me. That doesn't feel like love to me."

"That's…" His uncle swallowed. "That's entirely unfair, that characterization! You know I would acknowledge you, that I would do more, but…"

Adrian stood. He leaned forward. "If it were just me, maybe I'd continue on like this. I've been blessed with an overabundance. I try to take my share of burdens. But one day, I will have children. I have a brother; I have parents. A woman was married to me by force. They all deserve better. I cannot ask everyone else to shoulder your burdens, too."

"Is that how you see this all?" His uncle stood. "I took you in when you were a boy."

"I already had a place to stay. I visited you, and you made me your page," Adrian corrected. "And then your secretary. You asked me to pose as a valet, but did nothing to help with the problems that resulted."

There was a longer pause. He could see his uncle's knuckles tremble. Finally, Denmore exhaled.

"Adrian. It will ruin us both, the truth—me and Bishop Lassiter alike. If they knew that my sister had progeny like you…"

Adrian pulled back, and his uncle flinched.

"I mean, if they knew that I asked my own nephew to serve as a valet! That I did something so ungentlemanly as to spy on another man to obtain an advantage... It will ruin me."

Adrian just shook his head. "If you didn't want your actions to ruin you, you shouldn't have done them."

His uncle just shook his head.

"Consider," Adrian said. "Once you're ruined, it won't hurt you to invite my mother and her husband out for a visit. You may even find yourself better off."

Adrian was still sitting in his office, staring off into a distant nothing, when his brother tapped on the door.

"Adrian?"

He had put off this conversation for far too long. Grayson had woken him the morning Camilla left and witnessed his panic.

They'd had the opportunity to speak since, but they just hadn't done so. Largely by Adrian's design.

He had excused himself as too busy. And he *had* been busy. There had been documents to purloin and telegrams to track down. There were filings and business still to be done. His older brother had waited patiently, giving Adrian glances that said *I told you so* when they met over breakfast. Grayson hadn't needed to know precisely what had happened to know that it had been so irregular as to require an annulment.

Now their uncle had arrived—a shocking occurrence—and had left.

There was no getting around this moment. "Come in." Adrian sighed.

Grayson tossed Adrian one of the apples he was holding before seating himself on the edge of the desk. "So," he said. "Our dear uncle comes all the way from Gainshire—a two-hour journey—to visit his nephews. How unusual." Grayson took a bite of his apple, crisp and new, and chewed it slowly as if he were contemplating.

"Go ahead." Adrian sighed. "I know you're going to subject me to a long string of questions that culminate in your looking at me and *not* saying 'I told you so.' You might as well do it."

Grayson made a face and chewed faster.

No point waiting. Adrian bulled on ahead. "To answer the questions I know you are going to ask: Yes, Denmore *did* ask me to do something for him. He asked me to pose as a valet to find out information. And—don't look at me like that—I said yes. Yes, it did all go to hell and back, and yes, there was a wedding at gunpoint, and yes, Denmore did refuse to help —multiple times—and yes, he *did* just come here to ask me to give up on seeking an annulment, because it might make him appear less than perfect in the public eye."

Grayson swallowed his bite of apple.

"No," Adrian said, "he did not ever say please."

"I wasn't going to ask." Grayson took another bite.

"Oh, I don't mind." Adrian picked up his own apple. "You want to say it. 'I told you so.' Just like that. Go ahead."

His brother chewed and swallowed again, then slowly pushed to his feet and came to stand near Adrian. He reached out and slowly set his hand on Adrian's head. "You utter nincompoop," he said steadily. "I have never wanted to say 'I told you so' to you. All I ever wanted was to know that you were safe and secure and happy. How hard is it to understand that I don't want you hurt?"

Adrian stared up at him. Grayson gave Adrian's forehead an affectionate rub.

"Stop that." Adrian batted his hand away.

"I wanted to see if you were doing well," Grayson said, "because I care about your well-being, and it is obvious you've had a difficult time of it. *Not* because I wanted to tell you so."

Well. Adrian blew out a breath and took a bite of his own apple. It was sweet and just a little tart, and the juice running down his chin gave him an opportunity to think.

"This is awkward," he said finally. "I've spent days avoiding you because I was trying to figure out what to say when you so prominently did not tell me 'I told you so,' and now you've gone and said something kind and gracious instead. It's maddening."

Grayson just shrugged. "How dreadful of me. Would it make you feel better if I said 'I told you so' now, just so you could feel vindicated? You're the one who's had the month of gunpoint weddings and suchlike. I'll defer to your wishes."

"It feels petty to ask for it."

"You should be *more* petty, not less so. Let me go ahead. 'Adrian, I told you so.'" Grayson even managed to get the tone right.

"Oh, it doesn't work like that! You can't just throw it out with no context. It is supposed to come after we've had an entire argument about how I'm too trusting."

"That sounds reasonable. You *are* too trusting."

"You were supposed to tell me that you used to be more like me. That you didn't want me hurt the way you were. That you were only trying to protect me."

"All of that sounds like something I would say," Grayson agreed. "Consider it said."

"*Then* you'd say 'I told you so.'"

"Right. Now we're getting to the good part." Grayson gestured expansively. "Please. Go on."

Adrian looked down, examining his hands, and then looked up. "And *I* would say that nothing has changed. Maybe I should learn to be less trusting, but I knew when this whole thing started that it might not turn out well."

"Really." Grayson raised a single eyebrow.

"I didn't *tell* you I knew it. Just because I didn't want to admit that you were probably right doesn't mean I didn't *know* it."

His brother smiled. "I'll keep that in mind for every future argument we have. Please, finish."

Where had he been? Right. "I care about you, too." Adrian said. "I just wanted…" He looked up into his brother's eyes, and felt all the helpless impotence of the last few weeks. "You'll be gone on your telegraph cable laying trip soon. I have so much—so many advantages. *I* didn't go to war. I've never gone hungry, not really. I have so much, and I don't know why it's come to me. I'm alive, and I *shouldn't* be—and I thought if…if…" Adrian trailed off.

"If what?"

"If I could get Denmore to keep his promises, I could make it up to you."

Grayson just frowned. "Make *what* up to me?"

"I could make up for the fact that I stayed here in comfort, and…"

"And our brothers died?"

Now that it was said aloud, it sounded silly. It was impossible to ever make that up. Nothing Adrian did could ever change that.

He shut his eyes. "You're right. It's stupid."

Grayson reached over and set a hand on Adrian's shoulder. "So. In your imagination, you thought I was going to be petty enough to say 'I told you so' but not petty enough to interrupt you three sentences into your monologue?"

"Idiot."

"My apologies. I'm not good at moments like this. I don't know what to say, except..." Grayson's hand tightened on Adrian's shoulder. "Adrian, they were your brothers, too. Not just mine."

Adrian felt a hard core of emotion in his chest. He squared his jaw, resisting it.

"You cannot make up for their deaths, because they were not your fault. The only thing that brought me through the war was knowing that at least you were here. That you were safe."

"But I have *so* much." Adrian looked at Grayson. "I just want—I want..." He couldn't finish his sentence. For a long moment, he struggled. "You're my brother," Adrian finally managed. "I want you to have the world."

"I know." Grayson put an arm around Adrian. "But I have *you*. If you take the world for yourself, it will be enough for me. I promise."

~

In the end, there was nothing left for Adrian to do but to tell fifty truths and one half lie.

The truths were easy. Adrian swore during the hearing that was held that he was, in fact, the grandson of the Duke of Castleford and the nephew of the Bishop of Gainshire. Why yes, he had proof—here were his parents' marriage records.

The gossip would go around. The truth would come out. Acknowledgment or no, his uncle wouldn't be able to hide the connection.

The questioning went on for hours.

Yes, Adrian said, his uncle had requested that he look into the matter of Bishop Lassiter. Why yes, he had proof as to that, too. Here was the telegram requesting his presence at Denmore's house; here were the telegrams they exchanged, where his uncle insisted that he complete his investigation.

The lie was harder. Adrian had never been good at lying.

"Did you consummate the marriage?"

Adrian thought of Camilla. Of the way she smiled at him, of the way he had asked her to be his when he had returned from his uncle, of the brilliant wave of delight that had lit her features.

He'd taken that from her—the joy she had in believing that she had been chosen. And he could give it back.

Adrian was a terrible liar; he did his best. "I am the nephew of Bishop Denmore. We have discussed church matters before. I knew that if the marriage was consummated, the marriage could not be annulled. We both deserved better." It was not exactly an answer, but they did not realize it.

They did not hear *we both*—not truly. They heard that Lady Camilla—that was how they referred to her throughout the proceeding—deserved better.

They were not wrong. They were just not right in the way they thought they were right.

He did not speak to Camilla at the proceeding; they were interviewed separately, to see if there were discrepancies in their stories. He caught sight of her at the end of a long hallway once, though. Her head tilted toward him; his whole body turned to hers.

They didn't exchange a word. Just that long glance shared from a hundred yards away.

But there was one person he *did* speak to.

It was on the final day when Adrian was delivering testimony. He left the room for a brief respite, and was trying to gather his scattering thoughts when a man came to stand in front of him.

"You!" Bishop Lassiter glared at Adrian. "You! I've been called here to account for my doings, and it's *all* your fault."

It really wasn't. Bishop Lassiter, Adrian suspected, bore the lion's share of the responsibility for his own undoing, with unnecessary added help from Rector Miles.

Still. Maybe his conversation with Grayson enabled Adrian to be just a little petty in the moment.

"Why, thank you." Adrian smiled at him. "I'm delighted you noticed. I was hoping you would."

"You were the worst valet I have *ever* employed."

"I know." Adrian tried to look sympathetic. "And that was true even *before* I publicly exposed you as a criminal."

Lassiter just looked more enraged. "You were supposed to be a nobody! That was the entire point of making her take your name!"

Yes. Lassiter had decided that Adrian was expendable all those weeks ago, when he'd forced them to marry. Adrian had vowed he would learn otherwise. It felt surprisingly satisfying to bait the man.

"Yes," Adrian said, still pretending to commiserate. "That *was* where you went wrong."

"Do you understand that I could be defrocked for this? It's just a few thousand pounds! It's not even really stealing."

"Embezzlement," Adrian said with a sunny smile. "Performing an irregular marriage. That all sounds terrible. I hope you are defrocked, you and Rector Miles both."

For a second, he actually thought the man would hit him. Lassiter was certainly angry enough to do so. But a clerk came into the hall to call Adrian back.

"Do have a nice day!" Adrian said.

The moment passed.

Several days later, the news came that Bishop Lassiter had

stepped down from his duties at the request of his peers. Rector Miles followed the next day. Adrian and his brother toasted the news with champagne.

Adrian went up to Harvil for a few days. The first plates were in production and he needed to see the results. Besides, he had realized that he needed to ask his artists for a very personal favor.

Shortly after he returned, the results of that favor in hand, a group in Surrey announced that they were breaking ground on a charitable institution—Martin's Home for Women—for those who had nowhere else to go. The money, apparently, had come from a sizable donation from a wealthy, elderly woman.

Adrian kept copies of these news reports in a folder; one day soon, he hoped, he would be able to discuss them with Camilla.

He felt more ambiguously the next week, when Bishop Denmore announced that he would also be resigning his position. Adrian sent his regrets; he received no response.

Fifteen days after Adrian did his best to lie and claim that he'd never made love to Camilla, he received a notice delivered in person by his solicitor.

The petition to annul the marriage of Lady Camilla Worth and Mr. Adrian Hunter had been granted. The marriage was deemed void for lack of consent. *Congratulations,* said his solicitor. *It's as if you have never been married.*

Adrian read those words as if from the end of a long tunnel.

It was as if he had never been married.

He thought for a long moment about everything that had transpired—from the moment he'd first seen Camilla in the rectory to now. Then he got out pencil and paper.

Cam, he wrote. *I'm sure you've heard by now. We are no longer married in any sense. I am sure that you have a thousand things you might like to do—I have seen in the gossip columns that your sister wishes to launch you into society at large—but if you could find the time, I should like to call on you.*

The response he received was swift.

I am not taking callers, Camilla said, *as I have some personal matters I wish to attend to before I open myself up to social visits.*

That being said, pursuant to those personal matters, I should mention that I am traveling quite often by train these days. If you should have a day or so free, I would welcome your company on a journey.

His reply came easily. *Tell me where to meet you,* Adrian said, *and I'll be there. Wherever it is.*

CHAPTER TWENTY-SIX

When Adrian met Camilla at the train station early the next morning, she was wearing a dark purple traveling gown with even darker trim, and a hat with a dark veil.

Adrian was not well versed in such things; he'd never had any desire to learn which gown was intended for what purpose. What could he say? This one fitted her perfectly. There was a luster to the fabric. It must have been expensive, because crowded though the station was, people flowed around her as if they recognized that she was a woman of quality and not to be trifled with.

Funny, that it had taken her wearing this gown for others to see that in her. The entire concept of women of quality seemed sorely lacking, especially if anyone imagined that it might ever have excluded Camilla.

It felt like ages since they had seen each other. It had been far too long. He could only guess what she thought of him, and didn't know why she'd asked him to accompany her on a journey. He didn't know anything at all, except that he never wanted to go so long without seeing her smile ever again.

Only her clothing had changed; she lit up in delight as he approached, her expression so reminiscent of their times together that his heart squeezed in his chest.

"Camilla." He inclined his head in greeting, then remembered abruptly. "Oh, for God's sake. Should I be calling you 'Lady Camilla' now?"

She giggled—an actual giggle, as if he'd tickled her ribs. "Don't be ridiculous. We're friends, aren't we? Just Cam is fine, as always."

"Where are we headed?"

Her hand went to her hip; she frowned and opened up the large bag she carried at her side. "'You need new clothing,'" she muttered in tones that did not quite sound like herself. "'Think nothing of the cost, I promise. We'll never notice, but you couldn't possibly continue on without at least seventeen thousand utterly useless gowns.'" She rolled her eyes as she spoke.

"Your pardon? Is there a problem?"

"Pockets," Camilla said grimly. "Pockets are the problem. That gods-be-damned seamstress that my sister insisted was the best in town made my dresses without pockets, and then explained that it would ruin the line of my silhouette to have them bulging out with who knows what. So *now*, I have no place to put train tickets except in this *stupid* bag that I'm forced to carry *everywhere*—" She shook a massive bag at him. "Here." She held out two tickets. "We're going to Somerset today. The journey isn't so terribly long; we'll arrive by mid-morning, as long as we don't miss the train."

There was nothing for it. Adrian held out his arm. "If you don't mind?"

She took it.

"I told Judith you were likely coming along," she said. "Judith doesn't like the idea of my little journeys—she's made Theresa accompany me thus far, but now that I am a lady

326

whose marriage is safely annulled, I convinced her that no such company was necessary."

He wanted to ask why they were going to Somerset. He wanted to ask if she remembered the last time they had been alone together—when they'd kissed—or the time before that, when she'd promised that she would be his and that she would make him very happy.

They were in the midst of a crowd of hundreds. He set his gloved hand over hers. "How are you getting on with your family?"

Her lips pursed, and she let out a sigh. "It's…I suppose it's good, really? I'm still adjusting to the idea of them. There are all these rules, and honestly, I have not had to be a lady in far too long. It's all very constricting. I'm destined to be an eccentric. I kept correcting our solicitor on questions of ecclesiastical law, you know. He hated me at the end. He told me if I thought I knew the law so well, I should consider taking articles, and so I said I would." She smiled sunnily. "And then Benedict is apparently doing so at the moment, so he said I should come along and do it with him."

He laughed. "What did they think of that?"

"Luckily for me, I appear to not be the only eccentric in the family." She gave him a bright smile. "All these years, I had no idea what was happening with any of them. But it was touch and go from time to time. They had scarcely any money at all, not until recently. And the entire household is in a constant uproar. Judith was seventeen when this mess with my father happened; she was raised in luxury, and for all that she struggled thereafter, she simply cannot see that she just assumes things *must* be a certain way because they *were* for her growing up. Theresa, on the other hand, was raised by the docks in near-poverty. She learned that ladies are *supposed* to act a certain way, but she never believed she personally would be *expected* to do so until she was much,

much older. So Judith and Theresa are constantly at odds. They love each other dearly, but there is no reconciliation. Judith wants Theresa to have the chance to become just like Judith, and it hurts her feelings that Theresa doesn't want it."

They had reached their train. He found their car and then handed her up. The car was relatively empty; Adrian took off his hat and coat and sat on the other side of the seat from her.

"I'm sorry to sound as if I'm complaining," Camilla said. "I really am delighted to get to know my family again, and they've been nothing but welcoming. I don't regret a minute. But it is bewildering to find yourself in the midst of five-year-old arguments that you don't completely understand."

"I can imagine."

Camilla looked down at the floor. "Within the first three days, Judith was saying things like, *Theresa, if you don't learn to do such-and-such, Camilla will never be able to marry well.* Which was extremely awkward. You see, I do not think I will ever have a chance to marry better than I did the last time, and the one thing I specifically asked Judith for was the chance to be unmarried from him."

His heart clenched at that. He had been looking for an opportunity to bring up what they'd been to each other, and here it was. Adrian leaned forward. He thought of what he had in his pocket. All he had to do was—

The door to the car opened, and a man in a brown suit set an attaché case onto the luggage rack. He removed a newspaper, put on a pair of spectacles, sat down, and began reading.

Oh. Damn. Adrian tried not to feel impatient. There would be time, after all.

He pulled back, shifting subtly in place. "Go on, then. How did it all turn out?"

"It took three days for Benedict and Theresa to pull me into their pact."

"Your younger brother and sister, right? What pact?"

"Ah, don't you know? Everyone tries to use us against each other: 'If you don't behave like a marionette with no free will, your sister will lose her chance to *also* behave like a marionette with no free will. Do you want to be the one who does that to her?'"

Adrian laughed outright. The man with the newspaper looked up, sniffed, and pointedly went back to reading.

"So the three of us are now all in agreement. None of us wish to behave like marionettes, and thus, we cannot be used as weapons against each other."

"That seems fair."

"And that, in turn, hurts Judith's feelings again. She loves her husband, but..." Camilla swallowed. "Would you believe she set up a trust in my name? She owns a business making clockwork, and she tries not to be difficult, but... I suspect that Judith just wants us all to have the chance to marry marquesses the way she did, and I don't know how to tell her that she can keep her marquess. I don't want one."

The train started moving, and with it, the hiss of the steam engines and the screech of the gears filled the car. It provided a little cover for their conversation.

"No?" He leaned forward an inch. "Who do you want?"

Her cheeks pinked a little, but she looked out the window. "I have no intention of becoming an object of curiosity in polite society. They'd let me go to a few of their balls and they would gawk at me and ask me if I had *really* been married and if the marriage had *really* been annulled and what I had been doing beforehand." Camilla shrugged. "They would want me to feel ashamed of where I have been, and I have had a lifetime's worth of shame. I don't want to marry a man who will forgive me for what I have done. I want someone who will treasure me for it. You know what I want."

"You want to be chosen," he said in a low voice. "You want someone who thinks of all the women in the world and decides that he wants you above any other. You want a long, slow falling in love."

Her eyes fluttered up to his. Her cheeks were rosy, and the way she looked at him made him want to take her in his arms, and damn the other passenger.

"A point of clarification," Adrian asked. "Precisely how long a falling in love were you hoping for? My parents took three years. As for me, that sounds rather excessive."

She colored further. "I should like to reach our destination, at a minimum. Any time before then would be too fast."

"I see."

"Longer than that, I suppose, is up for debate." She grinned at him. "But I've spent this entire time talking of myself. Tell me about you. What did your brother think? Have you started producing the plates for the exhibition? When *is* the exhibition, and would you mind horribly if I came?"

God, he had missed talking to her. He had missed hearing her voice; he had missed seeing the glow in her eyes as she drank in his every word. He'd missed the way she laughed and the way she looked at him and the way she reached out at one point and tried to remove a piece of fluff from his lapel, and the way his whole body responded to that touch of her finger on fabric.

He had missed everything about her.

"I didn't ask before. Why Somerset?"

She looked down. "Well, since we couldn't talk to one another before the annulment, I decided to put my time while I was waiting to good use. You know how I felt about looking back."

He nodded.

"I've been looking back," she confessed. "I went to visit

Mrs. Marsdell—the woman who taught me to crochet. She was dead. I left flowers on her grave. I visited my uncle; he apologized, believe it or not, and I had the pleasure of seeing him very embarrassed. He had no idea what was going to happen, but that is no excuse for what he did. I visited his cousin, who was terrible. I went up to see Kitty; she's settling quite well into her new position, and she's so happy to have her daughter with her that I cried for her. I thought it would...help, perhaps? If I saw everyone who had once mattered to me."

He knew he should ask if it had helped in truth. Still, some dark impulse made him ask this instead: "Did you visit James?"

Somehow, the idea of her talking to the footman who had promised to love her and left her to the care of Rector Miles made him feel just a little angry.

Her lip quirked up. "No," she said simply. "Not him. He didn't deserve me, and when I thought back over that time... There was nothing I wanted to look back for. But I did go to see Larissa." Her eyes dropped. "I mentioned her to you once. We were particular friends. Or at least I thought we were. I always did wonder what had happened to her, after her parents separated us. She's... Um, how shall I say this?" She glanced across the car at the other occupant.

Camilla had mentioned that she had practiced kissing with Larissa.

"We were both very young," Camilla said. "But she has apparently taken Mrs. Martin's path."

"She's found a sweet young thing?"

"Someone a little older than her, actually. We hugged and she said she was sorry I was sent off, but that without me, she might never have realized that..."

"That like Mrs. Martin, she had no use for men?"

"Are you shocked?"

"Someday, I will tell you about my great-great-uncles. And... Never mind; I'll let her tell you herself. Who are we here to meet, then?"

She cast him a coquettish glance. "Can't you guess?"

He really couldn't.

"I'm going back and revisiting everywhere I ever stayed," Camilla said. "Everyone I wanted to love. Who do you think is left?"

He wracked his brain, trying to remember. He had absolutely no idea.

She had arranged to have a hired cart waiting for them at the station. The day was beautiful—just a few fluffy white clouds under a bright, sunny sky. He took the reins when she offered, and she pointed down the dry dirt road leading south. "That way, please."

They drove out of town.

There were no houses in the direction she had pointed them. Maybe there was a hamlet over the next rolling hill; maybe their destination lay ten miles distant.

After half an hour, she stopped the cart and opened the massive bag she had complained about earlier. She produced a bottle of soda water and some meat pasties. "Here," she said.

"You want to stop here for a rest?"

"I want to stop here because it's our destination."

Adrian looked around. He looked up, at the blue sun-kissed sky, and around them, at the landscape. There was a small copse of trees and the sound of a running brook. The grasses were green and the last late flowers made a riot of color.

"Here?" he asked dubiously. "Who are we visiting here?"

"Adrian," she said. "Isn't it obvious who I'm visiting here?"

"No. Not at all."

She gathered up her bag and stepped down from the carriage. "Don't be silly. It's you."

Oh. *Oh.* "And we couldn't have visited in London?"

"We could have," she said, "but this is prettier, and I have fewer sisters present." She winked at him. "In fact, there's nobody present here at all, and what my sisters don't know won't shock them."

After that, there was nothing to do but tie the horses to a nearby sapling and follow her into the field. Little insects flew up underfoot as they walked.

He reached out and took her hand, entwining it in his. "I never got to do this," he said. "Not at any point when we were together. We were always so intent on holding ourselves out as not married."

She did not pull away. She just smiled. "And how do you like it?"

"I like it very well. I find myself never wanting to let go."

Another shy look over her shoulder. "Adrian. You know you don't have to."

"I do, Camilla." He looked at her. "I'm afraid to tell you—but I do. I have to let go now. I had a long talk with Grayson. He urged me to find a way to be happy for myself, and the thing that would make me most happy right now is if I let go."

The look on her face—the way her eyes widened, the way her lips parted just a little bit—made him almost regret relinquishing her hand. Almost. But he did. He pulled away from her.

"You see," he said softly, "if I do not let go of your hand, I cannot reach into my pocket—my tailor, by the way, is kind in the matter of pockets—and take out…" He found what he had been searching for, and made a fist around it, and held his arm out. "This."

He opened his hand.

Her eyes widened even further.

"I didn't think you would want something ostentatious," he said. "And it turns out, I know some excellent artists who are skilled in enamel work. I asked them to put together a design while we were waiting for the annulment."

She did not move to take the ring from him. "Adrian." Her voice shook. "Is that an enamel tiger?"

"Yes," he said, "and I hope you'll forgive the few small stones, but I wanted to make sure that our tiger was crowned in the sparkliest of dreams."

"I love it." She looked up at him. "Is it intended for me?"

"Give me back your hand. No, without the glove."

She smiled, baring her hand. He slid the ring on her finger, gold and radiant for all to see. Her eyes shone.

"Camilla," he said, "I love you. I love you more than any other woman in the world, and I want you by my side for decades and decades. I choose you above everyone else. Will you please make me the happiest of men by giving me your hand in marriage?"

Her eyes sparkled. "That was so good," she said. "That was the best marriage proposal I've ever received."

"Oh, you've received a lot of them, have you?"

"Yes," she said. "Last time you had to marry me, you said 'no.' This was a thousand times better."

Adrian shook his head. "Will you please answer me?"

"Well, you *said* you wanted a long, slow falling in love. Getting a bit impatient, aren't you?"

He couldn't help himself. He laughed. Then he took a step toward her and wrapped her in his arms.

"Yes," she said. "Yes, yes, yes. I love you. I love you. I want you, and only you. I want you forever."

And then he was kissing her, laughing and holding her, with the sun all around them.

~

"I'm sorry it has taken so long."

Theresa stood beside Judith in the solicitor's office. They had been ushered into a side room and asked to wait. The room they were in was lined with books, books, books, and more books. Oddly, however, it smelled nothing like the General Register Office had smelled. *That* had stunk of must and ink. This was a slightly more pleasant smell—old paper and tea.

"I didn't mean to make you wait several weeks to see the letters—such as they are—but between Camilla's hearings and everything else..."

"Of course," Theresa said. "You've been busy. And I've enjoyed going about the country with Camilla by train. We've been to ever so many places. I get to pretend that I'm a lady while I'm doing it."

"Theresa, you *are* a lady." Judith said this with a smile and a shake of her head. "I do wish you'd believe it."

Let them call you whatever they want, the dowager marchioness had told Theresa. *Just keep the truth in your head, and you don't need to tell them they're wrong.*

"I suppose," Theresa answered dubiously.

For some reason, this just made Judith look all the more determined. "Whatever it takes, Tee. I'll give you whatever you need until you can finally believe it."

Someday, Theresa suspected she and her sister were going to have a giant row—larger than their usual, regular-sized rows—about the whole *lady* thing. Not today.

The door opened behind them, and an errand boy entered with a folder in hand. "Here they are, my ladies."

My ladies again.

But it didn't matter what the errand boy called her, if he

gave her what she wanted. The folder he handed over was exceptionally thin.

Theresa eyed it askance. "Anthony has been gone for almost a decade, and that's all his correspondence?"

Judith just rolled her eyes. "Nobody will ever accuse our brother of being an avid letter-writer. I did tell you they were letters—such as they are. I'll leave you to them, then."

Letters, such as they are turned out to be a good description of her elder brother's terse missives. The first could be summarized as, "hope you are all well, I'm not dead yet," spread over four sentences with a handful of connecting words.

The second was a little better. He made stupid excuses for his inattention to his family, and said unbelievable things about love. Ha. If he really loved them as much as he claimed, he would write more. Still, Theresa immediately recognized the part Judith had feared would set her off.

When she's old enough to understand, tell Tee-spoon that I send her all my love, as does Pri.

Theresa stopped reading, her heart giving a sudden twinge. Priya was the name of Theresa's imaginary sister.

When Theresa was a child, and her father had first been convicted of treason, she remembered throwing tantrums that had scared even her with their ferocity, demanding that her sister—not Judith, not Camilla, but her *other* sister —appear.

They had scared her at every moment up until this one. She remembered believing with every fiber in her being that she had actually had a sister named Priya.

It had taken her years to be convinced that no such person had ever existed. That her memories were fallible, stupid things. That she'd invented a sibling to pass time on a boring voyage, and then convinced herself that she *did* exist out of sheer obstinacy.

Judith had needed to show her their family Bible with marriage lines and birth dates and everything. Finally, at the age of eight, Theresa had accepted that it had all been in her imagination.

Looking at those words on the page—seeing Anthony write the name out like that—was a blow. Anthony was no doubt an idiot about a great many things, but he would know that his fifteen-year-old sister wouldn't want to play a game remembering an *imaginary* sister. Anthony communicated nothing at all in these stupid letters. No pleasantries. No information. Just excuses. And still he'd mentioned Pri.

There was only one possible explanation. He wasn't telling her about an imaginary sister.

At fifteen, Theresa understood something she had missed at eight. A family Bible, with marriage lines and birth dates, was not proof that her father had not sired another child. Marriage had nothing to do with that.

She read the line again.

...send her all my love, as does Pri.

Judith must have assumed that Anthony was humoring Tee's long-ago imagination. God, for all that Judith was older, she was in many, many ways so incredibly naïve.

For the first time in ten years, Tee realized the truth. She had been lied to. Not on purpose, not by Judith, no—but she had been lied to. For almost a decade, she had been told that her memory was false. That her mind was dangerous. That she had constructed a fable and believed it, and that she needed to be wary of every last thought that she had, lest they lead her astray.

Her father had been in India. Theresa could fill in the explanation that Judith had missed. Her father had had a mistress—of course he had—and his mistress had a daughter, because that was what happened. That daughter had, for some reason, been on the journey that the three-year-old Theresa had embarked upon.

Theresa had been allowed to meet her because she had been deemed too young to understand the truth. And when she had come back and cried about her missing sister, everyone who knew the truth had lied to her. Her father. Anthony.

They were all liars.

Theresa read the line once more. *...As does Pri.* Oh, that hurt, to hear that Pri was sending *Theresa* love. *Her* sister remembered her. *She* hadn't spent all this time believing Theresa was a figment of her imagination.

It was one thing to discover that her father and brother had betrayed their country. It was another to discover that he'd betrayed *her.* He had allowed her to believe her mind was her enemy her entire life.

Anger came first—anger at Anthony, then at Judith, then at herself, for those years when she'd believed that something was wrong with her. Anger hit her like a wave, so powerful that she almost screamed with the heat of it.

Disgust followed. She was disgusted with her father. She was disgusted with Anthony. She was disgusted with the entirety of England, a country that wanted her to be a lady, when being a lady meant closing her eyes to what was happening around her.

Finally, there came one last emotion—a memory that she'd never quite been able to push away. That feeling that someone loved her. Someone understood her. She had a sister who knew her and had loved her. She had a sister who knew what it was like to never grow up to be a lady. She had a sister who had been abandoned by the family in a more dramatic and painful way than Camilla.

Theresa was the only one who would care that she existed.

Judith was right. Theresa had grown up. She'd grown out of her tantrums. She'd gained nothing from the ugly rage that she'd indulged in as a child.

Theresa had a sister who needed finding, and Theresa was good at finding sisters.

Now, all she needed was a plan.

Ten minutes later, Judith returned to the room. "What did you think?"

Theresa smiled. She wasn't a lady, but she had learned to play one. Now, with possibilities boiling in her mind, pretense had become necessary.

"He really is the worst correspondent," Theresa said dryly.

They laughed together, and Judith didn't realize.

Theresa could wait as long as necessary. All she had to do was hide the fact that she was done with England. She was utterly done.

≈

Adrian returned with Camilla to her sister's home just before dusk. Camilla conducted Adrian to a parlor, then disappeared for a moment as she sent for her entire family to join them.

Adrian couldn't help but be nervous. Of all the ridiculous situations to find himself in. But Camilla came back, drifting to stand by him, and she introduced him to her family, one by one, as they entered.

Lady Ashford was the last to enter the room. She looked at Adrian in confusion, then at Camilla, beaming by his side.

"What is going on?" she asked.

"I have delightful news," Camilla said, all smiles. "Mr. Adrian Hunter asked me to marry him—and I said yes."

Lady Ashford blinked. She looked at the two of them

once more. Adrian reached out and took hold of Camilla's hand.

"Oh, for the love of goslings," she said. "We spent *weeks* on the annulment. Why?"

"I wanted to choose him," Camilla said. "I wanted him to *know.*"

"Normally, one does not annul a marriage to someone one intends to marry. I am a puddle of bafflement."

"Oh, Judith," Camilla said on a sigh. "Have you met Theresa? Benedict? Anthony? Yourself, even? Since when does one of your siblings do things the *normal* way?"

"Hooray!" said Lady Theresa Worth behind her. "I'm not the worst sister any longer!"

~

They were not married by special license. The banns were called. It took weeks upon weeks upon endless weeks—weeks of planning, weeks of signing marriage settlements with Judith and Christian grumbling over the details with Grayson—before they were married.

That also meant weeks in which Camilla met Adrian in her sister's home, weeks during which they stole kisses against walls. During those weeks, the china exhibit was held; Camilla stood to the side and watched the responses to her fiancé's newest china collection with gladness in her heart. There were vases, ringed in roses, and wide bowls with gold-plated rims.

In pride of place, there stood the plates that Adrian and his cohorts had made. She would never tire of those tigers.

Neither, apparently, would England. They sold the entire initial run before the exhibition was over, and Camilla cheered when people clamored for more.

After those weeks of waiting were over, Camilla stood in the church, surrounded by those who loved her best.

She had dreamed of marriage ever since she was twelve years of age and had been shunted off to the first family who reluctantly took her in.

Over the years, she had told herself that it didn't *have* to be marriage, and it turned out that it wasn't *just* marriage that she celebrated here. Not any longer.

Camilla stepped into the aisle on the day of her wedding and looked around her.

Her brother and sisters were here. Larissa and her companion had come down to London via train, on Camilla's invitation, and the correspondence they had exchanged in the weeks before had revitalized their friendship. Next to her sat Kitty with her daughter on her knees, smiling at Camilla with her heart in her eyes.

There were Adrian's relations—his parents, whom she had just met this last week—and a mountain of cousins and friends who she was gradually getting to know. Practically everyone from Harvil had turned out for the occasion, and they all watched the ceremony in delight.

One person was all Camilla had ever wanted. One person, just one, who promised not to leave her. She had told herself she didn't need love. She would have settled for tolerance and a promise that she would have a place to stay. And yet the one thing she had never done was stop hoping—hoping that one day, she would have what she wanted.

Camilla made her way down the aisle, on the arm of the brother-in-law who had taken over the role as gruffly protective guardian.

Adrian waited for her, and they could neither of them stop smiling.

They had wanted a morning wedding this time. The

sunlight danced among the pews, lighting his face with a joy that she could scarcely believe she had inspired.

She listened with tears stinging her eyes as the ceremony proceeded.

"Adrian Hunter," the vicar was saying. "Do you take Camilla Worth to be your wife? Will you love her, comfort her, honor and protect her, and forsaking all others, be faithful to her as long as you both shall live?"

She hadn't thought she needed anything except one person, and here she was with an entire horde of friends. She didn't need the gown of lace and pearls that her sister had demanded she commission. She didn't need the trousseau that had been sent ahead for their honeymoon trip. There was only one thing she needed.

"Yes," said Adrian, looking into her eyes. "Yes, I do."

He'd chosen her, and she'd chosen him. Camilla smiled up into Adrian's eyes, holding his hands so tightly that she thought she might never let go.

"I do," she said, when it was her turn.

And then the wedding was over—for a second time—and Adrian kissed her in full view of the world.

AFTER THE (SECOND) WEDDING

Theresa had not dared to proceed too swiftly. If she'd acted as quickly as she wanted, she would have been suspected. Suspected and stopped.

It had taken her week after careful week to research passage on ships. To figure out how to remove money from the trust that had been set up for her without her sister's knowledge, to creep down to the shops and sell some of the sparkling gowns that they'd made for her. It was easy enough —she ruined her dresses often enough that they would never wonder why one had disappeared.

Theresa wasn't a child any longer. The last time she'd thought of running away, she'd had a bit of food and nothing like a plan.

This time, though… This time, she didn't know if she'd ever return.

On the night when Theresa Worth left London—and England—for good, she packed in the dark. She'd already marked the gowns she'd be taking—good, serviceable ones that wouldn't set her apart as too wealthy. She'd memorized the list of things she needed to take because she didn't dare set them forth on paper, lest she be discovered.

Petticoats and bloomers. A heavy cloak and mittens, for when it got cold at sea. Two hats, no more. And jewels to sell. It all made a heavy pack; it would join the more prosaic trunk of remedies and provisions that she'd arranged to be delivered to the *Edelweiss* a few days earlier.

She removed the last horrifically embroidered cushion attempt from her wardrobe. The Trent raven-slash-horrible farming tragedy looked up at her.

She could stay here and try to be that misshapen bird. Or she could go.

She took the note she had written the day before, the one she'd been carrying in her pocket all day, and set it next to the cushion on the bed. She'd not wanted to give too many clues; they'd find her, if they could. If they found her, they would try to convince her to come back.

She had the words of her note memorized by heart.

My dear Judith, Camilla, Benedict, Christian, and Adrian—

My love for you is like a field going to rot. It will grow without bounds. You cannot burn it out, I promise you, no matter how much you may want to afterward.

But I love my family—all my family—and I cannot stay here any longer.

Your loving sister,

Theresa

She'd sobbed as she wrote it. Her breath choked in her chest as she set it on her desk. She set another note next to it, her vision clouding in acute misery.

My dear Dowager Marchioness of Ashford—

I don't remember my grandmothers. Any of them. I don't remember my mother.

I will remember you, your lessons, and your love, all my life.

I hope you can find it in your heart to forgive me for leaving like this.

Your adoring,

Theresa

There was no point dilly-dallying. The ship wouldn't wait for her.

She hefted the valise she'd packed and looked around the darkened room where she'd spent the last year and a half. This life was comfortable. The room was warm. There was always enough coal, always enough food, and where she was going, none of that was a given.

But comfort was a cage, and she wouldn't accept it. Not any longer. Not like this.

Her chin rose. There would be time for feeling sorry on board the ship. She gathered all her resolve and slipped out of her room.

A clock ticked in the hallway. A stair creaked—lightly—as she crept downstairs. But the kitchen was dark and empty, and as she made her way to the servant's exit—

"Theresa?"

She stopped, cursing under her breath. She turned in place. "Corporal Benedict." She looked at her younger brother with every ounce of command that she could muster. "Go back to bed."

But she didn't have a real army, and he didn't really have to obey her. He kept coming until he stood next to her. "Where are you going in the middle of the night?"

"Where do you think?" She straightened and glared her younger brother in the eyes. "I'm going to give you what you wanted."

"What *I* wanted? What do I want? Why are you carrying a valise?"

"Will you *please* whisper? You'll wake the household

otherwise. I'm giving you what you want, Benedict. You don't want to be a lawyer. You heard Captain Hunter talking. He takes on those who wish to learn what he does for a fee. Christian will gladly pay it. No sitting in a stuffy office looking at stupid papers for you any longer."

Benedict shook his head. "They'd never let me. And what has that to do with your valise?" His eyes narrowed. "Why are you sneaking about in the middle of the night? And why are you trying to distract me in the name of Captain Hunter?"

She reached out and touched her brother's cheek. "Don't you see? You've shown you're good at finding sisters. And reading clues. You're good at listening. I'm giving you an excuse. You'll need to go looking for one again, and this time, you won't have to stay in England to do it."

His jaw wobbled. He must have understood what she was saying. When he spoke next—in a whisper, as she'd told him —it sounded almost like a wail. "But all my sisters are *here.*"

Theresa's heart constricted. "No." Her voice was rough. "No, they aren't. Not even now. And no, they won't be. I'm leaving. I have to."

He exhaled slowly. He didn't ask questions. He knew what she was like when she was serious, and she was serious now.

Judith had never seen it, but for all their differences, Benedict and Theresa had always been much alike. Neither of them belonged in this comfortable place. They both knew it.

"Are you going to stop me?" Theresa asked.

"I've never been able to stop you from doing anything." Now his voice shook, but he kept it at just that.

She squeezed his arm. "You know what we have always been."

"We're an army of two."

Theresa nodded. She refused to cry. Generals didn't cry. "That's right. We're an army of two, even if we're separate."

He didn't ask where she was going or what she planned to do. He understood that if he knew those things, he'd tell Judith.

"When will I see you again?"

"I don't know."

"Well, sir." His voice shook. "Bon voyage."

She took a step toward him. "None of that *sir* business. You make your own orders now."

He nodded. "When you see me next, I'll make you proud."

They embraced—his arms came around her impossibly hard—and Theresa imagined that he squeezed those two tears out of her. They didn't come out on their own. *That* would be ridiculous of her.

"Go back to bed," she said. "Don't lock the door behind me. You'll come under suspicion." So saying, she slipped out into the dark.

The street was utterly quiet. A chilly little autumn breeze swirled over her, and she slipped on her gloves and began to walk, swinging her valise.

It was heavy. She hadn't realized how heavy it was until she'd gone one street, then the next. It felt as if her clothing had turned to bricks and her fingers to ice. She switched the valise to one hand, then the next, then carried it in two. Her shoulders slowly began to burn.

It was going to be a long, painful two miles to the docks, she thought.

A noise behind her caught her attention—the rattle of wheels against cobblestones. She retreated into the shadow of the stairs, huddling against the stone wall of a house as a carriage came into view.

If she was very still and very small, maybe they wouldn't see her.

But the carriage stopped in front of her. A footman—oh, damn it all, an *Ashford* footman—hopped off the back of the conveyance and opened the door.

Theresa had planned for this eventuality, too. She'd get in the carriage. Pretend to go willingly. She'd have to scramble and abandon her valise, of course, but damn, that valise was heavy. She'd be delighted to leave it.

But it wasn't Judith who stepped out. It was the dowager marchioness. She approached Theresa slowly, as if she were a skittish animal.

"Theresa, dear," she said, as if they were meeting in the yellow parlor, "why are you walking to the docks?"

Theresa sighed. "Damn Benedict and his eternally running mouth."

The dowager sighed. "Don't talk about your brother that way. He didn't tell me a thing. It's simply that I'm not an idiot. I *did* tell you months ago that I knew your habits. Do you think I wouldn't *notice* what was happening underneath my very nose?"

Theresa felt her chin set. "I'm not going back."

"I know. I told you I knew your habits. If you're going to be *you*, do it well. Running off by yourself, with a handful of notes that will be discovered by the servants? Your family would never live this down. That was a poor choice."

Theresa didn't have time to argue. Her teeth ground together. "I realize that. Nonetheless, I am not going back."

The dowager just shook her head. "And yet on the other hand, you have a perfectly acceptable alternative." She held out her arm. "You could be embarking on a world tour with your elderly grandmère."

Theresa blinked. She frowned. "I could?"

"I have access to funds you will never be able to tap," the dowager said. "I've instructed my girl to gather your note and deliver it along with my own letter to my son in the morning. And I really would prefer that you remain among the living, which is quite often *not* the case when young women without funds travel on their own."

Theresa blinked. "But I have over a hundred pounds on my person."

"So intelligent, and yet still so little sense." The dowager nodded. "I saw you looking up routes to the Orient in the newspaper the other day. I assume we're going to find your brother, Anthony? He was such a nice boy."

"Eventually." Theresa hadn't let herself say the words aloud. She was going to find him eventually, and tell him what she really thought. By then, maybe she would have sorted out her tangle of love and anger. "But not at first. I'm going to find my *other* sister." Theresa glanced defiantly up at the dowager. "They told me I made her up, but I've discovered I didn't. She's real. She's illegitimate. And she's half Indian."

"Well, then." The dowager just nodded. "Our work is certainly cut out for us. Come now, don't you think my coach will be a better way to get to the docks?"

Theresa looked at the conveyance. She thought about her aching shoulders.

Very, very slowly, she nodded.

"Excellent. Where are we heading, then?"

She'd not let herself say the words until now.

"We'll go to Brest first." Theresa had been on a ship when she was a tiny child, and her memories of it were as diffuse as water-color paintings. Still, she thought of the feel of sea wind against her face. She remembered salt spray against her cheeks, ocean waves, and an open vista of sky and water. She remembered the sight of land—a green peak rising sharply from the sea...

"Then, around the Cape of Good Hope to Calcutta. From there, we'll find passage to Hong Kong. And after that? Wherever the trail leads us."

"Well," said the dowager. "This will be interesting."

TEASER: THE DEVIL COMES COURTING

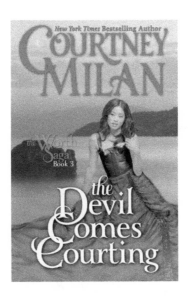

Captain Grayson Hunter knows the battle to complete the first worldwide telegraphic network will be fierce, and he intends to win it by any means necessary. When he hears about a reclusive genius who has figured out how to slash the cost of telegraphic transmissions, he vows to do whatever it takes to get the man in his employ.

Except the reclusive genius is not a man, and she's not looking for employment.

Amelia Smith was born in Shanghai as a child and was taken in by English missionaries. She's not interested in Captain Hunter's promises or his ambitions. But the harder he tries to convince her, the more she realizes that there *is* something she wants from him: She wants everything. And she'll have to crack the frozen shell he's made of his heart to get it.

Click here to find out more about *The Devil Comes Courting*.

OTHER BOOKS BY COURTNEY

The Worth Saga

Once Upon a Marquess

Her Every Wish

After the Wedding

The Pursuit Of...

~coming soon~

The Devil Comes Courting

The Return of the Scoundrel

The Kissing Hour

A Tale of Two Viscounts

The Once and Future Earl

The Cyclone Series

Trade Me

Hold Me

Find Me

What Lies Between Me and You

Keep Me

The Brothers Sinister Series

The Governess Affair

The Duchess War

A Kiss for Midwinter

The Heiress Effect

The Countess Conspiracy

The Suffragette Scandal

Talk Sweetly to Me

The Turner Series

Unveiled

Unlocked

Unclaimed

Unraveled

Not in any series

A Right Honorable Gentleman

What Happened at Midnight

The Lady Always Wins

The Carhart Series

This Wicked Gift

Proof by Seduction

Trial by Desire

AUTHOR'S NOTE

I got the idea for this book many years ago when I was reading ecclesiastical law for fun, because that is a thing that I do.

Specifically, I was reading about annulments, because there is an idea that is sometimes promulgated in historical romances that annulments are relatively easy to obtain as long as you don't consummate the marriage. This is not actually true; annulments are terribly difficult to obtain, even if you have never had intercourse, and most of the ways that people claim you can annul a marriage are, in fact, not accurate.

So yes—to the best of my ability, what Adrian and Camilla discover about annulment over the course of the book is correct.

- You *can* annul a marriage for lack of consent, but the standards for "lack of consent" back then do not track what we consider to be a lack of consent today.
- What Adrian says about not holding yourself out

to be married is true—if you told people a woman was your wife, even if you were married at gunpoint, the ecclesiastical courts might claim that you had consented to be married after the fact.

- If someone tells you that they can determine virginity on physical inspection, they are lying to you.

- Like just about everything else in life, it was a lot easier to get a marriage annulled if you had power and money. I exaggerated the degree to which that mattered in the two stories of Miss Laney Tabbott and Jane Leland, but it still mattered.

I got the idea for some of the specifics of this book back when I was writing *The Suffragette Scandal* in 2014, when I wrote this line: "It would be like the Archbishop of Canterbury calling a select club of his compatriots 'Bad, Bad Bishops'." For some reason, the phrase "Bad, Bad Bishops" just tickled the heck out of me, and it became the code name for this book.

There are two things mentioned in this book that are purposefully ahistorical. One is the underglazing colors that Adrian describes. I purposefully tried not to say too much about the production of china in this book because this is not a book about the production of china, but basically, the colors that can be used under the initial glaze were historically quite limited because the glaze needs to be fired at an incredibly high temperature. That temperature means that chemical reactions occur, and a dye that might start out as one color would turn into something else at heat.

As our knowledge of chemistry progressed, the colors we can use have been expanded. Adrian (and the business that his family runs) have historical access to minerals that would allow them to have a broader spectrum of underglaze colors.

The second thing I mention will be a much larger issue in the third full-length book in this series. I mention that Grayson wants to lay a transpacific telegraph cable. In reality, that cable was not laid until early in the twentieth century. There was, however, no reason it could not be put down earlier. There will be more about Grayson and the telegraph in the third book.

ACKNOWLEDGMENTS

I have so many people to thank for this book. First, for those who had a direct hand in its creation—Lindsey Faber, Rawles Lumumba, Louisa Jordan, Martha Trachtenberg, and Wendy Chan—my unending gratitude for working with me on impossible deadlines that were endlessly delayed.

Special thanks to those friends of mine, who were there for me when I needed them most. Rebekah Weatherspoon, Alisha Rai, Bree Bridges, Alyssa Cole, Rose Lerner, Erica Ridley, and Tessa Dare were all there during the hardest times of the last ten years. Lucas Watkins and Chris Walker listened to me and believed me.

My dog, my cat, and Mr. Milan all gave me snuggles when I needed them, and I needed a lot of snuggles.

And there's you, my readers. I will thank you, but first, I owe you an apology. I said something at the end of *Once upon a Marquess* like "I'm not the fastest writer…" And I said something like maybe this book would come out at the end of 2016?

I had no idea how slowly things were going to go. I am so sorry.

359

I've talked a little about why things went slowly for me—and the dedication for this book is a little personal, even for a book dedication.

All of my books have aspects of who I am in them, and I don't think this one is much different. But I wrote the first few scenes that appeared in this book—the ones that took place in the rectory—a few years ago, shortly after I'd written *Once Upon a Marquess*. Maybe I should have known then that there was a problem.

Sometimes we write books to challenge ourselves, but sometimes our challenges show up in our books.

I hope I am never that slow a writer again. I often say that I hope this book was worth the wait; in this case, the wait was pretty darned long, and so that may create too high a standard. All I can say is that if I had tried to publish what I had sooner, it definitely *wouldn't* have been worth it.

I didn't know that this needed to be a book about hope until I had found mine.

So finally, I'd like to thank myself. I know it's a little gauche, but I have been writing romance for ten years now because I always believed in hope, even if I didn't know the reason for it.

I'm glad I found the reason.